PALACE CIRCLE

American heiress Delia Chandler leaves Virginia
to marry Viscount Ivor Conisborough. Soon she is
holding dinner parties for Winston Churchill and
Wallis Simpson and attending glittering balls with
Prince Edward. But beneath the dazzling façade
there lies a world steeped in scandals and secrets.
Drenched in glamour, secrets and scandal, *Palace
Circle* is an irresistible combination of real
historical events and masterful storytelling.

PALACE CIRCLE

PALACE CIRCLE

by

Rebecca Dean

Magna Large Print Books
Long Preston, North Yorkshire,
BD23 4ND, England.

British Library Cataloguing in Publication Data.

Dean, Rebecca
    Palace circle.

A catalogue record of this book is
available from the British Library

ISBN 978-0-7505-3191-7

First published in Great Britain by HarperCollins Publishers 2008

Copyright © Rebecca Dean 2008

Cover illustration © Gordon Crabb by arrangement with
Alison Eldred

Rebecca Dean asserts the moral right to be identified as the author of
this work

Published in Large Print 2010 by arrangement with
HarperCollins Publishers

Magna Large Print is an imprint of Library Magna Books Ltd.

Printed and bound in Great Britain by
T.J. (International) Ltd., Cornwall, PL28 8RW

*For all those who work for and support
the Brooke Hospital for Animals in Cairo.*

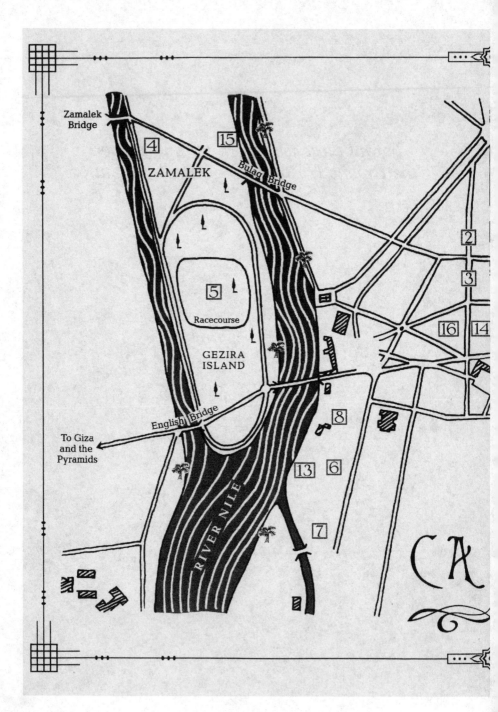

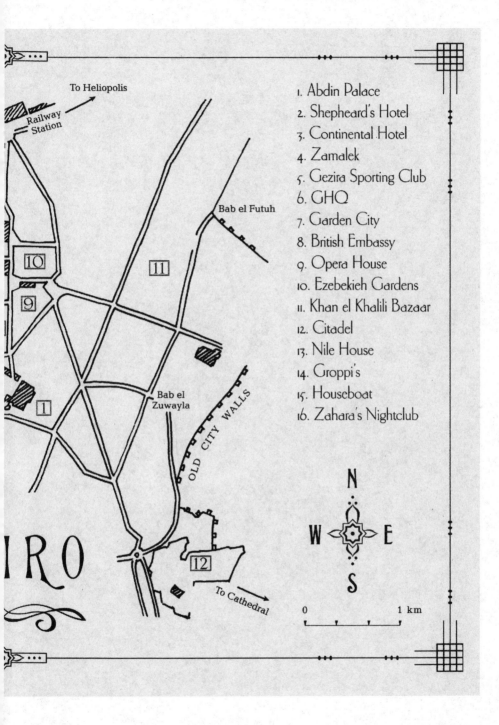

To Heliopolis

Railway Station

Bab el Futuh

10

9

11

Bab el Zuwayla

OLD CITY WALLS

1

IRO

12

To Cathedral

1. Abdin Palace
2. Shepheard's Hotel
3. Continental Hotel
4. Zamalek
5. Gezira Sporting Club
6. GHQ
7. Garden City
8. British Embassy
9. Opera House
10. Ezebekieh Gardens
11. Khan el Khalili Bazaar
12. Citadel
13. Nile House
14. Groppi's
15. Houseboat
16. Zahara's Nightclub

N
W   E
S

0   1 km

PART ONE

Delia

1911–1930

ONE

Sans Souci, Virginia, April 1911

The first rays of the rising sun filtered through the half-open shutters of the vast bedroom. Eighteen-year-old Delia Conisborough stirred slightly, her tumbled hair a glorious flame-red against the pristine whiteness of lace-edged bed linen.

The man beside her, snoring gently, didn't move and, much as she loved him, she did not want him to. This was the morning that, as a bride of four days, she was to leave her childhood home and embark on the long journey to England and a lifestyle very different to anything she had previously known. There were goodbyes to be said. Not to people. They would come later when the Chandler clan descended on Sans Souci to wave them off as they left by train for Richmond. From Richmond there would be a longer journey to New York and then, most exciting of all, the five-day Atlantic crossing aboard the *Mauretania*, the most luxurious liner afloat.

Still trying to come to terms with the realization that her surname was no longer Chandler but Conisborough and that she had a title, Viscountess Conisborough – though Ivor had explained to her she would generally be referred to as Lady Conisborough – she swung her legs to the floor, her silk nightdress swirling about her ankles. It wasn't yet six o'clock and she had at least two hours in which to say private goodbyes to all her favourite horses and all her favourite places – as well as to Sans Souci itself.

The bedroom she had been sharing with Ivor for the last three nights was not the bedroom she still regarded as being hers. That bedroom lay in the opposite wing of the house and she padded barefoot along the corridor towards it, plaiting her hair into a single waist-length braid as she did so.

'Mornin', Miss Delia,' said Sam, one of the servants who had been at Sans Souci for as long as she could remember, as she passed him outside her father's room. 'Ah sure am sorry you be leavin' us.'

'I'm sorry too,' she said, not at all abashed at being clad only in her nightdress. 'But my husband has promised we'll be back for visits.'

She flashed Sam a dazzling smile and, if she had been dressed, would have hugged him. No one ever stood on ceremony at Sans Souci. The easy-going intimacy between family and servants was taken for granted, though Ivor had not been able to accept it.

'Great Scott, Delia!' he'd said disbelievingly when first witnessing the familiarity that existed between the Chandlers and their staff. 'You won't be able to behave like that towards household staff in England. They would think you had taken leave of your senses!'

Now in her old bedroom she smiled at the memory, pulling her nightdress over her head and then dragging her ankle-length riding skirt and her riding jacket from her closet.

16

Though she was only eighteen she had enough sense to know that it was her so-different American ways that had captivated her new husband. He certainly hadn't married her for her money. A handful of other aristocratic Englishmen, those with vast estates and little money to maintain them, had married American heiresses, but Ivor Conisborough did not fall into that category. Twenty-two years her senior, he not only came from an exceedingly distinguished family, he was also distinguished in his own right, having been a financial advisor to King Edward VII, who had died a year ago, and now financial advisor to the about-to-be-crowned King George V. As a consequence of his position and his aristocratic family lineage he was very much a part of the royal circle. A royal circle of which she, as his wife, would also soon be a part.

Feelings of excitement and anticipation flooded through Delia as she pulled on her riding boots. Ivor's visit to Virginia – and his subsequent acquaintanceship with her father – had changed her entire future. As daughter of one of the leading families of Virginia she would, of course, have married well and always lived comfortably, but there could be no comparison between the life she had expected and the life she was now about to lead.

Chandlers rarely saw any reason to leave Virginia and it was a foregone conclusion that, if she hadn't married Ivor, her future husband would have been a distantly related Chandler cousin, perhaps Beau Chandler, who was a cousin twice or three times removed, she could never remember which. Beau was handsome enough to commit suicide for and fun into the bargain, but as his interests didn't extend much beyond drinking and gambling it was always fun of short duration. With Beau there would have been regular trips to White Sulphur Springs, a fashionable spa, and maybe even the occasional trip to Niagara, but there would have been no crossing of the Atlantic and none of the sophisticated social life that lay ahead of her in London. A social life that would, in a few weeks' time, include attending a coronation in Westminster Abbey.

In the stables she took her time saying goodbye to her father's horses. Her father had always been a keen horseman. A member of the Deep Run Hunt, he had taught her to ride before she could walk. When Ivor had asked her to marry him, it had been her only query. 'I shall still be able to ride?' she had asked, her heart slamming hard against her breastbone.

'You'll be able to ride every day in London,' he had said reassuringly in the clipped, cultured English accent that sent tingles down her spine. 'Many of my late wife's friends ride daily on Hyde Park's Rotten Row. It's a bridle path with stabling near by. And if you want to hunt–'

'I shan't,' she had said, before he could finish. 'Pa hunts. I never have.'

'You may change your mind when you find friends disappearing to Leicestershire every November,' he'd said drily. 'We'll wait and see. One thing is certain: once it is seen how you take a horse over a five-foot fence, no one will doubt what a superb rider you are.'

18

She had wanted to ask how far Shibden Hall, his family seat, was from Leicestershire. She knew it was in Norfolk but had no idea how far Norfolk was from Leicestershire or how far both counties were from London.

'But London is where we shall be spending most time,' she said now to her horse, Sultan, mounting him unaided.

Riding bareback, she cantered out of the cobbled yard and past the paddocks. It was a glorious spring morning, the air thick with the scent of heat to come and the grass still dew-wet. On mornings like these it seemed to her that the lush rolling Virginian countryside was as vast as all eternity. The softly rounded peaks of the Blue Ridge Mountains were hazy in the distance and nearer were belts of thick woodland edging a swift-running river and half a dozen creeks. She knew the names of all the trees. Red maple, tulip, blackgum, sassafras, hickory, dogwood and sourwood. In autumn their leaves were a blaze of colour. Now, in April, it was wildflowers that were at their best.

By the edge of the nearest creek she could glimpse the delicate pale mauve of wild geraniums and, beyond them, flashes of maroon-red trilliums and swathe after swathe of marsh marigolds, their deep-yellow petals glinting like gold.

She slowed Sultan to a walk, and with the reins slack in her hands she stared at the landscape she loved. The trouble was, she also loved Ivor and Ivor's life was in London – and not only London, for he was just as familiar with Paris and Rome and St Petersburg as he was with New York and Washington.

That she was the wife of such a distinguished cosmopolitan man thrilled her. The moment she had been introduced to him she had been bowled over; but he was of her parents' generation, not hers. Even when her father told her their visitor was a widower it had still not occurred to her that he might show romantic interest in her.

It had been her Aunt Rose, her mother's spinster sister, who had set out to catch his eye. Her mother, when Ivor had extended his stay in Virginia, had thought that perhaps Rose had a chance. Her father had always been far more perceptive.

'Lord Conisborough's marriage was childless,' he'd said when Delia had ever so casually brought up the subject of her Aunt Rose's hopes and aspirations. 'When Conisborough marries again it will be to a woman much younger than Rose. He'll want an heir and, because of his age, he'll want one fast. Poor Rose. I'm afraid she's going to be out of luck again.'

She had, indeed, been out of luck and when it became known that Lord Conisborough had asked for Delia's hand in marriage, Rose had been poleaxed – and she hadn't been the only one.

Delia, too, had hardly been able to believe it.

Her father had believed it, though, and had done so gleefully. 'An English viscount! A peer of the realm! Dammit, girl! I *told* you he'd be looking for a young wife! Wait until the *New York Times* gets hold of this! They'll have to describe us as Virginian aristocracy! The whole of Richmond will be bowing and scraping to us as if there's no tomorrow!'

20

Her mother had been far more restrained. 'He's been widowed for only such a short time, Delia,' she had said, seated beside her daughter on the edge of her bed and holding her hand. 'And he is so much older. I'd hate to think you were marrying because your head had been turned by the thought of an English title.'

'It hasn't,' she'd said adamantly. 'I'm marrying him because I'm in love with him. I'm marrying him because he's different to any other man I have ever met or, living in Virginia, am ever likely to meet. He's cultivated, sophisticated, intelligent – and *very* good-looking. Don't you think he is very good-looking?'

Her mother had thought of Ivor Conisborough's chiselled features, the aquiline nose, the faint hollows under the cheekbones, the well-shaped mouth that betrayed an arrogance that could never be wholly hidden, the dark blond hair, arrow-straight and silkily smooth, and had, with a marked lack of enthusiasm, agreed with her.

As she turned Sultan's head in the direction of Sans Souci, Delia thought her mother's lack of enthusiasm might have been because Ivor was such a complete opposite to her father. Always chewing on a plug of tobacco, her father was on the short side, no more than five foot eight or nine, but broad shouldered and barrel-chested. Most comfortable in shabby, well-worn riding clothes, he seldom wore anything else and wherever he went there was a ruckus of noise and laughter.

Ivor was tall, at least two inches over six foot, favoured Cuban cigars and was accompanied on all his travels by a valet. His starched collars were

21

higher than anyone in Virginia had ever seen and he always wore either a homburg or, in deference to the Virginian heat, a straw hat, with his fashionable lounge suits. Exquisitely tailored though they were, Delia privately thought he never looked quite at ease in them. He was a man who suited formal clothing. In the frock coat and top hat he wore whenever they visited Richmond, he looked superb.

Unlike her father, he never spoke unless he had something pertinent to say and there was something in his manner that commanded immediate respect. Even Beau, who had volubly declared he had no intention of fawning to English nobility, had referred to Ivor as 'Your Grace' on first being introduced to him.

By then Delia had been conversant enough with the way to address and introduce Ivor to know that Beau had made a social gaffe.

'Refer to me as Ivor or as Conisborough,' Ivor had said to him, tired of giving the instruction to Delia's army of relations. 'Only dukes are addressed as "Your Grace", and then only by servants or anyone with whom they are having non-social communication.'

Unused to Ivor's clipped way of speaking, Beau interpreted the remark as a put-down and, refusing to let Delia persuade him otherwise, had vowed he would never forgive it. When she had married Ivor a month later in Richmond's St James's Episcopal Church, Beau had been noticeable only by his absence.

Despite the sumptuousness of her silk and satin wedding gown, with its high bodice encrusted

22

with seed pearls and its slim skirt and lavish train glittering with crystal beads, it hadn't been quite the extravaganza she had always imagined her wedding would be – or the wedding her mother had always planned for her to have – because it had all been so sudden.

'It is impossible for me to return to England for the coronation and then travel back to Virginia for a winter or a spring wedding,' Ivor had said to her father in the tone of a man accustomed to getting his own way. 'And it would be highly inappropriate for Delia to travel back to England with me without doing so as my wife. Even if she were to do so, a wedding in England, without her family present, would cause comment and is not what she wants.'

It hadn't been what her father wanted either; hence the speedy wedding that had set tongues wagging all over Virginia.

As she neared the hill that gave a perfect view of Sans Souci, Delia urged Sultan into a canter, still thinking of her husband and the intimidating effect he had on people. Sometimes even she felt, a little intimidated by him, but common sense told her that it was natural when her respect for him was boundless and when he was, in so many ways, still a stranger to her.

Cresting the hill, she reined Sultan to a halt. This was the view she most wanted to say a lingering goodbye to.

Set against a background of evergreen trees, Sans Souci lay cradled in a bowl of hills that were, in comparison to the blue haze of the distant mountains, lushly green. Near to the house were the paddocks and then, a little to one side, the stables and the barns: the yearling barn and the brood-mare barn and the barn where all the winter foodstuffs were stored, and then, beyond the barns, the neat precision of the apple orchards.

And dominating everything was the house.

It was a three-storey brick-built colonnaded manor house, its elegant Georgian windows flanked by pale yellow shutters, a flight of stone steps leading up to its double front doors. The sun shimmered on its slate roof and honeysuckle fragranced the porch where her father and his friends liked to sit in the evenings, frosted mint juleps conveniently to hand.

It was the only home she had ever known and suddenly the prospect of leaving it caught at her throat. Sans Souci meant, in French, 'without care', and her mother had ensured that since the day she had entered it as a young bride, it had lived up to its name.

Delia's hands tightened on Sultan's reins. Though Ivor had told her they would be spending most of their time in London, she was sure that Shibden Hall would begin to play a large part in their married life once she had given Ivor an heir, and she was determined to turn it into the kind of home her mother had created at Sans Souci. A home that, however impressively splendid, was also glowingly welcoming. A home with fresh flowers in every room. A home where everyone who entered it instantly felt at ease. Most of all, a home where Ivor would want to be whenever he could get away from London and his court commitments.

As she gazed in deep thought across the open meadowland towards Sans Souci, the double front doors opened. For a heart-stopping moment she hoped it would be Ivor's distinctively tall figure that would emerge. She had been gone for nearly two hours and he would be up and dressed by now and wondering where she was. The thought of him walking into the meadows to greet her, as impatient to be with her as she was to be with him, sent excitement singing along her veins.

In high elation she dug her heels into Sultan's flanks, but then saw that it wasn't Ivor stepping out onto the colonnaded porch: it was two of the servants hauling out black travelling trunks starred with Cunard passenger stickers.

Her disappointment was intense, but swiftly overcome. Any moment now the luggage would be loaded into one of the many horse-drawn buggies that would accompany them when they left Sans Souci for the local train station. It meant she hadn't much time in which to bathe, breakfast and change into her travelling clothes. And though Ivor wasn't yet in sight, somewhere within Sans Souci he was waiting for her.

At full gallop she jumped the treacherously high split-log fence that marked the beginning of Chandler land, eager for the opportunity, aboard ship and away from the prurient eyes of her family, to get to know her husband better. Eager to embark on the new, exciting life awaiting her in England.

TWO

The country that was to be her home wasn't remotely as Delia had anticipated. When, after a windy transatlantic voyage, the *Mauretania* neared land she had expected to see white cliffs topped by springy green turf. Instead she had been faced with a forbidding-looking city of grey stone. The greyness of Liverpool was something she had never experienced before, not even in New York.

The train journey to London had also been a disappointment. She had seen no picturesque houses with thatched roofs and doors framed by roses, no children skipping around maypoles, no men morris dancing on village greens; she'd glimpsed only distant church spires and fields of cows huddled miserably together in heavy rain. By the time their train steamed its way into King's Cross Station she'd realized that the reality of England was going to be very different to her naively idealized picture-book expectations.

Her new home, though, was far from disappointing. Tall and imposing and with a splendid portico, it was situated in an elegant square only a few minutes away from Buckingham Palace. However, she was taken aback by the stiff etiquette that greeted her. The staff – a veritable army of white-capped maids and liveried footmen – had all lined up to greet her when she stepped out of the

Conisborough Rolls-Royce, their reaction one of unanimous disbelief.

Ivor had already warned her what to expect. 'Be prepared to meet with a little bemusement, sweetheart,' he had said as they neared the house. 'Whatever the staff are expecting, it won't be an eighteen-year-old with flame-red hair who uses expressions such as "a cracking good one", "I'm mighty glad", "real soon", and – don't deny you've said this, because I've heard you – "schucks".'

'I'll have you know,' she had retaliated with mock archness, 'that I've been tryin' real hard to drop all my Virginian slang. I just haven't gotten to replace it yet with an acceptable cut-glass English accent.'

Beneath his blond moustache his austerely straight mouth had twitched with amusement and, happy that she amused him, she had squeezed his hand lovingly.

Nothing could have been further removed from the easy-going atmosphere of Sans Souci than the formality of the Cadogan Square house. Over the next few days Delia made a determined effort to inject a little Virginian friendliness into her new home. There were occasions when Ivor cleared his throat or pursed his lips in disapproval, but it was disapproval she took no notice of. Bellingham, the butler, soon became her adoring slave and wouldn't allow a word of criticism to be said about her below stairs. She had arrived at Cadogan Square without a personal maid but she had rejected Ivor's suggestion that she should interview and hire a suitably experienced young woman; instead, having taken a great liking to Ellie, one of the young parlourmaids, she had asked that Ellie be allowed to fill the position.

Ellie was a chatterbox, something Delia was grateful for; and since she still knew no more about Ivor's first wife than she had on the day he proposed, she was glad that Ellie didn't hesitate to talk about her.

'Lady Olivia spent very little time in London, my lady,' Ellie said one day when Delia had pressed her for information. 'She much preferred being at Shibden Hall.' It was a piece of information that had startled Delia.

Somehow she had never thought of Olivia as spending a great deal of time away from Ivor. She certainly would never want to.

Then there was the mystery about why, among the many family portraits adorning the walls of the Cadogan Square house, there wasn't one of Olivia.

Again, it was Ellie who told her.

'There used to be one, my lady,' she had said as she brushed Delia's turbulently fiery hair until it crackled, 'only it's been taken down.'

'Taken down?' Delia had turned away from her dressing table. 'But why, Ellie?' she'd asked. 'For what possible reason?'

With an awkwardness she rarely displayed Ellie had said, 'I think, my lady, his lordship thought it best. I think he thought you wouldn't want to be constantly reminded that he had once been married to someone else.'

That Ivor should have been so sensitive to her feelings had taken her breath away and she had instantly forgiven him for the long hours he spent away from her at the Palace, the House of Lords or his gentlemen's club in Pall Mall.

One friend, Sir Cuthbert Digby, had even ushered Ivor away to Buckingham Palace only minutes after he had escorted her into the house. She had tried not to be cross about it, but she had been alarmed at the realization that if the aged Sir Cuthbert was typical of Ivor's friends, then their wives were all going to be as old as her mother or, even worse, her grandmother.

Gwen, Ivor's elder sister and his only close relative was nearer to fifty than to forty. And her husband, Pugh, was even older. Though she had speedily become deeply fond of Gwen, Delia very much wanted to make friends with people of her own age – and feared it unlikely she was going to be able to do so. A comfort was that Ivor left her in no doubt that his friends had all taken her to their hearts.

'Cuthie thinks you're a delight,' he said, preparing to leave in a hurry for the Palace. 'And lovemaking in the morning is going to have to come to an end, sweetheart, if this is how late it makes me.'

She laughed, knowing he was teasing, and helped him into his frock coat.

He reached for his top hat, gave her a swift kiss and was gone.

She was just going to ring for Ellie when she saw that in his hurry Ivor had left his appointments diary behind. She picked it up, about to run after him with it. A photograph fell from between the diary's pages, and as she knelt to retrieve it she saw that it was of a woman far too young to be Ivor's mother and far too old to be a niece or a godchild.

She sank back on her heels, knowing the photograph could only be of Olivia. She had expected Ivor's late wife to have been lovely and dignified. What she had not expected was for her to have been shatteringly beautiful.

Dark-haired, dark-eyed and dazzling, she was wearing a diamond tiara on her upswept, intricately arranged hair. Her eyebrows were strongly marked and dramatically winged. Beneath them, heavily lashed eyes stared out boldly with an expression of sultry insolence. Her cheekbones were high, her darkly lipsticked mouth sensually curved. The evening gown she was wearing was cut low, revealing a full bosom and emphasizing a wasp waist. In addition to the diamonds in her hair, there were diamonds at her throat, her ears, her wrists and on her fingers. Even in a photograph she glittered and shone, the epitome of exotic, *soignée* glamour.

Trembling violently Delia turned the photograph over. *All my love, darling Ivor, is for you and you alone* was written in an extravagant flourish in mauve ink.

Trembling even more violently she slipped the photograph back into the diary.

That Ivor had obviously loved his first wife was something that had never troubled her. She had been too confident of his love to allow herself to become jealous of a much older woman who was now dead.

But that had been before she had realized how

30

staggeringly beautiful Olivia Conisborough had been. And before she had realized that though Olivia's portrait had been taken down, Ivor still kept her image where he would see it frequently.

As she heard the front door close she placed the photograph back into the diary with unsteady hands and then put the diary back where she had found it.

It was something she knew she would never be able to speak to Ivor about and, no matter how deep her shock, it was something she was determined to come to terms with.

A week after her arrival in England she met a friend of Ivor's whom she instantly liked. They were walking along Piccadilly when Ivor came to such a sudden halt she almost tripped. A second later a man she judged to be in his early thirties walked up to them. As toughly built as a heavyweight boxer, he was wearing a dove-grey lounge suit and his matching grey homburg was tilted at a rakish angle. There was a devil-may-care air about him that reminded her of Beau and that she found unexpected in someone who was obviously on friendly terms with her statesmanlike husband.

'Jerome, I would like to introduce you to my wife,' Ivor said, an odd note in his voice. 'Delia and I were married in Richmond, Virginia. Delia, Sir Jerome Bazeljette.'

Something crossed Jerome Bazeljette's handsomely swarthy face that was as indecipherable as the expression in Ivor's voice.

'My congratulations, Lady Conisborough.' He shook hands with her and raised his hat, and she saw his hair was black as a gypsy's and thick and curly as a ram's fleece. 'And to you, Conisborough, as well, of course,' he added.

To Delia's mystification the conversation then came to a standstill.

Delia, who never had any compunction about launching into conversation with anyone, beggarman or king, said pleasantly, 'Have you ever visited Virginia, Mr Bazeljette?'

'No.' He was clearly startled by her disarming directness. 'I haven't. Is it one of the states south of the Mason–Dixon line?'

There was genuine interest and friendly feeling in his voice and she responded to it sunnily. 'It most certainly is. And Virginians never forget it. We still fly the Confederate flag at Sans Souci.'

'Sans Souci?'

There were gold flecks in his brown eyes. 'Sans Souci is the name of my family home, Mr Bazeljette,' she said, thinking what a very attractive man he was.

Ivor put a quick end to the conversation by saying, 'We must be on our way, Jerome, before Piccadilly Circus is treated to a rendering of "Dixie".'

It was a remark that could have been taken humorously, but there was a hard edge to his voice that caused Delia to suck in her breath.

'Perhaps I will have the pleasure of hearing "Dixie" sung another time,' Jerome said, and something in his expression indicated that he too had caught the undertone in Ivor's voice. Turning his attention to Ivor he said crisply, 'Sylvia is on the Riviera, as I think you know. I'm not sure when she intends returning,' and without waiting

32

for a response he raised his homburg once again and sauntered on his way.

The minute he was out of earshot Ivor said tightly, 'It isn't up to me to tell a man when his wife intends returning to London, but I can promise you, Delia, that Sylvia will be here in time to present you at Court.' A pulse was beating at the corner of his jaw and there were white lines around his mouth. 'And Jerome is a baronet,' he said as they began walking again in the direction of the Ritz. 'Anyone bearing the title of "Sir" is either a baronet or a knight. Referring to him as Mr Bazeljette was a great solecism. In conversation, the surnames of baronets and knights are never used, except by their men friends. Only their Christian names are used with the prefix of "Sir".'

Delia bit her lip, not because she was distressed at being spoken to in such a way, but because she was so furiously angry she wasn't sure she was going to be able to control her voice.

'And just how,' she said spiritedly as they entered the Ritz, 'was I supposed to know that? And how am I to address Sir Jerome's wife when I meet her?'

'Until you are on intimate terms with her – which you will be very quickly, for it is Sylvia who will be presenting you at court – you address her as Lady Bazeljette. Wives of baronets and knights are never formally addressed by their Christian names as that indicates that the lady is the daughter of a duke, a marquis or an earl.'

It was all so ridiculously complicated that Delia rolled her eyes to heaven.

Fortunately Ivor didn't see her.

As they were led across the opulent dining room to a table overlooking the terrace, she took a steadying breath. 'Why is it Sylvia who is presenting me at court, Ivor?' she asked, trying to put the conversation on a friendlier footing. 'I'd much prefer it if you were to present me.'

The change of subject had the desired effect.

He gave a slight smile. 'A presentation can only be made by a lady who has herself been presented. And as Sylvia has no daughters of her own, presenting you will give her great pleasure.'

Delia didn't protest any further. If Lady Bazeljette was as likeable and as amiable as her husband, then she was only too happy to put herself into her hands.

Two days later her hopes that she was already pregnant were ended. For a few hours she was plunged into gloom but then common sense reasserted itself. Not everyone was like her cousin Bella, who had become pregnant on her honeymoon. It might well take two months, maybe three, before she was able to give Ivor the news he so wanted to hear. For the moment, though, he was, she knew, going to be disappointed.

He wasn't just disappointed. He was devastated.

'I thought young women your age fell for babies easily,' he said, staring at her as if perhaps she had made a mistake. 'Dear God, it isn't as if we haven't tried hard enough, is it?'

The crudity was so unexpected – and so unlike him – that she gasped.

'I'm sorry, sweetheart.' He pulled her down onto his lap, hugging her tightly. 'It's just that I was so hoping for good news. Perhaps next month, eh?'

'Yes,' she said, her head against his chest. 'Perhaps next month.' But as his lips brushed her hair, her own disappointment took on an entirely different quality, for he had made her feel as though she had let him down – and letting Ivor down was the very last thing in the world she wanted to do.

The following week Delia was at Madame Colette's, the dressmaker Gwen had recommended.

'It's a great shame Sylvia is still not back from the Riviera,' Gwen said as she watched Madame Colette adjust, with pins and tucks, the white satin gown Delia was to wear for her presentation at court. 'She always leaves things to the last minute, but as Ivor said she was so thrilled at having been asked to present you, I really do think she should have kept us *au fait* with her travel plans.'

Already nervous at the thought of appearing at Buckingham Palace before King George and Queen Mary, Delia became even more so.

'If she don't arrive back in time, could you present me, Gwen?' she asked anxiously.

'No, darling, I couldn't.' Gwen's voice was filled with regret. 'All the paperwork for your presentation is already with the Lord Chamberlain and the name of the person presenting is Lady Bazeljette.' As an afterthought she added, 'And it's "doesn't", Delia, darling. Not "don't".'

Unlike the occasions when Ivor corrected her speech, Delia was unperturbed. Ever since their first meeting Gwen had shown nothing but maternal affection towards her and when Gwen

35

pointed out her mistakes Delia knew she did it to be helpful – and that the helpfulness was always meant in the kindest possible way.

When the pinning and tucking were done to her satisfaction, Madame Colette asked for Delia's white satin embroidered train to be brought out and temporarily attached to the gown so the full effect could be appreciated.

'Lady Conisborough's fan will be the one I carried when presented.' Gwen, appallingly flat-chested but majestic in a dress of grey silk worn with a wide-brimmed black hat decorated with a red rose, eyed Delia's hand-span waist with satisfaction. 'And also, she will be wearing the family tiara.'

'And other jewellery?' Madame Colette asked, not wanting anything to be chosen that would fight with the purity of the gown's neckline.

'A three-strand pearl necklace,' Delia said, 'and pearl drop earrings.'

'Ah! Another family heirloom, Lady Conis-borough?'

Delia shook her head. 'No. They were a honey-moon gift to me from my husband when we were in New York.'

'And a perfect choice for a presentation at court, if I may say so, your ladyship.'

When the fitting was completed, Gwen insisted that the two of them had tea at Fortnum & Mason.

As Delia walked into the St James's restaurant wearing a royal-blue walking costume, the short bolero jacket worn over a high-necked, heavily flounced white chiffon blouse, the ankle-length skirt skimming prettily buttoned shoes, her wide-brimmed, blue and emerald peacock-feathered hat at a seductive angle, she felt every inch a viscountess.

Gwen exchanged pleasantries with several other ladies taking tea and then, within minutes of their sitting down at a window table, Jerome Bazeljette strolled up to them.

'Good afternoon, ladies,' he said in his easy, affable manner, oblivious of the many female heads that had turned to watch him admiringly as he crossed the room.

Gwen's middle-aged face flushed rosily.

'Do please join us, Jerome,' she said in a manner that indicated he was a far closer family friend than Delia had thought. 'I believe you have already met my new sister-in-law?'

'I have indeed.' He took a seat at the table and smiled across at Delia. 'Though sadly these surroundings are no more suitable for a rendering of "Dixie" than our previous surroundings were.'

Gwen blinked in bewilderment and giggles fizzed in Delia's throat.

'I'm curious about Virginian high society, Lady Conisborough,' he continued. 'Is it very different to high society here, in London?'

Delia fought down a rush of homesickness for her beloved Virginia and said, 'Yes, totally different. In Virginia nearly everyone in polite society is somehow related to everyone else. And no matter how distant that relationship may be, it will be known. Genealogy is a very popular pastime in Virginia. Nearly everyone indulges in it. And because of that, class doesn't matter in the way it does here.'

'Good heavens!' Gwen straightened her napkin, hardly able to believe that things were so different on the other side of the Atlantic.

'And we're Republicans.' Delia thought it was something Gwen might need reminding of. 'Our public life doesn't revolve around a monarchy. Here in London, Ivor's life, and the lives of nearly all the people he has contact with, revolves around what is happening at court. And if it isn't court affairs that are being discussed, it's politics.'

'But, my dear, that's only natural.' Gwen ignored the decadent-looking pastries on the cake stand. 'Ivor's position as a financial advisor to King Edward put him right at the heart of British political life. Isn't that so, Jerome?'

Jerome nodded and in the light of the chandeliers – fully ablaze even though it was a sunny afternoon – his curly hair gleamed blue-black.

'King George, however,' Gwen continued, 'is far more conservative than his late father – and far less cosmopolitan. You won't find King George constantly in the casinos of Biarritz and Monte Carlo, or incessantly at fashionable spas such as Marienbad and Carlsbad.'

'Though you will find me at them,' Jerome interjected drily.

'That's true,' Gwen said scoldingly, but with much affection, 'and why Sylvia condones such behaviour I can't imagine.' She turned to Delia. 'Sylvia is the most scintillating creature. As a society hostess no one can hold a candle to her – not even Margot Asquith.'

Margot Asquith was the Prime Minister's wife

and having met her at a dinner party the previous evening, Delia realized that she was a woman who tolerated neither fools nor anyone not fiercely intelligent and bitingly witty. The prospect of acting as her hostess – which Ivor had told her she would have to do in the not-too-distant future – filled Delia with terror.

'Tell us more about Virginia,' Gwen said. 'Do Virginians eat very strange food?'

Grateful for the change in the conversation, Delia took a sip of tea and said, 'Some of it may seem very strange to you, Gwen, but it ain't strange to Virginians. We eat soft-shell crabs and shad roe and fried chicken and watermelon and home-cured ham – and it's all absolutely delicious. And compared to life here, everything is easy and informal.'

She told them about the glorious Virginian countryside; about how, in May, the scent of flowering dogwood filled the air, and how, from Sans Souci's shaded porches, there were hazy views of the distant Blue Ridge Mountains. She told them about her father's horses – particularly Sultan – and she told them of the sultry summer heat that was so different from anything she had so far experienced in England.

'Though today is delightfully balmy,' Gwen said in defence of English weather. 'May is often the loveliest month of the year in England. And now I really do have to go. I have a beauty appointment at the House of Cyclax in twenty minutes. I'm so sorry, Delia, because I'd thought we could take a cab together and that you could have been dropped off at Cadogan Square, but now there isn't enough time for that and I'm going to have to go straight to South Molton Street.'

Delia smiled, not at all put out. 'That's no problem, Gwen. You can take a cab and pop off to your appointment and I'll walk home.'

Gwen's china-blue eyes widened in horror. 'Good gracious, you can't do that, Delia! It's too far – and even if it wasn't, you couldn't walk there alone!'

Delia was just about to protest that she most certainly could when Jerome said, in a voice that brooked no argument – not even from Gwen, 'No need to worry, Gwen. I'll see Lady Conisborough safely back to Cadogan Square.'

'That would be wonderfully kind of you, Jerome.' Vastly relieved, Gwen allowed him to usher her out of the restaurant and out of the building, saying to both of them as she stepped into one of the horse-drawn cabs that were lined up outside Fortnum's, 'And I'll see both of you this evening at dear Cuthie's birthday party.'

As the cab began to draw away she leaned out of it in order to call to Jerome: 'Only please don't allow Delia to walk all the way to Cadogan Square, Jerome! It's much too far!'

Jerome merely waved until the cab was lost in a sea of other horse-drawn cabs, horse-drawn buses and a scattering of open-topped motor cars and then said to Delia, 'Is it too far? It's about three-quarters of a mile, maybe less.'

She flashed him a wide smile, saying teasingly, 'That's nothing to a Virginian. We walk that far to get from the house to the stables.'

He chuckled and then, in happy companionship, they set off in the direction of Hyde Park Corner, and Kensington.

'How are you settling into life as part of the Palace circle?' he asked as, on their left-hand side, they reached the park which backed on to Buckingham Palace.

'I ain't–' she corrected herself swiftly – 'haven't met their Majesties yet. That won't happen until I've been presented at court. I've been to a dinner party at which the Prime Minister and his wife were fellow guests, though. And I've met Sir Cuthbert a few times, and Lord Curzon.'

'Cuthie can be a bit of a fusspot but Curzon is a splendid fellow. He was Viceroy of India until a few years ago – and that made him one of the most powerful rulers in the world. Can you imagine it? At thirty-eight he held the destinies of millions in his hands.'

'He must have looked magnificent in vice-regal robes and mounted on an elephant,' she said, laughter in her voice. 'Just think how he must miss them.'

'The robes or the elephants?'

'The elephants.'

They were both laughing now and suddenly the homesickness that had never quite left her, vanished. She had, at last, found a friend, and it was a good feeling.

As they cut across a corner of Green Park he said, 'And who will be presenting you at court, Delia? Gwen?'

Her eyes flew wide open in startled surprise. 'No. I'm to be presented by...' She came to an awkward halt. Ivor had told her that she must address Sylvia – and presumably speak of her – as Lady Bazeljette until they were on terms of good friendship, but saying she was to be presented by Lady Bazeljette, when Lady Bazeljette was his wife, seemed far too formal, especially as she and Jerome had somehow slipped so comfortably on to first-name terms. 'Your wife is going to present me,' she said, amazed that he didn't already know.

He couldn't have looked more shocked if she had said that the Dalai Lama was going to present her.

'Sylvia?' he said. 'Ivor has asked *Sylvia* to present you?'

'Yes.' Her amazement was fast turning to alarm. 'There's nothing wrong with that, is there, Jerome?' And then, assuming his incredulity to be due to the fact that Sylvia was probably still on the French Riviera, she said reassuringly, 'Ivor is confident that she will be back in London by the time I am to be presented.'

'Is he, indeed?' His voice sounded almost as grim as Ivor's had been when Ivor had said that it wasn't up to him to tell a man when his wife intended returning to London.

Seeing the consternation in her cat-green eyes he said swiftly, 'And Ivor is right, of course. If Sylvia has said she will present you, nothing on earth will prevent her.'

For a minute or two there was silence between them and then, as they skirted Hyde Park Corner, she said, unusually subdued, 'I'm findin' English titles, and just who is connected to whom – and how – quite difficult, Jerome. And if

42

I'm findin' it difficult now, what is it goin' to be like when I'm in the company of royalty – as Ivor tells me I often will be?'

'Just remember that King George is addressed as "Sir", as is the Prince of Wales. Queen Mary is addressed as "Ma'am". And you never speak to royalty without having been spoken to first. You also never leave any function that royalty are at, until they have left first. And if the King and Queen should visit Shibden – and they did when Olivia was alive, for Ivor is on very close terms with King George and Sandringham is close to Shibden – then from the moment they enter the house until they leave it, they are regarded as being the owners of it.'

'But what on earth does that mean?' she asked, her alarm spiralling.

He flashed her an amused grin. 'Well, for one thing it means that you and Ivor will relinquish your seats at the top and bottom of the table and sit at the side with the rest of your guests. Don't worry about etiquette around royalty. Ivor will see that you don't come to grief. Other things are a bit trickier.'

She groaned and his grin deepened.

'You need to understand that London high society is a complex web of cliques and sets, Delia. Some are intellectual. Some are more rackety and Bohemian. Ivor, for instance, belongs to the former and I belong to the latter. And while we are on this subject, there is something I need to warn you about.'

She waited expectantly and he said, suddenly serious, 'I'm telling you this because I prefer to tell you myself rather than for someone else to tell you – and once you begin making friends in London you will most certainly be told. I have the reputation of being a philanderer – a rather notorious one, I'm afraid. And before you protest the reputation can't possibly be deserved, I have to tell you that it is.'

'Oh!' She couldn't think of anything else to say, but a lot of things now made sense, for it explained the tension that so clearly existed between Jerome and Ivor, for Ivor, so upright and honourable, would quite obviously find Jerome's reputation one hard to come to terms with.

She knew she should be shocked by his disclosure, but what she said was: 'I *knew* you reminded me of my cousin Beau!'

His crack of laughter was so loud that people walking nearby turned to look at them disapprovingly.

Neither he, nor she, cared.

'Some day,' he said, 'you'll have to tell me about cousin Beau.' He quirked an eyebrow, suddenly serious again. 'I don't know about marital fidelity in Virginia, Delia, but marital fidelity among the British aristocracy is not a highly esteemed virtue. It's accepted practice to marry for commonsense reasons and to find love afterwards, and that goes for wives – once they've produced an heir – as well as husbands.'

'But that's ... that's outrageous.'

'I'm rather glad you think so. However, it happens and everyone knows it happens. At every weekend house party in the country, bedrooms are allocated with a nod to who is presently involved

44

with whom – long walks down corridors in the middle of the night not being popular. There is only one fundamental requirement and it is that though everyone knows about it, one mustn't be caught out.'

'Or the gig will be up?'

He burst into laughter again. 'Yes, Delia. Or the gig will be up.'

The frank nature of their conversation prompted her to ask something she'd longed to ask, but had previously thought might be too personal. After all, Ivor had said that Sylvia had no daughters. It was equally possible she had no sons either and that the Bazeljette's marriage was as childless as Ivor's marriage to Olivia had been. 'Have you children, Jerome?' she asked. 'You haven't said.'

'I thought you were never going to ask. Yes, I do have a child. I have a son, Jack.'

He stopped walking and reached into his waistcoat pocket, withdrawing a small snapshot. 'He's three. Do you think he looks like me?'

Though small, it was a formal, studio portrait. Standing on an oriental rug by the side of a decorative Chinese pot holding an aspidistra, was a confident-looking little boy. His hair was dark and curly and, still being worn long, hung in ringlets any girl would envy. His eyes were as dark as his father's and full of bright intelligence. He was wearing a sailor suit and knee-high white socks and shoes.

'Oh, he's a *cracking* little boy!' she said sincerely. 'You must be very proud of him.'

A doting expression crossed his face as he said, 'I am,' and slid the photograph carefully back

45

into his waistcoat pocket.

They were now at the corner of Cadogan Square and as he walked her to the foot of the steps leading to the Grecian-pillared portico of the Conisborough mansion, she said, 'Ivor may be home from the House of Lords by now. Would you like to come in and say hello to him?'

He shook his head. 'No. I'll catch up with him this evening at the Digbys'. Goodbye for now, Delia.'

She wished him goodbye, impatient to know if Ivor was home, and when Bellingham opened the door to her with the words, 'His lordship is in the drawing room, your ladyship,' she dragged off her peacock-feathered hat, sent it spinning on to the first available surface and ran for the drawing room, eager to have her husband's arms around her once again.

THREE

Despite the fact that a maid or a footman was likely to walk in on them at any moment his kiss was deep and passionate and she slid her arms up and around his neck, responding to him ardently and with all her heart.

When at last he raised his head from hers he said, 'I have good news, sweetheart. Sylvia arrived back in London an hour or so ago. She'll be at Cuthbert's birthday festivities this evening.'

'Oh, what a wonderful surprise for Jerome!'

'A surprise? Probably not, Delia. He most probably went to meet Sylvia from the boat train.'

Still held in the circle of his arms, she shook her head. 'No, he didn't. Gwen and I met up with him unexpectedly while we were having afternoon tea at Fortnum's and then, because Gwen had to leave rather hurriedly for an appointment in South Molton Street, he walked me home.'

Ivor raised his eyebrows, his slate-grey eyes startled. 'He walked you home? From Piccadilly? What an extraordinary thing to do. And since when have you and Jerome become on first-name terms with each other?'

'Since he joined Gwen and myself for tea at Fortnum's. I'm not quite sure how it happened, Ivor, but as it's mighty comfortable, please don't be cross about it.'

His arms dropped from her waist, but with relief she saw that though he was exasperated, he wasn't cross. 'It's the sort of thing I should have expected from Bazeljette,' he said disparagingly. 'He's far too Bohemian for truly polite society.'

Suspecting Ivor was referring to Jerome's faithless private life, and not wanting her husband to put an immediate end to their burgeoning friendship, she made no response, merely tucking her hand lovingly into the crook of his arm.

His light-coloured eyes darkened, though with desire, not anger. 'I've told Willoughby I won't be needing him for the next hour or two.' Willoughby was his secretary. 'And if you have already had afternoon tea you will not be wanting more. It's a situation I think we can take advantage of, don't you?'

47

Heat flooded through her for she knew what was now about to happen. Even though it was only late afternoon he was going to take her to bed. Her response was one of immediate willingness – and amusement. For in making love to her when it was still light, her handsome and oh-so-correct husband was himself behaving in a Bohemian fashion.

The mint-green satin evening dress Ellie helped her into a few hours later had not come from a London – or a French – fashion house, but was one that Ivor had bought for her in New York before they sailed. The three strands of enormous pearls he had bought on the same day, and which she intended wearing when she was presented at court, lay at precisely the right depth of the daringly décolleté neckline, and the soft-flowing drapery of the skirt fell fashionably straight, barely skimming her feet.

Ellie had brushed her Titian-red hair in a centre parting and then, allowing deep waves to frame Delia's face as low as the tips of her ears, had coiled the rest high into a chignon.

'I don't think I want any jewels in my hair,' Delia said as Ellie reached for a diamond hair ornament. 'There is an arrangement of white roses in the drawing room and I think one tucked in my chignon will look far better than jewels.'

It did. When her toilette was complete and Ivor walked into the bedroom dressed in white tie and tails, his stiff-fronted shirt fastened with mother of pearl studs, his dark blond hair shining like glass, the expression in his eyes at the sight of her was one of deep satisfaction.

'Will I do?' she asked, as she had always asked her father before going to a ball at White Sulphur Springs.

'You will be the centre of attention and I shall be the envy of every man there,' he promised as he escorted her out of the bedroom and along the broad corridor to the head of the magnificent, brass-balustraded staircase.

As they began to walk down it she noticed, for the first time, that on a prime position overlooking the stairs there was a faded area where a large painting must have hung.

Her hand tightened involuntarily on Ivor's arm for she had no doubt at all that the painting had been the portrait of Olivia.

'All right, sweetheart?' he asked, flashing her a quick glance.

She nodded, forcing a swift bright smile, grateful that the portrait no longer hung there; knowing how disconcerting she would have found those brilliantly piercing black eyes if it had done so.

Sir Cuthbert and Lady Digby's house was in Fitzroy Square, a different area of London to the one their own home was situated in. 'And not as convenient for either Buckingham Palace or the House of Lords,' Ivor said drily as the Conisborough Rolls-Royce crossed Oxford Street in the direction of Regent's Park.

Ivor's chauffeur made a couple of right-hand turns and as they neared Fitzroy Square Delia could sense Ivor's increasing nervous tension.

That he was impatient to show her off, thrilled her and her own nervousness ebbed into pleasurable excitement.

Once they had been received by Sir Cuthbert and his elderly wife, she soon realized that the term 'birthday party' had been a complete misnomer, for the 'birthday party' was a full-scale ball. In Virginia, the balls held at White Sulphur Springs were regarded as incredibly grand, but they were nothing in comparison to this gala.

Beneath a vista of glittering chandeliers several members of the royal family had gathered, though not the King and Queen. She had quickly learned that they rarely attended private functions in the evening. There was a scattering of foreign royals – she instantly recognized a Montenegrin prince and a Russian grand duke whom she had seen at the unveiling of the Queen Victoria Memorial. The rest of the guests were British aristocrats and politicians. A vast number of men were wearing military decorations – the Montenegrin prince was as heavily festooned as a Christmas tree – and all the women were heavily and sumptuously bejewelled.

Across the crowded room she caught sight of Jerome in deep discussion with the Prime Minister, and was relieved that there was at least one person present whom she knew well enough to be able to have a friendly conversation with.

She waltzed with Ivor. She waltzed with the Montenegrin prince. She waltzed with Lord Curzon. When she wasn't dancing, Ivor introduced her to so many people that her head span. Just when she was thinking that she might be able to speak with Jerome, Ivor's hand tightened on her arm and he said, with a throb in his voice she had never heard before, 'Sylvia has arrived. So you need have no more worries about your presentation. Let me introduce you to her.'

In happy anticipation she allowed him to lead her through a throng of people to a dark-haired woman who was seated on a spindly-legged gilt chair, her face turned away from them, one hand languidly holding a fan of ostrich feathers.

She looked like a queen holding court, for though she was seated there was a semicircle of gentlemen around her, all paying her avid attention. Her gleaming hair was drawn into a flat coil on the crown of her head. Her midnight-blue sequinned gown was very slim-fitted, very *soignée*. Even before she turned her head at their approach, Delia knew her face would be spectacularly beautiful.

Ivor cleared his throat. 'Sylvia ... I would like to introduce my wife. Delia, Sylvia, Lady Bazeljette.'

As Sylvia Bazeljette turned, Delia was aware of three things.

The first was that she had been right in her assumption, for Sylvia Bazeljette was the most beautiful woman she had ever seen.

The second was that Ivor had been wrong. Her worries were not now at an end. They were escalating with such speed that she could no longer breathe; for the third thing was that the face of the woman now regarding her with mocking amusement, was the face in the photograph that had spilled from Ivor's diary.

51

Jerome's wife was the woman whose photograph Ivor needed to see on a daily basis. Jerome's wife was the woman who had written on the back of the photograph that her love was for him, and him alone.

It was all too bewildering for her to take in.

'How lovely to meet you at last.' Sylvia's husky voice was like cracked ice and the smile on her beautifully curved ruby-red lips was condescendingly patronizing. 'Ivor tells me you are to be my protégée.'

Delia gasped, bewildered no longer.

With utter certainty she knew that Sylvia Bazeljette had been Ivor's mistress. The knowing expression in her sloe-dark eyes told her so as clearly as words. Ivor's barely suppressed impatience in the Rolls-Royce had not been because he was impatient to show her, Delia, off. It had been because he was impatient to see Sylvia again. When Jerome had warned her of the lack of marital fidelity among British aristocracy, it was to prepare her for this moment.

The realization was so earth-shattering that she swayed.

Jerome, not Ivor, steadied her.

He had appeared out of nowhere and now gripped her elbow, saying nonchalantly to Sylvia and everyone standing in the semicircle around her, 'It's devilish hot in here, isn't it? I think the heat is proving too much for Lady Conisborough. It might be as well if I were to take her outside for a breath of fresh air.'

And without waiting for Ivor to answer he propelled her away from the group. Only when they had stepped though open French windows onto a blessedly empty balcony did he swing her towards him, saying fiercely, 'How, in the name of God, do you *know?*'

'Her photograph is in Ivor's diary.' She began to shiver. 'I thought it was a photograph of Olivia.'

He swore beneath his breath and she said, 'I don't understand, Jerome. Was it after Olivia's death that ... that...' She wanted to say, 'that my husband and your wife became lovers,' but she couldn't.

He didn't finish her sentence for her. Instead he said brusquely, 'You're cold. I'll go to the cloakroom for your evening cloak.'

'No!' She put a hand on his arm, appalled at the thought of being left alone on the balcony. 'I'm not cold, Jerome. It's the shock. I thought Ivor kept the photograph where he could see it every day because, despite his being so much in love with me, he was also still grieving for Olivia. And I could understand that...'

'Stay here,' he said, his voice charged with emotion. The anger he felt towards her husband and his wife was so intense he thought he was going to explode with it. 'I'm going back to give your apologies to Lady Digby. I shall say I'm escorting you home as you have a headache, and that I am doing so, instead of Ivor, as the King has asked him to speak in an unofficial capacity to one of her guests. The Montenegrin royal will be a good choice as it's common knowledge he returns to the Balkans tomorrow.'

'What about Ivor?' she said, knowing she

couldn't possibly face her husband until they were in the privacy of their own home.

'I'll give him the same message, and publicly, so that there is no gossip about you leaving with me. He'll pick up straight away on the Montenegrin red herring. And when we leave there's no need for us to walk the length of the ballroom. There's a small side staircase a few yards to the left of the French windows.'

Without waiting for a reply he was gone, the French windows swinging shut behind him.

She closed her eyes, knowing that the very worst thing about what had happened was that there was no question of her having put two and two together and making five. Though Jerome hadn't said so specifically, it was too obvious that he knew his wife had been Ivor's mistress for her to have made any mistake about it.

From beyond the closed doors came the sound of laughter and the buzz of animated conversation. And then the orchestra struck up into a deafening Strauss waltz.

She dug her nails into her palms, knowing that she was going to have to come to terms with the fact that she would regularly be meeting with her husband's ex-mistress. Even worse, that Sylvia would be presenting her at court.

She bit her lip so hard that she tasted blood. She had thought Ivor sensitive, yet in having asked Sylvia to present her at court he had behaved in a way that was unimaginably cruel. She remembered Jerome's shock – the way he had said in stunned incredulity, 'Ivor has asked *Sylvia* to present you?' when she had told him what the arrangements for her presentation were.

She tried to think how she would feel, being accompanied to Buckingham Palace by a woman who was as intimately acquainted with Ivor's body as she was; a woman who knew exactly how he kissed; how he always shouted at his moment of climax.

It was a situation so far removed from anything she had ever previously experienced that she didn't have the slightest idea how she was going to handle it. All she wanted to do was go home and wait for Ivor to return. When he did, he would, she was sure, make everything all right. He would explain about the photograph and how he had forgotten it was still tucked in his diary. He would explain how, after Olivia's death, he was so stupendously lonely that he had embarked on an affair with Sylvia. She tried not to think of how Sylvia was Jerome's wife and that Ivor's having an affair with her was the action of a cad. She would come to terms with that later. For now, all that mattered was that Ivor reassured her that she was the one he loved with all his heart and that his feelings for Sylvia were in the past.

The French windows opened and Jerome stepped onto the balcony again, her cloak over his arm. 'We can leave without causing gossip, Delia,' he said, slipping the evening cloak around her shoulders. 'Clara Digby sends her sympathy and will call on you in the morning. Are you ready to make the short walk to the side stairs?'

She nodded and he took her arm.

Jerome's motor car was parked in the square and there was no chauffeur. He opened the front passenger door for her. 'I always drive myself,' he said, knowing very well that Ivor never did so. 'I hope you'll feel safe.'

'I shall.' She managed a wobbly smile and something terrible trembled within him.

As she huddled deeply in her warmly lined cloak he cranked up the car.

A few minutes later they were driving out of the square and into Fitzroy Street and she said with touching simplicity, 'Is it because Sylvia has been unfaithful to you, that you are unfaithful to her?'

He crossed Howland Street and continued into Charlotte Street, fighting the temptation to say yes and gain her sympathy, knowing that if he did she might, in a little while, even turn to him for comfort.

With any other woman – especially a woman so overwhelmingly desirable – it was a ploy he wouldn't have thought twice about using. Delia, however, was different. In the short time they had known each other he knew she would become a friend and, unscrupulous as he was about many things, he was always punctiliously truthful to his friends.

'No,' he said. 'I'm unfaithful to Sylvia because being unfaithful is in my nature. I'm sorry if I disappoint you, Delia.'

She shook her head to show that it didn't matter to her; only Ivor mattered to her. Ivor, whom she suddenly felt she didn't know at all.

Jerome changed gear. 'Would you like me to take you somewhere you can get your thoughts in order before going home? We could drive out to Hampstead if you'd like?'

She shook her head. 'No. I want to be in the house when Ivor arrives. I want him to explain about the photograph to me – and I want him to tell me that I need never spend time with Sylvia again after she presents me at court.'

They were driving down Park Lane, Hyde Park dark and mysterious on their right-hand side.

He frowned, his face grim.

She was so young, so far from home – and her situation was far more catastrophic than she yet realized. He said unhappily, 'If you ever need me, you've only to telephone my club, the Carlton, and leave a message for me there.'

'Thank you – and thank you for bringing me home,' she said, as he turned into Cadogan Square. 'And don't worry about me, Jerome. You told me this afternoon that marital fidelity wasn't a virtue highly esteemed among the British aristocracy, but my marriage is far different. Whatever the situation that existed in the aftermath of Olivia's death, it isn't one that will continue. Ivor loves me now and he will be as faithful to me as I shall be to him.'

He brought the car to an abrupt halt, knowing that he should say something – and being unable to bring himself to do so.

With the breath hurting in his chest he walked around the car and helped her step from it.

She squeezed his hand tightly and then, without another word, ran across the pavement and up the steps.

If Bellingham and Ellie and the rest of the servants were intrigued by her arriving home unescorted by Ivor they gave no indication of it.

57

Bellingham was as imperturbable as ever and when Ellie removed the white rose from her hair and unpinned her chignon, she did so swiftly and silently.

Later, when Ellie had left her, Delia seated herself at her dressing table and stared at her reflection in the mirror. The face looking back at her was not the face of the carefree young girl who had left the house three hours ago.

White lines of tension edged her mouth. She had told Jerome that whatever situation had existed between Ivor and Sylvia after Olivia's death, it was one that existed no longer, but as she remembered the expression in Sylvia's voice and in her eyes, fear flickered in her chest.

Sylvia's demeanour had not been that of a woman whose lover had fallen in love elsewhere. Her expression was one of a woman whose lover's marriage was of no consequence whatsoever.

It would, though, be of consequence to Ivor. Of that she was sure.

She looked towards the small clock that stood on her dressing table. It was now an hour since Jerome had escorted her home, and with luck Ivor had already told Sylvia that no matter what her expectations to the contrary, their affair was over.

Fraught with tension, Delia began brushing her hair hard. Then, from the street, she heard the sound of a car door closing. She held her breath, the hairbrush motionless in mid-air. Moments later the front door opened.

Slowly she lay the brush down.

There was a sound of muted male voices,

though whether Ivor was speaking to Bellingham or to his valet she couldn't tell. Quite possibly he was telling his valet he wouldn't be requiring him.

There came the sound of his tread on the broad sweeping staircase.

She remained where she was sitting.

The door opened and their eyes met in the mirror.

He smiled and closed the door behind him. 'I take it you've recovered from your headache,' he said, walking towards her while undoing his tie. 'It was a great shame it attacked when it did. Sylvia was most concerned.'

She didn't believe that for a moment, but she said, surprised at how steady her voice was, 'I didn't have a headache, Ivor. I left the ball because I'd had a shock.'

'A shock?' He tossed the bow tie onto her dressing table and said, intrigued, 'What kind of a shock?'

'The other day when you left in a hurry for the Palace, you forgot to take your appointments diary with you. I picked it up, intending to run after you to give it to you, and a photograph fell from it. I thought it was a photograph of Olivia, and that despite us being so happy together you were still grieving for her. But tonight ... tonight I realized the photograph wasn't of Olivia. It was of Sylvia.'

'I have photographs of lots of my close friends in and among my personal possessions, Delia. The photograph I have of Sylvia isn't one that need cause you concern.'

Not rising from the vanity stool she turned

59

around to face him. 'There was a very personal message on the back of the photograph,' she said, her voice no longer so steady. 'It said, "All my love, darling Ivor, is for you and you alone."'

She waited.

A pulse began to throb at the corner of his jaw.

She licked lips that were suddenly dry and said, 'And so ... and so I know that she was once your mistress, and though I wish that you had told me ... and that you hadn't arranged for her to present me at court ... I do understand. Or at least I think I understand.'

Despite his sophistication he had the look of a man who was cornered; a man who couldn't decide on the best course of action. With sudden certainty she knew she had to assure him that she wasn't going to let Sylvia destroy their happiness. She had to let him know that she was mature enough to understand how such a thing could have happened.

Speaking very fast she said, 'My uncle, Ellis Chandler, was widowed when in his early forties and he almost immediately began a most unsuitable relationship with a showgirl from White Sulphur Springs. One of my aunts was very scathing about his behaviour and my mother was very cross with her, telling her that it was simply Ellis's way of coping with his grief. And so I know that unsuitable affairs are something newly widowed men sometimes have.'

Instead of being grateful for the allowances she was so obviously trying to make for him, he said explosively, 'For God's sake, Delia! Sylvia isn't a White Sulphur Springs showgirl! And there is no

60

similarity whatsoever between me and your uncle!'

It was so very much the opposite of what she had expected that she gasped.

He rubbed the back of his neck in a short, sharp, convulsive movement and then, when he had regained control of himself, said tautly, 'I'm sorry, Delia. I shouldn't have spoken like that. And I'm very, very sorry that I've been unfair to you.'

'Unfair to me?' The conversation was veering so far from the course she had expected it to take, that she felt dizzy. 'Unfair to me in what way, Ivor?'

'Unfair in that I married you without telling you of my commitment to Sylvia.'

'Your *past* commitment,' she said, her voice so strained she barely recognized it. 'Surely you mean your *past* commitment, Ivor?'

He shook his head and panic bubbled in her throat. Vainly trying to see things from his point of view, she said, 'I understand what a shock our marriage must have been to Sylvia, Ivor. And I understand that because of your friendship with her you feel that you still have some kind of commitment to her, but...'

'No, Delia.' The expression in his eyes was one of deep regret for the hurt he was about to cause. 'Sylvia and I were never merely friends.'

She blinked, bewildered. 'I don't understand.'

'We were always lovers,' he said and then, as if unable to bear the pain of her shock and disbelief, he turned away from her and walked across to one of the tall windows.

She didn't speak. Couldn't speak.

He lifted the curtain and looked out. 'We've been lovers since before my marriage to Olivia. Since before Sylvia's marriage to Jerome.' He let the curtain fall and turned towards her again. 'I would have told you when we'd been married for a little longer, when you had gained a little sophistication and come to understand how things are in my world.'

'You married me when you were in love with someone else?' She felt at the edge of a bottomless abyss. 'You married me without loving me?'

'It's true I had an ulterior motive when I asked you to marry me, but that doesn't mean I don't love you, Delia. In my own way, I do. You're a joy to look at and a joy to be with – and you amuse me immeasurably.'

She was over the edge of the abyss now, and falling. 'But I'm not your soulmate.' Against her fiery hair her face was deathly white. 'Sylvia is your soulmate. You love her more than you love me.'

'I love her differently.' He paused, seeking for words. 'She's my intellectual equal,' he said at last. 'And for twenty years we've been bound together by hoops of steel. It's a situation that has to be accepted, Delia.'

Her heart drummed against her breastbone. Of all the scenarios she had imagined when on her way home with Jerome, none had been as terrible as this.

She said incredulously, 'And you won't give her up?'

He shook his head. 'No. I'm sorry.'

She wanted to fly at him, claw his face, scream at him that he *had* to give her up; but she didn't. She was too numb, too stupefied with shock – and besides, she knew it would be of no use. In the short time they had been married she had come to realize that beneath Ivor's suave charm there was a side to him that was absolutely implacable and that tears, scenes and demands would always be powerless to move him.

She realized also that what he was doing was giving her a choice. She could accept her position – a newly married woman whose husband had a long-standing mistress – or she could refuse. And refusing would mean marital separation and eventual divorce.

With options such as these, there was no real choice at all.

She was going to have to make the best of the hand fate had dealt her, but it wouldn't be the Delia Ivor had married who would do so, the loving, trusting, carelessly happy, naive Delia. It would be a new Delia. A hardened Delia. A Delia who would hold her own in the glittering, cynical, amoral world she had been plunged into.

'There are just two things I want to know,' she said, as all her wonderful castles in the air tumbled to the ground. 'If you have loved Sylvia since before your marriage to Olivia, and before her marriage to Jerome, why did you marry Olivia and not Sylvia?'

He took a silver cigar tube from the inside pocket of his black tailcoat and removed the cigar from it. 'Olivia was the only daughter of the Duke of Rothenbury,' he said, cutting the end off the cigar with the cigar-cutter attached to his watch chain. 'Sylvia's father, though a millionaire, was in commerce – not that many people now remember that. The distinction was one that mattered to me at the time. What is the second thing you would like to know?'

She began to shake, not knowing how it was possible to feel such pain and live. 'You said you had an ulterior motive in marrying me.' It was all she could do to force the words past her lips. 'What was it?'

He lit his cigar and blew a plume of blue smoke upwards.

'I wanted an heir,' he said simply. 'And I still do.'

Time wavered and halted and would, she knew never be the same again.

She remembered the time at Sans Souci when her father had said of her Aunt Rose's hopes of catching Ivor, 'When Conisborough marries again it will be to a woman much younger than Rose. He'll want an heir and, because of his age, he'll want one fast.'

She thought of all the times he had made love to her so passionately. Had it always been only because of his need of an heir? She knew that she would never know – and that she would never know in the future either.

The only thing she could ever be certain of was that he didn't love her in the way she deserved to be loved – and that her heart was broken.

FOUR

'I think I'll wear the Poiret embroidered gold silk tonight, Ellie. It's only four weeks until Christmas and it will make me feel suitably festive.'

'The house will soon be looking suitably festive as well, my lady,' Ellie said chattily as she opened the doors of Delia's vast armoire to take out the evening gown. 'The head gardener always sees to it that there's an enormous fir tree in the hall here at Shibden and in past years, when Lady Olivia was alive, all the staff were allowed to help decorate it.'

'Were they?' Delia continued opening an array of jewellery boxes. 'That's interesting. I didn't know that.'

'I don't suppose his lordship thought to mention it, my lady.' Ellie laid the gown on the bed. 'Everyone always enjoyed it very much, though.'

Her meaning was clear and Delia didn't disappoint her. 'If it has become a tradition it is one I shall keep,' she said, trying to decide between an emerald necklace and a diamond one. 'Do you know if the Prime Minister has arrived yet?'

'He arrived about fifteen minutes ago, my lady.' Ellie helped her into the dress. 'Mrs Asquith is in her room, being attended to by her maid. His lordship and the Prime Minister are having a private conversation in the Blue Room.'

Delia breathed in as Ellie fastened the gown's

tiny hooks and eyes, not remotely surprised that Ellie knew the exact whereabouts of the evening's most important guests. 'And Sir Cuthbert and Lady Digby?'

'Still in their room. Parkinson said that when he arrived Sir Cuthbert looked a little tired.'

Parkinson was Shibden Hall's butler and, like Ellie, missed nothing.

'And most of the other guests?' Though Delia had hostessed weekend house parties before at Shibden Hall, this was the first the Prime Minister had attended and she was anxious that everything ran smoothly. The last thing she wanted was for someone to cancel.

'Yes, my lady.'

'And the Damnyankee?'

Ellie grinned, knowing that though Delia often used the expression in a derogatory way, in this case she was using it with deep affection. 'The Duchess of Marlborough hasn't arrived as yet, but she has a reputation for lateness.'

'Ah, well. There ain't nobody like her for niceness and so her faults can be easily overlooked.' It wasn't often now that Delia's speech lapsed into a Virginian drawl, but when it did it always made Ellie laugh.

She giggled now as Delia handed her the emerald necklace.

'And Sir Jerome and Lady Bazeljette?' she asked as Ellie fastened the necklace around her throat, not betraying by a flicker what it cost her to utter Lady Bazeljette's name. 'Have they arrived?'

'Not yet, my lady.'

Delia fastened her emerald pendant earrings,

knowing there was not the slightest chance of Sylvia forgoing a weekend at Shibden.

It was an issue she and Ivor had fought long and hard about. 'She didn't visit Shibden when Olivia was alive,' Delia had said furiously. 'I know, because Jerome mentioned to me that he was never invited here and, though he fudged the reason, that can only have been because Olivia put her foot down about having Sylvia beneath Shibden's roof.'

'And she could get away with it because she was a duke's daughter,' Ivor had said. 'You, sweetheart, can't pull the same rank. And if she *isn't* invited here by you, it will cause just the kind of gossip you are so anxious to avoid.'

No longer in awe of him, as she had been in the days when she had thought him noble and honourable, she had thrown a book at his head.

Such scenes were blessedly rare, partly because they were together far less than she had imagined they would be. This was not because his time was spent with Sylvia, but because as financial advisor to the King his workload was a heavy one. The necessity of having to adjust with great rapidity to a life centred at court and among the royal set had given Delia little time to brood. First there had been her presentation. She had insisted Ivor make known to Sylvia her awareness that she was his mistress and that, though Delia realized she had absolutely no option but to be presented at court by her, she had no intention of speaking to Sylvia on the subject, then or ever.

This he had done and, from then on, whenever they met there was no trace of condescending

67

amusement in Sylvia's violet-dark eyes. Instead, beneath a veneer of exquisite politeness, there was a frosty hauteur which Delia returned in full measure.

The presentation had been her baptism of fire and, with steely resolve, she had survived it magnificently. After that, thanks to the inner strength that now never let her down, nothing held any terrors, not even the awesome ceremonial of the coronation. In her crimson and ermine robe she had looked – and felt – so grand, she had doubted if anyone in Virginia would have been able to recognize her. The length of the gown's train and the width of the ermine on it denoted rank and, as a viscountess, her train was one and a quarter yards long, the ermine two inches wide. That Sylvia Bazeljette's train was far shorter and the ermine trim far narrower gave her a stab of satisfaction she didn't even try to be ashamed of.

Three weeks after the coronation, she and Ivor had been in attendance at the investiture of Edward, Prince of Wales, at Caernarvon Castle. It had been another occasion of medieval ceremony with the seventeen-year-old, golden-haired prince looking almost a child beneath the weight of his robes and fleurs-de-lys decorated crown.

She had been so enraptured by the spectacle she had clutched Ivor's arm, saying breathlessly, 'Oh, isn't it a cracking occasion, Ivor! I'm so glad I'm here!'

He had patted her hand and smiled down at her and it was almost as it had been before she had known of his infidelity. Almost, but – to her continuing distress – not quite.

She now took a last look at herself in the three-way mirror and liked what she saw. Emeralds were perfect with her flame-red hair and the gold silk was so seductive on her youthful body she couldn't imagine anyone, even Sylvia, outshining her.

There was a knock at the door and Ellie opened it to Gwen.

'Darling, nearly everyone is gathered in the drawing room and it's time for you to make an appearance,' she said as she swept in, her angular frame resplendent in an evening gown of beaded grey silk, a pearl and diamond necklace hanging to her waist. 'I've just seen Margot Asquith and she's looking very dramatic, but then she always does. She was wearing a full-length scarlet cloak when she arrived. You will remember that her Christian name is pronounced without the "t", won't you? I only mention it because I'm sure you are nervous and Americans do have such trouble with English names. Pugh once had his name pronounced Pug by the American Ambassador. I believe he quite lost control, thundering, "Pew! *Pew!*" until someone brought him a very large brandy.'

Delia chuckled. 'I'm not surprised my country-man was stumped. The difference between the spelling and pronunciation of some names is enough to give anyone a headache. Unless you heard Cholmondeley and Dalziel and Geoghegan spoken, you'd never know how to say them. And I'm not nervous, Gwen. Truly.'

Gwen cocked her head to one side. 'No, you're not, are you? For a girl so young you really do have the most enormous self-composure as well

69

as the most delightful vivacity. You are becoming a great social asset to Ivor – and he knows it.'

'Does he?' Delia quirked an eyebrow and then, arm in arm with her sister-in-law, she walked downstairs to meet her distinguished guests.

There were twenty to dinner. The Prime Minister and Mrs Asquith. The Duke and Duchess of Girlington. Consuelo, Duchess of Marlborough. The Earl and Countess of Denby. Gwen and her husband. Sir Cuthbert and Lady Digby. Lord Curzon. Mrs Marie Belloc Lowndes, a renowned novelist and a close friend of Margot Asquith's. Winston Churchill, First Lord of the Admiralty, and his wife, Clementine. Sir John Simon, Solicitor-General. And Sir Jerome and Lady Bazeljette.

As Delia took her place opposite Ivor at the head of the table, he flashed her one of his rare smiles and she knew he was pleased with the way she looked and with her social confidence.

Within minutes, Sylvia caused controversy. Well aware that Marie Belloc Lowndes was a committed supporter of the suffragette movement and that Ivor and the majority of the other guests, particularly the Prime Minister, Lord Curzon and Mr Churchill were anti-suffragist, she said sweetly, 'I understand you took part in the last Votes for Women march dressed as Queen Boadicea. Was it not rather chilly for you, Marie?'

'I wasn't bare-breasted, Sylvia.' Marie took a sip of her wine. 'And if you are hoping to embarrass me, you've failed.'

Mr Asquith, whose government was refusing to give way in any shape or form to suffragette pressure, cleared his throat.

His wife, who was tired of having the windows at 10 Downing Street smashed, and certain the suffragettes meant to cause her husband bodily harm, said raspingly, 'Really, Sylvia. Isn't it enough that we have to contend with suffragette nonsense in our public lives without having it made an issue at house parties as well?'

Sylvia, wearing a glittering, black, off-the-shoulder gown, shrugged carelessly and Delia saw her eyes meet Ivor's.

She felt a rush of anger, certain the remark hadn't been said in order to embarrass Marie, but to lure Delia herself into making comments that would infuriate Ivor and distance her from the Asquiths.

She admired the suffragettes hugely and avoiding Sylvia's trap was an agony; but just when she thought she couldn't bear it for another minute, the First Lord of the Admiralty ignored the very broad hint that the subject should be dropped, by saying pugnaciously, 'Women don't need the vote. Not when their fathers, husbands and brothers can represent their views.'

'But do they?' Viola Girlington lifted her naked shoulder expressively from a sea of indigo tulle. 'Girlington doesn't represent *my* views.' She looked across the table to where her husband was seated between Consuelo Marlborough and Clementine Churchill. 'In fact, I'm not sure he knows them,' she said, the amusement in her voice taking the sting from her words. 'As for dearest Marie dressing as Queen Boadicea, the image is one I would love to sculpt.'

'I'd love you to do that,' Jerome said, 'especially

if the representation was bare-breasted.'

There was general laughter and, as Viola was a serious artist of exceptional talent, the conversation veered away from women's suffrage and towards the arts.

Jerome caught Delia's eye and he gave her a discreet wink, indicating he well knew that she had exercised restraint only to avoid giving Sylvia satisfaction.

As the footmen cleared the first course away, she determined to join the Women's Social and Political Union as soon as she could. If Ivor didn't like it – which he wouldn't – then he could just go whistle.

Consuelo changed the subject by saying in her gentle voice, 'Do you know that Lord Croomb's bride-to-be is an American?' She smiled at Delia. 'We Americans are soon going to be no longer a minority on this side of the Atlantic.'

'I understand the bride is worth millions and the groom is land-rich and cash-strapped,' Sylvia said with a throaty laugh, turning towards George Curzon, who was seated on her right. 'Which surely makes the arrangement more of a business merger than a marriage.'

There was more laughter, but Consuelo didn't laugh and, knowing that her mother had forced her into her marriage purely for the title and that on the marriage the duke had collected millions of dollars in railroad stock from Consuelo's father, Delia didn't laugh either. She was fond of Consuelo and knew she was desperately unhappy.

Seeing the expression in Consuelo's eyes it struck her that perhaps Sylvia wasn't quite as overwhelmingly popular as she had thought – at least not with other women. There was a venom that, though she tried hard to hide it, was glimpsed all too often.

The knowledge cheered her. She didn't want Sylvia to be well liked. She wanted her to be heartily loathed.

By the time dessert was served, the conversation had turned to politics, as Delia had known it would considering the political positions of most of the men present.

'It would seem Europe is rapidly arranging itself into two opposite camps,' George Curzon said, prodding at his Pêches à la Reine Alexandra. 'On the one hand is the Triple Entente of Britain, France and Russia; on the other the Triple Alliance of Germany, Austria-Hungary and Italy. What will be the outcome, do you think?'

He was looking towards Herbert Asquith as he spoke but it was Winston Churchill who answered him. 'War,' he said with vigour. 'And we must be prepared for it. Isn't that so, Prime Minister?'

Asquith gave a heavy sigh and Delia, who had now met him several times and become quite a favourite with HH, as he had asked her to call him, realized he had been hoping for a relaxing weekend away from government matters. Not very tall, he had a rock-like build and massive head, neck and shoulders. Turning a little wearily to his First Lord of the Admiralty, he said, 'The Foreign Secretary is to make a proposal to Germany and Italy that a conference be held here, in London. That should settle things. We none of us want war, Winston, do we?'

73

Winston looked as though he very much wanted war, and, by the expression on his face, so did George.

As the talk continued, with the Countess of Denby saying silkily, 'With foreigners increasing their armies, I'm all for a big navy,' Delia experienced a moment of deep self-awareness.

Though not happy – happiness while Ivor continued his relationship with Sylvia was impossible – she was exhilarated. How could she not be when she was playing hostess to such distinguished, powerful, clever people? She wondered what it would be like to have nothing more stimulating than a weekend at White Sulphur Springs to look forward to, and shuddered. Much as she still missed her mother and Sans Souci, she knew she could never live there again, not when she enjoyed her life as Viscountess Conisborough so much.

With Jerome's help she had boned up on European politics so that she not only understood the conversations taking place at her dinner table, but was also able to take part in them. Republican to the core, she nevertheless enjoyed the theatricality of royal ceremonial, and despite finding a dinner at Buckingham Palace to be a surprisingly dull affair, the experience was one she wouldn't have wanted to miss. Neither would she have wanted to miss visiting nearby Sandringham, where she had met the Prince of Wales. He was only a year her junior and the two of them had got on like a house on fire.

It was the same with nearly all Ivor's friends and acquaintances. Though she worked hard at being agreeable to them, it was their children with whom she had instant rapport. One of the Duke and Duchess of Girlington's daughters, Daphne, was exactly her own age, for instance, and breezily rackety and unconventional. The Prime Minister's daughter-in-law, Cynthia, was also great fun.

The only thing marring her life was Sylvia's presence at nearly every event or social function they attended. Making this marginally easier for her was Ivor's impeccable behaviour whenever Sylvia was at Cadogan Square or at Shibden. At Shibden house parties, many of their guests made night-time visits to rooms other than their own, but Ivor never roamed. What he did elsewhere, of course, was very different.

One of the greatest shocks she'd had to overcome was the realization that Jerome had been speaking the absolute truth when he told her that in smart society amorous intrigues were the norm. Sir Cuthbert, for instance, was embroiled in a passionate affair with Lady Denby, something to which both of their partners, as they engaged in banter across the dining table, seemed supremely indifferent. It was well known that the Duke of Girlington gave most of his affection not to his wife, Viola, but to Violet Vanburgh, an actress, and that his supremely beautiful wife had her choice of lovers. Even HH was known to prefer spending time with the daughter of Lord Sheffield rather than with Margot – though as Margot was so formidable and sharp-tongued it didn't come as too much of a surprise.

She glanced across at Winston and Clementine. They had not been married long and so far there had been no whisper of any infidelities; nor did

Delia think there ever would be. Jerome, of course, was the most blatant of adulterers. After a long affair with Princess Sermerrini, a member of the Royal House of Savoy, he was now conducting affairs with two married ladies, saying that it was more challenging than conducting an affair with only one.

Just back from a European holiday – he had been to Berlin and Rome and come home via Paris – he was now leaning back, a brandy glass in one hand, his swarthy skin and gypsy-dark curls setting him apart from the other men, all of whom were either elderly and white-haired or, as in the case of Ivor, George and Winston, had mouse-fair hair worn glassily smooth.

As she watched, she saw the Prime Minister exchange a meaningful glance with Jerome and wondered about their relationship, for though Jerome wasn't a member of the government he was obviously on surprisingly easy terms with Mr Asquith.

Winston ceased being pugnacious and cracked a joke and as the champagne flowed and anecdotes and witticisms whizzed back and forth across the table, Delia knew everyone was enjoying themselves hugely. After the meal, Ivor was unconventional in that he saw no reason for ladies to leave the table while the men passed around the port. Once gathered in the drawing room, Gwen asked George Curzon if he would recite Tennyson's 'The Revenge: A Ballad of the Fleet'.

'For considering dear Winston is First Lord of the Admiralty, I think it would be most appropriate,' she said as Ivor gave a mock groan. 'Especially as our navy could very soon be facing enemy ships.'

'Quite right, Gwendolyn.' Curzon rose to his feet, struck a suitably grave posture and began sonorously:

At Flores in the Azores Sir Richard Grenville lay,
And a pinnace, like a flutter'd bird, came flying
   from far away:
'Spanish ships of war at sea! We have sighted
   fifty-three!'

At the last words of verse ten, 'Fight on! Fight on!', the cheering nearly took Shibden's roof off.

Once Curzon's party piece was over, Consuelo insisted on Viola Girlington playing the piano and singing some lieder for them, which she did with heart-stopping skill and emotion, and then Sylvia said in a falsely sweet voice, 'Your turn now, Delia. We've never heard you sing, but I'm sure your voice is exquisite.'

Delia, well aware Sylvia had only made the suggestion because she assumed she was tone deaf, hesitated just long enough to see confirmation that she had been right slide into Sylvia's eyes and then she said in an exaggerated southern drawl, 'What a crackin' good idea. Ah'll be only too happy to oblige.'

Ivor, annoyed at the accent and knowing that after Viola any other singer was likely to sound dreadfully banal, frowned warningly.

Delia ignored him and crossed the room to where Viola was still seated at the piano. As she

77

whispered in Viola's ear and as he saw the change on Viola's face, his consternation grew.

Delia faced her audience. 'This is especially for Consuelo,' she said, and launched into an exuberant, full-throated rendering of 'Dixie'.

Consuelo squealed protestingly. Jerome burst out laughing. When it came to the chorus everyone, even Winston, whose mother, like Consuelo, had been born on the wrong side of the Mason–Dixon line, joined in with gusto and great foot stamping. Everyone, that is, except Sylvia – and as all her other guests, including the Prime Minister, clapped and cheered, Delia no longer cared about Sylvia.

Later, long past midnight, when all their guests had gone to bed, Ivor said to her, 'It was a splendid evening, Delia. It's a long time since I've seen the Prime Minister enjoy himself so much.'

'Then why are you looking so grave?'

He looked down thoughtfully at the cigar he was holding. 'Because Winston has asked me to go to Germany.'

'Go to Germany?' Her eyes widened. 'Whatever for?'

'Because I have highly placed friends in German financial circles. One of them, Albert Ballin, is as close to the Kaiser as I am to King George. Winston wants me to have an informal conversation with him about the pace of Germany's shipbuilding programme. It's just possible a man as influential as Ballin will be able to persuade the Kaiser to bring it to a halt. If it isn't, sooner or later it will almost certainly lead to war.'

Delia drew in a sharp breath. When Winston

78

had uttered the word 'war' she had thought it merely typical of his desire to shock, not a serious possibility.

'When do you leave?'

'Monday morning.'

She remembered the glance Jerome and the Prime Minister had exchanged and said hesitantly, 'Do you think Jerome was doing something similar when he was in Berlin and Rome? Do you think he was speaking informally to influential people on HH's behalf?'

'Jerome a diplomatic negotiator? I don't think so, Delia.' He chuckled. 'The only reason for Jerome to go to Berlin would be to see one of his many mistresses. The same applies to his jaunt to Rome – unless he's considering converting to Catholicism.'

Still chuckling, he walked with her from the drawing room, leaving it to the maid to turn down all the lights.

It was a moment of closeness that was repeated quite often as the cold spring of 1912 melted into a hot summer, but, for Delia, it wasn't repeated often enough. There was something so coolly distant in Ivor's personality, so remote and detached, that she doubted their relationship would have been much different even without the added complication of Sylvia.

There were times when she would have liked to say as much to Jerome, but at their first meeting after her realization that Ivor's affair with Sylvia wasn't going to end, they had made a pact not to talk about their respective spouses unless it was absolutely necessary. Not doing so meant that the time they spent together was enjoyable. Though her Episcopalian upbringing ensured that the extra-marital affairs of other friends shocked her, Jerome's affairs never bothered her, probably because he never took any of them seriously. She teased him about them unmercifully and he teased her for her lack of lovers when nearly all her married women friends had at least one.

As the year wore on, the optimism she had gained from Ivor's irreproachable behaviour whenever Sylvia was their guest, faded, for he was quite ruthless in spending time with her on other occasions.

In September, when Sylvia was again enjoying a month-long vacation in Nice, he took an equally long vacation in nearby Monaco. In November, when Sylvia went to Market Harborough for a month to enjoy the beginning of the foxhunting season, he went too, accompanied by Lord Denby and Cuthie, who were both addicted huntsmen. Ivor wasn't, and Delia knew that the only reason he was spending four weeks riding hard over the Leicestershire countryside in appalling weather was because then he would be spending time with Sylvia.

It was a situation she had no choice but to accept, but it caused her a lot of deep unhappiness. Her constant hope was that when she became pregnant and Ivor had the son and heir he craved, things would change and Sylvia would begin to play a less and less important part in his life. By the beginning of 1913, however, the longed-for baby still hadn't materialized.

'I'm beginning to think I'm as barren as Olivia was,' she said bleakly to Jerome as they strolled in St James's Park. 'And if I am, Ivor will divorce me in the hope of a bit more luck in marriage number three.'

'Has he said he will divorce you?' There was surprise in Jerome's voice. 'It sounds a bit too Henry VIII for Ivor.'

It was a sunny day and Delia was carrying a parasol. She twirled it thoughtfully. 'No. He's never said as much. I'm just worried that he might want to. But divorced men aren't received at court, are they? The social stigma would matter a great deal to him.'

'And would put an end to his position as financial advisor to the King,' Jerome said drily, 'so I wouldn't worry about the possibility too much.'

'But I do. In any case, I want a baby just as much as Ivor does!' With a sudden outburst of emotion she swung to face him. 'It would be too cruel to have a marriage that isn't the kind of marriage I yearn for and to have no children either! I couldn't bear it, Jerome! Truly I couldn't!'

He took hold of her free hand and squeezed it hard. 'You're only twenty, Delia. You'll have babies. I'm sure of it.'

There was such fierce certainty in his eyes that she was almost convinced.

Aware that she was beginning to attract attention from passers-by she steadied her breathing. 'Sorry for that outburst,' she said as she began walking again. She flashed him an apologetic smile. 'Do you think Jack's nanny would mind if we took him off her hands for an hour or two? We could go boating or to the zoo.'

Taking his six-year-old son out on afternoon excursions was something they often did. At first, she had been reluctant to even meet Jack, terrified she wouldn't be able to look at him without being reminded of Sylvia, but when they finally met she had felt a vast wave of relief. He was as raven-haired as Sylvia, but as Jerome was raven-haired too it was a similarity she was able to cope with – and there were no other similarities. He didn't have her violet-dark eyes. He didn't have her perfect pre-Raphaelite features.

His brown eyes had the same gold flecks as Jerome's, his hair was just as curly. Even his fun-loving, equable nature was like Jerome's. Feeling his small hand in hers whenever they were on one of their little excursions always brought a lump into her throat, and the time the three of them spent together was very precious to her.

'The zoo, I think,' Jerome said as they exited the park and he hailed a cab to take them to Chelsea. 'Jack's having a love affair with the chimpanzees.'

She laughed as he opened the cab door for her, grateful that Sylvia was so indifferent as to whom her son spent time with; grateful that the world held someone she loved being with so much – Jerome.

In the summer she made a trip home to Virginia, explaining to her parents that Ivor hadn't been able to accompany her owing to his royal duties. For weeks she spent long hours riding the countryside she loved and jumping every high fence in sight. She even spent a weekend in White Sulphur

Springs and was amused by Beau persistently introducing her as 'ma second cousin, Viscountess Conisborough. Her husband, the Viscount, is on real friendly terms with England's King, don't ya know.'

While she was away, Jerome was ill. His letter was dismissive of it. In his usual bold handwriting he wrote:

It was nothing to worry about. Just one of those childish ailments that affect adults badly. Is there much talk in Virginia about the ruckus in the Balkans?

'Hardly any,' she had written back, and added, to amuse him:

Which isn't surprising when you consider that most Virginians don't know where the Balkans are. My bad news is that my mother is very ill and I am going to remain in Virginia, probably until Christmas and maybe even longer.

When she returned to London in February, it was to discover that in her absence Sylvia had acted as Ivor's hostess at Cadogan Square.

'And did you make love to her here?' Her rage and pain were so intense she felt she was going to explode. 'Did you make love to her in my bed?'

'Hysteria doesn't suit you, Delia.' His voice and eyes were as chilly as the North Sea. 'If Gwen had been able to act as my hostess for the very important dinner I gave, then she would have. As she was indisposed with influenza, Sylvia did so instead. You are making an undignified scene

83

over nothing.'

'Your mistress publicly acts as if my home is hers and you call it nothing?' Her face was as white as a sheet. 'Who were your guests? Were Margot and HH among them? Was George Curzon?'

He remained frigidly tight-lipped and she whirled away from him, hurrying blindly from the house, intent on finding comfort in the arms of the one person who never failed her.

Four months later, as the political crisis deepened, she was serenely uncaring for she was happier than she had been for almost three years. She was pregnant.

Ivor was ecstatic, though not so pleased as to stay in London when Sylvia departed for one of her regular trips to Nice.

'He's gone to Monaco,' she said bitterly to Jerome. 'It doesn't look as if anything is going to change, does it?'

'No,' he said wryly, feeling her crushing disappointment like a knife twisting in his heart. Morning sickness, coupled with Ivor's long absences, brought her social life almost to a halt. When the many predictions of war with Germany were fulfilled a few months later Delia barely saw even Ivor for there was an immediate banking crisis of major proportions and, as a member of the Privy Council, he was constantly in meetings of one kind or another. It was Jerome she missed most, though, for within days of war being declared he was off to his home county, Somerset, in order to volunteer with the North Somerset Mounted Infantry.

She lunched occasionally with Margot Asquith, who was a great admirer of Sir John French, the leader of the British Expeditionary Force. 'With French in command it will be over in six weeks and the Boche knocked into a cocked hat,' Margot said to her forcefully the day after the Expeditionary Force sailed. 'Pray God it is, Delia, for I have four stepsons of military age and two of them are married with children.'

Two weeks later came the shocking news that after engaging the enemy at Mons, French's army had suffered a massive defeat and was in retreat.

'So much for the war being over by Christmas,' Gwen said with rare waspishness. 'Thank goodness Ivor is too important to be called upon to fight.'

By the end of August there was another huge defeat to come to grips with when Russian troops were routed on the Eastern Front in a battle at Tannenberg.

Heavily pregnant and unable to bear either the sight of the ever-growing casualty lists or the company of fraught and anxious older friends who had sons of recruitment age, Delia left Cadogan Square for Shibden Hall.

She wrote to Jerome, who was still in barracks in Somerset.

At least it is quiet here. In fact it is so quiet it is almost impossible to believe that a few miles away such terrible carnage is taking place. If only America would come and help England then perhaps the war really would be over in a few short months. How I wish you were here with me, enjoying the incredibly beautiful weather and the amazing sunsets instead of preparing to leave for heaven knows what horrors in France – I just pray that a miracle will happen and that you won't have to go.

Even as she wrote the last few words she knew Jerome would not be praying for the same thing. Every letter showed only too plainly how much he was itching to see action.

By the end of September the Prime Minister had called for another 500,000 men to enlist.

'How long does Winston think it will go on for?' Delia asked Clementine when Clementine telephoned to ask how she was, only to be told that the First Lord of the Admiralty's opinion was that it would go on for a very long time.

In the first week of October Ivor drove to Shibden, insisting that as Delia was now only a month or so from giving birth it was high time she returned to Cadogan Square. 'You can't run the risk of going into labour here and having only the local doctor attend you,' he said bluntly. 'You need to be within reach of your gynaecologist. Apart from which,' he said, looking more tired and tense than she had ever seen him, 'I have news which I hope you are going to take in your stride.'

Her heart almost ceased to beat as she thought of all the young men they knew who were in France. 'Who has been killed?' she asked fearfully. 'One of the Prime Minister's sons? The Denbys' elder boy?'

'No. It's not that sort of news. I'm sorry for alarming you, Delia.' He poured himself a whisky and soda. 'I have to go to America. Needless to say, it's the very last thing I want to do when you are so near to giving birth, but I'm going as a member of the Privy Council and I can't possibly cry off. I'm sorry.'

She waited for a feeling of intense disappointment, but it didn't come. Since she had become pregnant, all lovemaking between them had ceased and he spent far more time away from her than with her. It was a situation she was accustomed to.

'It don't matter,' she said, and for once he didn't criticize her for lapsing into her old way of speaking. 'I will have Gwen with me when the pains start.'

'Well, I wouldn't be with you then anyway,' he said with blunt truthfulness. 'Men only get in the way at a time like that. I would have liked to see our son within minutes of his arrival, though.'

His disappointment that he wouldn't be able to do so – unless the baby was very late in putting in an appearance – was so intense she squeezed his hand comfortingly.

'Don't worry, Ivor. He'll keep.'

He gave her his attractive down-slanting smile and, with an arm around her shoulders, he walked her out to the waiting chauffeur-driven car.

A week later he sailed on the *Mauretania* for New York.

The baby didn't oblige him by being late. Instead it was early.

On 30 October, two days before Jerome was due to leave with his regiment for France, she went into labour. While she was still able to, she made two telephone calls: one to Gwen and the other to Jerome.

Then, slightly apprehensive, she took a deep warm bath and waited to see what would happen next.

What happened next was six hours of torture she was quite sure she would never willingly undergo again.

'My goodness, what a lot of complaining over nothing,' said the midwife who had assisted her gynaecologist. 'Lady Fitzwallender was sixteen hours in labour and not a murmur. And no, Lady Conisborough, you can't hold the baby yet. Nurse still has to bathe and dress her.'

Delia watched with bone-deep joy as her crying daughter – her beautiful, magnificent, *wonderful* daughter – was bathed and dressed.

'Lady Pugh is ever so anxious to see you and to see the baby, my lady,' Ellie said, taking a tissue-wrapped shawl from a nearby tallboy drawer. 'Since her arrival ten minutes after you telephoned her she hasn't left the house once – and Sir Jerome Bazeljette is here as well. He came about an hour ago.'

'Show Lady Pugh in first, Ellie,' Delia said, well aware of the furore there would be if Jerome saw the baby first. 'And has Bellingham sent a telegram to his lordship?'

'Yes, my lady. Five minutes ago.'

The nurse took the shawl from Ellie and swaddled the bawling baby as efficiently as if she were a parcel.

Delia held out her arms, her face radiant as the

baby was placed in them. 'Don't cry, little darling. Don't cry,' she said gently and, as if by magic, the baby ceased crying and blinked up at her with hazel-green eyes.

'Shall I tell Lady Pugh she may come in now?' Ellie asked.

Delia nodded, not taking her eyes from her daughter's red, wrinkled, perfect little face.

When Gwen came in, Delia said with a smile of joy, 'It's a little girl, Gwen. Ivor will be disappointed, but I don't care. I've never been so happy in my life. Never, never, never.'

Gwen leaned over her, tenderly moving the shawl a little further from the baby's face in order to see her better 'Oh,' she breathed reverently, 'she's absolutely perfect! What girl's name did you and Ivor decide upon?'

'We didn't.' There was wry humour in Delia's voice. 'Ivor only ever made plans for a boy. However, I have decided on a name. She is to be Petronella. Petronella Gwendolyn. I don't think Ivor will object.'

'No, Delia. I don't think he will.' Gwen was so overcome at the baby being named after her that tears misted her eyes. 'And next time, when the baby is a boy, Ivor can do the naming. Oh dear. I mustn't cry over her, must I? And you must need to sleep now, Delia. Shall I tell Jerome that it is far too soon for a visit and that he should come back in a few days?'

With great effort, Delia tore her attention away from her daughter's face. 'No, Gwen. Jerome is leaving for France in two days. Please ask him to come in as you leave. Two visitors at the same time would be too tiring for me.'

It was a fib, but she didn't care. She didn't want Gwen with her when Jerome saw the baby for the first time.

Gwen kissed her on the cheek and left the room. Delia turned to the midwife and nurse, saying, 'You must both be famished. If you go downstairs with Ellie, Cook will make you a light meal.'

'Thank you, Lady Conisborough,' they said in unison, both more than ready to eat.

Seconds after they had left the room, Jerome entered it, resplendent in his cavalry officer's uniform.

'It's a girl, Jerome,' she said huskily as he crossed to the bed and looked down at the now-sleeping baby. 'I'm going to call her Petronella and she's the most wonderful thing that has ever happened to me, Jerome. Truly.'

He touched the baby's cheek very gently with the back of his finger. 'She's going to have your colouring, Delia,' he said, his voice thick with emotion. 'There is red in her hair.'

She smiled up at him. 'Would you like to hold her?'

He nodded, tenderly taking the sleeping baby from her arms.

When Ellie returned to the room five minutes later he was still holding her – not only with great competence, but with almost fatherly care.

FIVE

On the day Jerome and his regiment left for France, not even cradling Petronella eased Delia's disquiet. Unlike the vast majority of the population she hadn't been euphoric at the outbreak of war. Now even those who had been were anxious, as it became increasingly obvious that the war was going to be far more drawn-out than they had anticipated. For Delia it was much worse, for with a husband a member of the Privy Council and with one friend married to the Prime Minister and another to the First Lord of the Admiralty, she knew too much of the worries felt at the very highest levels to be comforted by the remorselessly upbeat propaganda being pumped out by national newspapers.

'Please, God,' she prayed time after time throughout the day, 'please, God, don't let Jerome be killed. Don't let him be injured. Please, God. *Please.*'

She was soon beset by another grim anxiety for there were rumours of German submarine activity in the Atlantic.

'They won't attack civilian shipping,' Gwen's husband said to her robustly. 'Such a thing is unthinkable, Delia. Ivor will be home safe and sound within the next couple of weeks. You're worrying your head over nothing.'

Despite his certainty she continued to worry,

her only distraction the gossip of her visitors.

'The Queen is visiting as many as four hospitals a day,' Gwen said, busily knitting a khaki-coloured sock as she sat at Delia's bedside. 'Seeing such suffering must be a terrible ordeal for her. I remember she was once so overcome when a footman cut his finger badly that she nearly fainted.'

'The Prince of Wales has been gazetted to the Grenadier Guards,' Clementine said when she visited, delving in her bag for the khaki shirt she was making as a contribution to the war effort. 'He must look quite odd, for he's only five foot three and the Guards are all six foot and over!'

They had giggled, and though Delia had tried to imagine the golden-haired, slenderly built prince in Guards' uniform, it had been an utter impossibility.

Clara Digby visited and was appalled to find Delia out of bed and seated in a chair by the window. 'Goodness gracious! When doctors decree that a new mother should remain in bed for ten days after giving birth, they mean ten days. And bed means bed, not a chair!'

'I've been in bed for five days, Clara, and I'm bored to tears. What is Cuthie's latest news from the Palace? Is it true the King has ordered that no more wine is to be served at meal times?'

Clara seated herself and said, 'Yes, he's decided that alcohol is not consistent with emergency measures for winning the war. How deadly dull Palace dinners are to be endured without the benefit of wine, I can't think. I don't envisage Ivor enjoying boiled water sweetened with sugar – which is, apparently, what was served yesterday evening –

do you? And when do you expect him home?'

Without waiting for an answer, she eased off her pale kid gloves. 'He must be exceedingly impatient to see his daughter – and not, I hope, too disappointed about her sex. Cuthbert barely spoke to me for six months after Amelia was born.'

She straightened the seam of her glove. 'Has Sylvia been to visit? It will look very odd if she doesn't. I saw her at the Denbys' a week or so ago – your name was mentioned and the tips of her claws showed. Muriel Denby put her in her place – as, of course, did I. Why men never see that side of Sylvia is quite beyond me. Young Maurice Denby is quite besotted with her. He's Muriel's youngest and due to leave for France this week.'

Delia let Clara rattle on, wondering, as she always did, just how much of a true friend Clara was. Clementine and Margot sensitively never brought Sylvia's name into the conversation. She also wondered in just what way the tips of Sylvia's claws had showed – what it was she had said about her – but she had far too much pride to ask. And Clara's remark about Ivor's possible disappointment at Petronella not being a boy had merely increased her own anxieties about how deep his disappointment was going to be.

When he had received the cable informing him of the birth, his answering cable had simply read:

RELIEVED ALL IS WELL STOP HOME
SOON STOP IVOR

The wording hadn't filled her with optimism.

93

An hour after Clara had left her, another cable arrived:

AM SAILING TODAY ON THE CARONIA
STOP IVOR

When he arrived five days later she was in the frost-covered walled rear garden, cutting long sprays of yellow-berried pyracantha to fill the Chinese vases in the hall.

It was a footman who hurried out to her with the news. 'His lordship has arrived, my lady. And he's gone straight to the nursery, my lady.'

Thrusting the pyracantha into his arms she dashed to the house, yanking her coat undone as she ran.

'His lordship is in the–' Bellingham began helpfully as she raced past him.

'I know, Bellingham! I know!' Tossing her tam o'shanter at him, she hurtled up the stairs.

Bellingham, by now well accustomed to his mistress's easy-going familiarity, gravely carried the tam o'shanter towards the cloakroom.

With a fast-beating heart Delia hurried along the corridor towards the nursery. 'Please don't be too disappointed, Ivor,' she whispered to herself. 'Please think Petronella is beautiful. Please. *Please.*'

She opened the nursery door.

Still wearing his travelling clothes he was standing by the crib, looking down into it with a bemused expression on his face.

She stood very still. 'Do you like her?' she said, unable to voice the words drumming in her brain:

Are you going to be too disappointed to love her?

'Like her?' He turned towards her and to her vast relief he was smiling. 'Of course I like her, Delia. She's beautiful.'

All her tension and fear ebbed away. Everything was going to be all right.

She crossed the room and stood beside him, taking hold of his hand and squeezing it to express her gratitude.

'Why Petronella?' he asked. 'I've never heard of it before. Is it a Chandler family name?'

'No. It's a Roman family name. And I chose it just because so few people will have heard it and because I like it.' She remembered how important having a son was to him and realized how magnificently he was overcoming his disappointment. 'We can change it if you want to, Ivor. I don't mind.'

'I don't want to change it. It suits her. Who does she look like, do you think? I don't see the faintest resemblance to myself in her – and I don't think she looks much like you either, except for her dark red hair.'

'Imagining that babies look like family members is usually wishful thinking. Petronella just looks like herself – and I'm glad. Think how awful it would be if she had your big feet or my father's nose!'

He chuckled and she said, 'Would you like to hold her?'

He shook his head. 'No, I don't think I should when she's sleeping. It would only disturb her. And I have to go straight on to Downing Street. Lloyd George is waiting for my report on my meetings with J P Morgan and other American bankers.'

Lloyd George, the Chancellor of the Exchequer, was not a man known for patience and she didn't try to dissuade him. Instead, linking her arm in his, she said as they left room, 'Where will we be spending Christmas, Ivor? Here, or at Shibden?'

'It's tradition for Christmas to be spent at Shibden, as you know.' He saw the expression on her face and added, 'Is there a problem with that?'

'Only that Norfolk is bitterly cold at Christmas and, as Petronella will still be only a few weeks old, I think it would be better if she wasn't taken to Shibden until the spring.'

They had reached the head of the stairs and he came to a halt, looking puzzled. 'But that isn't a difficulty, Delia. She'll remain here in the care of her nurse and nursery maids.'

'And I will be over a hundred miles away. I'm sorry, Ivor. I'm aware no one will think that unusual, but not being with her at Christmas would make me very unhappy. I should like to stay here.'

He hesitated and she knew he was thinking how odd it would look not spending Christmas at Shibden when the Royal Family would be at nearby Sandringham.

'If that is what you want,' he said at last, a little reluctantly.

'Yes, it is. Thank you, Ivor.'

With her arm still linked in his she walked downstairs with him, feeling more optimistic about her marriage than she had since its first few headily careless days, her mind racing ahead

96

with ideas for making Petronella's first Christmas the most splendid Christmas the Cadogan Square house had ever known.

In the New Year, with a very satisfying nursery routine established under Petronella's nurse, who wasn't at all disconcerted that Delia treated her as if she were a member of the family, Delia began socializing and riding again.

Every morning at eleven o'clock she trotted into Rotten Row, riding side-saddle on Juno, the thoroughbred Ivor had bought for her shortly after their marriage. Compared to riding in Norfolk, it was sedate – and certainly nothing like the gallops she had enjoyed in Virginia, where she had jumped five-foot-high snake fences with reckless élan.

Occasionally Sylvia would also be in the Row, her satin-black hair worn in a bun that met the back rim of her veiled hat and showed off the lovely long line of her neck. Her hat was always tilted at a provocative angle, the veil pressing against her face, her elegant riding habit fitting so perfectly Delia wondered if she were wearing anything beneath it.

They would incline their heads to each other and nothing more. The pretence that they were friends was never carried on if there was no one near by to observe it.

In February, Lord and Lady Denby's only son was killed in his first twenty-four hours of action.

By March, the death toll of officers in the Grenadiers and the Scots – two Guards' regiments packed with Ivor's friends or the sons of his friends – was so colossal Delia's fears for

Jerome's safety reached astronomical proportions. But in his letters to her he repeatedly told her not to worry.

As cavalry we don't suffer in the same way that the poor sods living twenty-four hours a day in the trenches do – and I have the comfort of your Fortnum & Mason's food parcels. I made myself very popular with my fellow officers by sharing out the pâté and caviar.

In April, when he came home on leave, his description of life at the Front was very different.

'It can't be expressed in a letter,' he said, his hand holding hers so tightly she thought he was going to break it. 'It's indescribable. Filth. Thigh-deep mud. The dead unburied. The injured lying with them for hours, sometimes days, before they can be carried to a field hospital. Constant cold. Constant pandemonium. And a constant feeling of near uselessness.'

His voice was bitter, his olive-skinned face pale with fatigue.

'Uselessness? But why? I don't understand.'

'Cavalry might have been the ace in the army's hand in previous wars, Delia, but no war has ever been on the scale of this one. How can cavalry successfully charge against machine guns and barbed wire and six-foot-deep trenches? More and more valiant horses are dying horrific deaths. In a charge near Ypres we lost one hundred and forty-four horses out of one hundred and fifty – and the number of men lost is almost beyond human calculation.'

She blanched.

'In the short time I have before going back to such a hell, I want to enjoy myself – and not talk about the war.' He gave a lopsided smile. 'How's Petra? As we didn't have the chance to celebrate her birth with champagne at the time, let's toast her now.'

Delia forced herself into a cheerful mood; a mood of loving gaiety that would enable him to forget, for a little time at least, the horrors waiting for him when his leave was over.

'Petra?' With super-human effort she banished the images he had conjured up, knowing that the minute he had gone they would resurface to give her endless nightmares. 'No one calls her Petra,' she said, managing to giggle. 'Not even Ellie.'

'Well, no one will keep calling her Petronella when she's older. It's too much of a mouthful. And better Petra than Nellie!'

This time her laughter was unforced. 'Just for you, Jerome – and because I would take a gun to anyone who called my lovely daughter Nellie, Petra it is.' She hugged him tightly, saying, 'God, but I've missed you, Jerome. I've missed you more than words can tell.'

The days after Jerome's return to the Front were spent in an agony of anxiety. The newspapers were full of accounts of the British spring offensive at Ypres and she knew that Jerome was in the thick of it. If Sylvia was similarly concerned she showed no sign. 'There's no need to worry about Jerome,' Delia overheard her saying at a house party at The Wharf, the Asquiths' country home on the upper reaches of the Thames. 'He always falls on his feet.'

At the beginning of May Delia discovered that she was pregnant again.

'Which is the only good news I've had for nearly ten months,' Ivor said. 'And, once again, I'm going to be in America for part of your pregnancy, though this time in the early part.'

'America? But why?'

'I'm going with a begging bowl,' he said grimly. 'We need American financing in order to keep armament production at its present level. I don't work only for the King nowadays, Delia. I work for the government.'

She tilted her head a little to one side. 'If the Atlantic is safe enough for you to cross it, then it's surely safe enough for me. Petra is seven months old and my parents still haven't seen her. We could sail together to New York and then you could go to Washington or wherever it is you have to go, and I could go down to Virginia. We could meet up again in New York for the trip home.'

'No,' he said, not even hesitating. 'I'm not going to allow you to take even the slightest risk. When the war is over, then we'll go to Virginia, Delia. And not before.'

He was implacable. Disappointment flooded her, but she knew better than to lose her dignity in an argument she couldn't win.

A week later she lost all desire to cross the Atlantic with her precious daughter.

'There's just been a wireless announcement that a German submarine has sunk the *Lusitania*, my lady!' Ellie said, coming into Delia's bedroom with her breakfast tray. 'It was on its way from New York to Liverpool carrying hundreds of

100

civilian passengers. Mr Bellingham says it's the worst wartime outrage he's ever heard of. His lordship left the house in a great hurry. He'll be going to Downing Street, I expect.'

Four hours later he returned home, his handsome features so grim they looked as if they had been carved in stone. 'Cunard is talking in the region of over a thousand drowned.' He poured a large whisky and added the merest squirt of soda to it. 'There'll be no more passenger sailings. The American financing will have to be carried out by telegraph.'

He drained his glass and then said unsteadily, 'The *Lusitania* was the sister ship of the *Mauretania*, Delia. What kind of hell have we plunged into when a liner carrying American passengers, who are neutral and not at war, can be blown out of the sea as mercilessly as if she were an enemy warship?' He covered his eyes with his hand. 'It's something I would never have believed.'

Two weeks later, despite it being the beginning of the London season, they went to Shibden taking Petra and her nurse – and Juno and his groom, Charlie – with them. The horse, accustomed to travelling in a horsebox, was no trouble. According to the nurse, who was travelling with Petra and a nursery maid in a separate car, Petra was.

'She's cried on and off the entire journey, my lady,' the nurse said as Delia lifted Petra from her arms the instant they had all stepped from the cars, in front of Shibden's porticoed entrance. 'I think maybe she's beginning to teethe.'

Though she knew Ivor would think it extremely undignified, Delia didn't hand Petra back to her

101

nurse, but carried her herself into Shibden and up to the rooms set apart as a nursery. She had every intention of taking an even greater part in her daughter's day-to-day care while they were in Norfolk and was setting out as she intended to carry on.

Within days, Ivor was summoned back to London for a meeting of the Privy Council. 'The war is going so badly we're at crisis point,' he said bluntly as she walked with him to his chauffeured car. 'Now he's no longer Chancellor but Minister for Munitions, Lloyd George is doing all he can to change the situation, but so far it isn't enough. I hate to say this, but I think the fault lies with Herbert. He was an excellent Prime Minister when we were at peace, but war is a very different kettle of fish. If Lloyd George were to make a bid for the premiership he would have my support.'

Delia was so deeply shocked, she was speechless. Long after the Silver Ghost had disappeared down the mile-long driveway she stood on the gravel, staring after it. Just as it was impossible to think of Buckingham Palace not being home to King George and Queen Mary, so it was impossible to think of 10 Downing Street not being home to HH and Margot.

Heavy-hearted she walked back into the house just in time to take a telephone call from Gwen. 'Darling,' Gwen said, barely intelligible because there was so much static on the line. 'I'm on my way to Hunstanton to stay with the Denbys and thought I would call in at Shibden and stay overnight. It's so long since I've been able to have a really good chat with Ivor.' The static drowned

102

out Gwen's next few words and then Delia heard, 'And so there will be two of us … so kind of you, darling.'

The line went dead before Delia could tell Gwen that Ivor was on his way back to London and that going out of her way to stay overnight at Shibden in order to spend time with him was pointless.

When she rang Gwen back, it was only to be the told by the butler that Gwen hadn't been at home all morning and would be in Norfolk for the next few days.

Faced with the choice of telephoning a whole host of Gwen's friends to see where she was, or of simply letting things stand, she decided to let things stand.

'Lord and Lady Pugh will be staying overnight,' she said to Parkinson. 'Please make sure the maids have a room ready for them.'

Much later in the day she put on her riding clothes and went to the stables. The horses Ivor and his guests rode looked towards her, hopeful of a late-afternoon ride.

'Sorry,' she said, as Charlie saddled Juno for her. 'I'm afraid I'm a one-horse woman, boys.'

That Juno was there to ride at all was an achievement, for Ivor's disapproval of her riding when she was pregnant was intense.

'I'll stop in three months' time,' she had said when they had had a heated argument over it. 'And I won't gallop hard. I promise.'

It was a compromise neither of them had been happy with but one which, as in so many other instances in their marriage, they had settled for in a spirit of give and take in order to keep their life together acceptably harmonious.

'And I didn't promise not to gallop,' Delia said, leaning forward to pat Juno's neck as they trotted out of the stable yard. 'I said I wouldn't gallop *hard.*'

All through May the weather had been beautiful, and even though it was now late afternoon, it was still sublimely warm, the sky a bright brassy blue flecked with wisps of snow-white clouds. She headed east over Shibden's parkland towards a narrow lane that led through flat countryside thick with grazing sheep. In the distance was a drainage mill, its slowly revolving sails looking, to the uneducated eye, like a windmill.

'The land is so low that without the drainage mills it would be underwater,' Ivor had said the first time he had brought her to Shibden. 'And don't keep using the word "river", Delia. In Norfolk, the rivers and lakes are known as broads. And always be careful when riding over the humpbacked bridge. It's treacherously steep.'

As Delia rode Juno at a careful walk over the bridge, the reed-edged water beneath it was as hard in colour as a stone and suddenly she became aware of the eerie stillness that presages a storm. She reined Juno to a halt, looking up at the sky, wondering whether to continue to the beach, which was still a mile or so away. The sky was still a vivid blue. The wispy clouds were still a snowy-white. Secure in the certainty that any storm was a long way off she urged Juno into a canter, looking forward to the day when she would be able to enjoy such rides with Petra riding beside her.

When she reached the beach it was deserted as

far as the eye could see. She gave a deep sigh of pleasure. Here, with the sea only yards away, the waves crashing rhythmically on miles of empty sand, she was at last able to ride as hard as she loved to, and without any disapproving eyes watching her.

By the time she turned Juno homeward the sky was beginning to smoke with the first hint of dusk. Now the sensation of a coming storm was strong. Indigo-rimmed black clouds rolled in from the sea and she knew she would be very lucky to reach Shibden before they broke.

She headed towards the bridge at a brisk canter and to her amazement saw that a horse ridden side-saddle was heading towards it from Shibden's direction.

'Whoever she is, she's an idiot,' Delia said to Juno. 'The only place she can be goin' is the beach, and by the time she gets there she'll be soaked to the skin.'

She slowed Juno down and squinted to see the figure more clearly. The only large country house within riding distance was Shibden and the only person who could possibly be riding out from Shibden – assuming, of course, that she had arrived there – was Gwen. Gwen, however, rarely rode these days and would certainly not come out with a storm about to break.

She reined Juno to a halt, sucking in her breath. The elegance of the rider, the provocative tilt of the hat, were unmistakable. When Gwen had said 'and so there will be two of us', the other person she had been referring to had been Sylvia, not Pugh. And only Gwen, of everyone she knew, would so artlessly bring Sylvia on a visit to Shibden, for Gwen, she was quite sure, was the only person in London who didn't know that Sylvia was Ivor's mistress.

She gritted her teeth together so hard they hurt. Having Sylvia as a guest when Jerome was with her and sixteen or twenty other people were there also, was one thing. Having her as a guest when the only other visitor was Gwen, was quite another. How, in the name of all that was wonderful, was she going to survive it? The only ameliorating circumstance was that Ivor was in London and so Sylvia's hopes of being able to parade her closeness to him beneath Gwen's blinkered eyes, and her very unblinkered ones, had been dashed. Presumably it was furious disappointment that had prompted her to take one of Ivor's horses and ride out uncaring of the storm clouds that were now rolling fast over their heads.

Delia spurred Juno into movement. If Sylvia wanted to keep riding away from Shibden, getting saturated in the process, she was welcome to. She, however, was going to head for home as fast as she could.

Sylvia was riding her horse at just as fast a gallop as she now was, but whereas she still had a couple of hundred yards to go, before needing to rein as she approached the bridge, Sylvia was nearly upon it.

Delia saw her rein in far too late for safety, saw the horse skitter at the sudden steepness as lightning streaked down. The horse, now at the middle of the narrow bridge, reared and then bolted, unseating Sylvia with such force that she went flying

106

over the low flintstone parapet, into the water.

As thunder cracked deafeningly, Delia urged Juno into an all-out gallop, bringing him to a halt within yards of the bridge. The rapidly deepening dusk, combined with black storm clouds and rain coming down like knives, made visibility practically zero. Hardly able to see where the reeds ended and the water began Delia slithered from Juno's back and hurtled onto the bridge for a better vantage point.

'Sylvia!' she shouted into the darkness as the rain plastered her hair to her head. 'It's me, Delia! Where are you?'

'I'm in the water!' The response was terror-laden. *'And I can't swim!'*

As another bolt of lightning streaked down, Delia saw the pale oval of Sylvia's petrified face, her blue-black hair indistinguishable from the inky blackness of the water. In the split second before thunder followed the lightning, the pale petrified oval disappeared beneath the surface.

Delia didn't hesitate. There was no time to take off her riding habit with its heavy long skirt; no time to struggle with riding boots that always needed an extra pair of hands to successfully remove them. As the rain sluiced down she lowered herself over the edge of the parapet and then, hanging on to the wet flint by her fingertips, took in a deep lungful of air and let herself fall.

Her cousin Beau had taught her to swim at White Sulphur Springs when she was thirteen and, until now, water had never frightened her. This time, though, as the water closed over her head, she was unable to kick freely with her legs

107

and rise to the surface like a cork, as she had when with Beau; this time she was hampered by cumbersome boots and a beautifully tailored Busvine riding skirt.

As she struggled to break the surface, the weight of the skirt acted like a force of gravity, pulling her down until she touched bottom. The deep mud of the broad sucked at her boots, debris swirling around her. Algae clung slimily to her face. Desperately she fought with the fastenings of her skirt. As she finally freed herself from the knee loop and the strap that ran through it to the hem to prevent the skirt from flying upwards, her chest was bursting and her ears felt as if they were about to explode.

Then, at last, she was free of the cumbersome material. A second later she was gulping in air and a second after that, without a flicker of hesitation, she dived beneath the surface again.

It was an easy search. Though the water had seemed much deeper when she had been certain she was drowning, it was only a little over twelve foot deep and as she had entered the water almost over the point where Sylvia had disappeared, she bumped into her motionless body immediately.

Seizing hold of her under her armpits, Delia kicked her way to the surface, hauling Sylvia's dead weight with her.

There was no resistance from Sylvia; even worse, when they broke the surface there was no spluttering from her either.

With one hand under Sylvia's chin to keep her nose and mouth clear of the water, Delia swam backwards.

Unlike a normal river, the broad had no banks to scramble up. It was edged by thick reeds and, even when she was able to stand, the ground within reach was not firm enough for her to lie Sylvia down on it in order to try to revive her.

Sobbing with exhaustion Delia fell into the squelching reeds, taking Sylvia with her. Then, as they sank ever deeper into the marsh, Delia circled Sylvia around the chest as tightly as she could with her arms, alternately squeezing her with a sharp upwards movement and fisting her forcefully in the middle of her back.

'Breathe!' she gasped as the thunder and lightning rolled away. 'Land sakes, Sylvia! *Breathe!*'

There was a gagging sound and a flicker of movement.

Delia summoned up all her remaining energy and jerked Sylvia round the chest so tightly and abruptly her arms nearly came from their sockets.

Two things happened simultaneously. Sylvia retched, spewing up water and vomit, and Delia heard the sound of hoofbeats.

'We're here!' she shouted hoarsely as Sylvia continued to gag. 'Here! Below you, in the reeds!'

The horses slowed to a walk to take the bridge.

'We're here!' she shouted again, certain it was a Shibden search party. 'To the right of the bridge! In the reeds!'

'Holy God, it's her ladyship!' The voice was Charlie's. She heard him vault from his horse and shout to the other horseman, 'Shine the lantern over the edge of the bridge, Dan!'

Dan, Shibden's head groom, did as he was bid. As the light fell on her, Delia uttered a devout

109

prayer of thankfulness, took her arms from around Sylvia and staggered to her feet.

'Don't mind me,' she gasped when the two men had made their way through the sodden reeds. 'See to Lady Bazeljette first. She's half drowned and is in a bad way.'

Then, as Charlie's arm went around her, her legs buckled and she lost consciousness.

How Charlie and Dan got her and Sylvia back to the house she didn't know and – fearful that the answer would be 'slumped across the horses like sacks of potatoes' – afterwards never asked.

It was enough to know that she was safe. That she hadn't lost her unborn baby. That Sylvia was alive.

'Though only just, according to the doctor, my lady,' Ellie said, taking a stone hot-water bottle that was beginning to cool from the bed and replacing it with a towel-wrapped hot one. 'He's still here and says he will be remaining with her all night.'

The bedroom was lamp-lit. Delia looked down at her lace-trimmed nightdress and saw that, though she didn't remember it, she had been given a hot bath. She wondered how many hot baths she'd had to have to get rid of the mud and slime she had been encrusted with, and said weakly, completely disorientated, 'What time is it, Ellie? Is it evening or the middle of the night?'

'Neither, my lady. It's just before dawn. Both Lady Pugh and the doctor insisted you shouldn't be left on your own, not even for an instant, and so I've been sitting with you ever since you were put to bed. You don't seem to be able to stop

110

shivering, my lady, and you've got a very high temperature. The doctor is worried you've caught pneumonia.'

Delia closed her eyes. Pneumonia. She wasn't going to give in to pneumonia. Not after all she had just survived.

When she next woke, aching in every bone of her body, the curtains had been drawn back and Ellie, still sitting by the side of the bed, said, 'Would you like a little breakfast, my lady?'

'I'd like some tea and perhaps a slice of toast.' She pushed herself up against the pillows, wincing. 'Has his lordship been informed of what has happened?'

'Yes, my lady. Though Lady Pugh couldn't give him exact details because neither you, nor Lady Bazeljette, was in any condition to tell anyone. She simply said that there was a storm, that it was deep dusk and that you and Lady Bazeljette were thrown from your horses, fell into the broad and were nearly drowned. He's on his way here and is expected within the next hour.'

'Is the doctor still with Lady Bazeljette?'

'I believe he's downstairs, having breakfast.'

To Ellie's alarm Delia threw back the covers and eased her aching legs to the floor. 'You can't get up, my lady,' she said, panic-stricken. 'The doctor gave strict instructions you were to remain in bed. He's forbidden all visitors, even Lady Pugh.'

Delia slipped her arms into her negligee and Ellie's panic grew. 'You can't mean to be leaving the room, my lady! The doctor said it was a miracle you hadn't lost the baby and that you still have to be very careful!'

111

'Stop behaving like an old mother hen, Ellie. I will be careful. All I am goin' to do is to walk fifteen yards down the corridor to whichever guest bedroom Lady Bazeljette is in.'

'She's in the Italian bedroom, my lady – and I doubt she'll be in any condition to appreciate your visit. She was more dead than alive when Dan carried her into the house.'

Delia took no offence at being spoken to as if she were a recalcitrant child. The familiarity that existed between her and Ellie was a familiarity she treasured – and she knew that Ellie was right. Bed was the only place she should be. The problem was, though, that if she stayed in bed she wouldn't be able to speak to Sylvia before Ivor arrived and there were things that needed to be said between them – not least the need for Sylvia's account of what had happened to tie in with the account she had decided to give.

Bennett, Sylvia's maid, opened the door to her with the words 'Her ladyship is allowed no visitors...' on her lips. They died the instant she saw who the visitor was. 'The doctor has given instructions that her ladyship has to have complete rest, Lady Conisborough,' she said, making a valiant attempt to carry out the orders she had been given.

'I shan't tire her, Bennett. I intend to stay only ten minutes. Perhaps you would like to take advantage of my being with her in order to go downstairs for a cup of tea?'

It was a dismissal and Bennett knew it.

'Well ... if you say so, your ladyship.' Unhappily she allowed Delia into the room and, even more unhappily, left it.

Sylvia was lying in the centre of a vast bed, propped up by a mountain of silk-covered pillows, her blue-black waist-length hair streaming loose. She looked like a beautiful ghost, her eyes darkly ringed, her skin deathly pale.

The only movement she made was a very slight turn of her head. 'Ah,' she said as Delia sat down in the chair beside the bed. 'It's you. I knew you'd come.'

'How are you?'

'Alive. Just. And for that I suppose I should say thank you.'

'You don't have to. I would have done the same for anyone.'

'Yes, you would, wouldn't you?' There was faintly amused mockery in her voice. 'Your behaviour is always admirable, isn't it? You discover you have married a man who is in love with someone else and you behave with a dignity far beyond your years – a dignity that earns you your husband's profound respect and that, in most circumstances, would have made him end his affair. You are so vivaciously unconventional – and speak with such odd familiarity to everyone from the Prime Minister down – and yet no one takes offence. Everyone is entranced by you. The Queen is fond of you – which is saying a lot because she isn't fond of many people and that includes half of her own family. The Prime Minister, a man with a weakness for women young enough to be his granddaughters, is more than a little in love with you. Instead of being ostracized by high society, no party is complete without you. You are not as I expected – and for that I hate you, Delia. And your

113

having saved my life makes no difference at all to that hate.'

The shocking words were said with such matter-of-factness that it was all Delia could do not to react emotionally.

'I never imagined for one minute that it would,' Delia said, struggling to be equally impassive. 'I'd like to know what I was supposed to be, though, for I can't see how I was supposed to be anything when my becoming Ivor's wife was such a surprise to everyone.'

With her head still laid heavily on the pillows Sylvia lifted a glossily perfect eyebrow. 'It wasn't quite such a surprise to me, Delia. Ivor needed to remarry – and to remarry a young woman – in order to have the son Olivia failed so spec-tacularly to give him. I had no desire to see him married to the debutante daughter of one of my friends – and English high society is such an elite, closed circle I am on terms with almost everyone. My last words to him before he sailed for America were that a New York heiress would solve our problems admirably. What I didn't expect was for him to marry a Virginian who, no matter how well regarded her family, could in no ways be termed an heiress – and a Virginian who, instead of being disconcerted at finding herself plunged into an alien way of life, threw herself into it with bewitching self-confidence.'

For the first time she moved, pushing herself up against the pillows. 'Having no family or contacts in England was supposed to ensure you would have no option but to be malleable when you discovered the true reason why Ivor married you.' Despite her obvious exhaustion her voice was withering. 'Olivia was never malleable. She made life as difficult as possible for Ivor – and for me. God, what a bitch that woman was! The public humiliations she made me suffer were endless. Not for one minute did she allow anyone to forget that my background wasn't aristocratic or that of landed gentry. The contempt Olivia put into the words *"nouveau riche"* had to be heard to be believed. By the time she died, Ivor could barely bring himself to speak to her.'

Her eyes held Delia's with chilly frankness. 'And nothing could have suited me better. I didn't want Ivor to be in love with Olivia – and even on the day he married her, he wasn't. You, however, are different.'

She paused, breathing in deeply, her finely drawn nostrils whitening. 'From the moment of my first conversation with him after I met you – at Sir Cuthbert's birthday ball – I knew he was more than a little in love with you. You weren't what he had wanted in a second wife – a pliant background figure – but you are so shatteringly beautiful and amusing it was a detail he overlooked. And you handle your relationship with him with the skill of a far older, far more experienced woman.'

Her eyes hardened. 'But you won't win him, Delia. What happened last night, in the storm and the darkness and that filthy, murderous water, makes not one iota of difference. Ivor may love you a little, but he loves me more. And that's the way I intend it to remain.'

She closed her eyes, so obviously unable to

115

continue talking that Delia rose to her feet. 'There's just one thing before I go, Sylvia,' she said quietly. 'And it's about last night.'

With great effort Sylvia opened her eyes, her expression wary.

'Gwen told Ivor that we were together when the storm broke and that our horses threw us more or less simultaneously into the broad. Unlikely though it may be, it's a version of events I'd like to stick to. I've no desire to become known as a heroine. Especially when the circumstances are as they are.'

The faintest of smiles touched Sylvia's beautifully shaped mouth.

'That's fine by me,' she said weakly, closing her eyes again. 'I don't want the embarrassment of the whole world knowing I owe you my life.'

As Delia opened the door, Sylvia said, 'And you were very brave, Delia. I'll give you that. We call it spunk in England. Is it something all Virginians have?'

'No, but I'm a Chandler, and all Chandlers have it.'

On that note she closed the door behind her.

Half an hour later Ivor's Rolls swept up Shibden's drive. Delia's bedroom windows were open and within a second of the car coming to a halt she heard him sprint across the gravel.

Her stomach muscles tightened. Thanks to Ellie, she knew exactly what Gwen had told him and since he believed both of them to have suffered similarly, whom would Ivor rush to see first? Her, or Sylvia? He always behaved with the utmost propriety in front of servants and as every servant in the house would know if he strode to Sylvia's room first, that alone was reason enough for him not to. He would also have to take into account the fact that Gwen was in the house. If he were to hurry to Sylvia's side first, even Gwen would finally realize the true nature of their relationship. Also, in order to reach Sylvia's guest bedroom he would have to pass her bedroom. And, last but by no means least, she was pregnant – and according to the doctor, still at risk of losing the baby.

As she heard him take the stairs two at a time, she was certain he would come to her first. She couldn't see how, in all conscience, he could do anything else.

She heard him round the head of the stairs and begin striding swiftly along the corridor towards the door of her room.

He reached it.

And passed it.

Seconds later, without even pausing to knock, she heard him throw open the door of Sylvia's room.

Very slowly Delia let out her breath. At the window, muslin curtains fluttered gently in the May breeze.

For four years she had lived in the hope of Ivor returning the love she felt for him. It was a hope often dashed, but it had never died. Only days ago, when he suggested that they spend time together at Shibden, it had burned so strongly she had felt certain that her long battle was almost won.

Now, with terrible finality, she knew she had lost. He loved her a little, but not enough. With

Ivor, Sylvia came first, and, even pregnant, Delia came a very poor second.

But she didn't come second with everyone.

She didn't come second with Jerome.

She heard Sylvia's door open and then close. As Ivor's footsteps strode down the corridor towards her, her thoughts were no longer about him or their marriage.

She was thinking of the letter she would write when she was next alone. The letter she would send to France. The letter she knew Jerome had given up all hope of ever receiving.

SIX

At Christmas Delia gave birth to a second daughter after a prolonged and difficult labour This time she had no name ready and waiting. This time, like Ivor, whose disappointment was profound, she hadn't even entertained the thought that the baby might be a girl.

'We could name her after your mother,' she said hesitantly, so weak from the birth she didn't truly care what name the baby was given.

A shutter came down over Ivor's austerely handsome face as it always did when mention was made of either of his long-dead parents.

'No,' he said shortly. 'I think not.' He paused and then said, 'What about naming her after your mother?'

'Bedelia? I don't think so. I found the name

118

hard enough to live with until I insisted it was shortened to Delia and two Delias would be highly confusing – as well as being highly unimaginative.'

'And you truly don't have any preferences?'

She shook her head, her mane of hair glowing like fire against the ivory-silk pillows.

'Then we'll call her Davina May. Davina as a mark of respect to David Lloyd George – who is certain to replace Herbert as Prime Minister within the year – and May after Queen Mary, who was christened May and, as you know, is still known as May by everyone on intimate terms with her.'

Delia closed her eyes. To name their daughter after a bullish, fiery-tempered Welshman was ridiculous, yet the name was both pretty and unusual and she liked the way Delia and Davina rolled off the tongue so easily when spoken together.

Eight weeks later, just as she was finally regaining her strength after Davina's birth, news came that Jerome had been badly injured. He wrote to her from the field hospital he'd been taken to.

I still have all my limbs, which I hope is as much of a relief to you as it is to me. Word is that I'm to be transferred to a hospital in Blighty where, with luck, I'll recover fast enough to be back at the Front for the final push.

'He's mad,' Delia said, when she next had lunch with Margot. 'How can he say *with luck* he'll be back at the Front for the final push? And how can there be talk of a final push when things are at such a stalemate? Month after month men are gassed, mined and mutilated, with no appreciable ground being taken. Things are just as bad as they were this time last year.'

Margot, her face white and strained, remained silent. Afterwards, when they parted, Delia regretted saying things which, though true, could have been taken as criticism of her husband's handling of the war.

A month later and Jerome was in a military hospital in Sussex. Delia could have been chauffeur-driven down to see him, but chose not to be. Wearing a sea-green bolero and matching ankle-length pleated skirt, a stiff white shirtwaist with close-fitting sleeves and a high neck, her only jewellery a cameo brooch worn at the throat, she went by train and taxi. Though she'd had two children, rigorous corseting ensured she still had a wasp waist and an hour-glass figure, and the admiring looks she received from men in uniform – and every fit man of military age was in uniform – were considerable.

It wasn't merely her deeply waving fox-red hair – topped by a saucily pert straw boater – that attracted attention, or the fact that she was taller than most Englishwomen. It was her breezy American manner, her blatant self-confidence and her unpretentiousness that set her apart.

When she walked into the hospital ward all eyes turned towards her.

'Whom are you visiting?' the ward sister asked, swiftly coming to greet her.

'Captain Bazeljette.'

'Ah.' The sister called a nurse away from her task of making an amputee a little more comfortable. 'Nurse – please escort Mrs Bazeljette to Captain Bazeljette's bedside.'

Delia cleared her throat. 'Lady Bazeljette is unable to visit on this occasion. I am Viscountess Conisborough – a close family friend.'

Though the ward sister's eyebrows rose only the merest millimetre Delia knew that, now it was known she was not Jerome's wife, giving him the kind of loving greeting she had intended was out of the question.

As the nurse led her down the long ward full of injured officers she was sickeningly aware that very few of them would ever walk again without the aid of crutches or an artificial limb. With rising panic she wondered whether Jerome had lied in his letter to her. Perhaps he had not told her the full extent of his injuries. Perhaps he, too, had been maimed for life.

As the nurse came to a halt, Delia steeled herself for the worst. She mustn't let horror show on her face in case he registered it as repugnance. She must be brave, as he had constantly been brave for so long.

'Captain Bazeljette, you have a visitor,' the nurse said sunnily, her manner completely different from that of the ward sister. 'And can I ask you not to stay any longer than half an hour, Lady Conisborough? We have to have rules. Wounded men tire easily.'

With a flick of her starched skirt she was gone. With relief that made her weak at the knees,

Delia saw that though Jerome's left arm, shoulder and leg were heavily bandaged, none of the bandaging ended in a stump.

'God, but you're a wonderful sight,' he said as she sat down as close to the bed as she could get.

So full of emotion that speech was beyond her she took hold of his hand and pressed it against her cheek.

His hair, far longer than army regulations allowed, tumbled low over his brow and curled tightly at the nape of his neck. A livid wound knifed down through his left eyebrow.

He read her thoughts and said gently, 'It could have been worse, Delia. I could have lost an eye. Of all the men in this ward I'm probably the one least grievously injured.'

'I know,' she said unsteadily. 'And I'm grateful. But such luck can't last, Jerome. You've been at the Front for almost eighteen months. The next time you could be ... could be...' She couldn't finish the sentence and instead said thickly, 'I want you to apply for a staff posting. You have influential friends.' Her voice was both urgent and pleading. 'It could easily be managed. And it isn't as if you haven't done your bit. You've been mentioned in dispatches for exceptional bravery. As a staff officer you could...'

'...Remain well behind lines and never be able to live with myself?' His voice was still gentle, but it was mulishly firm. 'No, Delia. It isn't an option.' He squeezed her hand. 'Tell me about the new baby. Ivor didn't seriously name her after Lloyd George, did he?'

Still distraught at the prospect of his returning

122

to the Front she managed only a glimmer of a smile. 'Yes, he did. Despite being so different in character, he and Lloyd George have become very close, though not so close that he has asked him to be her godfather. That position is reserved for you – and we're goin' to delay the christening until such time as you can attend it.'

'Thank you.' He paused and then said in a different tone of voice, 'And Petra, Delia? How is Petra?'

Her smile deepened. 'Very sassy. She's walkin' and talkin' and is full of mischief. I wish you could see her, Jerome. I wish I'd been able to bring her with me, but babies ain't' allowed.'

In spite of the pain he was in, an answering smile split his swarthy face. 'And is her hair still red?'

'Yes, but not Titian, like mine. It's more a russet red. And though her eyes are green, they're a hazel green, not cat green. I've brought a photograph.'

There was a locker by his bed and she propped the photograph against the jug of water standing on it, wondering if he would keep it there – and if he did, how he would explain it away to Sylvia.

As if reading her thoughts and with his eyes on the photograph, he said, 'I haven't seen Sylvia yet. She's in Scotland with the Girlingtons. Jack's been, though. My father brought him down.'

He dragged his eyes away from the photograph, his mouth tugging into a smile. 'He wasn't at all fazed by the bandages – not when I told him I still had an arm and a leg beneath them – and he was very admiring of the wound through my

123

eyebrow. He said it made me look like a pirate.'

Laughter fizzed in her throat. 'It does. Not an evil Captain Hook sort of pirate. A handsome swashbuckling pirate.'

'Your sort of a pirate?' An amber flame burned deep in his eyes.

'Oh, yes,' she whispered, her whole heart going out to him in love. 'Very much so, Jerome.' And, uncaring of who might be watching, she leaned forward and kissed him long and tenderly on the mouth.

Three months later he was back in France. A month after that, in July, the Somme campaign opened. It was the biggest British army ever sent into battle and families in every home in the country held their breath. Delia received regular field postcards from Jerome, but the censor saw to it that they told her nothing except that, at the time of writing, he had been alive. And the battle that had been meant to be so decisive simply went on and on and on, for month after month, in a seemingly endless series of partial actions. The casualty lists were so catastrophic that it seemed to Delia beyond the capability of the human mind to take them in.

In September, as a second big push on the Somme began, Margot's stepson, Raymond, was killed leading his men over the top.

Margot's grief was deep. 'What a waste, what a waste,' was all she could say, ashen-faced, when Delia went to 10 Downing Street to pay her condolences. 'Raymond should have had a staff job where he could use his brains, but no one of any sensitivity will take a staff job any more – it arouses both jealousy and the suspicion of cowardice. And there's another kind of cowardice too, Delia.'

She clenched her hands, the knuckles shining white. 'Too many of Henry's friends are no longer loyal to him. Not Winston. Not George. Not Ivor. All the three of them ever do is praise Lloyd George to the skies – and that's tantamount to trying to push Henry out of office. The consequence is that I'm losing all my friends. I had a dreadful altercation with Clemmie – she, of course, can only see things from Winston's point of view. I do hope the same kind of thing isn't going to happen with you, Delia?'

Delia, knowing that such an event was highly likely, murmured something placating and left heavy-hearted, sensing that their friendship would end the day Lloyd George stepped into HH's shoes.

The announcement that he was to do so came in the first week of December. 'Thank God,' Ivor said with vast relief. 'The war will now have a new direction. Even the King – never the most optimistic of men – now believes it could well be over by the spring.'

It wasn't.

When Jerome came home on leave in March, he said, grim-faced, 'Unless America enters the war, the fighting is going to go on until there isn't a man left standing.'

He was a major now and looked a decade older than when, three years ago, he had enlisted so exuberantly. His thick dark hair was flecked with grey, the lines running from nose to mouth were so deep they looked as if they had been carved there, his bone-weariness and exhaustion were so palpable there was no way they could be hidden.

'Heaven only knows what's happening on the Eastern Front,' he said bitterly to Ivor when he dined with him at the Denbys'. 'But the Western Front is a stalemate of cataclysmic proportions. An entire generation is being wiped out. It's kill or be killed. God knows how I'm still alive – I don't.'

On 6 April, the day after his leave ended, America entered the war. A month later Delia received a euphoric letter from her cousin Bella. It was addressed 'Darling Viscountess', because Bella loved to use Delia's title – however inappropriately – at every opportunity.

Isn't it wonderful that our American boys can now share in all the glory and the gallantry? Cousin Beau enlisted immediately and I can't tell you how handsome he looks in uniform. He's such a daredevil I just know he'll win all kinds of honours. He's as eager to go into battle as a child itching to go to a party, but we don't rightly know yet when American troops will be leaving for Flanders – and is Flanders in France or Belgium or is it in a bit of both? Or perhaps even a town? One thing is certain: once Beau arrives there the men will have to look to their laurels where their girls are concerned.

Delia lay the letter down, sick at heart at Bella's foolish naivety and appalling ignorance. Over half a million men had died on the Somme alone – and that was just the published figures. She thought of the amputees in the ward Jerome had been in.

126

Men in their early twenties, and even younger, who would never walk again. Men who, unable to work again, would be reduced to selling matches or to beggary. And to Bella the war was one of battlefields set neatly outside towns where, the fighting for the day over, gallant soldiers returned as if from the office to flirt with pretty mademoiselles.

'Don't be too hard on her,' Ivor said when she voiced despair that Bella wasn't better informed. 'Three years ago that was how nearly everyone thought things would be. All that matters is that if American troopships reach France without being blown out of the water by German submarines, the end of the war will be in sight.'

At the end of June American troopships did reach France safely, but as the weeks passed, Delia could see no dramatic change taking place. If anything, things grew worse. The Germans began making Zeppelin raids over London, bringing the war onto home ground and involving civilians in a way no one had ever previously thought possible. One bomb fell on a school, killing a roomful of children. Another crashed onto a railway station, hitting a train.

Postcards from Jerome, written in pencil and with nearly every sentence blocked out by the censor, still arrived with thankful regularity. Though he had fought tooth and nail against accepting a staff job, a staff job, behind lines, was what he had now been assigned and, on her knees, Delia thanked God for it every night.

'Has Jerome said what he intends doing once the war is over?' Ivor asked on one of the rare

127

evenings when he was home and dining with her. 'The world won't be the same place and, knowing Jerome, he'll adapt accordingly.'

'He's going to enter politics. He's already spoken to Lloyd George, who has promised him that at the first post-war election he'll be adopted as the prospective Liberal candidate for some promising constituency.'

Ivor wasn't as surprised as Delia had expected him to be. 'It's something he should have done ten years ago,' he said. 'He's got the right manner. People like him. I suspect they'll vote for him in droves.'

If he lives, Delia thought fiercely, but she did not put the thought into words; for though Jerome had been detailed to a staff job she knew it didn't mean he would stay in it or, while in it, not put himself into a dangerous position when visiting the Front.

In October, on Petra's third birthday, Delia held a party for her in the ballroom at Cadogan Square, complete with a Punch and Judy man and a conjuror. Jack, who was now ten and at a preparatory school in Sussex, was home for half-term and he called in unexpectedly when the party was in full swing, accompanied by the nanny who still looked after him whenever he was at home.

'Ooh, Jack, *Jack!*' Petra squealed, hurling herself towards him and fastening hands gooey from iced cake around his legs. 'Come and see the man taking rabbits – live real rabbits – out of his hat. Can I have one of the rabbits to keep, Mama? Jack is going to stay, isn't he? You are going to stay, aren't you?' And letting go of his legs to grab hold of his hands, she dragged him across the floor to where a dozen children, under the eyes of their accompanying nannies, were laughing and cheering as the conjuror drew a live dove from his hat.

Davina, twenty-two months old, was standing chubby-legged as near to the conjuror as she could get, not clapping and cheering noisily like the other children, but simply staring at the dove in round-eyed, grey-eyed wonder.

Watching her, Delia's heart contracted with total, unequivocal love. Where Petra was exuberantly outgoing, demanding constant attention and entertainment, Davina was quite happy with her own company as long as she had bricks or tiny toy figures to play with, or had crayons and paper. Delia bit her lip, wondering what a third child would have been like – a third child that, after Davina's difficult birth, she'd given up hope of conceiving.

For a long time her obstetrician's words to Ivor – that it was unlikely she would be able to conceive again and, if she did, her life would be at risk – stirred up her old fears that Ivor would divorce her.

He made no such suggestion.

'Divorce is simply not socially acceptable,' he'd said. 'Not for a man in my position. I've had two rolls of the dice where trying for an heir is concerned. The first, my marriage to Olivia, resulted in no children at all – and a great deal of personal misery. The second, our marriage, has resulted in two daughters – and two daughters

129

are simply what I'm going to have to settle for.'

He hadn't troubled to disguise his bitter disappointment and she hadn't troubled to hide her vast relief. If he *had* wanted a divorce, it would have made it well-nigh impossible for her to spend time with Jerome. It was only because she was safely married, and because her husband was viewed as being Jerome's close friend, that regular contact with Jerome aroused no adverse public comment.

As the conjuror began using Jack as a prop, withdrawing coloured silk handkerchiefs from the back of Jack's jacket and from his sleeves, Delia tried to think of life without Jerome, and couldn't. He had become her best friend at their first meeting and, now that her inability to give Ivor a son had made her husband even more distant, Jerome had become far, far more to her. He had become the central person in her life.

Sudden uproar cut across her thoughts. From Jack's pocket the conjuror had withdrawn a live mouse. Nannies and nurses screamed and scattered. Toddlers shrieked. Jack shouted – though it was a shout of delight.

Aware that it was time she intervened, Delia walked swiftly across the polished floor, determining that the instant the party was over she would telephone Fortnum & Mason's and order another food parcel for Jerome – one including his favourite Fuller's walnut cake and Tiptree Little Scarlet strawberry jam.

Christmas was spent at Shibden, and over the holidays King George and Queen Mary paid one of their very rare social visits. It was a visit and disruption Delia could well have done without, entailing, as it did, the menu having to be submitted for approval in advance – ensuring that Cook had hysterics – and a swarm of police outside the house on the day of the visit, plus detectives on duty in the house. The Queen unbent enough to ask after Delia's charity work in the City's orphanages and the King discussed with Ivor the difficulty of America's restrictions on the loans taken out with them.

'That the money can only be spent to pay for war supplies bought in the United States is criminally constricting,' he said, so deeply anxious that he was oblivious he was discussing a political subject in front of his wife and his hostess. 'We don't exact similar conditions on the loans for supplies that we make to our allies. Difficult though such trips now are, I fear you are going to have to cross the Atlantic again, Conisborough. The US Secretary of the Treasury needs appraising of just how critical our financial situation is. Complete financial disaster would be worse than defeat in the field and he must be told that – in no uncertain terms.'

Later, when their royal visitors had driven the short distance back to Sandringham, Delia knocked on the connecting door between their bedrooms.

'Will you really have to risk crossing the Atlantic again?' she asked when Ivor opened the door to her.

Though he had dispensed with his evening jacket he was otherwise fully dressed and she was

131

suddenly very conscious of being clad only in her nightdress and peignoir.

'Perhaps. It will be up to Balfour.'

Arthur Balfour was the British Secretary for Foreign Affairs.

'The difficulty is,' he said, frowning deeply and talking frankly to her as he had always been in the habit of doing where his work was concerned, 'America now has its own vast war needs and supplies to think about and, as a consequence, the supply of credit to Britain could well begin to dry.'

'But not when we're allies! Surely now that we're allies we'll be able to rely on increased lines of credit?'

'Maybe.' He shot her his familiar down-slanting smile. 'Perhaps it's you, not me, Balfour should be sending to speak to America's Secretary of the Treasury. His name is Mr McAdoo.'

It had been a long time since, in Ivor's company, she had giggled, but she giggled now. 'It sounds like something out of a comic-strip cartoon.'

His smile deepened and a new expression entered his eyes.

Seeing it, knowing what it portended, knowing she couldn't bear to have her emotions thrown into turmoil yet again, she said swiftly, 'I'm sure if you go to America your trip will be successful. Goodnight, Ivor.' And before he could try to detain her she walked back into her own bedroom, closing the connecting door firmly behind her.

All through the cold months of the spring the fighting continued without the least sign of any good news. On the Eastern Front, the Russian armies had ceased to exist as a fighting force. On

132

the Western Front, the French troops were so diminished in number they could no longer be relied upon for any operation that involved an attack on a grand scale, and US troops were still not fighting in any great numbers. In March, when the Germans opened a massive offensive, King George was so certain a German victory was imminent that he rushed to France in order that his presence might bolster the flagging morale of the British armies.

Jerome's staff job hadn't prevented him from being injured again, though this time there was no evacuation to a military hospital in England. Instead, he spent several weeks in a hospital near Boulogne and then, in June, suffering from a limp that would be permanent, he was back in the thick of it.

So as not to think, Delia kept herself so busy with charity work that she was in danger of collapsing from exhaustion. It was better, however, than reading the casualty lists in *The Times;* reading that a soldier who had just been killed had been the last surviving brother of three or four others.

'Their poor mothers,' Gwen said unsteadily, time after time. 'To lose not one son, but all their sons. What fortitude they must need to bear such unimaginable loss.'

In September it looked as if the tide was turning, but just when her spirits were higher than they had been for four years, Delia received news that Beau had been killed.

Even though she hadn't seen him since she had visited Sans Souci the summer before the outbreak of war, when she had enjoyed a family reunion at White Sulphur Springs, the news poleaxed her. He had been part of her childhood; part of her youth. For weeks her thoughts were full of Virginia and the glorious, carelessly happy days of the past; days in which her many cousins – particularly Beau – had played such a great part.

'When the war is over and the Atlantic is safe to travel again, the very first thing I'm goin' to do is visit my folks,' she said to Ivor. 'My parents aren't gettin' any younger and I want Petra and Davina to be able to remember them.'

The war came to an end in November and the country erupted in an orgy of celebration. Church bells rang. Fireworks exploded. Ivor ordered flags be hung out of every window of the Cadogan Square house and then, after going to the House of Commons to hear Lloyd George read the armistice terms, he took Delia to Buckingham Palace where King George, in khaki, and Queen Mary, glittering in jewels, stood on the balcony waving to the crowds.

Although common sense told her differently, Delia half expected life to return to the rhythms and certainties of the pre-war days. It didn't. Many of their aristocratic friends who, like them, had both palatial mansions in town and even more palatial stately homes in the country, gave up their town houses. They still entertained, of course, but house parties were now more often weekend events, not week-long events.

In town, the young thronged nightclubs. Jazz

was king. American music was everywhere. Black musicians ceased being a novelty and became the norm. It was a social scene Ivor disliked and had no time for. Delia, however, via her growing friendship with the Prince of Wales, often night-clubbed, for nightclubbing was Prince Edward's favourite occupation and whenever he indulged in it he liked to be surrounded by a large party of friends.

'And Ivor can't very well forbid me from accepting such invitations,' Delia said to Jerome in the spring of 1920 when they had escaped for an illicit picnic on the North Downs, 'not when they come from a man who will one day be his king.'

'Edward doesn't have the look of a king.' Jerome, lying on the grass with his weight resting on one elbow, bit into a leg of cold roast chicken. 'He looks every inch a fairy-tale prince – slender, blue-eyed, golden-haired – but he lacks gravitas and, in my book, gravitas is a necessary quality for a king.'

Delia set down her glass of white wine, smoothed her fashionable mid-calf-length skirt over her knees and circled them with her arms. 'Ivor thinks it a necessary quality too. He's hoping King George will live to be at least ninety.'

'Which, considering how old his grandmother was when she died, he may well do.' He put the chicken leg down on a napkin and lay flat, his hands beneath his head. 'Did Ivor give you any idea how long he might be in Paris?'

'No. He said the Peace Conference was likely to go on for months. You're an MP – what's the inside gossip?'

'That it will go on for months.' He shot her his wide, easy smile. 'I don't think Lloyd George will want Ivor in Paris for months on end, though. He wants his thoughts on the financial implications of what is happening in Egypt. If we grant Egypt independence – and the strength of feeling is such we may have to – it has to be done in a way that will maintain our control of the cotton trade – and of the canal. Without Suez, we lose our strategic link with India.'

Delia's conversations with Ivor were nearly always about his work, which meant they were nearly always about politics. She didn't want the same situation arising with Jerome. Egypt didn't interest her one little bit and she'd no intention of wasting one of their precious afternoons together talking about it.

She lay down beside him, her head next to his. 'Let me tell you about Virginia,' she said dreamily. 'Let me tell you how utterly wonderful it was takin' Petra and Davina there. If only you had been with us everythin' would have been absolutely perfect.'

He rolled over, pinning her beneath him, his eyes hot with desire. 'One day,' he said, lifting a stray tendril of fiery hair away from her face, 'one day we'll go there together.'

Her hands slid into the curly thickness of his hair. She didn't want to talk about one day, because she knew that one day was never going to come. Divorce was out of the question for Jerome because of Jack. 'Maybe when he's older, Delia,' he said. 'But a divorce while he's still at Eton would be disastrous for him.' And recently Jerome had become an ambitious Member of Parliament, making divorce unthinkable for a whole lot of new reasons.

Delia no longer cared. Her marriage to Ivor was not one of unmitigated misery. She respected his intellect and his huge capacity for hard work. She enjoyed the prestige of being his wife. She valued the way he shared his political concerns with her and knew he held her in very deep affection. It made for a marriage far more compatible than the marriages of most of her friends.

The situation – that Sylvia was his long-term mistress and that Sylvia's husband was now her lover – was odd, but no odder than many of the other entanglements at court, and in their case the relationship was honest. Ivor not only knew about her relationship with Jerome, he was deeply grateful for it made his own affair with Sylvia far easier. The only person who disliked the arrangement was Sylvia. And Delia didn't give a rat's behind for Sylvia's feelings.

In 1921 she visited Virginia again and was there when her mother died unexpectedly from a heart attack. In 1922, taking Petra and Davina with her, she holidayed with the Denbys in their villa at Rolle, on the shore of Lake Geneva. Jerome arranged to be in Switzerland at the same time, introducing Jack to the thrills of sailing, and afterwards spending a few leisurely days at Nyon, the neighbouring village to Rolle.

Away from the eyes of London society, it was an arrangement that worked beautifully. Jack amiably coped with eight-year-old Petra and seven-year-old Davina following him everywhere. For Delia, the hours walking with Jerome along the flower-scented lakeside were magical. Sometimes they wandered around the sun-lit ruins of Nyon's Roman amphitheatre. Sometimes they sailed. It was a blissful few days, and when Jerome announced his intention of buying a villa at Nyon Delia was ecstatic.

By the time 1923 dawned, Delia considered herself a very happy and fortunate woman. She had a husband whose company, on the social occasions when it was necessary for them to appear together, she found congenial. She had two healthy, delightful daughters. She had a lover who was also her best friend and who, amazingly, considering his reputation, was faithful to her. She enjoyed a privileged position in the most elite echelons of society. Though not an inner member of the fast Prince of Wales's set, she enjoyed an easygoing friendly relationship with him. He liked American women and was as far removed in character from his staid, stuffy, dutiful father as it was possible to get.

Life was fun and Delia never expected it to change.

When it did, things happened so suddenly she was left gasping.

She had just arrived back in Cadogan Square after visiting the National Gallery with Cynthia Asquith.

Ivor was in the main drawing room, his back to her as he poured himself an extraordinarily large whisky.

Without turning to face her, he said, his voice queerly abrupt, 'I'm afraid I'm to go to Cairo as an advisor to Fuad who, with British backing, has become King. It isn't a case of being there a few months. It's a diplomatic posting that is likely to extend for several years. Because of its nature it's essential I have my family with me. We are to leave in a month's time.'

'Leave? Leave England to go to *Egypt?*'

Delia stared at his back, unable to take in the enormity of what he was telling her.

'Yes. I'm sorry, Delia.'

Still not facing her he drained the whisky glass. Always a moderate drinker, his doing so showed her how deeply shaken he was.

She dragged a purple cloche from her recently bobbed hair and threw it onto the nearest chair.

'It's impossible,' she said flatly. 'Wild horses wouldn't drag me from England to live in Egypt. There's still some kind of a revolution going on there, isn't there? And you couldn't go.'The band around her heart that had felt so tight at the prospect of being so utterly separated from Jerome, eased as she prepared to play her trump card. 'You couldn't go,' she said in a voice of sweet reason, 'because you wouldn't be able to survive living so far away from Sylvia.'

He turned round and she felt the world tilt beneath her feet. His face was ashen. His light grey eyes filled with unspeakable pain.

'Sylvia is in love with Theo, Girlington's elder son. Our affair is over, Delia. Finished. And I don't want to speak about it. I don't think I'm ever going to be able to speak about it. As for the revolution, there isn't one any longer – not now Egypt has been granted partial independence. What is necessary now, under the new king and his government, is for Britain to retain as much influence as possible – which is why I am being sent there.'

'I won't go.' Her voice sounded to her as if it were coming from miles away. 'You can't make me. Just because your life has been so unexpectedly and shatteringly disrupted – how long has her affair with the Earl of Grasmere been going on, anyway? – you can't expect me to disrupt my life.'

'I'm sorry, Delia,' he said for the second time. 'But this isn't open to discussion. To use one of your favourite phrases, the gig is up. I leave for Egypt in a month's time. And you and our children – unless you prefer to make other arrangements for them – are coming with me. Now, if you'll excuse me, I would like to be alone.'

As she made no effort to leave him, he strode unsteadily past her, out into the hallway. Seconds later she heard the front door open and then close.

Still she didn't move; couldn't move.

Egypt.

How could she possibly continue seeing Jerome with any kind of regularity if she were in Egypt? There was no way it could be done. It was impossible. And what would happen to them once they saw each other only once, or perhaps twice, a year?

The answer came as with the roar of waves crashing on a beach.

He would be unfaithful. How could he be anything else? By his own admission he wasn't faithful by nature. By being faithful to her for so long he had amazed both her and himself. Once Europe and the Mediterranean separated them, his old habits would reassert themselves and there would be nothing, absolutely nothing, she would be able to do about it.

She never drank whisky: had never drunk it in her life.

She crossed to the drinks cabinet.

Egypt. It was a death knell. There would be no more Shibden Hall – and she had grown to love Shibden. There would be no more gay nights out with Prince Edward and his friends. There would be no more country-house weekends. No more riding on Norfolk's glorious beaches or on Rotten Row. No more entertaining politicians, bankers and industrialists in Cadogan Square's magnificent dining room. And above all, there would be no more Jerome.

She poured herself a whisky as generous as the one Ivor had just drunk.

The villa Jerome had bought in Nyon would remain, by her at least, unvisited.

She drank the whisky in three shudder-making gulps.

The way of life that meant so much to her was over – and a dreadful premonition told her she would never be so happy again.

SEVEN

Five weeks later Delia was standing by the rail of a P&O liner as the ship eased its way along the Egyptian coastline towards Alexandria. Ivor was in their state room, dictating letters to his secretary, Mr Willoughby. The new nanny she had hired shortly before sailing was a few feet away with Petra and Davina.

'When will we see the pyramids, Nanny Gunn?' Petra asked impatiently as they stared at a strangely flat countryside.

'And when will we see camels?' Davina asked, clinging to Nanny Gunn's hand.

'I'm not sure when we will see the pyramids, Petra.' Miss Gunn, who came from Inverness, had a delightfully soft Scottish lilt to her voice. 'And there will be camels in Alexandria, Davina.'

Listening to her, Delia was sure that Kate Gunn was going to be a great success. Unlike the children's previous nanny she was young and pretty and more than capable of coping with children who had long left the nursery behind them.

As Petra and Davina continued to chatter and as Kate Gunn answered their eager questions with gentle imperturbability, Delia continued to stare unseeingly towards land, her thoughts full of Jerome.

Was he already missing her as fiercely as she was missing him? Where was he? Who was he with?

142

Her kid-gloved hands gripped the rail tightly. He had promised that he would visit Cairo often – but how long would it be before his first visit? And until he did, would he remain faithful to her? At the thought that he might not she felt a knife twist in her heart. It was a situation she would have to understand. How could she not, under the circumstances? The pain of it, though, would be more than she could bear.

As tears stung her eyes, she heard Davina shouting, 'I can see a camel, Mama! *I can see a camel!*'

Blinking her tears away, Delia pretended to share her daughter's excitement, reflecting that she had unsuspected talents as an actress.

Even though they had two private carriages, the train from Alexandria to Cairo was unlike any train she had ever been on. The rear carriages not only had people packed in them like sardines, but even had people travelling on the roof. The heat was stifling; the smell of poverty overpowering.

'Why are all the men on the roof dressed in dirty nightshirts, Mama?' asked Petra. 'Now we're in Egypt, Papa won't have to wear a night-shirt, will he?'

'No, Petra. Of course not.' At any other time Delia would have begun to explain about the nightshirt-wearers' dreadful poverty. At the moment, though, she felt far too out of sorts.

'And what about shoes?' Davina asked, noticing that the people she could see from the train window didn't have anything on their feet. 'Will Papa still wear shoes?'

Ivor, who had been deep in conversation with Mr Willoughby in the second of their two carriages, now chose this moment to rejoin them.

'Of course I shall still wear shoes!' he snapped, deeply irritated. 'Miss Gunn, will you kindly keep my daughters occupied and see to it that they refrain from making such unsuitable remarks?'

'Yes, my lord,' Kate Gunn said, unruffled. She withdrew two drawing books and a pack of crayons from the carpetbag she never went anywhere without. 'Would you like to draw a scene we can see from the train window?' she said to the girls. 'When they are finished we'll send them to your Aunt Gwen. I don't suppose your Aunt Gwen has ever seen a camel.'

At Cairo a large reception committee greeted them. In heat that seemed to come out of the ground in waves they drove from the station, Kate Gunn, Petra and Davina in the car following Delia, Ivor and an Egyptian dignitary. Mr Willoughby and Myers, Ivor's valet, rode in a third car, the reception committee bringing up the rear.

'Your villa is in Garden City, Lord Conisborough,' the Egyptian said in excellent English as their car turned into a road in which trams, battered cars, horse-drawn gharries, donkey carts, overloaded mules and stray sheep fought chaotically for space.

'Not Cairo?'

Delia was aware of Ivor's shoulders stiffening.

'Garden City is part of Cairo, Lord Conisborough,' the dignitary said reassuringly. 'The British Residency and most of the ministries are situated there. It is a very elite part of the city. The very best part. The grounds of your villa run down to the Nile.'

Ivor visibly relaxed.

'We are now in Ibrahim Pasha Street,' the man continued. 'On your right is Shepheard's Hotel – very famous, very elegant. At the far end of the street is Abdin Palace, where tomorrow your lordship will have an audience with King Fuad. Now, however, we turn right. The building on the left is the Opera House – and very shortly we will be crossing Soliman Pasha Street, Cairo's Oxford Street.'

Soliman Pasha Street, with its tiny shops and its goods spilling out into the street, didn't look at all like Oxford Street, but Delia kept her thoughts to herself and, despite her heartache, began to look around with interest.

In front of them a camel, ridden by a small boy, was swaying with stately dignity down the centre of the dusty, acacia-lined road. By the edge of the street there was a man with a monkey and then they were passing a group of women carrying gaily coloured bundles on their heads. An overcrowded tram went past with people balancing precariously on its running board. There were shoe-shine boys and veiled women and small boys begging.

And then the trains, the beggars and street vendors were left behind and they were driving along a spacious avenue lined with sycamore trees. They turned and came to a halt in front of high wrought-iron gates. Seconds later two young boys in spotlessly white shirts opened the gates and the family was driven into the grounds of their new home.

The house was long, low and palatial and Delia

gave a sigh of relief. Shaded verandahs and balconies that reminded her a little of Sans Souci looked out over immaculately kept lawns, and beyond the house was the magical sweep of the river. She could see a steamboat ploughing upstream and dozens of much smaller boats plying backwards and forwards, each with a distinctive triangular white sail.

'Welcome to Nile House, Lord Conisborough, Lady Conisborough.' An imposingly tall, very dark-skinned man wearing a royal-blue garment edged with gold braid stepped towards them and bowed deferentially. 'I am Adjo. I have the honour of being Nile House's cahir.'

'Cahir is a head housekeeper,' the Egyptian who had accompanied them from the station said helpfully in a low voice to Delia.

As Adjo bowed once again Delia flashed him a brilliant smile and said, with the same easy familiarity she had always treated Bellingham and Parkinson, 'Could we please have afternoon tea, Adjo? And could someone show Miss Gunn the children's rooms?'

'I want a room facing the river, Mama,' Petra said urgently. 'And it's so hot I want a cool white nightshirt to wear and–'

'And why were those little boys begging?' Davina cut across her.

Wishing heartily that her children understood there were occasions when they should be seen, and not heard – and that this was one of them – Delia drew in a deep breath, about to silence them. She wasn't quite quick enough.

Ivor who had transferred his attention from

Adjo to the dignitary now whipped round, his eyes glacial. 'Miss Gunn, take the children to their rooms *at once!*'

Kate Gunn's response was as unflurried as it had been when on the train. 'Yes, my lord,' she said serenely. 'Come along, Petra, Davina...'

Adjo clapped his hands and a young man slid quietly into the room then led Kate Gunn, Davina and Petra from it.

At another clap from Adjo two young men rolled in a white-naperied tea trolley. In a little dish there were slices of lemon and when Delia lifted the lid of the teapot she saw that the tea was Earl Grey.

'Thank you, Adjo,' she said gratefully, aware that the kettle must have been boiling even before their car had turned in at the gates. 'You're a treasure.'

He bowed his head and she thought she saw a gleam of amusement in his eyes.

Only after she had been in Cairo for several months did she discover that Adjo, in Egyptian, meant 'treasure'.

The next morning Delia asked him the correct name for the garment he, and so many other Egyptians, wore.

'The word for such traditional clothing is a galabiya, my lady,' he said gravely. 'And it is worn by all classes of Egyptians, not just the fellahin.'

'The fellahin?'

'The poor, my lady.'

'And the name for the close-fitting red hats with a tassel that I saw so many people wearing

147

when we drove through the city?'

'Sometimes they are called a fez, and sometimes a tarboosh – and only men wear them, my lady.'

'But you don't wear one, Adjo. Is that because you are a cahir?'

Adjo folded his hands in front of him. 'No, my lady. It is because I am not a Muslim. Only Muslims wear the tarboosh and I am a Copt.'

'And is a Copt a Christian?'

'The Coptic faith is one of the earliest forms of Christianity in the world, my lady.'

Delia enjoyed her conversations with Adjo and, despite her heartache over Jerome, she began to settle down to her new life. Meanwhile, Petra and Davina were enjoying almost limitless freedom, for they were having no schooling at Nile House and neither were they attending a local school.

'The only local school of excellent repute is the Mère de Dieu and the girls can't attend until they are twelve,' Delia said reasonably when Ivor complained.

They were on their way to the High Commissioner's birthday party. As the limousine purred its way down Garden City's main boulevard, Ivor said, 'One of King Fuad's Egyptian advisors, Zubair Pasha, has suggested that Petra and Davina might like to have lessons with his daughter, Fawzia. She's nine, like Petra, and the arrangement would be for the girls to be chauffeured to Fawzia's home every morning. It isn't far. Only the other side of Garden City.'

'And Davina?' Delia asked doubtfully. 'She's a

148

full year younger. Will she be able to keep up?'

'I don't know,' Ivor said truthfully. 'But as there seems to be no other suitable alternative we'll simply have to give it a try and find out.'

'Fawzia has an older brother,' Petra said to Delia after she and Davina had finished their first week of lessons with Fawzia. 'He's fourteen and he's very moody. I don't like him.'

'Well, that doesn't matter too much, does it, honey?' Delia was in the middle of writing a letter to Jerome and she laid her pen down reluctantly. 'He's so much older than you that you'll never have much to do with him.'

'No. I suppose not.' Petra hesitated and then said wistfully, 'He goes horseback riding out by the pyramids and sometimes Fawzia goes with him.'

'Horseback riding?'

Petra now had her full attention. Delia suddenly knew what would lift her spirits. She would begin riding again. Hard, fast, challenging gallops. The kind of riding she had been accustomed to as a young girl in Virginia. The kind of riding she could do in the desert.

Making her daughter almost as happy as she was making herself, Delia said, 'There's a hotel out by the pyramids called the Mena House and it has stables and horses for hire. We'll go there on Saturday and I'll arrange for you to have riding lessons. If Fawzia's brother can ride out by the pyramids, then so can we.'

Petra threw her arms around her mother then ran away to tell Miss Gunn. Delia picked up her

149

pen, eager to share her new resolution with Jerome; knowing that though riding in the desert wouldn't put an end to the ache in her heart, it would at least ease it.

Delia quickly developed such a pleasant routine that, if she hadn't missed Jerome so much, she would have enjoyed life in Cairo even more than she had enjoyed life in London. Though there was formality at the Residency, and almost stultifying formality at Abdin Palace, in all other aspects life was now far more relaxed.

Mornings were spent either riding south beyond the pyramids over hard-packed desert sand, or swimming in the Mena House pool. Later Delia would meet with friends for coffee at one of the two Groppi's tea rooms, where the ice cream and honey-drizzled pastries were to die for. Other days she would have coffee on the terrace at Shepheard's where there was a grand-stand view of snake-charmers and jugglers and conjurors in the street below.

During the heat of the afternoon she rested at Nile House between silken sheets in a bedroom shaded from the sun, the air cooled by the gently rotating mahogany paddles of a giant ceiling fan. Late afternoons were often spent at the Gezira Sporting Club, which was set on an island in the river and where there was always a wonderfully competitive sporting event taking place. Ivor played tennis there two or three times a week and they both enjoyed the polo matches. Early evening was cocktail time. Dinner was often formal, either at the British Residency – the home of the

British High Commissioner, where 300 could be seated for dinner comfortably – or at Abdin Palace, where the Oriental splendour was quite stupefying. If there was no formal function then she would dine with friends at Shepheard's or the Continental, sometimes, though not often, doing so with Ivor. She was soon one of the diplomatic community's most successful hostesses, with everyone prizing an invitation to Nile House.

Jerome, accompanied by Jack, but never by Sylvia, visited at least three times a year. On such occasions Ivor often found a pretext for being in Alexandria. When such a pretext was impossible, Jerome would announce he wanted to sightsee further down the Nile and, as Ivor would then find he had vital business at Abdin Palace, no eyebrows were raised when Delia acted as his guide.

During these excursions Jack remained in Cairo, good-naturedly enduring Petra's blatant adoration.

On Ivor's annual visit to England, Delia always accompanied him, taking Petra and Davina with her. For a few short weeks she was then able to renew her friendships with Clementine Churchill and Margot Asquith – and spend time with Jerome.

Their long separations never became any easier. Though none of her friends told her, she was sure there were occasionally other women in his life; women he didn't love, as he loved her, but who were there nevertheless.

'For how much longer are we to remain in Cairo?' she asked Ivor despairingly at the end of 1928. 'Surely the Prime Minister can find someone to replace you?'

'He could certainly find someone to replace me as a financial advisor to King Fuad, but he couldn't find anyone to replace me when it comes to acting as a mentor to Prince Farouk. The years I've spent earning Farouk's trust can't be thrown away, Delia. When he comes to the throne, he has to come to the throne a friend of Britain. It's the Prime Minister's belief – and King Fuad's – that I have great influence with Farouk. That being the case, it's my patriotic duty to remain in Cairo. I'm sorry, Delia. Believe me, I wish things were different.'

She'd turned away to hide her tears. For Ivor, Egypt was made tolerable by the presence of Kate Gunn who, now that Petra and Davina were too old to need a nanny, had replaced Mr Willoughby as his secretary. For Delia, there was no such comfort. The only thing that made the passing years bearable was that Petra and Davina loved Egypt and had no desire to live anywhere else.

Unlike their mother, they never counted days off a calendar in the weeks leading up to their annual visit to London and both of them had been so appalled at the thought of going to school in England that Ivor had arranged for them to attend the Mère de Dieu school in nearby Samalik Street. Davina and Fawzia were still there but Petra now went to the lycée.

'When she leaves the lycée,' Ivor said, 'Petra can finish her education in England, at either Oxford or Cambridge.'

By the time Petra celebrated her sixteenth birthday she showed no inclination to fall in with

Ivor's plan.

'I might be academically able enough to go, but I'm not interested enough,' she told her mother, with a touch of Delia's Virginian bluntness.

'Jack's at Balliol,' Delia said, trying to tempt her. 'He thinks you'd love Oxford.'

'By the time I went to St Hilda's, Jack would no longer be it Balliol.'

It was true and Delia knew that the battle was lost. When her elder daughter dug her heels in, nothing on God's good earth would make her change her mind.

The day after Petra's adamant refusal to apply for Oxford, Delia attended a garden party at the home of one of Cairo's leading socialites, Princess Shevekiar. The Princess, who had been one of King Fuad's wives until she had achieved the near impossible and obtained a divorce from him, was neither young nor beautiful, but she adored having young and beautiful people around her and was a great party-giver.

Delia was surprised to see that Fawzia's twenty-one-year-old brother, Darius, was among the guests.

During the seven years she had lived in Cairo, Delia had become very fond of Fawzia, whose mother had died before Fawzia had been old enough to remember her, but Darius was – as Petra had pointed out years ago – moody, and kept himself very much to himself.

Unexpectedly, he was now making a beeline towards Delia. She was forced to admit that, moody or not, he was extraordinarily handsome.

153

Like the vast majority of high-society Cairenese he always dressed in Western clothes and today he was wearing a grey-striped shirt and casual white trousers, a lock of his sleek black hair falling over his forehead.

He stood at Delia's side silently for a moment or two, surveying the other guests – nearly all British – and then said, 'Are the British going to live in Egypt for ever, d'you think?'

She was so startled that her eyebrows flew nearly into her hair and then, without waiting for a reply, he said tightly, 'They promised to leave in 1883. Did you know that? And they promised again in 1922 when they allowed us our so-called "sovereignty" and put Fuad on the throne. And they are still here. Are they ever going to go?'

'I don't know.' It was a question no one had ever put to Delia before. She tried to imagine Cairo without the British and couldn't. 'Don't the terms of the protectorate state that Britain will leave the moment Egypt is capable of managing alone?'

'We're capable now!' His olive skin was tight over his sharp cheekbones. 'How'd America respond if it was in the position Egypt is? You would kick the British out, wouldn't you? And don't say you wouldn't, because a hundred and fifty years or so ago, that's exactly what you did do!'

Delia looked around and was relieved to see that the British High Commissioner wasn't within earshot.

'I don't think the situation was quite the same,' she said, not knowing if it had been or not. 'And you have to take into consideration the help Brit-

154

ain has given Egypt. All the hospitals, schools...'

'The hospitals and schools have been for the British, not the Egyptians. The British have never drilled a well to bring drinking water to one of our villages. They've never established medical services for Egyptians. They've never built schools, hospitals or public housing. They've never done *anything* to improve the living conditions of the ordinary Egyptian. They don't *care* how the vast majority of Egyptians live. They never even *see* how they live.'

It was an extraordinary outburst to be taking place when the British High Commissioner and his wife were only thirty yards or so away and when half of the other guests in Princess Shevekiar's garden were either high-ranking British advisors to King Fuad, or high-ranking British civil servants. Delia wondered if Darius was drunk.

'Westerners in Cairo don't know the real Cairo,' he said, his eyes narrowing. 'All they know is the British Residency, Shepheard's, Groppi's, the Gezira Club and the shops in Soliman Pasha Street.'

From a little distance away Princess Shevekiar caught Delia's eye and waved gaily. Too near for comfort, she saw Ivor in conversation with Mahmoud Pasha, the Egyptian Prime Minister.

'Seeing other parts of Cairo isn't an option, because it isn't safe,' she told Darius reasonably, wondering if what he'd said was true; determined she was going to speak to, Ivor about it at the first opportunity.

'It would be safe with me. I could show you what the city is really like. Where would you like

155

to go? The Citadel? The Muqattam Hills? The Old City?'

She could tell by the expression in his eyes that he was perfectly serious – and that he wasn't drunk. She also knew what Ivor's reaction would be if she were to tell him she was leaving the garden party in order to explore the less salubrious parts of Cairo with Zubair Pasha's handsome twenty-one-year-old son.

He would, quite naturally, forbid her to do any such thing.

'The Old City,' she said, deciding to merely leave Ivor a message saying she had left the garden party early and that he wasn't to worry. 'How are we going to get there?'

'By tram,' he said, and she could tell that he was expecting her to be so deeply shocked that she would cry off going.

She *was* deeply shocked, but she had no intention of showing it. 'That's fine,' she said equably, 'but not dressed like this. We need to stop at Nile House so that I can change into something a little less noticeable than a dress for a royal garden party.'

He nodded, seeing the sense of her suggestion. Five minutes later, after she left a message for Ivor with a footman, the two of them walked out of Princess Shevekiar's palatial gardens and Delia embarked on an afternoon that was to entirely change the way she thought about Cairo.

'I don't suppose you've ever been on a tram before?' Darius said as they stepped from the gharry that had brought them from Nile House to the Number One tram stop at Ezbekiya Gardens.

156

'No.' Delia was well aware that no one she mixed with socially had ever travelled by tram either. 'But I've always thought it looks far more exciting than travelling by car.'

Within seconds of boarding the tram she discovered that it *was* more exciting, for as it rumbled along the crowded streets it dipped and swayed like a ship in a gale. She also discovered that it was excruciatingly uncomfortable and that the smell of fish and stale body odour coming from their fellow passengers was almost more than she could stand.

'The only part of Old Cairo the tram goes to is the old Roman fortress of Babylon,' Darius said as she resisted putting a handkerchief over her nose, 'but since it's the very oldest part of Old Cairo, it's a good place to start.'

'Babylon? That's a bit Old Testament, isn't it? Why is it called Babylon?'

'No one knows for sure. It's thought that one of the Pharoahs brought prisoners back from Babylon in Mesopotamia and that they were later given the site as a free colony. They called it after their homeland.'

It was an interesting theory and one she doubted anyone else could have told her.

Once off the tram he took her into the old fort. It was her first major surprise, for she had expected to see only a few crumbling walls; instead, the walls were massive in parts and the sanded space they enclosed was massive too. There were alleyways and gardens and five churches, some of them pretty, some of them hideous, all of them Coptic.

'Over there,' Darius said, pointing across the courtyard they were standing in, 'is a lone synagogue that has quite a claim to distinction. The prophet Jeremiah is buried beneath it.'

She was about to ask if they could take a closer look at the synagogue, when Darius said abruptly, 'This isn't what I want you to see. I want you to see the people living outside the golden triangle of Garden City, Shepheard's and Abdin Palace. I want you to see the streets of Old Cairo. They aren't far away. Just a short walk.'

It was a walk from one world into another.

As they plunged into a zigzagging maze of medieval alleys, the first thing to meet her was the stench. Not just cooking smells, but smells of unwashed bodies, raw sewage and disease. The next things were the noise and the claustrophobia. Everyone was crowded cheek by jowl into alleyways so narrow, the balconies of the houses on either side so close together, that hardly any sunlight penetrated. Even with Darius at her side, protecting her, she was jostled and pushed in a way she had never experienced in her life before. The din was incredible. Everyone seemed to be shouting at the tops of their voices. Babies cried. Dogs barked. Donkeys brayed.

There were no other Westerners. Everywhere she looked there were only turbans, red fezzes, hijabs, and heavy, all-covering veils.

Heaps of rubbish were everywhere. Tawdry shops, some little more than holes in walls, sold fly-covered food. Ragged children had flies clinging around their eyes and their mouths. *She'd* flies buzzing incessantly around her eyes and mouth.

It was so hot, so stifling, so foetid, that she could hardly breathe.

'People here live two or three families to a room – rooms with no running water and no sanitation. Half the children die before they are five,' he said grimly, sidestepping a pile of rotting refuse. 'How many of your friends at Shepheard's and the Gezira Club are aware of that, do you think? And if they were aware of it, how many of them do you think would care?' His voice was taut with anger. 'Our King doesn't care that Cairo's poorest live like this, and wealthy land-owners like my father don't care either.'

Just when she thought she was going to faint with the heat and the claustrophobia and the pungent smell of human waste, he said tersely, 'Had enough?'

She nodded and they turned left into a crowded bazaar. 'Back to the fortress and a tram, I think,' he said, making no comment on the indescribable poverty they had just witnessed.

At the far end of the bazaar they reached a street that was a little broader, a little lighter, a little less crowded. Heat shimmered up from the ground and she watched Darius drop some coins and a beggar grab at them and shout a grateful *'Shukran! Alhamdulillah!'*

As a muezzin called the faithful to prayer, Darius said abruptly, 'Do you speak any Arabic?'

'I can say "good morning" and "good evening" and I know that *Shukran* means "thank you" and that *Alhamdulillah* means "thank God".'

'That isn't much after seven years.'

Not for the first time she noticed that he avoided

ever addressing her as Lady Conisborough and that, by any normal standards of conversation, he was blunt to the point of rudeness.

'Maybe not,' she said, aware that their relationship had turned into one that was different to any other she'd ever had. 'But as all the Egyptians I meet speak either English or French – or both – I've had no need to study Arabic. And it isn't an easy language to learn.'

'No, it isn't. But when you make your home in a city, it's polite to be able to speak a little of the language, don't you think?'

She nodded, wondering what Ivor's reaction was going to be when she announced she was going to learn Arabic.

Reading her thoughts, he said, 'You won't be the first member of your family to begin learning Arabic. Davina asked Adjo for lessons a long time ago.'

'She did?'

Her surprise was so obvious that he said, 'She didn't want her father to know in case he put an end to them.'

They reached the tram stop and with relief Delia saw that the tram going back to Ezbekiya Gardens wasn't as crowded as the outward tram had been. When they were seated on one of the dirty slatted seats, she said, 'Even though my husband is a friend of your father's, you don't like him, do you? I can tell by the expression in your voice whenever you refer to him.'

'You're right,' he said with stark honesty. 'I don't like him. I don't like anyone who is British, except for Davina who is, after all, half American

160

– and Jack.'

'Jack?' Delia felt as if the surprises of the after-noon were never, going to end. 'I didn't realize that when Jack visited Cairo you and he spent time together.'

He turned his head, his eyes meeting hers. 'That,' he said drily, 'is because when Jack and his father visit Cairo, his father so often then travels south, to Aswan. And when he does, you go with him.'

Aware that the subject needed changing fast, she said, with a bluntness equal to his own, 'Are you more than just a nationalist, Darius? Are you one of the students at King Fuad University that my husband says are hot-headed young revo-lutionaries who ought to be imprisoned?'

He didn't even hesitate. 'Yes,' he said grimly. 'I am one of the students your husband would like to see imprisoned. I want the British out of my country. I want Egypt to be ruled by Egyptians – not a king the British put on our throne and who is more Albanian than he is Egyptian. As long as Fuad is on the throne Egypt will never become independent.'

She looked behind them to make sure no one was sitting near enough to overhear.

A glimmer of a smile touched his mouth. 'Even if people overhear me, no one who travels by tram is going to take issue with what I've said. Except for the Palace circle, who've grown fat colluding with the British – a circle that includes my father – Egyptians want Egypt for Egyptians. It's as plain and simple as that.'

As the tram rattled and swayed and at every stop

filled with more and more galabiya-dressed fellahin, Delia remained silent, knowing that her own situation was no longer either plain or simple, for she couldn't tell Ivor that Darius was a revolutionary. If she did he would refuse to allow either Petra or Davina to visit Zubair Pasha's home again and their friendship with Fawzia, their only Egyptian friend, would be at an end.

Not only that, but she would have to admit to Ivor that she sympathized wholeheartedly with Darius's position, which was that the British should not still be in a country they had promised to leave years ago.

Even as it was, the sights she had seen that afternoon were going to make her relationship with Ivor once again unbelievably strained, for she was going to tell him about them and she was going to tell him that as an advisor to King Fuad he should be advising the King on how to drag his impoverished people from the middle ages into the twentieth century – something she was almost certain he didn't see as being any of his business.

At the thought of the unpleasant scene that would then take place her head ached. He would simply not understand; but Jerome would.

Jerome.

Longing for him overwhelmed her. Apart from brief interludes, they had been separated for seven years. How much longer was their separation going to last? How much longer could she remain the most important person in his life when he seldom saw her and when so many young London socialites were, she was sure, only too willing to take her place in his heart?

PART TWO

Petra

1930–1933

EIGHT

Petra was lying flat on her back next to Jack on the grass beside the tennis court at Nile House. They had just finished a hard-fought game – which he had won – and were both in a state of pleasant exhaustion.

'I don't think anyone else knows, apart from myself and Davina – and now you – but Darius is a very committed Egyptian nationalist,' she said, shading her eyes from the sun.

'I doubt it.' Jack swatted a fly away from his face. 'Fawzia probably just told you he was in an attempt to impress you.'

'How would her brother wanting to kick my father out of Egypt impress me? I think she was speaking the truth and I'm rather glad, as now I don't feel bad about not liking him.'

'Are you sure you don't like him?' There was teasing amusement in Jack's voice. 'Last year I thought you had a secret crush on him.'

Beneath her suntan she blushed, and in order to hide the fact she sat up so that her back was towards him. 'Last year I was fifteen and knew no better. I certainly don't have a crush on him now.'

'That's good. I don't think I'd like the thought of you mooning over Zubair Pasha's son and heir.' Though there was still amusement in his voice there was also something else. Something which caused her to blush even more furiously.

He rolled over to lie on his side, resting his weight on one arm, saying thoughtfully, 'Do you think Zubair Pasha knows of Darius's political inclinations?'

'God, no! He'd skin him alive if he did.' She hugged her knees. 'Zubair Pasha is very pro-British. If he wasn't, my father would certainly know and wouldn't be such close friends with him.' Her blush had safely receded and she turned towards Jack again. 'As it is, Papa is almost as close to him as he is to your father.'

'Which is why it's such a shame your father has meetings in Alexandria for nearly the entire length of our stay. They must both be bitterly disappointed, but it seems to be nearly always the way. Do you remember the last time we were here your father had to attend a meeting in Alexandria? I'm not sure, but I think my father caught up with him there for a few days. I didn't stop off in Alexandria with him because I had to be in London to sit my exam for the Foreign Office.'

'Is the Foreign Office the reason you're interested in Darius's politics?'

He plucked a blade of grass. 'No. It's just that as I've been out here for a few weeks at a time ever since you moved here, I've known Zubair Pasha's family for almost as long as you have and I've always liked Darius. I wouldn't like to see him end up in a British prison.'

'Land sakes!' The blood drained from her face. 'Is that what could happen?'

It wasn't often she used any of her mother's Virginian expressions and, despite the grimness of the subject, a smile twitched at the corner of his mouth.

'If he's joining the violent extremists, yes. If he's merely a member of the WAFD Party, then possibly not. After all, it's a pukka political party that stands on a platform calling for extensive social and economic reforms and full independence.'

'He may be a member of WAFD. I don't know. All I'm certain of is that his father doesn't know of his opinions.'

'And does your father?'

'Do you mean did I tell him what Fawzia told me and Davvy? Of course not. I'm no sneak. Besides, if my father were to suspect how anti-British Darius is, he'd probably forbid me to see Fawzia.'

Jack picked up his tennis racket and rose to his feet. 'How is the lovely Fawzia? I'm surprised she didn't leave the Mère de Dieu and go to the lycée when you did. She's bright enough.'

Petra stood up and brushed the grass from her tennis skirt. 'She may be bright, but she's also lazy. For all her Western attitudes, life in a harem, doing nothing all day but eat chocolates, would suit Fawzia down to the ground.'

He chuckled. 'You're wrong, Petra. Chocolates would make her fat – and Fawzia would die rather than become fat. And the women of King Fuad's harem are obliged to wear veils when out in public. Wearing a veil, and hiding her beauty, is not something Fawzia would ever do.'

Crossly, Petra picked up her racket and began walking back to the house. Fawzia *was* beautiful, but Petra didn't much like hearing Jack say so. She looked across at him. In his white shirt and flannels, his turbulently curly hair slicked back with brilliantine, he was head-turningly good-looking. Over the last year, since he had left Oxford and gone to the Foreign Office, he had become a very sharp dresser. Like his father, however crowded a room, he stood out in it. She just didn't want him standing out from the crowd with Fawzia at his side.

As they neared the terrace Davina stepped through the open French windows and shouted good-naturedly, 'Come on, you two. Hurry up and get changed. You're going to be late for lunch and, as Papa is away and Uncle Jerome is here, we're eating Virginian fashion. Fried chicken and lemon pie.'

Petra's crossness vanished. Her mother was always in an exceptionally good mood when Jack and his father visited. Later on they were all going to the Gezira Sporting and Racing Club where Jack had been invited to play polo.

'The Prince of Wales played polo at the Gezira when he visited Cairo in 1922,' Delia said chattily to Jack as lunch was served. 'It was way before we came here, but it's still talked about.'

She was wearing a new calf-length lemon silk dress and a heavy amber necklace. Her fiery-red hair had been tamed into a cap of fashionably sleek, head-hugging waves.

'That's only because one of the other players was Seifallah Youssri Pasha,' Davina said, helping herself to green beans in a mustard sauce. For her Uncle Jerome's benefit, she added, 'Youssri Pasha was one of the club's first Egyptian members – and he still plays a mean game of polo. If

168

you're Egyptian you have to be royalty or an intimate friend of royalty to be a member of the Gezira. Darius is only a member because his father is such a close confidant of the King. He'll be playing this afternoon.'

'Interesting,' Jack said, his eyes meeting Petra's across the table.

She knew very well what he was thinking. Why on earth was Darius playing polo at the Gezira, when the club epitomized the foreign domination he hated?

'And talkin' of the Prince of Wales,' Delia said, bringing the conversation back in the direction she had initially been trying to steer it. 'Everyone in Cairo was mightily disappointed that he didn't play polo when he was here last spring on his way back to London after tourin' Kenya and Uganda. He viewed some antiquities and that was all. Even Ivor didn't get a glimpse of him. What is the London gossip, Jerome? Is the gig really up between him and Freda Dudley Ward? Gwen wrote me that he now has eyes for no one but Lady Furness.'

Petra was intrigued to see that Jerome looked distinctly uncomfortable. 'For goodness sake, Delia,' he said in fond exasperation. 'Do you really expect me to discuss such a subject in front of Petra and Davina?'

'It won't shock them. You forget they live in Cairo. They're quite used to scandal.'

Davina and Petra both raised their eyebrows. Scandals were never discussed in front of them. The very thought would have thrown their father into a fit. Neither of them was about to say so, though. Not when the conversation was becom-

169

ing so interesting.

'Well, if you must have scandal over the lunch table, yes – Gwen is quite right and doing a good job of keeping you up to date.'

'She may be' keepin' me up to date, but she doesn't have access to as much inside gossip as you. Do King George and Queen Mary know of David's latest infatuation?'

'Who,' Davina asked, 'is David? I thought you were talking about the Prince of Wales. His name is Edward.'

'He's known as David to his family and friends, honey.'

'And are you one of his friends?' Davina was clearly impressed

Petra rolled her eyes, annoyed at having her mother sidetracked.

Delia, who never minded being sidetracked, said breezily, 'He treated me as a friend before I left England for Egypt. There are only a few months' age difference between us and he likes Americans. Freda-Dudley Ward has an American mother and I'm guessin' Thelma Furness is either American or half American.'

'American,' Jerome said. 'Her father was US consul in Buenos Aires. Her mother is Irish-American and *her* mother was Chilean and re-portedly a descendant of Spain's royal house of Navarre. Which is why Thelma is pronounced the Spanish way: Tel-ma.'

Petra gave a deep, exasperated sigh. From her rare visits to Virginia she knew how fascinated Virginians were with family trees. Her late grandmother had been familiar with the family

170

trees of nearly everyone she ever met and it was a fascination her mother shared. If they weren't very careful the conversation was going to veer off onto Spanish royalty and she would be left no wiser about the Prince of Wales's current love life.

'The King and Queen, Uncle Jerome,' she said, prompting him in a way she could never have done if her father had been present. 'Mama wanted to know if they know about Lady Furness.'

He quirked an eyebrow in her direction. 'Ah, yes. The answer is that I don't think they do. Not yet. And now that you're sixteen, Petra, I think you're old enough to drop the honorary "uncle" title. Unless your mother has any objections, of course.'

He looked across at her mother. Delia's eyes held his for such a long beat of time that Petra actually thought she was going to object – which would have been pretty odd, for even when he had been a small boy Jack had never called Delia 'Aunt' – and she knew her mother didn't really like her and Davina referring to Jack's mother as 'Aunt'.

'Of course I don't,' Delia's voice was filled with the warmth it always held when Jack and his father visited. 'So silly to use it when you are most definitely not her uncle.'

'No, indeed.'

Petra wasn't sure, but she thought her mother blushed. As this was patently ridiculous, she wondered if her mother had been wise to serve hot spicy chicken when the temperature was over ninety degrees.

'And what is the gossip about Margot?' Delia

171

asked. 'How is she coping with widowhood?'

'She spends most days at the House of Commons, in the Ladies Gallery.'

'And the Churchills?'

'I haven't seen Clemmie for quite a while. Winston is very hang dog. To be honest, I quite understand his depression. Unemployment is escalating – George Curzon's son-in-law, Oswald Mosley, was recently given responsibility for solving the problem, but the Cabinet has blocked every scheme he's put forward. I suspect that by the time I get back to London he will have given up the battle and resigned. In Germany, unemployment is even worse. It's so bad Winston thinks it will result in that ruffian Hitler coming to power.'

Petra stopped listening. London gossip about the Prince of Wales was riveting. London gossip about politics wasn't. Jerome, however, was a Liberal Member of Parliament and it was only to be expected that politics was one of his favourite topics of conversation.

For the rest of lunch she wondered how she was going to get used to dropping his honorary title of 'Uncle'. It was all very well for her flamboyantly unconventional mother to agree to his suggestion that she should now call him Jerome, but she knew that her father would never agree. He would insist that if Jerome felt the title was inappropriate she would in future have to address him as Sir Jerome – which wouldn't be easy considering he had been as close to her as family ever since she had been in her cradle.

From the other side of the table Jack gave her a

172

wink. Knowing he was reading her mind – as he did uncomfortably often – she flashed him a broad grin. It was a common joke between them that when her father wasn't there and Jerome had to make do with her mother's company, the atmosphere and conversation always bordered on the risqué.

'It's because Mama is an American,' she had once said a little apologetically to him. 'And not just an American, but a Virginian. She seems to think she can say whatever she pleases to whomsoever she pleases – and she's always embarrassingly affectionate to people. Bellingham and Parkinson have always been treated as members of the family – and she's no different with Adjo. He now speaks to her as if she's an equal, not an employer, much to my father's fury.'

'However bizarrely free and easy she is, it works,' Jack had said. 'All the homes you've lived in have had the most welcoming atmosphere I've ever experienced. And there are never any staff problems, are there? No one who's worked for your mother ever wants to leave her.'

Petra was brought back to the present moment by her mother saying in a voice that brooked no argument: 'I'm not surprised the Denbys are divorcing. He's an awful screw.'

'Screw?' Davina said.

'Mean with money, pet. Never marry a man who is mean with his money, because he'll be mean with his affection as well.' And deeming it an appropriate note on which to end lunch, Delia rose to her feet.

The heat was always so intense in the early

173

afternoon that it was customary for everyone to retire to their rooms and, with ceiling fans softly whirring, to sleep until it was cooler

Petra didn't. She had far too much on her mind. Sleeplessly she stared up at her bedroom ceiling, replaying the scene by the tennis court when Jack said he didn't like the idea of her mooning over Darius. Had he meant that now she was sixteen he would far prefer her to be mooning over him? And if he had, how did she feel about that?

Though everyone referred to Fawzia as being her closest friend, Jack was really her best friend and had been so for as long as she could remember. Could best friends become romantically involved? And if they could, would she want to become romantically involved with him?

She thought of the way his hair curled in the nape of his neck when he didn't slick it into submission with brilliantine. She thought of his finely chiselled mouth and firm jaw and the slight cleft in his chin. She thought of his perpetual good humour and the way he made her laugh and of how happy she always was in his company.

And then she thought of Darius.

She didn't *like* Darius, but he certainly had an effect on her. Just what the nature of that effect was, though, she couldn't decide. It certainly wasn't romantic in the way she envisioned romance. She thought of the narrow slanting eyes set above high cheekbones; of the intensity in his lean, dark face; of the blue sheen to his night-black hair. Her mother had once said that Darius reminded her of Rudolf Valentino. There was the same panther-like grace about him; the same

174

sense of power under barely controlled restraint.

She would much rather be with Jack than with Darius.

But it was Darius she couldn't get out of her head.

The Gezira Sporting and Racing Club had four polo grounds and it was on ground number one that Jack and Darius were to play.

'Though on opposing sides,' Petra heard Davina say to Jerome. 'Jack will be playing on the Visitors' Team. They usually lose against the home teams.'

'They may very well win today,' Jerome said drily. 'Jack is a barbarian on the polo field.'

Davina giggled, but Petra didn't. She was sure that if any rider proved to be a barbarian it would be Darius and she didn't want Darius riding hard at Jack in an effort to cause him to pull out or, at the very least, to unhorse him.

The stand was crowded with Cairo's crème de la crème. Delia was in her element. 'Don't you just wish you were goin' to play today?' she said to Jerome. 'I know I do. The minute we have a women's polo team I'll be first on the field!'

Happy at having her girls at either side of her she acknowledged a nod from the British High Commissioner and then shot a dazzling smile in the direction of Zubair Pasha who, with Fawzia, was walking towards them.

'Seeing Jack and Darius on opposing teams is quite an event, isn't it?' Delia said as he and Fawzia seated themselves.

'It is indeed, Lady Conisborough.' Zubair Pasha, always affable, beamed broadly. 'And making it even more special is that Fawzia is to present the winning trophy.'

Petra leaned forward and looked towards Fawzia. Fawzia met her look and grinned, her self-satisfaction so evident she was positively purring. Petra smiled back, happy for her. The presenter of a trophy had hundreds of eyes focusing on her and no one loved being the centre of attention more than Fawzia.

When the eight riders trotted onto the field and lined up in positions of play, Petra saw that Jack had been allotted the Number Two position, a position needing a keen eye and high manoeuvrability. In the opposing team Darius was Number Three, the tactical leader, a position always given to the team's best player.

'Having been a member of a crack cavalry regiment, you must be an excellent polo player also,' Zubair Pasha said to Jerome.

'I carry a nine-goal handicap.'

Zubair Pasha was impressed. 'Then I should like to see you play. Though not for the Visitors,' he added with a chuckle. 'With Darius.'

As one of the mounted umpires prepared to start the match by bowling the ball hard between the two teams, the atmosphere became electric and all chatter ceased.

Moments later Darius made a long powerful hit, feeding the ball to his Number Two and a roar of applause went up.

From then on, play continued at terrific speed. There were groans from the Residents' supporters and cheers from their rivals as the Visitors' Number Four player made a back-handed stroke, shooting the ball away from their goal and towards his own team mates. Galloping hard, Jack secured the ball and, despite Darius riding his sweating pony hard at him, scored a goal.

Petra rose to her feet, clapping hard and cheering till she was hoarse. Only when she sat down did she realise that Fawzia, too, had been on her feet – and was still on them.

'I think Fawzia has a crush on Jack, just as Petra has a crush on Darius,' Davina said to Delia under cover of the applause. 'Have you seen the expression on her face? Her eyes are on him the entire time.'

Petra opened her mouth to protest that she most certainly did not have a crush on Darius and then closed it again. It was better that her mother believed it. She didn't want Darius's politics to mean she was forbidden contact with Fawzia.

As one chukka followed another, with both Jack and Darius changing their exhausted ponies after each one, Petra realised that Davina was right and that Fawzia was most certainly not rooting for her brother's team. Despite the close proximity of her father, she was rooting for Jack.

In the sixth and final chukka, with the Residents' team way ahead on goals, both Jack's and Darius's riding became more and more fearless and aggressive.

'Land sakes!' Delia said anxiously to Jerome. 'I hope Jack doesn't unseat Darius. Darius would never forgive him.'

'They're both going to be unseated if they aren't careful,' Jerome said tautly, and then, barely before he'd finished speaking, Darius broke away from the pack at a full gallop, thundering down on Jack, who was in possession of the ball.

The crowd rose to its feet.

Jack tried to twist his pony away but was a split second too late. The impact was enormous. Both Jack and Darius were sent flying to the ground. Fawzia screamed. Umpires raced to the scene. As Jack and Darius continued to lie prone in sickeningly unnatural positions, Zubair Pasha and Jerome simultaneously made hurried exits from the stand.

'Oh God!' Delia said devoutly. 'Oh *dear* God!' She had a hand at her throat and her face was ashen.

The atmosphere was no longer electric. As first-aiders ran to join the umpires and as Jack and Darius's team members slid from their saddles, the air was filled with dread. Fatal polo accidents were not unknown and, as neither Jack nor Darius showed any signs of movement, everyone was gripped by the worst possible fear.

Fawzia had her hands clenched to her mouth.

Davina looked as if she was about to be sick.

As for Petra, time stood still. In a moment of blinding clarity she knew that if Jack was dead, her life would have lost all meaning.

'You can't die,' she whispered fiercely, knowing her whole world was on the line. 'Move, Jack! For God's sake, *move!*'

He moved.

The sob of relief she gave came from the profoundest depth of her being.

An ambulance drew up and men with stretchers ran across the field. As Jack was helped into a sitting position, Darius opened his eyes and Jerome turned towards the stand and gave them a thumbs-up. With her heart hammering in her chest, Petra watched as Jack was helped to his feet and Darius, now conscious and with what appeared to be a broken leg, was placed on one of the stretchers.

As the body language of those on the field indicated that no great harm had been done to either player, the relief in the stands was palpable.

'Thank God,' Delia was saying over and over again. 'Thank *God*.'

Petra was thanking God too, but she was also aware that during the entire drama every iota of her concern had been for Jack and that Darius had barely entered her thoughts.

NINE

Within weeks of the polo match Delia dropped the bombshell that she had arranged for Petra to leave the lycée and that for the next two years she was to attend an international school for girls at Montreux.

'It's all arranged, honey.' On this issue, if on no other, Delia was determined to have her own way. 'And before you kick up a fuss, let me tell you that it's either Montreux or a finishing school in New England.'

Unaccustomed to meeting with such implacability from her usually indulgent mother, Petra was appalled.

'Don't be,' Jack had written back to her when she had poured out her woes to him in a letter.

Montreux is only a little over forty miles from Dad's villa at Nyon. We'll be able to meet up far more often than when you're in Cairo. And think of the skiing you'll be able to do. You'll have the time of your life.

Knowing that Jack wouldn't let her down and that he would be at his father's villa at every opportunity he could, she allowed herself to be shipped off to Montreux.

It was far more fun than she had anticipated. Only when she found herself surrounded by dozens of girls all her own age and from similarly privileged backgrounds, did she realize just how circumscribed her life had been in Cairo. There, she'd had only Davina and Fawzia to gossip and laugh with, but Davina had barely left childhood behind her and outside of school Fawzia was allowed very little freedom. It was a situation that didn't give the three of them much racy subject matter. Within days of settling in at the Institut Mont-Fleuri she discovered that the conversation was hardly ever *not* racy.

She was in a class of ten and they were split up into two dormitories. Inevitably, late-night talks after lights-out ensured that she became far closer to the four girls she shared a dormitory with, than to the other five girls.

She wrote to Jack.

Suzi de Vioget is French, and manages to be sen-

180

sationally attractive without being classically beautiful.

She paused there, wondering whether to mention that Suzi had celebrated her seventeenth birthday by ridding herself of her virginity with the Mont-Fleuri ski instructor. On reflection, it was information she decided not to share with him. She didn't want him thinking she was getting up to the same kind of fun and games.

Magda von der Leyen is a member of the German aristocracy and her mother has just married for the umpteenth time. It doesn't matter what male name is mentioned, if he is over forty and has a title, at one time or another he's been Magda's stepfather.

Annabel Mowbray is English and is the great-niece of a friend of my mother's, Lady Denby.

Boudicca Pytchley is also English. She was conceived in Coventry and is named after Queen Boadicea. She has a terrific crush on the Prince of Wales and our dorm is plastered with pictures of HRH launching ships, shooting big game and looking dinky in a kilt at Balmoral. When she escapes from Mont-Fleuri and comes out (we're planning on all three of us being presented at court on the same day) she's determined to capture his attention and become the next Queen. I rather hope she does, as she says she'll attend the coronation bare-breasted in tribute to her namesake.

Life with Suzi, Magda, Annabel and Boudicca as friends was far from dull. Though an eagle eye was kept on them, it wasn't always eagle enough – as Suzi's adventure with their ski instructor had shown. One of the most exclusive boys' schools in the world, Le Rosey, was at nearby Rolle and, despite all the efforts of staff at Le Rosey and Mont-Fleuri, a great deal of fraternization took place.

'Which is exactly what my mother hoped there would be when she sent me here,' Annabel said to Petra when the five of them had set off for an illicit assignation with five Le Rosey eighteen-year-olds. 'Every pupil at Le Rosey is either royal or rich as Croesus. Snaring one of them as a future husband would reassure my mother that my fees here had been worthwhile.'

Talk about boys was almost non-stop, but Petra never talked about Jack. That a family friend had a villa at Nyon was known both to her friends and to the staff. What was also known was that her mother visited Nyon three or four times a year – always visiting the school when she did so – and that there was absolutely nothing extraordinary about Petra making occasional visits to Nyon.

These visits only ever occurred when Jerome was also at Nyon. 'It just isn't on, now that you're seventeen for the two of us to meet at the villa when there is no one else there but the staff,' Jack had said when, with Suzi's seduction of the ski instructor in mind, she had made the suggestion. 'Your father would regard it as a gross breach of trust and I have too much affection and respect for him to want that to happen. What we can do, though, is to meet up in Montreux or Rolle. That way our meetings can be completely above board.'

He was right – and she knew he was right – but she was disappointed all the same. The meetings they had in Montreux coffee shops and Rolle restaurants were full of fun and laughter, but they were not steamily romantic. And steamy romance was what she craved.

If it was also what Jack craved he gave no sign of it. As her first year at Mont-Fleuri gave way to her second year, he was posted to the British Embassy in Lisbon and there were no more gloriously carefree meetings at Nyon. Every so often, when Jerome was at Nyon and, in his role as family friend, he took her out for a coffee or a steamer ride, he would let slip that as well as working hard, Jack was also socializing hard.

'Ever since the war, Portugal seems to have become a haven for most of the exiled royalty of Europe,' he said to her one time as they strolled companionably together towards the lakeside. 'The daughter of the Marquis de Fontalba is featuring large in his letters at the moment. If anything should come of it his mother would be enormously pleased.'

She had bitten her lip and made no response. The daughter of the Marquis de Fontalba may have been featuring large in the letters his father was receiving from Jack, but she made no appearance at all in the letters Petra was receiving from him. She tried to take this as a sign that he wasn't seriously romantically involved with anyone, but as the months went by she couldn't help wondering whether her belief that he felt the same way about her as she did about him, was wishful thinking and nothing more.

'Do I know if Jack is on the verge of becoming engaged?' Delia repeated, surprised, when she visited Nyon shortly before Petra was due to leave the Institut. 'What an odd question, honey. If he had, surely he would have written and told you? You two are close buddies, aren't you?'

'Well, of course we are. I was asking because he's going to be in London for my coming-out ball and I'm thinking of introducing him to Magda.' There was no way she was going to tell her mother the real reason. If Jack did have someone else she didn't want her mother to know about her own hopes. 'I think Jack is probably just Magda's type.'

'Maybe he is, but Magda is still a smidgen away from her eighteenth birthday and Jack is twenty-five. It wouldn't be a good idea, Petra. Trust me.'

It was a remark she took note of, for if that was her mother's opinion of the seven-year age difference then, if things did work out between her and Jack, it would clearly be safest not to tell her – or at least not to tell her at the outset.

Delia's visit to Switzerland had been one she had made alone. 'It's term time for Davina,' she explained. 'And as there has been another violent outbreak of anti-British feeling in Cairo, your father has felt it his duty to remain on the spot.'

It was an explanation that Petra, hugging her, saw nothing odd about.

Mont-Fleuri hadn't given permission for her to stay at the villa for the duration of Delia's stay there, but they had given her extra time off during the day and extended the time she was allowed to stay out in the evening. To ensure they could enjoy each other's company for the longest time possible, Delia booked dinner at a restaurant close to the school.

184

Jerome had come from London to meet up with them. Aware of how hungry Delia always was for royal gossip, he said, as the waiter filled their glasses, 'George Curzon's daughter, Alexandra, has become a firm part of the Prince of Wales's set since she married the Prince's best friend, Fruity Metcalfe.'

'I don't suppose her sister and her husband are.' Delia, resisting with great difficulty the temptation to reach out and touch his hand, smoothed her napkin across her lap.

'Gwen wrote me that Tom was so disgruntled at having his blueprint to end unemployment rejected that he's left the Labour Party and formed his own political party – and that it's causing quite a furore.'

'Most things Mosley does cause a furore.'

He sounded amused, as he always did when in her mother's company. Looking at him, Petra realized that for a man in his late-forties he was still startlingly attractive. A scar ran through his left eyebrow, but didn't detract from his good looks. A souvenir from an old war wound, it only served to make him look even more dashing. His immaculately-clipped moustache showed no hint of grey and his hair, though silvered at the temples, was still thick and curly. That he had retained his looks so well pleased her, for it was a favourable indication that in twenty years' time Jack too would still look just as good as he did now.

Though the conversation was already beginning to follow what was, to her, a boringly predictable pattern, the name Mosley attracted her attention.

'I thought the Mosley who had married a

Curzon was called Oswald, not Tom?'

'He is.' Delia took a sip of wine and then added, 'Only he's known as "Tom" to family and friends. And Alexandra is known as "Baba".'

Petra raised her eyes to heaven. Why her mother's friends couldn't go through life with the name, or the diminutive of the name, they had been christened with she couldn't begin to imagine. Fruity and Baba. They sounded like something out of a nursery rhyme.

She let her attention drift and it wasn't until the dessert trolley made its appearance that she caught up with the conversation again.

'... and so Aunt Rose, who is a friend of Wallis's aunt, has asked me to do all I can to ease Wallis and her husband into London society. There is precious little I can do while still in Cairo,' Delia continued. 'But perhaps you could do something, Jerome?'

'I'll do my best.'

Not for the first time, Petra was aware that Jack's father always did everything he could to please her mother. 'I'll need to know a little about Aunt Rose's friend's niece,' he said with his indefatigable good humour. 'What is her background, do you know?'

'Some of her mother's relations live in Virginia, not too far from Sans Souci. Bessie Merryman, her aunt, visits them regularly – which is how Aunt Rose got to know her. Wallis, though, was born in Baltimore. She divorced her first husband – an American who, from Aunt Rose's account, was absolutely ghastly – and her second husband is British and a partner in a firm which buys and sells ships.'

At the expression on Jerome's face, Petra stifled a giggle.

After playing for time by choosing a raspberry pavlova from the dessert trolley, he said with remarkable restraint, 'Forgive me for saying so, Delia, but the Simpsons don't sound very promising material. As she is a divorcee, an invitation to a royal garden party is out of the question and I can't quite see the Digbys taking them up – or anyone else for that matter.'

'I shouldn't think Wallis would want to be taken up by an old fogey like Cuthie anyway. What I had in mind was an introduction to the more raffish elements of the Prince of Wales's set. I thought perhaps she could be introduced to Thelma Furness, a fellow American who must be about the same age...?'

Delia didn't finish the sentence. She just let it hang in the air, hopefully.

'I'll do my best, but bear in mind that Thelma Furness has eaten better men than me for breakfast.' There was teasing humour in his voice. 'Still, if that's the danger you want me to face...'

To Petra's amazement, her mother giggled in exactly the same way Suzi de Vioget often giggled.

It was most disconcerting.

Just as she had realized a little earlier what a seriously attractive man Jack's father still was, so she now realized that her mother was still bewitchingly lovely. It was a loveliness enhanced by the American freshness, vitality and wholesomeness she'd never lost, and by the glorious

187

colour of her hair which would, Petra suspected, still be as red – by fair means or foul – when she was in her dotage.

She turned her thoughts to her immediate future. In another few weeks she would be leaving Mont-Fleuri and, much as she wanted to return to Cairo, she wouldn't be – at least not straightaway. Being presented at court and enjoying a London season afterwards was essential for a girl of her family background, and as she would be sharing all the fun of being a debutante with Annabel and Boudicca, she was looking forward immensely to all the razzmatazz.

'Your mother was a married woman when she was presented,' her Aunt Gwen said to her fondly as they waited for the third fitting of her presentation gown. 'Under normal circumstances she would have been presented by her mother-in-law but as your grandmother was dead – I do wish she had lived long enough for you to have known her – Sylvia presented her.'

'I didn't know that. How odd. They never spend a lot of time together, do they? I don't think Sylvia has visited Egypt once in all the time we've been there. I expect they'll be meeting up now Mama is in London. She's happy as a lark at having the excuse to be here for my coming-out season.'

'And I'm as happy as a lark that she's here. She's so full of life and high spirits she makes even me feel young.' Her age-spotted hand patted Petra's. 'Now we're going to have a rehearsal today with shoes, feather and fan, aren't we? I'm so glad you haven't opted for one of the fashionable high-fronted gowns. An evening gown should always be becomingly low – especially when you have a nice bosom to display. Your mother looked exquisite in her presentation gown – and I came with her to her fittings as well. She was fresh from Virginia and rather shy and nervous. It's hard to believe that now, isn't, it?'

For Petra, it wasn't hard. It was impossible.

Ever since they had arrived back in London together, Delia had socialized with fury, making contact with all her old friends and with lots of new ones, including Wallis Simpson.

'Wallis had absolutely no need of anyone's help in becoming acquainted with Thelma,' Delia said, returning to Cadogan Square from an early evening cocktail party at the Simpsons' Bryanston Square flat. 'She's an old friend of Benjamin Thaw's and Bennie is married to Thelma's sister. I like her a lot – Wallis that is, not Consuelo Thaw. Consuelo is far too...' She paused, seeking the right word. 'Too unconventional,' she said at last. 'Your father wouldn't approve of me spendin' time with her, and as for you, Consuelo is completely off-limits. If she should show signs of taking you up, scoot away fast. Don't ask me why, honey. Just trust me.'

She shrugged herself out of a small chinchilla shoulder cape. 'Thelma is in a different category – mainly because the Prince of Wales thinks she's the bee's knees and so it's impossible for anyone to get away with snubbing her.' Delia reached into her handbag for her cigarette case. 'I wonder when he's going to end his unhealthy fascination for married women and start payin' attention to someone he can marry? Perhaps when you've been presented you could catch his eye. My cousin Beau would have loved the idea of my bein' mother-in-law to the future King of England.'

She paused, the cigarette case in her hand, her eyes brilliant with memory.

'And are you back on hobnobbing terms with Prince Edward?' Petra asked, before her mother could go on a reminiscing jag about her girlhood at Sans Souci and about how, if it hadn't been for Ivor visiting Virginia in 1911, she might very well have ended up marrying Cousin Beau.

'I'm not sure "hobnobbing" is the right word, pet. I've known David – I can't refer to him as Edward, he hates it – far longer than most of the other people in his present set and that counts for somethin', but there's a fly in the ointment and the fly is that the King regards your father as a friend and has done for twenty-odd years.'

She lit a cigarette. 'David,' she said, after blowing a thin plume of blue smoke into the air, 'is never one hundred per cent comfortable with people whom his father is also on easy and relaxed terms with. He's nervous of his father learnin' too much about his extra-curricular activities with unsuitable married women.'

'Then there's no chance of his coming here to a cocktail party and of my being able to invite Boo?'

'Boudicca?' Delia's eyebrows rose. 'Honey, she's eighteen. No matter how crazy she may be about him, HRH would barely register her presence. He only takes an interest in women who are around the thirty mark and married. And talking of your friends ... is Jack going to be in London in time

190

to act as your escort at Annabel's pre-presentation party?'

'Yes.' Her heart slammed as it always did when Jack's name was thrown unexpectedly into the conversation.

Delia decided against the cigarette and stubbed it out. 'I've told Lady Mowbray there's nothing untoward about his being your escort and that he's such an old family friend he's almost like a bro'—' Her rush of words came to an abrupt end as she coughed so hard Petra thought she was going to choke.

'Do you want some water?' she asked in concern. 'You really should stop smoking, Mama. Coughing like a tramp isn't very elegant.'

Delia, still coughing, shot her a glance so aggrieved Petra wanted to laugh. Instead she crossed the drawing room to the art-deco cocktail cabinet and hastily-poured a glass of soda water.

'Here,' she said to her mother 'Drink this. Now what was it you were going to say?'

Delia drank and then, made an expressive gesture with her hand. 'I can't remember. I think I was just about to point out that even pre-presentation parties are an ideal opportunity for husband-hunting and so attending one with Jack as your escort is probably not very sensible. It will give the wrong signals. People might assume things and I wouldn't want them to. If you are going to stick to your decision not to try for Oxford and to husband-hunt instead, then you need to hunt a young man with far more wealth and position than dear Jack has, or is ever likely to have.'

Petra sucked in her breath and when she had

recovered herself said, truly shocked, 'That's the most snobbish thing I've ever heard you say!'

Delia looked suitably discomfited. 'And probably the most unnecessary as Davina tells me you still have your sights set on Darius. Now if I were *really* uppity I'd object to the idea of an Egyptian son-in-law even though he is a Copt – but I don't, or at least not much. What I want, though, is for you to meet lots of other eligible young men. Marryin' the first person you think you've fallen in love with isn't sensible. It's too easy to make a mistake and, when your father is a friend of the King, mistakes of that kind aren't easy to rectify.' As if she was afraid she had said a trifle too much, she added swiftly, 'And now I must hurry and have a bath. I'm having dinner at Margot's this evening and I'm tight for time.'

And before Petra could pursue any of the interesting points she had raised, she whirled from the room, taking her chinchilla cape with her.

Petra crossed to the cocktail cabinet again and mixed herself a pink gin – a vice her mother was unaware she had acquired – then she flopped onto a sofa, to ponder things over. As her mother was so eccentrically opposed to the idea of her having a romantic relationship with Jack, it was exceedingly useful that Davina had so innocently led her to believe that she was still carrying a torch for Darius.

She took a sip of her cocktail. That her American, Republican-reared, unconventional mother was, in reality, a conventional dyed-in-the-wool snob when it came to a question of who was, or was not, eligible as a son-in-law was a pro-

192

found revelation. If her dreams were to become reality, she and Jack would need all her father's support in order to overcome her mother's objections. That they would have it she didn't doubt. For one thing, he and Jack's father were friends, and for another, when it had come to his own marriage, he had not cared that her mother hadn't either grand family connections or wealth.

Her mother, she reflected, was quite obviously being influenced by her many friends who were also bringing out daughters or granddaughters that season. Lady Denby, for instance, a very old chum of her mother's, was cock-a-hoop that Annabel, thanks to Le Rosey, had snared a White Russian prince and was already officially engaged and sporting an emerald the size of an egg on her left hand.

The prince in question, Prince Fedya Tukhachevsky, was the elder brother of one of the eighteen-year-old Le Rosey boys they had made such good friends with in their last year at Mont-Fleuri. He was reasonably attractive and great fun and Annabel was, she knew, sincerely in love with him. Petra also knew that if it hadn't been for his title, there was little chance Annabel would have been marrying him. It was the prospect of becoming Princess Tukhachevksy that had rolled the dice in Fedya's favour.

If Petra had wanted, she could have made a far more prestigious conquest. Mohammed Reza was an exceptionally handsome Persian-student at Le Rosey, who had never troubled to hide the fact that he had a crush on her. Because of Jack she had given him no encouragement, but she knew every single one of her Mont-Fleuri class mates would have, for Mohammed Reza was the elder son of the Shah of Persia and his future wife would one day be an empress.

Well aware of the uproar there would have been at Cadogan Square if it had become known that she had actively discouraged the attentions of the future ruler of Persia, she turned her thoughts to Jack.

He had promised months ago that he would be in London for her presentation. She had ringed the date in red on a calendar kept beneath her pillow.

Apart from the snippets of information his father gave her – information which was always of a kind she'd rather not have had – it was hard to come by any other gossip about Jack's social life in Lisbon. He wrote to her mother almost as regularly as he wrote to his father, but Delia's only comment, when she asked about Jack's latest news, was, 'it's no doubt the same news as in his letters to you, honey, and isn't it dandy how he's become such a success as a diplomat?' This wasn't the kind of information she was after.

She finished her pink gin and remained on the sofa, deep in thought.

Very, very occasionally Jack wrote to Kate Gunn. After she had replaced Mr Willoughby as her father's secretary, Ivor had instructed the girls to address her as Miss Gunn. Davina had done so ever since, but in answer to one of the letters Petra had sent in her early days at Mont-Fleuri, Kate Gunn had written:

Isn't it wonderful that your father has been able to arrange for me to move into one of the Garden City flats set aside for British Government personnel? It's the first home of my own I've ever had and I'm thrilled to bits with it.

Love,

Kate

P.S. Please don't write 'Dear Miss Gunn', 'Dear Kate' would be much nicer and friendlier.

Petra decided she would write to Kate, not only asking if she knew whether Jack was enjoying a heavy romance while in Lisbon, but also confiding why such information was so important to her. It would be good to have someone to talk openly with. Sometimes not doing so with anyone made her feel as if she was about to explode.

She jumped to her feet, intent on writing the letter immediately. Seconds later, as she crossed the hall towards the foot of the staircase, she came to an abrupt halt. Bellingham was opening the front door to a visitor – and the visitor was Jack's mother.

Considering how close their two families were and how Jerome was always popping into Cadogan Square, Sylvia's unexpected arrival should not have been disconcerting. The trouble was, she was always disconcerted when faced with Sylvia. Brought up to address her as Aunt, she had only ever thought of her as Lady Bazeljette. Even reminding herself that Sylvia was Jack's mother didn't help, for apart from his dark hair he looked nothing like her.

'Nonchalante et froide' was how Suzi de Vioget

195

had described her when Sylvia had been spending a few days at Nyon and the two of them had accidentally run into her in a smart Montreux café. 'Very beautiful, of course, especially for her age, but not, I think, very *sympathique*.'

Now, remembering her manners, Petra greeted the woman she hoped would one day be her mother-in-law.

'Aunt Sylvia, how nice to see you!' she said, forcing warmth and welcome into her voice as Bellingham sent a footman upstairs to inform her mother of Sylvia's arrival.

Sylvia tilted her head a little to one side, regarding her with interest, as she always did. It was an interest Petra had never been able to understand, for it was never followed up in any way. 'You're looking well,' Sylvia said in her cracked-ice voice. 'Being back in London obviously suits you.'

Willowy as a woman twenty years her junior, she was wearing a dove-grey grosgrain suit, grey suede shoes and a small hat with spotted veiling. A silver fox fur, complete with head, was casually draped over one shoulder and there were large, opulent black pearls at her ears and around her throat.Her eyes were heavily mascaraed; her flawless skin was as pale as porcelain; her lips were a glossy japonica-red and her perfume was heady and exotic. Petra found the mix of restrained elegance – the suit could have been tailored only in Paris, by Mainbocher or Chanel – and the blatant sensuality in the way that it was worn, deeply disturbing.

Good manners necessitated that she accompany Sylvia into the downstairs drawing room

196

until her mother came and as she led the way she said, making small talk, 'You must be looking forward to Jack's visit to London. I expect it's an age since you've seen him.'

'Jack?' His mother's pencil-thin, beautifully arched-eyebrows rose as if she were trying to place him. 'Yes,' she said at last. 'Possibly.'

Not for the first time Petra wondered what on earth her mother found to talk about when in Sylvia's company – not, she reminded herself, that her mother often was in Sylvia's company. Though Jerome had come out to Cairo often, Sylvia had never done so. 'The heat wouldn't suit her,' Delia had said when she had once queried why this was.

She decided to launch into family gossip and hope for the best. 'Davina's begun doing voluntary work in a Cairo orphanage,' she said, drumming up the only item of interest she could think of. 'It's something she's always wanted to do.'

'Voluntary work?' Without removing her silver fox, Sylvia seated herself on one of the room's many sofas. 'But surely she's still at school?'

'She does it at weekends.'

'How extraordinary.' The expression on Sylvia's exquisite face was one of bafflement. 'I'm surprised your father is allowing it.'

'I don't think he agreed easily, but Davvy can be outstandingly persistent when she wants.'

The conversational ball wasn't batted back. A silence fell.

Just as she was wondering what would engage Sylvia's interest, she saw that Sylvia's eyes had turned in the direction of the cocktail cabinet.

'Would you like a drink, Aunt Sylvia?' she asked,

with a touch of her mother's breezy manner. 'A Martini? I've just learned how to mix them.'

'Then I hope you've discovered that the secret is to mix them very dry.'

Taking this to mean that a dry Martini would be gratefully received, Petra crossed to the cocktail cabinet, glad of the diversion.

Sylvia rearranged her fur. 'Is Delia going out this evening? I only ask, as she isn't expecting me.'

Petra was tempted to say that her mother was out every evening – often with the racy Prince of Wales's set. Instead, she said: 'I believe she's dining with the Countess of Oxford and Asquith. How do you like your Martini garnished, Aunt Sylvia? With an olive or a twist of lemon?'

'A twist.'

The door opened and Delia entered the room, looking sensational in a halternecked evening gown of turquoise slipper satin.

'Sylvia!' She looked more startled than Petra had ever seen her. 'How unexpected!'

'It is rather, but then so is my news.'

Petra handed her the Martini. Neither Sylvia nor her mother looked towards her. It was as though she had become as invisible as a maid or a footman.

'Has something happened to Jerome?' Delia's voice was taut with fear. 'To Jack?'

The last possibility froze Petra to the spot.

'No. Theo has just told me his father has terminal cancer. It's come as rather a shock. I hadn't anticipated Theo succeeding to the dukedom quite so soon. However, that being the case, I have made a quite major decision.' She paused, took a sip of her Martini and said, 'I thought you should be the first to know, Delia, that in order to marry Theo, I'm going to divorce Jerome.'

Petra gasped.

Delia sank down onto the sofa facing Sylvia's. 'You can't mean it,' she said, sounding as if she'd been punched hard in the chest.

'But I do.' Sylvia looked completely unperturbed. 'Theo has wanted me to divorce Jerome for aeons. Until now I've never seen it as being in my best interest. I always thought Jerome would reach a position of distinction in the government, perhaps even become Prime Minister, but now the Liberals are no longer in the political mainstream it simply won't happen. That being the case, rather than face a future as the wife of an MP who will never enjoy a title any higher than that of a baronet, I prefer to seek a divorce and become a duchess.'

'The divorce...' Delia licked her lips. Petra wasn't surprised. Her mouth, too, was dry with shock.

'The divorce...' Delia said again. 'Has Jerome agreed to it?'

'He doesn't yet know I want one. And in case I've given a different impression, I shall be the one doing the divorcing and I shall be doing so on the grounds of his adultery.'

'Sylvia ... if you're intendin' to do what I think you are intendin' to do... If you're intendin' to name names...'

Sylvia cleared her throat and looked in Petra's direction. Delia looked towards her too.

'Please leave us, Petra,' she said stiffly, as if she

199

was having trouble moving her mouth. 'And what Aunt Sylvia has said is private. You're not to repeat it to anyone, d'you understand? Not even to Aunt Gwen.'

Giddy with the enormity of what she had just heard Petra nodded that she understood.

As she began to walk unsteadily from the room, Sylvia said: 'Naming names won't be necessary, Delia. Jerome will simply book into a hotel with a blonde. The hotel register and a private detective will do the rest.'

'It will ruin his reputation.' Her mother sounded as though she was having difficulty breathing. 'It will destroy his political career.'

'Maybe so,' Sylvia sounded bored, 'but the alternative is for him to divorce me on the grounds of adultery, and if he did I wouldn't admit to adultery with Theo. I'd admit to adultery with the lover who preceded him.'

Petra reached the door and closed it behind her. Then, as she leaned against it, trying to stop her legs from trembling, she heard her mother say with such passionate vehemence her scalp prickled. 'You can not, absolutely *can not*, ruin the career of such a distinguished man by dragging his name through the divorce court!'

Petra forced herself to move towards the stairs, wondering which of her friends' husbands her mother was referring to and wondering why Sylvia had told her mother she was seeking a divorce even before she told Jerome.

She walked into her bedroom, all thoughts of writing to Kate forgotten.

The person she wanted to write to was Jack.

200

And she couldn't. Not only because she had promised her mother she wouldn't reveal to anyone what she had just heard, but because her telling him that his mother was about to ask for a divorce would be totally inappropriate. It was news that should be given to him only by his mother or, if she couldn't face the task, his father.

As Petra thought of Jack's reaction, the breath hurt in her throat. The next few weeks, weeks she'd been looking forward to for so long, were going to be very difficult – and not just for the people most closely involved.

She hugged her arms to her chest, thinking of her own personal difficulty. It was one that was all too clear. With his parents' marriage in such disarray, Jack wasn't going to be in any mood to embark on a long-overdue love affair with her.

And she, God help her, had no desire to embark on one with anyone else.

TEN

Annabel's party was great fun – but Petra wasn't escorted to it by Jack. His telegram read:

LEAVE POSTPONED STOP
SEE YOU IN JUNE

It was a great disappointment, but life had become such a whirl of feverish activity Petra didn't have time to brood. Just as they had always

201

planned, she, Annabel and Boudicca were being presented at the same court. It was an evening court, which made it seem all the more glamorous. As Ellie helped her to dress and her mother and Aunt Gwen stood by ready to help with her Prince of Wales feathers, her jewellery and her fan, she felt quite sorry for all the debutantes who had been allotted an afternoon time slot.

'Now remember, darling,' her aunt said anxiously, 'when you have been presented and before you back away from their Majesties and from the room, *your train must be securely draped over your arm.* Otherwise you will trip over it – and why doing so is such a rarity I shall never know.'

'And when Ellie has secured your headdress, do one last practice curtsey,' Delia said, equally anxiously. 'A full curtsey in full fig is trickier than walkin' a tightrope blindfold.'

'Stop! Please! You're making me even more nervous than I already am. Ellie, you will make sure the feathers won't come adrift from my headdress when I make my low curtsey, won't you? And what if they do?' she added in real panic to her mother. 'Do I leave them where they fall? Do I pick them up?'

'You do nothing, honey. A gentleman-in-waiting will be only feet away from you and he'll sort out any disaster. And if a disaster seems imminent – say your train isn't just as it should be and it looks as if there's a danger of it tripping you up – he'll adjust it. That's why calamities are such a rarity.'

Her mother helped Ellie secure her headdress and Petra gave a sigh of immense satisfaction.

Worn slightly to the left side, with the centre plume the highest of the three, she felt like a queen.

Her gown was an absolute dream. Made of pearly-white chiffon over satin, short-sleeved and low-necked, and with white roses embroidered on the bodice and skirt, it looked like a cloud. It also, when the heavy train was attached at the shoulders, looked like a wedding dress.

Once again she thought of Jack.

The purpose of coming-out and the almost non-stop parties and balls that followed until the end of July, when the season ended, was to meet as many eligible men as possible and make a suitable marriage. And a suitable marriage meant marriage to someone rich and titled.

Boudicca's daydream was to attract the attention of the Prince of Wales. As it was also the dream of a very large percentage of that year's debutantes, it wasn't one that was likely to be fulfilled, and Petra was certain that by the end of the season Boo would be engaged to a lesser mortal – though one her parents would deem eminently suitable.

Annabel was already well on the route to becoming Princess Tukhachevsky and so didn't have to bother about husband-hunting.

And as she already knew very well who she hoped to marry, Petra had no intention of husband-hunting either.

'Your gloves,' Aunt Gwen said, handing them to her as her mother fastened around her neck the pearl necklace she had worn for her own presentation.

'There!' Delia, resplendent in a tiara and

dripping with diamonds and emeralds, stepped back to look at her. 'You are stunning, darling. Absolutely the bee's knees.'

'You look beautiful too, Mama,' she said truthfully. 'I just wish Papa and Davvy were here to see us.'

'That they aren't you can blame on nasty Egyptian politics. Your father isn't the High Commissioner but you would think he was, the way the Prime Minister relies on him. As for Davina, she couldn't possibly have travelled on her own and there was no one leavin' Cairo for England who could have chaperoned her. Even if there had, being here would have been no fun for her when she's too young to be invited to any of the balls and parties.'

In lieu of her father, Gwen travelled with them to Buckingham Palace, in the Conisborough Rolls. By the time they entered the Mall the stream of Rolls-Royces and limousines was seemingly endless and for long periods – sometimes twenty minutes at a time – they were at a standstill. The standstills weren't boring, though, for the Mall was crowded with sightseers who had come to see the long line of cars and their occupants.

'It's like being in a zoo,' Petra said, vastly amused as a woman with a toddler in her arms pressed so close to their car that the child was able to bang on the window.

'It will be like this all the time for whoever Prince Edward marries,' her mother said, cheerily blowing a kiss in the direction of the snotty-nosed infant.

She was wondering why her mother never referred to the Prince as 'David' in her Aunt Gwen's presence, when her aunt said, 'I think you're wrong about that, Delia, dear. The Prince always has outriders. And I have to say that I wish we had outriders, too. I find it unnerving hearing what the hoi polloi are saying about my gown and jewels.'

Fifteen minutes later, as they ascended the palace's grand Carrera marble staircase, Petra saw both Annabel and Boudicca ahead of her. At the top of the stairs she was shepherded with all the other girls into an anteroom full of stiff gilt chairs. There were thirty, perhaps forty, girls in the room and there was no opportunity for her to huddle together with Annabel and Boo or to chat with them. Under the stern eyes of palace lackeys they were all lined up according to the importance of their father's title and all she could do was to give them a small, excited wave.

After what seemed to be an age there came the sound of the national anthem being played in a room close by.

'That means the King and Queen are entering the Throne Room,' said the girl next to her. 'Any minute now and the girls at the head of the queue will be going in to be presented.'

After handing her presentation card to a footman, girl after girl was escorted from the anteroom. Petra watched Annabel hand over her card and then raise her hand to her headdress to check that it was secure. Boudicca was so nervous she dropped her card and a gentleman-in-waiting had to retrieve it for her.

At last it was her turn. At the entrance to the Throne Room a gentleman-in-waiting spread out her train. Another handed her presentation card to the Lord Chamberlain.

The room ahead of her seemed vast. On both sides were tiers of seats, every one occupied. In front of her, set on a dais beneath a scarlet canopy, were the thrones and, standing, the King and Queen. A little to the left of the King was the Prince of Wales and a little further distant, in glittering gowns and uniforms, were minor royals and other notables.

The Lord Chamberlain announced her name and seconds later she was in front of King George and Queen Mary. Almost sick with nerves she made a full court curtsey, her left leg behind her right leg, her knee bending until it almost touched the floor. Then, holding the position, she made a low bow and, most difficult of all, rose without losing her balance. Her relief, when her second curtsey had been successfully executed, was enormous and must have shown on her face, for she was quite sure she saw a rare glimmer of amusement touch the corner of the King's mouth.

Afterwards, in a room on a different floor of the Palace, there was champagne and small cocktail pies called Windsor pies, and she was at last able to grab a few words with Annabel and Boudicca.

'I wobbled,' Annabel said, not sounding too distraught about it. 'I wobbled so badly my mother said my Prince of Wales feathers were dipping and bobbing as if they were still on the ostrich.'

'I didn't know Prince Edward would be present!' Boudicca was flushed and starry-eyed. 'I was so busy looking at him I hardly noticed the King and Queen. Didn't he look absolutely spiffing in court dress? He's more handsome than any film star. Oh, I do hope he noticed me – and that he remembers me.'

'I don't think he noticed anyone,' Annabel said, cruelly forthright. 'I thought he looked bored to tears – as if he was wishing he was out night-clubbing.'

Annabel's mother sailed up to them resplendent in a stomacher of diamonds that rarely left the family vault. 'Who are you talking about?' she demanded, having caught only the tail end of the conversation. 'If you are talking about the Lord Chamberlain, of course he wasn't bored. Now say goodbye to Boudicca and Petra. We have an appointment with a photographer and are already late.'

Reminded that they also had similar appointments, Boudicca and Petra bade each other a hasty goodbye.

As the family Rolls sped towards the Chelsea studio of London's most prestigious society photographer, Delia said with satisfaction, 'What a day! And to think that I shall be doing all this again when Davina is presented.'

Petra looked across at her, startled. 'Are you sure Davvy wants to be presented?' she asked, sounding a note of caution. 'She doesn't like being the centre of attention and she has no friends in London.'

'Which is why she needs to be presented and have a London season. That way she'll make lots of suitable friends.' Davina making suitable friends was one subject Delia was firm about. 'That is what the whole exercise is about. A wide social circle will help her adjust to life back in England when your father is recalled.'

'Recalled?' Petra stared at her mother. 'Is that going to happen? I mean, is it going to happen *soon?*'

The Rolls was speeding along Chelsea Embankment and beneath a brilliant moon the Thames glittered on their left-hand side like black silk.

Delia made an exasperated sound in her throat. 'Well, of course it must happen soon, Petra. When your father went to Egypt as a British advisor, he went believin' he would be there for four or five years, six at the most. That was ten years ago. What has kept him there is the very troublesome political situation, and the fact that not only has he such a good relationship with King Fuad but the King believes he's a good influence on young Farouk. It is a relationship that is a great help to the present High Commissioner and so your father's length of tenure just keeps being extended and extended. It can't, however, be extended for ever. Enough is enough. He intends being back in London by the end of the year and even if he isn't, *I* certainly shall be. I've enjoyed seeing all my old friends again and I don't intend remaining in virtual exile any longer than the end of this year.'

There was underlying steel in her voice and Petra sank back against the Rolls' hide upholstery, stunned.

That her father's tenure as a British advisor to King Fuad would eventually come to an end was obvious and yet until now she'd never taken onboard what it would mean to her. Somehow she'd thought of the end as being so far in the distance that it needn't be worried about. Now she realized how very wrong that assumption had been.

When her parents left Egypt, Nile House would no longer be her home. She wouldn't be able to return there. And if she couldn't return to Nile House, how could she return at all? Where would she live?

Her plan had always been that she would return to Cairo at the end of the season – though she hadn't really thought about what she would do then, with finishing school and her presentation behind her. Most girls were engaged at eighteen and her hopes were pinned on becoming engaged to Jack. As his diplomatic posting was in Lisbon, it hadn't occurred to her that she would be spending the obligatory year or eighteen months of their engagement anywhere else but in Egypt with frequent visits on his part to Cairo. After that, her life would be wherever he was then posted and she'd seen no reason why, with a few discreet words in high places, he shouldn't be given a posting in Cairo.

That was the ideal scenario. And even if it didn't come to fruition, she still had never imagined anywhere but Cairo as home.

'Does Davvy know you and Papa are geared to leave Cairo by the end of the year?' she asked as the Rolls came to a halt outside the studio.

'I've no idea, but though she's managed to worm her way out of going to finishing school, there's no way she's going to worm her way out of havin' a London season. It's probably tactless of me to say so, but though Papa has always thought you were the headstrong one, I rather think it will be Davina who will one day turn his hair white. Beneath her sweet and gentle demeanour Davina is *very* unconventional.'

As her mother swept into the studio before any other arrivals could add to the queue in front of them, Petra didn't know whether to be pleased her mother thought her unlikely to ever cause her father grief, or miffed. In the end she was miffed. It made her sound so dull. And to be thought of as dull in comparison to her little sister was the living end. Deciding that her mother had had too much champagne and didn't know what she was talking about, Petra prepared to have a photograph taken that would, with a bit of luck, find its way into *Tatler* and perhaps even into *Vogue*.

Dear Petra,

What a hoot having your photograph in Tatler! It isn't something I ever look at, but the High Commissioner's wife has just come back after a few weeks in London and brought a copy with her to show us. Papa says Mama is sending him a copy of the photograph so that he can frame it and have it on his desk. I expect it's the Prince of Wales feathers that make you look so regal. What on earth happens to them if you have to cross Buckingham Palace courtyard in a gale?

I've just come back from Abdin Palace having been dragooned into acting the part of an admiring spectator while Prince Farouk displayed his falconry technique. He's twelve but looks younger, probably because he's treated as if he's still a baby. Everything is done for him. I tried to chat to him about the orphanage I do voluntary work for – he will be the next king, after all, and you'd think he'd take an interest – but he simply said anyone not having parents was very lucky. Which has to be the most stupidly flippant remark I've ever heard. Darius said I have to remember he's only twelve and still a child. I'm trying to, but he made me very *cross (Farouk not Darius).*

I'll be glad when it's August and you come back to Cairo. It will still be stiflingly hot, of course, but that doesn't matter. We can go to Mena House and swim in the pool. It's the first year I can remember when Papa hasn't moved to a rented house in Alexandria to escape the worst of the summer heat, but the situation is such he feels it his duty to stick things out here, and so obviously I'm here with him. Things are never dull. A water buffalo trampled a fence and got into the Nile end part of the garden yesterday. Adjo got it out again, though not without a great deal of hollering and arm-waving. It was all tremendous fun. Better than a Charlie Chaplin film.

I'm thinking of asking Papa if I can train as a nurse. The problem is, though, where I would do the training. And don't say London. I can't bear the thought of living in London. What I'd really like to do, of course, is to become a doctor, but I don't have your academic ability and the exams would be completely beyond me. It's all a bit of a problem but I'm sure it will sort itself out eventually.

Lots of love,
Davvy

As it was so obvious Davina didn't have a clue that plans were being made for her to have a London season – and, worse, that her father was

211

certain the present year was going to be his last in Cairo – Petra wondered how she should break the news. A letter seemed very blunt, and a phone call, with the call having to be directed through operator after operator, through country after country, wasn't much more satisfactory.

After mulling the problem over for several days she decided to do nothing in the hope that perhaps the situation would be a little different by the end of the summer. Her mother often made extreme remarks off the top of her head and, with a bit of luck, the remarks she had made while on the way to the photographer would prove to be no more than wishful thinking.

As Petra attended a frenetic round of cocktail parties, dances and coming-out balls – often barely knowing the debutante whose ball it was – she enjoyed herself hugely. At every ball, party and event she went to, Annabel and Boudicca were there too and, as if they weren't seeing enough of each other every night, they also met up nearly every day, either at Gunter's tea shop or at the soda fountain at Selfridges. The only drawback to the fun they were having was the sheer tiredness that accompanied it, for it was rare for them to get to bed before four in the morning.

Petra's own coming-out ball was held during the first week of June and both Magda and Suzi came to London to attend it.

'Find me a glorious duke who owns half of England,' Magda said as the five of them sunbathed in the rear walled garden at Cadogan Square, drinking cocktails, 'and I'll be a happy girl.'

'Every English duke I know is a crusty old

man.' Petra swirled her ice cubes round with her finger. 'What you need is a young and dashing heir-presumptive.'

'Whatever.' Magda, superbly sophisticated in a black sun-top, black shorts and white plastic-framed sunglasses, rolled from her tummy onto her back, barley-gold hair streaming fan-like over the grass. 'As long as home is a ducal palace and the income is in six figures, I don't mind. Have I told you my mother is getting divorced again? It will be the *sixth* husband she's discarded. My grandmother says it borders on carelessness.'

They all giggled. Magda's racy mother was a favourite subject of conversation.

'She was a guest at Berchtesgaden last month,' Magda continued, taking off her sunglasses and closing her eyes. 'I'm simply keeping my fingers crossed that she isn't setting her sights on our beloved Führer.'

'*Your* beloved Führer,' Petra said chidingly. 'He certainly isn't *our* beloved Führer. We all think he's a horrid little man and can't understand why you Germans are getting so excited over him.'

Magda opened her eyes. 'He's making us feel like a nation again,' she said easily. 'When we lost the war, we lost our pride. Hitler is giving it back to us.' She sat up, reached for the glass of Tom Collins perched precariously near to her and said, changing the subject, 'A Tom Collins tastes even better, Petra, if you add strawberry schnapps to it. They sell schnapps in London, don't they? I'll try to get you a bottle.'

That her father wasn't in London for her coming-

213

out ball was a great disappointment to Petra, but as it was common knowledge that there had been a fresh violent outburst of anti-British feeling in Cairo, no one was surprised that Lord Conisborough was remaining in the troubled city.

'His not being here leaves us with a sticky problem,' she said to her mother while Delia was supervising the unloading of acres and acres of fresh flowers from a van as large as a removal lorry.

'Here come the hydrangeas,' Delia said as the delivery men began bringing pots of blue hydrangeas into the house. 'I'm going to stand those in all the fireplaces.'

'You're not listening to me, Mama. I said that Papa not being here for my ball leaves us with a sticky problem.'

'Which is?' Delia didn't take her eyes off the flowers being unloaded from the van. 'D'you think the carnations will look right with the lilies and roses? I'm beginning to wonder if I made the right decision when I said I would arrange them myself, with a little help from Gwen. Lady Mowbray had Constance Spry do the flowers for Annabel's ball and they were absolutely cracking.'

'The flowers will be fine. What won't be quite so fine is that for the first dance of the evening, when my father should be doing the traditional thing and waltzing me around the ballroom, he won't be there for me. And I don't have a brother. I don't even have a cousin. It's a problem I'd like a solution to. Have you any ideas?'

She had finally caught her mother's attention. 'You're right, honey. How on earth did I overlook a thing like that?' She frowned, deep in thought, and then said, 'Perhaps Winston could stand in for Papa?'

'No,' Petra said firmly. 'I don't mind the fact that so many family friends are going to be guests, but I am *not* going to endure Mr Churchill as a stand-in for Papa. For one thing, I'm far taller than he is. I'd look ridiculous.'

Sheaves of scarlet late-flowering tulips were carried past them, their scent heavy and sweet.

Her mother chewed her lip. 'Dear Pugh would never be able to complete a circuit of the ballroom. His gout is far too bad. Now, if only dear Cousin Beau were alive...'

Petra prayed for patience.

'But as he isn't,' her mother continued, happily oblivious of her reaction, 'we'll have to look elsewhere.' She paused for a second and then said, 'What about Sir John Simon? I don't think Britain has ever had a Foreign Secretary who is such a wonderful dancer. His predecessor, the Marquess of Reading, was a calamity on the dance floor.'

Petra hesitated. She quite liked Sir John Simon, but there was a drawback to his standing in-for her father. In his early sixties, tall, lean, patrician-faced, austerely handsome and imposing, he *looked* like her father. And that would, she knew, only make her father's absence even more obvious.

'No,' she said firmly. 'Not Sir John Simon.'

'Well, Lord Denby is out. He's been sick since March. And Cuthie Digby can barely walk any more, let alone dance.'

Petra decided to put her mother out of her misery. 'The proper person to stand in for Papa,

215

is Jerome. I know he's not an uncle or a cousin – but then neither is anyone else who has been mentioned – and he's always been as good as an uncle. I can't think of anyone I'd rather have acting as a stand-in father than Jerome.'

Instead of looking pleased that the problem was solved, her mother looked aghast.

'Why the shock?' Petra asked as the two delivery men, having carried the last of the flowers into the house, vaulted into the cab of their van. 'Papa wouldn't mind. If you'd realized the problem earlier and spoken to him about it, I'm sure Jerome is the person he would have suggested. I'll ring Jerome and ask him if he'll be Papa's stand-in now, shall I? And I'll think about what waltz I want the orchestra to play. I think I'd like something nice and old-fashioned. Perhaps "Roses from the South" or "On the Beautiful Blue Danube".'

By the end of the afternoon, the house was en fête. Blue hydrangeas massed the fireplaces; delicately coloured carnations twined around the magnificent brass-balusters of the grand staircase; ornate arrangements of lilies and roses graced every available highly polished surface. The first-floor drawing room, its floor waxed to a high sheen, had been turned into a ballroom and all around the walls were small gilt chairs hired for the occasion. A vast marquee erected in the rear garden was the supper room and the air inside it was heavy with the scent of the flowers decorating the damask-covered, silver-laden tables.

Before the ball there was a formal dinner party

at which her mother's friends, not hers, were the guests. Among them was Margot Asquith, now in her early seventies and as caustic-tongued as ever. Another of her mother's old friends, the former Duchess of Marlborough and now Madame Jacques Balsan, had journeyed all the way from her home on the French Riviera. Though at least twenty years younger than Margot, she was still nearly fifteen years her mother's senior, and not for the first time Petra marvelled at the way her mother had always made a friend of her father's friends, despite the fact they were nearly all a generation older than she was.

She wondered if her mother had sometimes found that difficult, and if that was the reason, with her father far away in Egypt, that Delia had begun spending so much time with the Prince of Wales and his friends – all of whom were about her age – and many of whom were fellow Americans. Was it because her mother was taking advantage of the fact that her father wasn't around to criticize her for doing so? And was that why she was so careful never to refer to the Prince of Wales as 'David' when in Gwen's company?

It was an interesting thought, as was the realization that so many of the people who had played such a large part in her mother's life were now dead.

'No George Curzon and no Herbert Henry,' her mother said sadly, making sure that all the name cards were in the right position on the dinner table. 'Which is a great loss. They always made every party they attended a special occasion.'

Both Lord Curzon and the Earl of Oxford and

Asquith had died during the years she had been in Egypt and Petra had no memories of either man. Not wanting her mother to become gloomy – as she sometimes did when her Cousin Beau cropped up in conversation – she said brightly, 'But at least you are good friends with one of Lord Curzon's daughters. You see an awful lot of Baba, don't you?'

'Yes.' Her mother straightened Winston Churchill's place-setting card. 'And if it wasn't for Tom Mosley being such a political wild card I'd probably see far more of Cimmie, as well.'

During dinner Petra was seated between her Uncle Pugh and Winston Churchill. On any other occasion she would probably have enjoyed Winston's rumbustious conversation, but she was too keyed up with anticipation to really appreciate it.

At ten o'clock, with the dinner over, guests began to pour into the house. Magda and Suzi, who were staying with Annabel, were among the first to arrive, but there was a seemingly endless stream of other debutantes and Petra was staggered to realize how many of them she now counted as close friends. The point her mother had made when discussing why she wanted Davina to be presented was obviously a valid one. It really did provide a girl with as wide a circle of suitable friends as possible. And though she wasn't interested in any of the 'eligibles' – the veritable army of upper-crust young men who had been invited – it was great fun to recognize nearly all of them from previous balls and parties and to be, for one evening at least, the absolute centre of attention.

She knew she looked sensational. Her mahogany-red hair was just as thick and naturally wavy as her mother's and she wore it fashionably short, with deep waves framing her face and a cluster of curls in the nape of her neck. Unlike many other debutantes, she'd elected not to wear her virginal white presentation gown for her party. The dress she had wanted to wear was long and slinky in bias-cut gold satin, with a halter neck and a plunging neckline.

Her mother had vetoed it instantly. 'Land sakes, Petra!' she had said, appalled. 'It looks like one of Thelma Furness's gowns! Wear that and the label "fast" will be one you'll never lose.'

'So what can I wear?' she had said exasperatedly, knowing full well that Magda's gown would be halter-necked and virtually backless, and that it would cling to every voluptuous curve.

'Chiffon would be a good choice. Perhaps floral chiffon. Or floral chiffon and tulle.'

It hadn't been a suggestion that had excited her. It was Lucille, her mother's favourite dressmaker, who had come to her rescue by designing a starkly simple, straight as an arrow, foot-skimming gown in mint-green taffeta, with a wide, slashed neckline and huge puffed sleeves. It crackled as she moved and amid a sea of pale pastel and floral gowns she stood out in just the way she had wanted. Her only ornamentation was a huge white rose pinned in her hair.

Her mother had looked at it with an odd expression, as if she was remembering something from long ago, and then had given herself a little shake and said, 'Unusual, honey. But it certainly works.'

Catching sight of herself in one of the giant mirrors lining the walls, she too thought her choice of dress certainly worked.

Everything else was working too. The orchestra her mother had hired was terrific. Gunter's had done the catering and the menu for supper included quail, lobster, chicken in aspic, asparagus and, to follow, Charlotte Russe, traditional English trifle, and strawberries and cream.

Jerome did an exquisite job waltzing her around the floor. Annabel clung to Fedya Tukhachevsky's side like a limpet. Suzi hadn't sat out one dance – and was somehow ensuring that all her partners were not only startlingly handsome, but were heirs to their father's vast estates. Petra hadn't seen her dance with a younger son even once. It was as if she could sniff them out at a mere glance.

Magda hadn't danced – and nor did it seem as if she intended to dance – with anyone's son. In a gown of silver lamé shimmering with crystal beads, her barley-gold hair coiled in a plaited knot in the nape of her neck, her every dance partner was a distinguished older man. Winston was quite obviously utterly bewitched by her. Sir John Simon couldn't take his eyes off her. Neither, though, were bachelors. And Petra was sure that only a very distinguished, exceedingly rich bachelor was going to seriously engage Magda's attention.

Despite having bowled over more eligible young men than the average girl would meet in a lifetime, Petra knew that none of her highly agreeable dance partners would ever seriously engage her own attention. Only Jack was capable of doing that.

And Jack was hundreds of miles away.

Wishing with all her heart that he could see her as she looked now – which was absolutely *stunning* – Petra lifted a glass of champagne from the tray of a passing waiter and decided, as the orchestra had launched into a tango, to take a breather between dances even though Boudicca's brother's name was marked on her dance card.

Jerome, an excellent dancer despite his barely noticeable limp, was performing some very nifty Argentinian footwork with Magda. It wasn't a performance any of her previous partners would have been able to give. At the thought of Winston executing a tango, Petra giggled.

'Rupert Pytchley is searching for you,' her mother said, looking oddly out of sorts as Jerome and Magda caught her attention. 'And don't giggle when you're not in conversation with anyone. It looks as if you've had too much champagne – and you haven't, Petra, have you?'

It was her third glass of champagne and Petra rather thought that perhaps she had. She didn't say so, though. Instead, she said, 'I'm just going to stand outside the room for five minutes and get a little air. Jerome doesn't seem at all put out about Aunt Sylvia wanting a divorce, does he? News that they've separated has already begun to spread. Aunt Gwen told me about it "in confidence" about an hour ago.'

Her mother said nothing, but as she looked across the dance floor to where Jerome and

221

Magda were continuing with their cabaret-worthy performance, there were lines of strain at the edges of her generously curved mouth and her eyes looked bleak.

As Petra walked from the ballroom she knew she shouldn't have brought up a subject that would cause her mother distress. Divorce in their social circle was not to be undertaken lightly and there was no telling what the effects of it would be on Jerome's career. It was reason enough for her usually carefree mother to be looking so concerned.

Outside the ballroom the air was refreshingly cool, heady with the fragrance of the pink and white carnations garlanding the staircase. The now muted strains of tango music came to an end and the orchestra began playing 'Love is the Sweetest Thing'. Just then the doorbell rang.

From where she was standing, at the first-floor curve of the grand staircase, Petra saw Bellingham cross the marble-floored hall. Idly she wondered who the late arrival would prove to be. It was close to one o'clock and nearly time for the supper to be served. Certain it was going to be a male friend of her mother's – none of her fellow debutantes would be arriving at such a late hour – she turned towards the ballroom again.

As she did so, she heard the sound of the door opening. And then the voice she'd been longing to hear for months and months.

'Good to see you again, Bellingham,' Jack said cheerily. 'I'm a bit late, but better late than never. I've come from Lisbon via Paris and the boat train was delayed.'

Petra spun round, her heart beating so hard

that for a second she had to rest her hand on the balustrade to steady herself.

As Bellingham closed the door behind him, Jack looked upwards.

Their eyes met.

His face broke into a broad grin.

'Sorry I didn't make it for your presentation, but the good news is that I'm not here on leave. I'm back in England for good.'

She gasped and then, as he took the stairs two at a time, she began to run down them. They met on the broad first half-landing and as he opened his arms she hurled herself into them, dizzy with joy.

His arms closed around her and she knew, even before he spoke, that things were going to be different between them.

'I've missed you,' he said, and the expression in his gold-flecked eyes sent her pulse racing.

Still in the circle of his arms, held in a way he had never held her before, she said with stark candour, her voice thick with emotion, 'All my life I've missed you when you're not with me – but I've never felt able to tell you so before.'

'And for the last two years, there have been things I've never been able to tell you.'

The throb in his voice told her she didn't have to ask what those things were.

For a long, long moment their eyes held and then, as the final strains of 'Love is the Sweetest Thing' drifted down the stairs towards them, he lowered his head, her arms twined around his neck and his mouth was hot and sweet on hers.

ELEVEN

It was the most transfiguring moment of Petra's life. She knew, deep in her bones, that what was happening between them wouldn't be a transient romance – a romance that would last only for the summer and not beyond. This was love. Just as she had known ever since she was sixteen that Jack was the only man in the world for her, she now knew that he had felt the same. Her age had been the only barrier to his telling her so – and her age was a barrier no longer.

As he lifted his head from hers she said, her voice wobbling with happiness, 'I wish you'd told me you were only waiting until now before letting me know that you loved me. I was so terrified I'd got it all wrong... Your father kept telling me you were seeing the Marquis de Fontalba's daughter. He thought you were about to become engaged.'

Amusement tugged at the corners of his mouth. 'You're quite right in that I love you – though it would have been more usual for you to wait until I'd told you so. As for Beatriz...' He paused teasingly and, seeing the apprehension in her eyes, said gently, 'Beatriz de Fontalba is an absolutely stunning girl and desperately in love with an Argentinian to whom, being neither titled nor wealthy, her father violently objects. She asked if I would act as a cover for the two of them and, as we are friends, I was happy to.'

224

'That's all right, then,' she said, her relief vast. 'And now I want you to waltz me round the ballroom in a way I'll never forget. Your father kindly stood in for my father where the first dance of the evening was concerned – and he did so splendidly – but if you whirl me round the floor it will be so magical I shall remember it to my dying day.'

'Best not to walk in there in such an intimate fashion,' he said as, arms around each other's waist, they walked up the stairs towards the ballroom. 'Not until we've put your parents wise to the situation.'

She missed her footing and his arm tightened around her, steadying her.

'There's something you should know,' she said, thinking it best to put him in the picture straight away. 'My mother isn't going to be as happy about our being in love with each other as you might expect. And it's only fair to tell you that she rather thinks I'm interested in Darius.'

He came to a halt outside the ballroom doors. 'Darius?' he said, staring down at her in baffled astonishment. *'Darius?'*

Giggles fizzed in her throat. 'It's completely accidental that she thinks so but – and this is a touch of the Beatriz's – I found it useful as it threw her off the scent where my feelings for you were concerned.'

'But why the devil did she need to be thrown off the scent about me? I would have thought she'd be over the moon if we married. Our families have always been so close that you were brought up calling my parents "Aunt" and "Uncle". And though I never did the same, I certainly always regarded your mother and father as being far more central to my life than many of my relatives. In fact the blunt truth is, I spent more time as a child with your mother, than I did with my own.'

He ran a hand distractedly through his thick curls. 'I think you've somehow got this all wrong, Petra. I reckon your mother was just concerned about you falling in love at such a young age. I don't think she'll mind having me as a son-in-law.'

Understanding flooded through her. Jack's explanation was entirely logical.

'Then we'll simply tell her that as long as we have her permission to become engaged, we're quite happy to wait until I'm twenty-one before we get married.'

'I've missed something here,' he said in mock mystification. 'Perhaps it was a proposal of marriage. Has there been one?'

She blushed furiously, and then, as the orchestra in the ballroom began playing a popular foxtrot, he lowered his head to hers and kissed her. 'Will you,' he said softly, 'please marry me, Petra?'

'Oh yes,' she said, her eyes shining, her face radiant. 'I've *always* wanted to marry you. I just thought that you were never going to ask!'

The ballroom doors burst open and a laughing, tipsy group of her guests spilled out, almost knocking them off their feet.

At that moment they were seen by several of the couples on the crowded dance floor. 'It's Jack Bazeljette!' a friend of his shouted. 'What ho, Jack! Typical of you to get here just in time for supper!'

As word spread that Jack had arrived, Petra saw

the news reach her mother. She saw Delia turn and look in their direction. And she saw her instant reaction. It was one of such pleasure and welcome she didn't have a single remaining doubt that Jack had been right.

Certain of all the happiness the future held for her, she walked into the ballroom at his side and five minutes later was waltzing with him to the unforgettably romantic strains of a Viennese waltz.

For the remainder of her party they behaved as if nothing exceptional had happened between them. Jack danced with several of her friends. She danced with several of the 'eligibles'. Annabel whispered to her that she thought Jack was 'absolutely brill' – and wanted to know what his prospects were. Fedya Tukhachevsky asked if he was Italian. Occasionally, as dancing continued after supper, their eyes met and her heart leaped with such violent desire she thought she would die of it.

As dawn broke and while she was dancing with Rupert Pytchley, Jack, who was dancing with Boudicca negotiated things so they were dancing next to each other. 'How about us all scarpering off for breakfast?' he said, speaking to both of them. 'Fedya has his car with him and I picked up mine en route from the station. We could be in Brighton by six-thirty.'

'Spiffing idea.' Rupert was always up for a bit of fun. 'There's nothing like an early morning swim after too much champagne. See if you can rope in Archie Somerset. He's somewhere in the garden with Boo and Petra's French friend, doing his best to cement Anglo-French relations.'

'And don't let's forget Magda,' Petra said.

'She'll never forgive me if we go without her.'

'Though don't invite her besotted dance partner!' Rupert called after Jack as Jack and Boudicca began dancing away from them.

'Why not?' Petra asked. 'Is there something wrong with him?'

'One hundred per cent,' Rupert said with deep feeling. 'He's my father.'

Piling into the two cars and roaring off to Brighton, while the rest of her party guests were milling into the marquee for bacon and eggs, kidneys, salmon kedgeree and coffee, was great fun. On the outskirts of Brighton, within sight of the South Downs, they stopped at a roadside café for bacon sandwiches and mugs of steaming tea.

'I think it's time some of us changed cars.' Magda, who had been squashed beside a canoodling Suzi and Archie all the way from London, looked at Jack with a meaningfully raised eyebrow. 'How about I sit in the front with you, Jack, and Petra does a stint in the back?'

'I don't think so,' Jack said pleasantly, a proprietorial arm around Petra's taffeta-clad shoulders. 'It might give the impression Petra isn't my girl – and, in case there's any doubt, she's very much my girl. Just thought you'd all like to know.'

Magda was unperturbed. 'Then I'll travel the rest of the way in Fedya's car and sit between Boudicca and Rupert. You'll have to crush your skirts up a bit, Boo. Why on earth did you opt for a crinoline instead of something slinky and svelte?'

'Because though slinky and svelte looks good on you and Petra, I'm too plump for it. What are we going to swim in when we get to Brighton? I

228

can't plunge in wearing my dress. The seawater would ruin it.'

'Take it off and go in in your undies,' Suzi said with French practicality as they headed back to the cars in all their evening finery, leaving a café full of bemused workmen behind them. 'I shall.'

Archie's roar of approval could have woken the dead.

On arriving in Brighton, the sea proved to be so cold that only Jack and Fedya stripped down to their underpants and plunged in. Archie and Rupert took off their socks and shoes and shouted encouragement as Jack and Fedya cleaved powerfully through the waves, headed in the general direction of France.

The girls slipped their feet out of their evening shoes, unclipped their suspenders, rolled their stockings down and then, lifting their ankle-length skirts knee high, paddled in the shallows, screaming at the cold and then screaming with a touch of real fear as it seemed neither Jack nor Fedya was going to give in and turn for shore.

'It's a male-pride thing,' Rupert said, shielding his eyes against the brightness of the early morning sun on the sea.

'But I can't *see* them,' Petra said, no longer enjoying herself one little bit.

'That's because of the waves. Don't worry, I can. And they've both turned. They're racing each other shore-wards now. Who is your money on? Fedya or Jack?'

It was Jack who waded out of the sea first. Petra raced into the water towards him, not caring that she was ruining the skirt of her taffeta evening gown by doing so.

Panting heavily, he came to a halt in waist-deep water and hugged her tightly against him. As she felt the reaction of his near-naked-body to hers and as her mouth pressed against his dripping-wet, salt-sheened flesh, an emotion she had never experienced before jack-knifed through her. She knew, without a shadow of a doubt, that a three-year engagement was going to be an impossibility.

Though Archie and Suzi never became a serious item, and though Magda never even troubled to flirt with Rupert, the jaunt to Brighton was the first of many the nine of them enjoyed together during the season. They became a little clique that no outsider – even when the outsider was someone Boudicca, Suzi, Magda, Archie or Rupert was seriously interested in – ever succeeded in becoming a part of.

In the Pytchley townhouse, Magda taught them all how to tango, to gramophone records. At a picnic on the North Downs she caused contro-versy by casually handing round a signed photograph of Adolf Hitler. It was the only time Petra had ever seen Jack close to losing his temper. At Cadogan Square Archie improved Petra's – and everyone else's – cocktail-making techniques. Whatever party or ball one of them went to, the others would be there also.

It was an arrangement that ensured she saw Jack almost constantly, without her mother's suspicions being aroused.

'Though we won't be pulling the wool over her

eyes for long,' Jack said, one arm lovingly around her shoulders, the other hand lightly on the wheel as he drove her home after an evening dancing at the Savoy. 'As soon as your father responds to the letter I've sent him I'll speak to her.'

'As long as Papa's reply is favourable,' she said, without any real fear that it wouldn't be. 'Then we can be engaged by the end of the season and married at Christmas.'

It was the first week in July and the Talbot's top was down, the night air warm and balmy, the sky star-studded.

As Jack turned right into Sloane Street, he said in amusement, 'There you go again. Making all the arrangements without first waiting to be asked. For all you know I may not want to marry you until you're an old lady of twenty-five.'

Her head was on his shoulder and she could smell the faint tang of his lemon cologne. 'By the time I'm twenty-five we'll have a house full of children,' she said dreamily. 'Four boys and a girl. Or would you prefer four girls and a boy?'

'I'd prefer to take things a step at a time and get engaged first.' He dropped a kiss onto her hair. 'Will your mother be waiting up for you, to ask where you've been?'

'No. She won't be in until the early hours. She's gone with her new friends, the Simpsons, and half a dozen other friends to a restaurant-nightclub at the Piccadilly end of Bond Street. It's a favourite haunt of Prince Edward's and Mrs Simpson is like Boudicca, she's desperate for chance meetings with him.'

That her mother's social life had become so racy

amused both of them. 'I sometimes think,' Petra had said when telling Jack earlier in the week about her mother dining at Quaglino's with a party of friends that included the Prince of Wales and Thelma Furness, 'that my mother tries to pull the wool over Aunt Gwen's eyes in much the same way I try to pull the wool over hers. You can bet your life that if Aunt Gwen asks who she's been dining with, she'll only mention the names of people she knows Aunt Gwen approves of, like Lady Londonderry, and conveniently omit the fact that the Prince – who Aunt Gwen does not approve of – and Thelma – who she most *definitely* doesn't approve of – were there as well.'

The car turned into Cadogan Square and a few moments later slid to a halt. Because they were so certain that her mother wasn't at home and wouldn't be twitching a curtain aside, they risked a long, lingering goodnight kiss.

'How soon will it be before we can expect a reply from my father?' she asked breathlessly as he reluctantly lifted his head from hers.

'Another week. Perhaps two. With luck, he may even send a telegram.'

It was a thought that hadn't occurred to her and for the next few days she left the house only with the greatest reluctance, terrified a telegram would arrive while she was out and that she would miss knowing its contents by a few hours.

'I think you're making a mountain out of an anthill,' Magda said. With Annabel at the wheel of the little Morris Minor that had been a birthday present, they were speeding towards Hyde Park on a motorized treasure hunt.

'Molehill,' Petra corrected automatically. Though Magda's English was nearly flawless, there were still times when she didn't get things exactly right. 'And I'm not making a mountain out of a molehill. You don't know my mother like I know her. She's not always rational and if she gets an irrational idea in her head – such as Jack not being ideal son-in-law material – then it can be the devil's own job getting her to think differently.'

'I think your mother is absolutely wonderful.' Boudicca was squeezed between Magda and Suzi on the back seat. 'I wish my mother was as young and as glamorous and as unconventional. And I just *love* your mother's Americanisms. You'd think after living in England for so long she would have lost all trace of American speech.'

'She hasn't lost all trace of it, because she doesn't want to. It makes her stand out and be different, and she enjoys that. And also,' she added as they drove into the park, 'it annoys my father. And for some reason I don't understand, she always takes a great deal of pleasure out of annoying him.'

'Are you sure this statue you are taking us to is the right answer to the clue: "A vulnerable point in Hyde Park?"' Suzi asked, changing the subject as Annabel headed in the direction of the Achilles Statue. 'I don't see any sign of the others heading this way.'

'Yes, of course I'm sure.' Annabel, still an inexperienced driver, crunched the gears. 'What else can it be? And Jack and Fedya aren't driving towards it because they haven't yet worked out the answer. Now do stop distracting me, Suzi. I've already come the wrong way. I should have driven down Park Lane.'

Five minutes later they had safely parked and walked to the foot of the giant monument. It had been erected in 1822 in honour of the Duke of Wellington and his companions-in-arms and was of Achilles, nude except for a cloak thrown carelessly over one arm. In one hand he was brandishing a short, leaf-shaped sword. In the other he was holding a shield aloft. Taped to the granite pediment was the next clue in the treasure hunt. As Petra, Annabel and Boo pored over it, trying to decipher where they should go next, Magda and Suzi, who knew too little about London's landmarks to be helpful, surveyed the statue.

'He's wonderfully muscular,' Magda murmured admiringly. 'Almost Teutonic.'

Suzi was less impressed. 'He may be muscular,' she said critically, 'but for such a heroic figure his fig leaf is tragically *petit*.'

The two of them collapsed into giggles and were still laughing when Petra shouted triumphantly, 'I've worked out the answer. We're being sent to the Reformers Tree Memorial. It's up near the refreshment kiosk. If we sprint we can win this treasure hunt hands down.'

Later, as Petra, Suzi, Annabel and Boudicca sprawled on the grass near the kiosk eating ice creams and as Magda leaned against a convenient tree, elegant in white bell-bottomed trousers and a short-sleeved navy sweater, Annabel said to her, 'So who is the man you are seeing, Magda? I know you are seeing someone. And as you so obviously don't want us to know his identity, he must be someone very interesting.'

234

Boudicca sat up sharply, her eyes flying wide. 'It isn't my father, is it? I know he made a complete donkey of himself over you at Petra's coming-out ball, but please tell me it isn't my father!'

'It isn't your father and it isn't your brother and it isn't anyone any of you are in love with. He does happen to have a wife, though. And because of that I think it best if I keep his name to myself.'

'That is absolutely not playing the game!' Annabel sat up too, so sharply she was at risk of sending her ice cream flying. 'I thought it was understood that we had no secrets from each other?'

Magda gave a throaty laugh. 'But you don't have any secrets to keep, Annabel. I, at the moment, do.'

Hoping that Magda's secret paramour wouldn't turn out to be one of her mother's friends, Petra shielded her eyes against the sun and said, as four figures strode towards them over the grass, 'Here come the others. Your fiancé is looking very miffed, Annabel. I've never known anyone who hates losing at anything so much. Is it because he's Russian, d'you think?'

As the summer progressed, the main subject of gossip was the Prince of Wales's love life. Because her mother was now considered to be part of the raffish Prince of Wales's set, it was gossip Petra grew increasingly uncomfortable with. It was a discomfort her friends – even the sensitive Boo – remained blissfully unaware of. As far as they were concerned, having a mother who knew at first hand who was currently uppermost in the Prince's affections was unutterably thrilling.

'I think it's *so* naughty of him to still see Mrs Dudley Ward when everyone knows of his liaison with Thelma Furness,' Boo said, speaking of the Prince as if he were a rather mischievous little boy.

'And *extremely* naughty of him to have abandoned Thelma on Derby Day in order to escort Amelia Earhart. Though I rather suspect that the first woman to cross the Atlantic on a solo flight would have the advantage as an interesting companion,' Magda said, tongue-in-cheek.

'And no hope of Amelia becoming Princess of Wales,' Annabel interjected. 'Like all his other lady loves she's married already.'

It was the kind of subject matter that could keep Petra's friends entertained for hours.

Another topic that she knew they discussed on the rare occasions she and Jack were not with them was the scandal of his parents' open separation and pending divorce.

'What makes it even worse is Sylvia's age,' her mother said exasperatedly after seeing Margot, who had gossiped about the Bazeljettes ad nauseam. 'By the time a woman is in her fifties she should be past wanting to flee a long-standing marriage in order to marry elsewhere. The damage she is doing to both her reputation and Jerome's is incalculable.'

Though Petra had always known that Sylvia was older than her mother, she'd never before realized by just how much. 'What of the Earl of Grasmere's reputation?' she asked, genuinely interested.

'Theo?' Her mother gave an unladylike snort. 'Theo's never given a damn about reputation. He's a screwball – which is just as well, because

236

I've come to the conclusion that Sylvia has bats in the belfry as well. To be quite honest, if I'd realized she was capable of behaving so unconventionally – and if circumstances had been different – there's a chance we might have been friends.'

Petra's eyes nearly popped out of her head. 'What do you mean "might have been friends"? I thought you were friends! You certainly never asked me to address anyone else I was unrelated to as "Aunt"!'

Her mother backtracked instantly. 'Is that what I said? Then it just goes to show what a state Margot's visit has left me in. Until today I hadn't seen her in a long spell and she's becoming very difficult to rub along with. Why do people get so querulous when they get older? If I do that, you have my permission to shoot me!'

Three days later, walking down Bond Street, Petra ran into Jerome.

His face creased with delight at the sight of her. 'Where are you going?' he asked affably.

'The Royal Academy. I know it's a bit late in the summer to be going to the Summer Exhibition, but this coming-out lark has meant it's the first opportunity I've had.'

'But you're not going by yourself, surely?'

She shook her head. 'No. I'm meeting Magda, Suzi, Annabel and Boo in the Friends' Room. Harrison dropped me off, but because I was early I thought I'd nip into Fenwicks.'

Harrison was her mother's chauffeur.

As he fell into step beside her, Jerome said with unusual gravity, 'I'm glad we've met up by accident like this, Petra. I've wanted to have a private word with you for some time.'

She came to a dead halt, saying in alarm, 'Because of my friendship with Jack?'

'Your friendship with Jack?' He looked startled. 'No, of course not.'

He was wearing a superbly tailored pinstriped suit, pale kid gloves and a hat. She wondered whether he was on his way to the Canton. Even dressed so traditionally, he still managed to exude an air of swashbuckling rakishness. Perhaps it was his olive-toned complexion. Or the angle he wore his hat. Or the thin white scar that knifed down through his left eyebrow. Whatever it was, it was quite obvious to her where Jack got his to-die-for-handsomeness.

'I wanted to talk to you about my separation from Sylvia,' he said as they began walking again. 'There is a lot of ugly gossip flying around and it concerns me that you might...' This time he was the one to come to a halt. 'It concerns me that you might...'

That a man she had known since birth – a man she was so deeply fond of and who was so effort-lessly sophisticated – should be struggling so hard to say something to her, filled her with a fear that was almost all-encompassing.

'It concerns me that after listening to some of the things that are being said, you might be disappointed in me,' he said at last.

The fear ebbed. She opened her mouth to speak and couldn't. She tried again. 'Be disappointed in you? *Disappointed in you?* I could never be disappointed in you, Uncle Jerome. Not ever.'

It was the first time in two years that she had called him 'Uncle'.

The relief in his dark eyes – eyes that were so like Jack's – was so vast it brought a lump to her throat.

Impulsively she tucked her hand in the crook of his arm.

Her reward was to see his familiar, infectious smile.

'I'll walk you to the Academy,' he said, patting her hand with such affection that she knew, when Jack told him he wanted to marry her, they would receive his blessing in spades.

Almost before she had recovered from this emotional meeting, she knew that what she had said to Jerome was untrue and that she could be disappointed in him. And not only ordinarily disappointed, but crushingly, overpoweringly and cataclysmically disappointed.

The blinding revelation came the following day when she accompanied Aunt Gwen, who never liked going anywhere by herself, to a jeweller's in Hatton Garden in order to collect a tiara Gwen had left there for cleaning.

It was an old-fashioned jeweller's with little booths closed off by curtains, where jewellery could be shown to customers in complete privacy. As they waited for a member of staff to bring Gwen's tiara from the vault there came the sound of voices from a nearby booth. Voices Petra recognized.

Bewildered – and hoping that her hearing was playing tricks on her – she left Gwen to wait for the tiara and stepped back into the main body of the shop, from where she could see the adjoining booths. There was only one other that was occupied and the curtain had not been pulled fully across. Magda, dressed in lavender-blue silk, a peplum emphasizing the luscious curve of her hips, was holding her wrist high, entranced by the beauty of the diamond bracelet adorning it.

'Do you like it, sweetheart?' she heard Jerome say.

'It's *wunderbar, Liebling*. Absolutely *wunderbar!*'

Jerome moved, taking hold of her hand to kiss the back of it, and as he did, his shoulder edged the curtain even further to one side so that he too was clearly in view.

If either of them had turned their head they would have seen her watching them. They didn't. They were too wrapped up in each other.

Churning with emotions she couldn't even begin to analyse she stepped back into her own booth, pulling the curtain behind her. Grateful for the length of time Gwen always took over any transaction, she made sure they didn't leave the shop until Magda and Jerome were halfway down the street.

TWELVE

The dilemma Petra was left with was whether or not to tell Magda what she had seen. In the end she decided not to. If Magda put into words that she was sleeping with Jerome – and knowing

240

Magda, Petra had no doubt at all that she *was* sleeping with him – it would be just too stomach-turning. She couldn't have felt worse if it had been her father and Magda who were having the affair.

During the next few days, one question constantly gnawed at her. Was Jerome's behaviour with Magda a one-off, or was he in the habit of indulging in such liaisons? If he was, it certainly put a different light on his willingness to act the part of the guilty party in his divorce from Sylvia – and made his doing so far less of an admirable, selfless act.

The more she pondered it, the more she knew it was a question that she had to have answered. And the only person she could possibly ask – and who was such a long-time friend of Jerome's that she could be trusted to know the answer – was her mother.

Choosing her moment with her mother wasn't easy, for the season was now so far into its stride that her mother no longer attended – in the role of a chaperone – all the balls and parties that she, Petra, was invited to. It was something she was deeply grateful for, but taken together with her mother's own hectic social life, it did mean that opportunities for the kind of conversation she now wanted to have with her were few and far between.

She caught Delia at an unconscionably early hour one Friday morning. She was just slipping into the house after having been a guest at one of the last balls of the season and her mother, still in a floaty nightdress and negligee, was arranging a bowl of pink and white roses in the drawing room.

'What's the matter, Mama?' she asked, slipping

her swansdown evening wrap from her shoulders. 'Couldn't you sleep?'

'No.' Her mother looked preoccupied, as if arranging the roses was taking all her concentration. 'I seem to have gotten out of the habit.'

Petra pondered how best to launch into what it was she wanted to ask. As there didn't seem to be an easy way and as it was in her nature to be direct, she simply took a deep breath and said bluntly, 'I'd like to ask a rather odd question about Jerome.'

Her mother ceased what she was doing and turned to face her. There were dark shadows beneath her eyes and Petra realized Delia hadn't exaggerated about her inability to sleep. 'If it's about him and Sylvia, honey, I don't think it would be at all appropriate—'

'It isn't,' she said quickly before her mother could finish her sentence, 'or at least not directly.'

'Well, then...?' Her mother's forehead puckered into a frown.

'I just wondered if he had a bad reputation where women were concerned. It's just something I overheard.'

Her mother stared at her for a long time, as if not really seeing her, and then said, 'He used to have. Years and years ago, before you were born. Perhaps now Sylvia has left him so publicly he's just reverting to type.'

'Oh, I see.' It wasn't the answer she'd been hoping for, but she did her best to look as if it was of no importance.

Her mother showed no desire to continue with the conversation and so Petra forced a bright

242

smile and said, 'I must go to bed and get some sleep. I've a garden party to go to this afternoon.'

As she opened the door to leave, her mother said, 'The something you overheard. Did it include the name of one of your friends?'

Petra half turned, one hand on the glass door knob. 'Yes,' she said. 'It did.'

Her mother's face was blank of all emotion. 'And was the friend Magda?'

Petra nodded, and then, not wanting her mother to question her any further, closed the door behind her.

Petra deliberated about whether to tell Jack of his father's liaison with Magda. It was as difficult as she had found deciding whether to tell Magda that she knew. In the end she resolved to keep the knowledge to herself. Magda would soon be returning to Berlin and the affair would no doubt then fizzle out; plus, she felt Jack had enough on his plate where his parents' sexual activities were concerned. Surviving the revelation that his mother was hell-bent on divorce and marriage to a man twenty years her junior was difficult enough without also having to tackle the knowledge that his father was having an affair with a girl Jack regarded as one of his close chums.

Any doubts she may have had regarding her decision vanished completely when Jack met her the next day at the refreshment kiosk in Hyde Park. He was jubilant at having received a letter from her father – a letter in which her father said he was delighted to hear they wanted to marry.

'He's given us his blessing and, rather than

doing so himself by letter, is leaving it to me to break the news to your mother.'

'Oh! *Fantastic!*' She threw her arms around his neck, kissing him full on the mouth.

An elderly gentleman walking past them, a bulldog at his heels, cleared his throat censoriously. Neither of them paid him an iota of attention.

'When will you do it?' she asked. 'Oh, please say you're going to do it straight away, Jack! I can't wait another minute before being able to tell the whole world that we're in love and going to get married!'

'What are your mother's plans today? Do you know?'

With their arms around each other's waist they began walking across the park in the direction of Knightsbridge.

'She's lunching with Wallis or Baba. I can't remember.'

'Baba Metcalfe?'

Petra nodded.

Jack looked bemused. 'I wonder what your father is going to say when he next visits London and finds your mother so firmly entrenched with the Prince of Wales's set? They're all at least twenty years his junior, aren't they?'

'Thirty years in the case of Baba. And they all nightclub like mad. I'm sure other debs don't run the risk of running into their mother when they go to the Embassy or the Kit-Kat Club. Haven't you noticed how difficult it makes things?'

As they left the park and crossed the busy main road, she said, 'I think it would be best if I made myself scarce for the next hour or so. I don't think the hopeful bride-to-be should be within earshot when the kind of conversation you're about to have with my mother is taking place. And *please* remember to tell her we don't want a long engagement. A wedding at St Margaret's, Christmas week, would suit perfectly.'

'Followed by a honeymoon in Cairo?'

She hugged his arm tightly. 'Oh, darling Jack! A honeymoon in Cairo would be *bliss*.'

'I thought it would be proper to ask Ivor's permission first.' Jack smiled broadly at the woman who had been almost a surrogate mother to him ever since he was three, and drew Ivor's letter from his inner Jacket pocket.

'Permission?' Delia was in the drawing room, waiting for Harrison to bring the car around to the front of the house. Aware that Jack's arrival would now delay her in her departure for her luncheon appointment – and being far too fond of him to care – she fumbled in her lizardskin clutch bag for her cigarette case. 'Permission for what, Jack?'

'Permission to ask for Petra's hand in marriage.'

The clutch bag slid from Delia's knee to the floor. An engagement book fell out of it. A gold powder compact rolled across the carpet towards his feet.

He made no move to retrieve it. Her reaction had left him too rigid with shock.

'Marriage?' The blood had drained from Delia's face. 'You've written to Ivor asking for

Petra's hand in marriage?'

'Under the circumstances ... his being in Egypt ... I thought that was the proper thing for me to do.' His smile had gone. All he felt was fast-escalating concern. 'He was very pleased, Delia.' He proffered Ivor's letter. She didn't take it.

Realizing he should have taken more notice of Petra's warning that her mother was likely to be highly irrational about their relationship, he said, 'He's given us his blessing and asked that I break the news to you...'

He broke off lamely, appalled by the obvious depth of her distress.

She was still holding the unopened cigarette case, her knuckles white.

'You can't marry Petra.' Her voice was hoarse. 'You can't, Jack. Trust me. It's impossible.'

'But why?' He'd never been more baffled in his life. Delia looked as if she had been dealt a death-blow.

'Because ... because ... because you *can't.*'

Against her Titian-red hair her skin was almost translucent.

He took a deep breath. 'That's obviously not the case, Delia,' he said reasonably. 'Once Petra is twenty-one she can marry with or without parental consent. As Ivor has already given us his blessing we can marry at any time. We wouldn't, however, wish to while you are so opposed. I just don't understand *why* you are so vehemently opposed. Have you heard some vile gossip about me? Because if you have, let me assure you it's untrue. I've never done anything despicable or dishonourable in my life.'

Delia gave a barely suppressed sob. 'Oh, Jack! I'm *sure* you haven't – and I've heard no gossip about you. None at all.'

'Then why...?'

She fumbled to take a Sobranie out of her cigarette case. He reached over and helped her.

'Thank you,' she said, her hand trembling violently as he offered her a light.

She inhaled deeply and cupped her elbow with her free hand, her arm pressed hard against her body, as if holding herself together against some kind of inner disintegration. 'My objections have nothing to do with you personally, Jack,' she said unsteadily. 'No woman could hope for a finer young man as a son-in-law. It's just that Petra has known you all her life – when she was a baby you often came with us when I took over from Nanny and walked her in the park in her perambulator. All through the years Petra was growing up in Cairo, you visited regularly. I think that somehow Petra has grown up *expecting* to marry you – and that isn't the best basis for a marriage, Jack. Especially when the girl in question is only eighteen years old.'

'We're in love, Delia,' he said flatly. 'I love her. She loves me. What better basis for marriage is there than that?'

She caught her breath. 'You're not lovers already, are you?'

'No.' His reply was quite unequivocal, though he was deeply shocked by the frankness of her question.

She let out her breath unevenly and then said, 'I want you to break off your relationship with Petra,

247

Jack. I want you to break it off until she is twenty-one. If, when she is twenty-one and has had the opportunity to meet lots of other eligible young men, she is still of the same persuasion as she is now ... well, if she is we shall have another conversation about it. Until then I think it best that you don't meet. Not even as friends. Is that understood?'

He nodded, knowing that it was useless to argue with her further. He wasn't agreeing, just signifying he understood quite clearly what her terms were.

There was a light knock on the drawing-room door and Bellingham entered.

'Harrison is at the front, my lady,' he said, mindful of the time she was expected at the Ritz.

'Thank you, Bellingham.' Still distrait she looked around her for her clutch bag.

Jack bent down and retrieved it, along with the contents that had spilled from it.

As she took them from him, putting her engagement diary and powder compact back into the bag, she said, 'Being in the Foreign Office will make it easy for you to arrange for another posting abroad. It's what I think you should do, Jack. And until another posting is arranged, perhaps it would be best if you took some leave and spent it abroad. France, maybe? Or maybe even America.'

Still looking incredibly strained – and not kissing him goodbye as she usually did – she walked from the room, leaving him feeling more bewildered, more shocked, and more crushingly disappointed than he had ever been before in his life.

Petra was waiting for him in the gardens in the centre of Cadogan Square. The instant she saw him she knew the kind of news he was bringing.

'She can't have objected!' she cried, running towards him. 'She can't have! Not when Papa has given us his blessing!'

'She has,' he said heavily, holding her close. 'And for the craziest reason.'

'That you're not yet earning enough money? That your position at the Foreign Office isn't yet one with enough status? That–'

'That I've been a part of your life for too long for you to be able to judge whether or not you are really in love with me. She wants you to meet more young men – and she wants me to go away for three years – after which time, if you still feel the same way about me, she says the subject can be discussed again.'

'Land sakes! You're not going to take any notice of such silliness, are you?'

'No,' he said, holding her even closer and kissing the top of her head. 'She's just stalling for time in the hope that one of us, or both of us, fall in love elsewhere. We know that isn't going to happen, so there isn't any sense in our spending three years apart.'

'What *are* we going to do?'

She stepped away from him a little so that her hands were pressed against his chest, and looked up into his face.

'I'm going to go to Cairo and speak to your father. I can't put your mother's objections in writing. He won't understand. The only difficulty

249

is that I don't have any leave due until the end of August.'

'That's only three weeks away. We can manage to still see each other, without my mother knowing about it, for the next three weeks. And then Papa will make her see sense. When Papa really puts his foot down everyone takes notice. Even King Fuad.'

With a decision made she felt a tad better; but only a tad. Her mother's response was so mystifying she didn't know how to even begin to understand. What if her mother failed to see reason? What if her father decided that a three-year separation was actually quite a good idea and rescinded his permission that they could marry? How on earth would they manage to live apart for three years? What if her mother was right, and Jack fell in love elsewhere during that time? She was willing to stake her life on the fact that she wouldn't, but how could she be so sure about Jack? He was wildly attractive and girls were always throwing themselves at him. It might be a temptation he couldn't resist.

Her fears only heightened the almost unbearable sexual excitement she felt every time she was with him. She wanted to bind him to her irrevocably.

As the weekend drew near – a weekend when she had been invited to Heathlands, Boudicca's country home in Hampshire, Jack said, 'Do you think you could get away with chucking Heathlands?'

'Easily. Boo wouldn't mind. What is it you have in mind?'

'A weekend by ourselves in Brighton. Depending on how things go when I see your father, it could be the last chance we have of being alone together for a long time.'

She hugged his arm, knowing exactly what it was he had in mind and not having even the slightest reservation.

'Where will we stay?' she asked, her face radiant. 'A hotel?'

'No. Archie has a small house on the seafront in the Lanes that his grandfather bequeathed to him. He tells me it's full of olde worlde charm and that there's a smashing little French restaurant only a few steps away.'

His voice changed timbre, becoming full of concern. 'If you have the slightest doubt about this, Petra, tell me. Because, if necessary, I'll do the Old Testament Jacob and Rachel thing and wait seven years for you.'

She giggled throatily. 'God, really? I'm very impressed, but a wedding at Christmas and a January honeymoon in Cairo is what I'm aiming for – and I don't want our plans put on the back burner for three years, let alone seven.'

'Neither do I,' he said grimly, a pulse beginning to pound at the corner of his strong jaw. 'And I'm going to do everything in my power to see that they aren't.'

Afterwards, when she looked back at that very special weekend, she was amazed at how little shyness she had felt; how wonderfully right everything had been. He had brought a bottle of vintage champagne and red roses, so many roses that every room in the house was scented with their fragrance.

She had bought a new nightdress in Harrods. It wasn't black or scarlet or blatantly erotic. It was a bridal nightdress in oyster-white silk satin; the kind of nightdress she would have packed for her honeymoon.

And a honeymoon was how both of them regarded their precious stolen hours in Archie's little house.

The evening they arrived, they dined in the candlelit French restaurant. Later, in Archie's oak-beamed sitting room, Jack put on a recording of Puccini's *Madame Butterfly*. The beautiful music drifted after them as he carried her up the stairs.

For the rest of her life, whenever she heard the heart-stopping strains of '*Un bel di vedremo*', she was transported back to the night they became lovers, the window open to the sultry night air and the sound of the sea.

No questions were asked of her when she returned to Cadogan Square on the Sunday night. Her mother merely said, 'How were the Pytchley clan? Blooming?' in a way that indicated she neither expected nor needed any real answer.

The following weekend – which was Magda and Suzi's last in England – was Annabel and Fedya's wedding day. It was a wonderfully grand and joyous occasion. Annabel's train was so long it stretched almost from the altar to the door of the fifteenth-century church, and the brides-maids' dresses were so full-skirted that Petra and

Boudicca, and Magda and Suzi, could barely squeeze down the aisle.

Delia was there, of course, and even though Jack was one of the groomsmen, they scrupulously avoided eye contact with each other.

'Flirt with me,' Archie said helpfully to Petra. 'I've always wanted to have a redhead look adoringly at me. Jack tells me he's setting off for Cairo next Saturday, to enlist your father's help in smoothing some rather troubled water.'

'Yes.' Petra wasn't sure just how much Jack had told Archie, and she didn't want any of her mother's many friends overhearing their conversation.

'Tell me about the racing car you've bought, Archie,' she said, changing the subject. 'Is it true you're going to start racing professionally?'

Two days later she was back in town, walking down Lower Sloane Street on her way to the hairdresser's. Walking towards her, on the same side of the street, was Theo Girlington.

She sucked in her breath and ducked her head, hoping that he wouldn't recognize her and that, even if he did, he wouldn't speak to her.

There was no real reason why he should.

She knew him to speak to only because he was part of the same, elite social circle as her parents. Since Sylvia's announcement that she was divorcing Jerome in order to marry Theo, she doubted if her mother had ever spoken two words to him, though as he was now a duke – and a duke with great material possessions – she was fairly certain her mother wouldn't have cut him completely.

'What ho! It's Petronella Conisborough, isn't it?'

As he halted in front of her and she was forced to come to a halt also, Petra was greatly tempted to deny it.

'I saw your father earlier today,' he said, grinning at her like the Cheshire cat in *Alice in Wonderland*. 'Not that I'm someone he likes to run into too often these days.'

She stared at him, remembering her mother's verdict that he was a screwball.

'You can't have,' she said, giving him a dismissive smile. 'My father is in Cairo.'

'Not Conisborough.' His grin widened even further. 'Your real father. Jerome Bazeljette.' There was absolutely no malice or mischief in his voice or his smile. He simply said it as a statement of fact – a fact he quite obviously thought she was well aware of. He gave a jolly laugh. 'In a rum kind of way we're almost family, what with me on track to becoming your half-brother's stepfather. Not that I imagine Jack will ever call me "stepfather". Can't blame him. I'm only ten years his senior, after all. Give my regards to your mother, Petronella. Goodbye and toodle-pip.'

He sauntered off down the street, happily oblivious of the effect his words had had on her.

Dazedly she stared after him. Jerome, her father? She wanted to laugh it off as being too ridiculous for words, but she couldn't.

She remembered her Aunt Gwen telling her how Jerome had been at the Cadogan Square house the day she was born; how he had held her almost immediately after her birth. She remembered how he had always been there for her; how, fond though he was of Davina, it had always been her he had singled out first; how it had always been her he had paid most attention to. She remembered the interest he had taken in her education, how the Institut Mont-Fleuri had been so conveniently near to his villa at Nyon, and the long periods of time he had spent at Nyon during her years at the Institut. She remembered their long walks together along the shore of Lake Geneva and how interested he had always been in her dreams and aspirations.

She remembered how, when she was sixteen and he had been visiting Cairo, he had suggested that, if her mother had no objections, she put an end to calling him 'Uncle'. She remembered the long, tension-filled pause and then her mother saying, 'Of course I don't. So silly to use it when you are most definitely not her uncle,' and the way, when Jerome had responded drily, 'No, indeed,' that her mother had blushed furiously.

She remembered how deeply concerned he had been that she might have heard gossip that would have caused her to be disappointed in him, and how his relief, when she said she could never be disappointed in him, had been so intense it had brought a lump to her throat.

She remembered how aghast her mother had been when she had suggested that, as her father couldn't be there, Jerome should stand in for him at her coming-out ball, and how, when it had come to the traditional opening father and daughter waltz, he had waltzed her proudly around the ballroom.

Other memories, too, came thick and fast, falling into place like the pieces of a jigsaw puzzle.

Jerome's constant presence in her mother's life; the way that though she'd been brought up to believe Jerome was her father's friend, her father always had important business elsewhere whenever Jerome visited Cairo. The way that it was then her mother who entertained him and dined with him. The way her mother had made so many lone visits when she, Petra, had been at school in Montreux, always staying with Jerome, at Nyon, when she had done so. She thought of how her mother's *joie de vivre* had vanished overnight when Jerome had begun paying attention to Magda, and she thought of her mother's horror when Jack told her that they were in love and wanted to marry.

Last, but by no means least, she thought of the two nights she and Jack had spent together in Archie's cottage.

The pit of hell that then yawned open at her feet was bottomless. She couldn't breathe. Couldn't move. One thought only pulsed through her brain and that was that she had to know the truth. And only two people could tell her. Her mother and Jerome.

She stared around her, looking for a telephone box. There wasn't one in sight and she began walking numbly towards the one in Sloane Square.

Once there she fumbled clumsily in her bag for money. Twice she dropped her sixpenny piece. By the time she dropped it into the slot she was so terrified of what she was possibly about to hear that her heart felt as if it were in her throat.

'Chelsea 3546,' Jerome's dearly familiar voice said. 'Bazeljette speaking.'

She pressed Button A. The coin fell into the box.

'It's Petra,' she said and then, without any preamble, 'I have to ask you... I have to know... Are you and my mother lovers?'

There was a stunned silence at the other end of the line and then Jerome said in a voice almost as unsteady as hers, 'Petra, my dear. This isn't a conversation we should be having over the telephone. You are obviously very distressed. Where are you? I'll come and meet–'

'I don't want to meet you, I just want to know the truth.' Tears coursed down her face. 'Are you and my mother lovers? Have you been lovers for years?'

There was a long silence and she knew he was trying to think of the right words to use. 'Petra, sweetheart,' he said at last. 'The answer is yes. You are old enough now to understand and I suppose someone who should have known better has told you. I love your mother dearly. I've loved her from the very first moment I met her and...'

With a cry of anguish she dropped the receiver and pushed blindly against the telephone-box door.

Jerome's voice calling her name followed her as the receiver dangled in mid-air. She took no notice of it. She hadn't asked her next question, 'Are you my father?' because she had to hear the answer from her mother.

Tears still raining down her face, she walked the short distance to Cadogan Square.

Her mother was in the drawing room, seated at her pretty Chippendale writing desk. She was wearing a pale mauve voile dress and her favourite item of jewellery, a three-string pearl necklace.

As Petra entered the room she turned to greet her with a wide welcoming smile. The instant she saw Petra's face the smile vanished.

'What on earth has happened, honey?' she said, in alarm, jumping to her feet.

'I ran into Theo Girlington in Lower Sloane Street.' Petra put her hands up, to forestall her mother from rushing towards her and hugging her. 'He told me he'd just seen my father.'

Delia came to an abrupt halt, her face whitening, and then she said, 'Unless Theo was hotfoot from Cairo he has bats in the belfry.'

'He wasn't referring to Ivor, Mama.' Petra's voice sounded to her as if it were coming from a million miles away. 'He was referring to Jerome.'

Time stood still.

Her mother tried to speak and couldn't.

'I spoke to Jerome, Mama. He told me that you and he are ... that for years you and he have been...' She tried to say the word 'lovers' but there was no way in the world she could utter it. 'Is he my father?' she managed at last, her voice cracking and breaking. 'Is what Theo Girlington said, true?'

Her mother's lips were now as white as her face. She looked as if she were in the seventh circle of hell, impaled on the past, paralysed by the present and unable to conceive of the future. 'I don't know,' she said at last, despairingly. 'It's a possibility, Petra. There was one instance, in the

258

early spring of 1914, when I went to Jerome for comfort, but our affair didn't start then. It didn't start until much later, after Davina was born. I'm so sorry, Petra. I never dreamed that there would be such complications.' She made a helpless, hopeless motion with her hands. 'That Jerome may be your father is something Jerome and I have never talked about ... never openly acknowledged ... and he may not be, Petra. Under the circumstances, though, I couldn't allow you and Jack to become engaged. Not when there was even the faintest possibility that Jack was your half–'

'Don't say it!' Petra clapped her hands over her ears. *'Don't say it!'*

She struggled to breathe, numb with pain. Her whole life was over. All her hopes and dreams were at an end. She had lost not only Jack, but her mother too, for things could never be the same between them, just as things would never be the same between her and Jack.

'I'm going back to Cairo,' she said, fighting to keep hysteria out of her voice. 'And I don't want Jack to ever know about this. Do you understand?'

'I understand, Petra dear, but you have to listen to me. You have to let me explain the circumstances...'

'No.' Petra's voice was hoarse. 'I don't have to listen to another word about you and Jerome. Not now. Not ever.' And turning her back on her mother she ran from the room.

She didn't stop running until she was once again in Sloane Street, and when she did, she had three things clear in her mind. One was that she couldn't possibly see Jack again, for it would be an agony she would never survive. The second was that because Jack would follow her to Cairo, she would stay not at Nile House, but with Kate. And the third was that she had two letters to write. A letter to Jack, irrevocably breaking off their relationship, and a letter to her father – and she was quite determined to continue thinking of Ivor as her father – telling him she had broken up with Jack for private reasons, and informing him that she was returning to Cairo but would be staying with Kate and on no account wanted Jack to be told where she was.

On the far side of the street was a travel agent. Hardly able to believe that the world was still turning exactly as it had been doing when she had seen Theo Girlington striding towards her half an hour earlier, she crossed towards it, knowing that the world, for her, would never be the same again.

Minutes later, in a voice scarcely recognizable as her own, she booked a reservation on a Channel crossing and a train to Paris; a reservation on a train from Paris to Marseille; and passage on a ship sailing from Marseille to Alexandria. Then, unable to face returning home, she walked into Hyde Park and on a bench beside the Serpentine sobbed and sobbed until she could sob no longer.

PART THREE

Davina

1934–1939

THIRTEEN

Davina boarded a tram packed to capacity and squeezed onto a wooden slatted seat next to a heavily veiled Muslim woman. The tram was travelling from the Muqattam Hills down into the city centre, and because she was the only non-Egyptian on board – and because of her sex and her youth – she immediately became the object of much suspicious and disapproving scrutiny.

She ignored it. She had just spent the morning – as she spent every morning – working as a volunteer at an Anglican orphanage tucked away in the tumble of streets at the foot of the Citadel. It was early afternoon and Cairo's March sun was uncomfortably hot. She wiped a bead of sweat from her forehead and tried to ignore the hen trapped in a wooden cage on the Muslim woman's knee. Later on, when it became a little cooler, she intended going to the Gezira Club with Fawzia to watch Darius play in the finals of the club's annual tennis tournament. Petra was also going, though not with them; she would be with a new group of friends she had made.

The hen squawked and its owner slammed a silencing hand down on the top of its cage. Davina averted her eyes and continued to think about her sister.

Ever since Petra had returned to Cairo the previous summer, the closeness that had always existed between them had become marred by a kind of strain that Davina couldn't understand. Petra rarely chatted to her in the old carefree manner and when she did chat, it was usually about something quite inconsequential and never about anything that mattered, such as why, when she had returned to Cairo so unexpectedly, she had stayed with Kate Gunn in order to avoid Jack, who had arrived in the city a couple of days after her.

All she had ever been able to get out of her on the subject was, 'We were about to become engaged and then I decided it would be a mistake. That's all there is to it, Davvy. Now if you don't mind, I'd rather not talk about it.'

And she hadn't. Ever.

Jack had been totally bewildered and deeply distressed by her action, as had been crystal clear when he had arrived in Cairo looking for her.

'I'm sorry, old chap,' she'd overheard her father say to him. 'She is in the city, but she doesn't want to see you. As I have to respect her wishes, I can't tell you her whereabouts.'

'But why is she behaving like this?' Jack had demanded. 'She must have given a reason! One minute we were perfectly all right – the next she'd bolted, leaving only a letter behind. And a letter that explained nothing except that she'd had second thoughts about marrying me and was ending our relationship.'

'Where relationships are concerned,' her father had said, with an edge to his voice Davina had never heard in it before, 'women often do the most inexplicable things.'

The tram was now trundling in the direction of

Abdin Palace. She wondered whether her father, who had had a meeting there with King Fuad earlier in the day, was still at the palace, spending some time with Prince Farouk. It was something he was always being encouraged to do by the High Commissioner and the King.

'You are the very best kind of Englishman,' the King had once said to Ivor in her hearing. 'And I want my son to grow up emulating all that is best in the English character.'

If any good had come out of the change that had taken place in Petra in the months since she'd been back in Cairo, it was that she had become much more aware of what a remarkable man their father was.

'I don't believe he's ever wanted to be in Egypt any more than Delia has,' she had once said. 'He's here simply because he feels it his duty to help Egypt find her way into the twentieth century.'

That Petra now nearly always referred to their mother by her Christian name was one of her new-found oddities. Another had been her decision to learn shorthand and typing.

'Because I'm not going back to London – and if I'm going to remain in Cairo I have to fill up my time with something other than parties,' she had said when Davina had queried why she was doing so. 'Kate taught herself shorthand and typing and she's going to help me do the same thing. Until I become proficient enough to be employed as someone's secretary the High Commissioner is letting me act as a general dogsbody at the Residency.'

And that was what she was still doing. Her

social life was now spent exclusively with the other girls who worked at the Residency and Davina rarely saw her.

As the tram rattled towards the Ezbekiya Gardens stop Davina rose to her feet and forged a way towards the door. Not only did she now see very little of her sister, she saw even less of her mother, for though their mother had returned to Cairo at the end of last year's London season, she had stayed on in Cairo for only a couple of months. At the end of October she had gone back to London, where the Bazeljettes were in the middle of their divorce, had returned briefly to spend Christmas in Cairo and had then returned again to London.

'She enjoys a different way of life in London,' Petra said when Davina had asked if she could shed some light on why their mother was now spending more time in London than she was in Cairo. 'Instead of mixing mainly with friends who are Papa's friends and who are all approximately Papa's age – friends such as Sir John Simon, the Digbys and Margot Asquith – she's become friends with the Prince of Wales's set. She and the Prince have always been chummy. There are only a few months' difference between them in age and though some of his friends are a good bit younger than she is – Baba Metcalfe, for instance, is only twenty-nine and Delia is forty-one this year – it doesn't seem to make any difference. She's unconventional enough to fit in very well.'

There had been such an odd inflection in her voice as she had uttered the last sentence that Davina was totally bewildered. It was almost as if

266

Petra didn't like their mother much any more. As this was clearly an impossibility she had shrugged the thought away, but it kept recurring at times when their mother's name came into the conversation and Petra again spoke of her with an odd expression in her voice.

Putting on the wide-brimmed sun hat she'd taken off when on the tram, she began walking towards Shepheard's Hotel. Besides being the most popular meeting place in British Cairo, it also boasted the finest English bookshop in the city and there had been a telephone call to Nile House that morning saying a book she had ordered had now arrived and was ready for collection.

Once it was tucked under her arm, she didn't linger. The distance between Shepheard's and Garden City wasn't far, but in a hot, noisy, dusty city such as Cairo, it was quite far enough when on foot – and unlike anyone else she knew, Davina far preferred to walk everywhere if she could.

It was her way of keeping in touch with what she always thought of as the *real* Cairo. And to Davina, the real Cairo was Egyptian, not British. As she made her way down Ibrahim Pasha street, towards its junction with Fouad El Auwal Street, she pondered the difficulty of living simultaneously in a world of crushing, grinding poverty – which was the world she saw in the streets and experienced at first hand via her voluntary work – and a world of luxury and privilege, which was the world she had been brought up in and which was epitomized by the exclusive sporting club she would be going to in a couple of hours.

The only other person she knew who had a foot firmly in two such very different ways of life, was Darius. Darius's loyalty was wholly to the most extreme wing of WAFD, the political party that wanted to negotiate the British out of Egypt. In private he expressed nothing but contempt for King Fuad. 'He's a mere puppet of your government,' he often said to her. 'And the reason your father spends so much time with the Prince is to ensure that when he inherits the throne, he, too, will dance to Britain's tune.'

She'd long been aware that her father's official role in Cairo as an advisor to the King also incorporated the role of being an unofficial tutor and mentor to Farouk. She wasn't happy about it, but she didn't think it was going to matter too much if, under her father's influence, the fourteen-year-old Prince grew up as pro-British as his father. She was quite sure that by the time he was King, WAFD would have peaceably freed Egypt from British rule.

Her thoughts were diverted by a rumpus in the street in front of her. In the midst of a sea of cars, motorbikes and sidecars, donkey carts and gharries, a bullock had come to a sudden and very determined halt. Half a dozen galabiya-dressed men were pushing on its haunches, all to no avail. As a gang of small barefoot boys whooped their way through the traffic to join in the fun she began walking faster, well aware that if she didn't get a move on she wasn't going to be ready when Zubair Pasha's chauffeur brought Fawzia to Nile House in order that they could go to the Sporting Club together.

There was a surprise waiting for her when she walked into the marble-floored hallway. 'Your mother has just arrived!' Adjo announced, a smile nearly splitting his ebony face in two. 'How long for, Missy Davina, I do not know. She's out in the garden. I think you are going to need to explain about the donkey.'

Davina had rescued the donkey a few weeks ago when, after being furiously whipped, it had collapsed in the street, unable to pull its cruelly heavy load a step further. She'd paid off its owner and, not knowing what else she could do with an animal so starved its ribs were sticking through its flesh, had hired another donkey cart and had paid the driver to take his cargo to Nile House.

Fortunately her father had been out when the cart and its pathetic load had rattled through the gates of Nile House. By the time he had returned, the donkey was installed in the long sloping rear garden beneath the shade of the jacaranda trees, water and alfalfa grass within easy reach.

Six weeks afterwards, its ribs were not nearly so visible, but Davina hadn't the slightest intention of exposing it again to life on the Cairo streets. What she could do for the countless other donkeys suffering similarly she didn't yet know, but she knew that she was going to do something.

As she burst out of the house and into the garden she saw that her mother was still in her travelling clothes – and was regarding the donkey as fixedly as the donkey was regarding her.

'Mama!' she shouted, running across the velvet-smooth lawn towards her. 'How smashing! Why didn't you let anyone know you were

269

coming?' Breathlessly, she hurtled into her mother's arms.

Laughing with pleasure her mother hugged her tightly and then, on releasing her, said, 'I assume you're responsible for this animal's presence in the middle of my garden. He can't possibly stay here, Davina. Nile House isn't a zoo.'

'No, it's a home. And a home is a sanctuary. And that is what this donkey – and donkeys like it – need.'

Her mother, who had often expressed horror at the condition of the city's donkeys and horses, looked at the donkey.

The donkey looked at her mother.

It was a battle Davina knew was already won.

'There's someone I must put you in touch with,' her mother said thoughtfully, stroking the donkey's muzzle. 'Her name is Dorothy Brooke. She came to Cairo a couple of years ago when her husband, an army general, was posted here. Finding former ex-cavalry horses living out their lives on the streets as exhausted, emaciated beasts of burden came as a pretty nasty shock to her. She's organized a committee to raise funds to buy those in the last stages of collapse so that they can die peacefully and with a little dignity. And yes, before you ask, I've already sent her a hefty donation. The thing is, Davina, if she feels so passionately about the cruel treatment of old cavalry horses, she'll be equally impassioned about the condition of the city's donkeys.'

Delia tucked her daughter's arm in her own. 'Donkeys, however, are not what I came back to Cairo to talk to you about.'

Davina felt her heart sink. 'If it's about my having a London season, I simply don't want to have one.'

'I know you don't, darling.' Her mother began walking her down the garden, towards the broad glittering river. 'I'm sorry, honey, but it's absolutely essential. You don't know anyone of your own age in London society – and you can't go through life not knowing anyone. By the end of your season as a debutante you will have made enough friends to see you through the rest of your life.'

'I have friends already. I have Fawzia and Darius and the people I work with at the orphanage...'

'Those are Cairo friends – and quite honestly not all the friends you are now making in Cairo are suitable, but we'll talk about that later. What I want to talk to you about now is having friends in London. Making contact with people so that you will always have plenty of invites to weekend house parties and balls and having a coterie of people to go to point-to-points with and to Ascot and to Cowes...'

'But I'm *never* going to want to go to weekend house parties and balls and race meetings and regattas! I'm just not like that! I don't see the sense in spending three months in London attending parties and dances that I don't want to go to. And I certainly don't want to suffer the silly rigmarole of curtseying to the King with feathers stuck in my hair. Petra may have enjoyed it, but I won't.'

'It isn't a silly rigmarole, Davina. It's ceremonial. There's a difference.'

271

'Well, if there is, I honestly don't see it.'

They came to a halt, staring out across the river, Davina mutinous, Delia rigidly resolved. From across the water there came the sound of lions roaring in the zoo on Gezira Island.

At last her mother said pleasantly, but with underlying steel in her voice, 'When I leave Cairo for London in four weeks' time, you will be leaving with me. And now, if I am to bathe and change before going to this evening's tennis tournament I have to hurry. Adjo tells me you are going with Fawzia.'

'Yes.' Davina nodded, knowing that though she had won the battle over the donkey, she had lost it where her presentation at court was concerned. When her mother made up her mind to something there was no moving her. However much she hated the thought of it, she was going to have to endure a summer in London doing all the things she most loathed. The only good thing about it was that she still had four weeks in which to get in touch with Mrs Dorothy Brooke.

'But you're so *lucky!*' Fawzia said as her father's chauffeur drove them in the Zubair open-topped limousine across the Kasr el Nil Bridge onto Gezira Island. 'I'd give anything in the world to be a debutante and be presented to King George and Queen Mary at Buckingham Palace! Think of all the parties you will be invited to! Think of all the rich, handsome, aristocratic, eligible young men you will meet!'

'I am thinking of them and I'm fairly certain that nearly all of them will be boring.'

Fawzia, wearing a knife-straight scarlet silk dress with a heavy, gold belt cinching her waist, shook her head disbelievingly, her cloud of dark hair so black that as it caught the late afternoon light it looked almost blue. 'You can't mean it, Davina. *No one* could mean it. Not if they were in their right mind.'

'Then perhaps I'm not in my right mind,' Davina said equably, knowing that Fawzia was never going to think the way she did no matter how many years they were friends. She turned to Fawzia suddenly. 'Why don't you ask your father if you can come to London with me? It would make the endless party circuit a bit more bearable for me and it's about time you saw British high society in action on home ground.'

Fawzia gasped, overcome at such a dizzying prospect. 'Oh, Davina! That would be marvellous! I'd so love to see London. And Jack is in London, isn't he? It would be so nice to see Jack again.' Her face fell as another thought struck her. 'But would my father agree to it? I'd have to be chaperoned. He never lets me go anywhere without being chaperoned. I know how you hate turning up at the club in a chauffeured car, but it's the kind of thing my father insists on. Don't take offence when I say this, but he doesn't think much of your mother's chaperoning skills – that you are allowed to wander around Cairo on your own shocks him to the core – and so he might very well not let me go.'

'Then we'd just have to assure your father that it wouldn't be my mother, but that it would be my aunt, Lady Pugh, my father's elder sister, who would be doing the chaperoning.'

Hope flooded Fawzia's delicately boned face. Her father's admiration for Lord Conisborough was boundless and would be equally boundless for all his blood relations. That being the case, he was almost certain to approve of Lady Pugh as a chaperone.

'Oh goodness! This would be so wonderful!' she said ecstatically as the limousine entered the Sporting Club's vast, immaculately kept grounds. 'Your mother is a friend of the Prince of Wales, isn't she? And so that means I'd very probably meet him. He's very attracted to dark-haired women. I've seen photographs of Mrs Freda Dudley Ward and Lady Furness and they are both very dark-haired. I'm far more beautiful than either of them and – oh, Davina! – wouldn't it be utterly heaven if he were to fall in love with me and I were to become the Princess of Wales!'

Remembering what Petra had let slip about the Prince's preference for mature, sexually experienced, married women, Davina thought this highly unlikely, but was too kind to say so. As far as she was concerned, Prince Edward could do far worse than fall for Fawzia – and she rather liked the idea of the future Queen of England being Egyptian.

As they walked to their seats in the crowded stand they drew a lot of male attention. Fawzia always turned heads wherever she went and Davina gave little thought to it, not realizing that her fair hair and slim figure – and the simplicity of the apple-green, white polka-dot cotton dress she was wearing – were drawing their own share of admiring glances.

She waved to Petra, who was seated with her friends a few rows behind them. Her mother and father had seats in the front row, in close proximity to Zubair Pasha. In a stand on the opposite side of the tennis court Davina could see the willowy figure of Kate Gunn.

There was a ripple of female excitement as Darius came out onto the court and Davina could well understand why.

He glanced up at the stand and she knew he was looking to see if she was there. She didn't wave, knowing how much he would hate it. Instead, as his eyes met hers, she gave him a discreet thumbs-up sign. Ignoring Fawzia and his parents he gave her a barely discernible nod and then turned all his attention to the game he was about to play.

Even though his opponent, the reigning champion, played like a demon, it proved to be one of the most one-sided finals in the club's history, with Darius putting in a nearly faultless display and winning 6–1, 6–3, 6–2.

Still breathing heavily, he accepted the trophy from the Deputy High Commissioner with an elation Davina knew had nothing to do with winning the match. His elation came from being Egyptian and from having beaten a British opponent so publicly and spectacularly in a club that permitted very few Egyptian members. In a sudden flash of insight she knew why, though wanting the British out of Cairo with every fibre of his being, he so regularly patronized the club. It was because being there, and thrashing British opponents on the polo fields and tennis courts, was his own private way of thumbing his nose to people like the High Commissioner and her father.

As he held the trophy aloft he was drenched in perspiration. It soaked his tennis shirt, sheened the harsh, Arabic planes of his face and ran in rivulets down his olive-toned neck. He was surrounded by people congratulating him and she didn't even attempt to join in the crush. She would be able to congratulate him later, when they were on their own together.

Leisurely she walked down from the stand, aware as no one else was, that while for his beaten opponent the tournament had been only a game, for Darius it had been much, much more.

Late that night she couldn't sleep. As she lay on her back in the darkness, the windows of her room above the terrace open, she heard her parents' voices drifting towards her. 'I think Ramsay Mac-Donald is a skunk,' her mother was saying of the Prime Minister. 'Insisting you remain here for another two years so as to maintain your relationship with Farouk until he is sixteen, is simply not fair. Surely that is a task for Sir Miles Lampson?'

'The reason Sir Miles replaced the last High Commissioner is that he has a more military cast of mind. And a military cast of mind isn't what Farouk needs. Which is where I come in.'

There was a long silence and then her mother said, her voice suddenly sounding strained, 'And just why did our government think a man with a more military cast of mind was needed here, Ivor?'

'The violent nationalist groups splintering off from WAFD are growing in such strength it's a necessity, Delia.'

'I hadn't realized things had got quite so bad.'

'It's bad in the sense that it's young educated Egyptians who are behind most of the street violence. Containing it isn't easy, and we've a lot to be thankful for in that the King is still resolutely pro-British. If he wasn't, it would be a very different matter.'

'Which is why it's necessary for you to continue being a positive influence on Prince Farouk, so that things don't go belly-up when Fuad dies?'

'Yes, Delia. I'm sorry. I know how much you hate being here.'

'Oh, it's not so bad now that I'm dividing my time between here and London. Though things in London aren't exactly a bowl of cherries.' Her mother's voice was bleak. 'Jerome is still carrying on his affair with Petra's German friend and she is in London far more often than she is in Berlin.'

Her father gave a heavy sigh and then said, 'There will be problems for Kate when I'm released from my posting here. Tongues wagging in Cairo are one thing. London is quite a different kettle of fish.' He gave a mirthless laugh. 'We haven't exactly made life easy for ourselves, have we, Delia?'

'No, Ivor.' Her mother's voice was full of an emotion Davina couldn't place. 'I think it's safe to say that we haven't.'

Not understanding the last part of the conversation Davina dozed off into a deep sleep, troubled only by thoughts of the violent nationalist groups splintering off from WAFD – and whether or not Darius had become a member of one of them.

FOURTEEN

Nothing made the journey to London pleasurable for Davina, not even travelling via Paris in order for her mother to make one of her regular visits to her favourite fashion designer, Madeleine Vionnet. All she wanted was to be back in Cairo, especially now that she had made contact with Mrs Brooke.

'Another few months and we'll have a hospital where our poor old war heroes will be able to meet a merciful end,' Mrs Brooke had said fiercely. 'At the moment the horses we are able to buy are only in temporary stabling, but we have made a start, Lady Davina. And when we have taken care of every old, exhausted ex-cavalry horse that is working ceaselessly in great heat – heat they were never bred for – then the next step will be ensuring there are ample water troughs and shade shelters in Cairo's streets.'

It was work Davina passionately wanted to be involved in and no number of beautiful evening gowns – evening gowns that even she knew made her look breathtakingly lovely – could compensate for the fact that she wasn't in Cairo helping to establish what Mrs Brooke had told her was to be called the Old War Horse Memorial Hospital.

Out of respect for her mother she suffered the ritual of 'coming out' with as good a grace as possible. Some events, such as attending the

278

opening of the Royal Academy Summer Exhibition followed by a Covent Garden grand opera in the evening, she enjoyed hugely. The vast majority of events, though – the never-ending round of parties at which she always met the same people – bored her to tears. The only ameliorating factor was the pleasure Fawzia was gaining from being her companion throughout the season, for her exotic looks made her the centre of male attention at every ball they attended, much to the displeasure of Davina's fellow debutantes.

'She hasn't been presented and so she shouldn't be invited to everything as if she has been,' was the general grumble.

Davina felt sorry for the grumblers. All of them were keen to snare a highly eligible suitor and it couldn't be easy for them knowing that Fawzia was receiving proposals of marriage nearly every week. She didn't, however, let her sympathy for them alter her insistence that anyone who invited her, also had to invite Fawzia.

'She's been presented to her own monarch, King Fuad, and that is all that matters,' she would say airily, neither knowing whether it was all right or not, nor caring.

Just when she was wondering whether she could take another week of partying, let alone last out until the end of the season, her mother said, 'You're going to Dartington House ball tonight, Davina, aren't you?'

'If you say so. I wouldn't be going to it if I had any say in the matter myself.' It wasn't in her nature to show exasperation, but sometimes she just couldn't help it. 'Why?'

'Because I'm having a rather special, small dinner party this evening. Prince Edward is going to be guest of honour and I thought, before you and Fawzia left the house, that the two of you might like to join us for cocktails?'

'Smashing. I haven't met him since I was a little girl and you took me with you to Sandringham. As for Fawzia ... she's been champing at the bit to be introduced. Who are your other guests?'

'The Metcalfes. Lord Denby. And Wallis Simpson.'

Davina didn't take the interest in her mother's social life that Petra did, but even she could see there was something a little odd about such a small dinner party – and the guest list. 'What about Mr Simpson?'

'Ernest has business affairs to attend to,' her mother said, looking deeply uncomfortable.

Davina frowned. Surely her mother wasn't setting up a discreet dinner party in order to facilitate an affair between her friend and Lord Denby? Wallis Simpson was, she knew, only a year or two younger than her mother and, according to her mother, very zippy, whereas Lord Denby was elderly and more than a little doddery. She said, still frowning, 'I'm sorry. I don't quite understand...'

'And neither do I, honey,' her mother said drily. 'All I know is that Wallis is just back from a trip to the States and David – Prince Edward – has asked me to arrange tonight's dinner party ... and has asked me to invite Wallis.'

Davina stared at her. 'You mean he wants Wallis to be introduced to him?'

'No, darling. Thanks to Wallis's friendship with Thelma Furness, the Simpsons and David are already on easy terms. They've been his guests at Fort Belvedere several timcs. I think tonight's dinner is to be more of a welcome-home party for her.'

'Oh! I see,' Davina said, not sure that she saw at all. She shrugged her shoulders. Her mother's friends and her mother's social life were, after all, nothing to do with her. She had other, more urgent things to think of, not least of which was how she was going to survive until the season ended at the beginning of August.

It was a dapper-looking Prince Edward who gave her her answer.

'Toynbee Hall,' he said helpfully when she had told him how she spent her free time when in Cairo. 'It's in the East End – in Commercial Street, Whitechapel – and it's the most radical centre for social reform that there is.' The Prince had the most unexpected accent, plummy vowels embellished with a dash of pseudo cockney and, at times, a pseudo American drawl. 'I know about the place,' he continued, 'because a friend of mine took me there not long ago on an incognito visit. It's a settlement house, the idea being that those giving aid to the poor should live among the poor. It's a good idea, don't you think? If I were you, I'd trot along there. I'm sure you could be useful.'

Davina was so astonished at such advice coming from such a source that she had to try hard not to let her jaw drop and then, realizing that her mother couldn't very well forbid her to do voluntary work at Toynbee Hall when it had

281

been the Prince who had suggested it, she gave him a beaming, grateful smile.

Informal and relaxed, he smiled back, his eyes puckering at the corners. Even wearing low-heeled shoes she was the taller, and while she could well understand why women all over the world considered him a pin-up to rival any Hollywood star, she didn't find herself physically attracted to him. He was too slightly built and, despite the premature pouches beneath his eyes, too boyish-looking. But she liked him. It would have been impossible for her not to when he had visited a place such as Toynbee Hall out of real, genuine interest.

The Metcalfes and Wallis hadn't yet arrived. Despite Fawzia doing all she could to make an impression on him and Prince Edward putting her at her ease by chatting about a trip he had made to Egypt, Davina could tell, by the way he kept looking towards the door, that his thoughts were elsewhere.

Bellingham entered the room to discreetly announce that the Pugh Rolls-Royce had arrived for her and Fawzia. Though it was the custom not to leave a room until the Prince had left it, he accepted their apologies with easy, almost American, informality.

Fawzia spend the rest of the night talking ceaselessly about him: how charming he was, how fiercely interested in Egypt he was, how handsome he was.

Gwen, who had a very low opinion of Prince Edward's dalliances with married women such as

Freda Dudley Ward and Thelma Furness, endured her rhapsodies with gritted teeth. Davina barely heard them. Even though she had yet to visit Toynbee Hall, she had already made up her mind to do whatever voluntary work Toynbee Hall could offer her, which would mean no more daytime debutante socializing. To say that her mother would not be pleased about it was putting it mildly. If it meant her own daytime socializing being curtailed, Fawzia, too, was going to be seriously upset.

She chewed the corner of her lip thoughtfully. Just because she didn't turn up at the daytime events they were scheduled to attend, that didn't mean Fawzia couldn't – especially as Gwen would be chaperoning her to them. Gwen couldn't be in two places at once, but that didn't matter a rap. Delia was so accustomed to Davina doing whatever she wanted to do unaccompanied, and going wherever she wanted to go unaccompanied, that she wouldn't worry about Gwen not being with her. All that mattered was that Fawzia was scrupulously chaperoned and that Zubair Pasha was given no cause for concern.

A few days later, telling Gwen and Fawzia that she wanted a little time to herself, she journeyed by bus and tube to a part of London she doubted any member of her family had ever visited. It was like being in another country.

As she walked up Whitechapel's Commercial Street she was strongly reminded of the difference, in Cairo, between the elegant streets and palatial villas of Garden City and the squalid, teeming areas beyond it. Commercial Street, too, was squalid and teeming. Even though she was wearing a very modest candy-striped dress and displaying no outward signs of wealth, she stuck out like a sore thumb – and knew it.

The vast majority of those bustling past her looked to be Jewish and spoke a language she didn't recognize. The small dark shops sold fruit and vegetables she couldn't identify. But something that was familiar was the smell in the air. It was the smell of unwashed bodies. The smell of cheap food being fried in cheap oil. The smell of poverty.

None of it came as a surprise to her. What did come as a surprise was the sight of Toynbee Hall. She had expected it to be a smoke-scarred building in keeping with the buildings around it. Instead, screened from the street by a block of dingy warehouses, it was fronted by an Elizabethan-looking gatehouse with an oriel window.

Intrigued, she stepped through the arched entrance and found a large Tudor-style, red-brick building, its walls covered in ivy. Set around a narrow quadrangle, the house had steep gables, tall chimney stacks and mullioned windows with lovely diamond-shaped leaded panes.

Deeply encouraged, she hitched her shoulder bag a little higher and walked towards the open door.

A few moments later she was standing in what she took to be the reception area, talking to a middle-aged woman in twinset and pearls, who eyed her doubtfully. 'Voluntary work? Have you

284

ever done any voluntary work in a critically deprived area? It's very practical work here in Whitechapel. It isn't just making cups of tea and handing out biscuits. And you do seem a little young, if you don't mind my saying so.'

Davina's eyes held hers steadily. 'I'm nearly nineteen and I've got lots of experience of working in extremely deprived areas.'

A troop of children clattered past.

'Have you, indeed?' the woman said, unconvinced, when the children had disappeared noisily from view. 'And just where was this?'

A pleasant-looking bespectacled man of about thirty, wearing tweeds that had once been very good and carrying a doctor's bag, hurried out of a nearby room and, with his free hand, scooped up a file from the reception desk.

Knowing that the woman was expecting her to say something foolish, such as 'the less fashionable part of Piccadilly', or perhaps even 'the less fashionable part of Knightsbridge', Davina said pleasantly, 'Cairo. The old part of the city. And no matter how horrific Whitechapel's slums, they can't be worse than the slums of Fustat or Khan el Khalili.'

'Cairo?' The young man turned towards her, his face alight with interest. 'Now that must have been educational, don't you think, Miss Scolby?' There was the soft burr of the Scottish Highlands in his voice and more than a hint of Celtic red in his hair. 'What kind of voluntary work did you do there, Miss...?'

Davina made a split-second decision not to say 'Lady Davina Conisborough'. 'Conisborough.

Davina Conisborough. And I helped out in an Anglican orphanage.'

'Then you're good with children?'

Miss Scolby, who had been startled when Davina had mentioned Cairo, pursed her lips, clearly not too pleased at having the interview taken out of her hands.

'Yes,' Davina said to him, untroubled by the woman's ruffled feathers.

'Then if you've got the rest of this afternoon free, come with me. My wife usually gives me a hand, but she's visiting her widowed mother in Scotland and won't be back until the end of the week. Do you have any nursing experience?'

She shook her head.

'It doesn't matter. I'm off to a local school to do a general medical inspection. The children are from five to eight years and some of them need a little reassuring. You look as if you might be quite good at that.'

'I am.' Davina was too much her mother's daughter to have any truck with false modesty.

He shot her a friendly grin. 'Then let's go.' And tucking the file under his arm he led the way out of the building, saying, 'I'd better introduce myself. My name is Fergus Sinclair. Aileen and I are fairly new to Toynbee. Would you like me to tell you about the work we're doing?'

'No, Davina,' said her mother when Davina came home. 'No, no and no. Occupying your time with a little charity work in Cairo is one thing. Acting as an unpaid nursing assistant in the East End of London is quite another. Heaven only knows

286

what you may have picked up from those children. Some of them probably had head lice.'

'They all had lice – and sores and rashes. And nearly all of them were malnourished.'

'Malnourished?' She had caught her mother's attention, as she knew she would.

'Malnourished,' she said again firmly. 'Men in the East End have been unemployed for so long now, all that's ever put on the table is bread and dripping and tea laced with condensed milk. And because the children are underfed, they're vulnerable to disease. Dr Sinclair and his wife are carrying out an inoculation programme in local schools and that is where I come in. East End children aren't used to seeing doctors – and they're certainly not used to the sight of a hypodermic needle. I'm to be what Dr Sinclair terms "a reassuring presence" – and I'm also to make myself useful to Mrs Sinclair, who is a State Registered Nurse.'

The conversation was taking place in her mother's bedroom and Delia was seated at her dressing table. She drummed scarlet-painted fingernails on its art-deco surface.

'It's not that I *mind* you doin' charitable work,' she said at last. 'I'm glad you have a well-developed social conscience and that you care about people less fortunate than yourself. This summer, though, when you're halfway through your season, just ain't the right time to be indulging in it.'

It wasn't often that her mother used the word 'ain't' and Davina knew that her lapse revealed just how upset she was.

Taking a deep breath she set about trying to

make her feel a little less upset. 'It actually won't make much difference to my season,' she said, sitting down beside her on the vanity stool and sliding an arm around Delia's waist, 'because if you let me help Dr Sinclair during the day, I promise you I'll go to every evening event I'm invited to.'

'And as most evening events don't finish until the early hours of the morning, when will you catch up on your sleep?'

'I'll manage.' She kissed her mother on the cheek knowing that she had, for once, got her own way. 'And to show you how much I love you, I'll put in an appearance at your cocktail party this evening. Where's Fawzia? If our evening is going to start a little earlier than usual she'll need to know.'

'Jack has taken her to an exhibition at the Tate.'

'Unaccompanied by anyone else?' This time it was Davina's turn to raise her eyebrows.

Her mother reached for her scent spray. 'Yes. It won't harm for once. They make a very attractive couple and if Jack should propose to her – and I don't see why he shouldn't, considering how many other proposals of marriage she's received since coming to London – then I think it would be a proposal she and Zubair Pasha should seriously consider.'

It was on the tip of Davina's tongue to remind her mother that Jack was quite possibly still in love with Petra. She didn't. On the few occasions when she'd spoken of Jack and Petra in the same breath, her mother had speedily changed the subject. A cloud of Jean Patou's Joy enveloped them and Delia rose to her feet.

If her mother wanted to do a little matchmaking she was, after all, quite entitled to do so – and Petra's heart wouldn't be hurt, for she'd made it quite clear that she realized she'd made a huge mistake in ever believing herself to be in love with Jack. Which, as far as Davina was concerned, was a shame, for Jack would have made the best brother-in-law she could possibly imagine.

The first person she saw when she went down for cocktails was the dark-eyed, dark-haired Baba Metcalfe. Baba was the daughter of the late Lord Curzon, a man who had been a close friend of her father's. Over the years, Davina had met her quite often. She had never met her husband, though – and he came as quite a shock.

Somehow she had imagined Fruity Metcalfe as being an easy-going, mild-mannered kind of chap. The powerfully-built man who removed his arm from around Baba's waist in order to shake hands with Davina, was far from being mild in any way.

As dark-haired as Baba, and abnormally pale-skinned, he had a fierce, almost overpowering intensity about him.

'We haven't met before, though I've known your mother for years,' he said, holding her hand in a strong grip for far longer than was necessary. 'She tells me you prefer the exoticism of Egypt to milk-and-water life in London.'

His piercing black eyes moved from her eyes to her mouth in a way that was so blatantly sexual she flushed scarlet.

Beneath a night-black moustache his lips parted in a smile – and she knew it was with satisfaction at the effect he was having on her.

'I prefer Egypt because I think of it as home,' she said stiffly, forcing herself to look away from his hypnotic gaze, terrified that if she didn't she would find her will – however much she didn't want it to – bending to his.

Baba was no longer anywhere near by. Across the room Fawzia was standing close to Jack. He was deep in conversation with Argentina's Ambassador to Britain and Fawzia was looking at him with an expression on her face that indicated Delia could have been right in thinking a proposal from Jack was one Fawzia might well accept.

'Have you ever travelled to Germany?' Baba's husband asked, his sexual magnetism coming at her in waves. 'I think you would like it. Under Hitler it's becoming very youth-conscious. Something it would do Britain good to emulate.'

She was just about to say that she had never been to Germany and to excuse herself and escape from him when Jerome walked into the room, his slight limp a little more noticeable than usual. On seeing them, he strolled towards them.

'Hello, Davina,' he said, giving her an affectionate smile. 'I haven't seen much of you while you've been in London. Perhaps it's something we can remedy. As for you, Tom, I thought you were still in Italy, paying homage to Mussolini.'

'And I thought you were in Germany, with Brunhilde.'

Jerome gave a slight shrug of his shoulders. 'If you're referring to Magda, I did go to Berlin to spend time with her earlier this year. I won't be going again. Unlike you, I'm not an admirer of Hitler and I don't like what's happening in Germany and, as Magda does, I won't be seeing her again. And now, if you'll excuse me, Tom, I'm going to steer Davina into a quiet corner in order to catch up on some family gossip.'

With his hand beneath her arm he propelled her as far away from Fruity as, in the confines of the drawing room, it was possible to get.

'Thank you for that, Uncle Jerome,' she said, her nerves still jangling. 'He made me very hot and bothered. I was well out of my depth.'

'I'm not surprised. Tom is a seducer on a massive scale. I suggest you steer well clear of him. Now, what are you going to have to drink? Do you do cocktails – it looks as though Delia's mixing some rather lethal gin fizzes – or d'you stick to champagne?'

'I stick to champagne. And why do so many people refer to Tom as Fruity? It doesn't suit him. It's too comic a nickname for someone who looks like a demon king.'

'The answer is, that they don't,' he said, amused. 'The only Fruity, is Fruity Metcalfe.'

'Then who have I just been talking to?' she asked, looking back to where the demon king had been joined again by Baba.

'Sir Oswald Mosley. Tom is his nickname. Far from being Baba's husband, he's her brother-in-law. His wife, Cimmie, died a couple of months ago.'

Her mother, looking sensational in a dress of lime-green chiffon that fitted close to her slim

291

figure yet floated as if in a breeze, was carrying two gin fizzes in Baba and Tom's direction. As she handed them the drinks, Davina saw Tom Mosley slide his free hand once again around his sister-in-law's waist.

If Jerome also saw what looked to Davina to be a shocking intimacy, he made no comment on it.

'Tell me how you are enjoying your first season,' he said with the kind of avuncular interest in her activities he'd always shown. 'In the general way of things your mother would have kept me in touch about it, but I haven't seen a lot of her lately.' There was deep regret in his voice and his gold-flecked eyes were no longer on her, but on her mother, who was again mixing cocktails with great expertise. 'It's something I intend to rectify.'

A few days later Aileen Sinclair returned from Scotland. She was tall, with a square-jawed, high-cheek boned face and a mass of dark hair. Like Fergus, she wore clothes that were good quality, but they had seen better days. Her mauve-flecked tweed skirt was faded, her pink twinset had suffered far too many trips to the laundry and her sandals were inelegantly flat and serviceable.

'We're going to make a wonderful team, Davina,' she said with a wide, friendly smile, and Davina knew instantly that she had at last found a friend who, unlike Fawzia, shared her passion for helping others.

'Fergus thinks you should be taught how to give inoculations and so I have a couple of oranges with me for you to practise on. Have you always wanted to learn a little nursing?'

'Yes – though when I was very young I wanted to be a doctor. And then I realized that I wasn't clever enough.'

'Then be a nurse. You could do your training at Guy's Hospital. For now let's have you practising puncturing these oranges.'

And with another wide smile her new friend passed her an orange and a syringe.

FIFTEEN

For the next two weeks she enjoyed every hour of every day. Before anyone else was awake she left the house and travelled to Whitechapel on public transport. While Fawzia spent her time in the company of Gwen, and sometimes also in the company of Jack, Davina accompanied Fergus and Aileen Sinclair on their tireless mission to bring healthcare to Whitechapel's slums.

At first she had thought that such work was what Toynbee Hall was all about.

'Heavens, no,' Fergus said with a chuckle when she put her assumption into words. 'Toynbee has a far broader aim. It's a social workshop, Davina.'

He called a temporary halt to the seemingly endless stream of lice-ridden children filing into the treatment room and, wrapping his hands around a mug of tea, said, 'One of its prime aims is educational. There are year-round day classes for the unemployed – all free, of course. There are also weekly debates – often with leading political figures as speakers. When that happens the Hall is packed to overflowing.'

He put his mug of tea down, took his glasses off and pinched the bridge of his nose. 'One of our central tenets is that the provision of education should be a two-way process. How can politicians, for instance, fight poverty and unemployment if they never meet with these conditions face to face? By living for a few weeks at Toynbee they do so. It's education on a grand scale. Men with the experience of Toynbee behind them are men who can truly make a difference.'

He gave a wry grimace. 'I just wish more of this country's useless aristocracy would follow their example instead of spending their time drinking cocktails and going to balls so lavish the cost of even one of them would provide an adequate meal for half of Whitechapel. How they can live as they do, in their vast houses and on their vast estates, while most British people have neither bath nor heating is beyond my ken.'

At the stricken look on her face he gave an apologetic grin. 'Sorry. I didn't mean to go off on a rant. It's just that it's something I feel very passionate about. I think we'd better start work again or we'll be here till midnight and Aileen won't want that. Usher in our next snotty-nosed patient, will you?'

Afterwards she knew she should have told him then and there about her privileged background, but she hadn't, and later she didn't know how to bring the subject up again.

There was something else, too, that had begun preying on her mind.

Whitechapel was an area of Jewish immigrants. The language she'd heard on the streets the first time she had walked from Aldgate East station to Toynbee Hall, and that she had not been able to understand, was Yiddish. Synagogues stood at nearly every corner. And vicious attacks on Jews, by members of Sir Oswald Mosley's new and growing British Union of Fascists, were a daily occurrence.

'And it will only grow worse,' Aileen had said to her gravely. 'Like Hitler, his fascist rhetoric appeals to bullies and thugs, especially when they can parade around in Blackshirt uniforms, paramilitary style, and give stiff-armed, Nazi-type salutes.'

Whenever Davina thought of Sir Oswald Mosley she dug her nails as deep into her palms as they would go, certain that if Fergus and Aileen were to discover that Mosley felt able to drop in for cocktails at her home whenever the fancy took him, they wouldn't want anything further to do with her.

'Have you given any more thought about applying to Guy's for nursing training?' Aileen asked her one day when they were taking a lunch break. 'It would mean Fergus and I would have to manage without you – and we'd miss you – but we'd still be able to see quite a bit of each other. Things aren't quite as draconian for student nurses as they used to be. You are now allowed out of the hospital grounds occasionally.'

They were sitting on a bench in Toynbee Hall's quadrangle. Beside them was a tub of brilliant orange nasturtiums and a bee was hovering over the blossoms, darting into the heart of first one flower and then another.

Davina took a deep, steadying breath and then said, 'I am going to apply for nursing training, but not at Guy's.'

'Not at Guy's?' Aileen stared at her, dumbfounded. 'But Guy's is the most famous teaching hospital in the world! You can't possibly consider applying anywhere else. Especially not when you're a Londoner!'

'I'm not really a Londoner, Aileen. Though I was born here, it isn't my home. I'm only here for the summer because ... because it's the season and my mother insisted on it.'

Aileen blinked, her grey-green eyes baffled. 'Your mother insisted on you being in London during the summer season? You're not making sense, Davina. Why is the summer season any different to the autumn season or the winter season or–'

'I mean the London season, Aileen. It's a class thing,' she added unhappily. 'Presentation at court and ... and all that.'

Aileen's jaw dropped. 'You mean you're a debutante? You're one of those young women whose photograph appears in *Tatler?*'

Davina nodded and waited for a chill to descend.

It didn't.

'But how on *earth*,' Aileen asked, 'do you manage when you're working with Fergus and me for such long hours every day? Don't debutantes have to go to lots of parties and grand balls and to

296

Henley and Ascot and places like that?'

With thankful incredulity Davina realized that instead of being appalled by what she had told her, Aileen was intrigued.

'Yes. But because I'm working here my mother has let me off the Henley and Ascot stuff. I still have to go to other debutantes' coming-out balls, though. It would be awfully bad manners not to.'

'Dear heaven! How much sleep are you getting?'

'Not much.'

Their eyes held and then simultaneously they burst into laughter.

Later, when they were packing up their medical equipment after an afternoon working in a run-down primary school, Fergus said to her, 'Just out of curiosity, Davina. Who is your father? He must be fairly well-heeled if you're a debutante.'

Secure that her background wasn't going to affect the friendship she enjoyed with the Sinclairs, she said, 'Viscount Conisborough. He's a British advisor to King Fuad. That's why I can't apply to Guy's. I'm going to have to do my training in Cairo.'

The Sinclairs stared at her as if she'd said she was going to have to do it on the moon. Dazedly Fergus put his stethoscope into his doctor's bag and fastened it shut.

'Ye gods,' he said, severely winded. 'And does your father know the kind of work you've been doing these last few weeks – and where you've been doing it?'

Always scrupulously truthful, Davina hesitated. Since she'd begun working at Toynbee Hall and keeping her mother happy by going to parties and balls in the late evening, she hadn't had a minute free for letter writing. 'I'm not sure. I'm certain my mother will have told him. And he won't object,' she added as she saw the expression on Fergus's face. 'I've always done lots of voluntary work.'

'I've heard of Conisborough.' They were now all packed and ready to leave the little cramped room that had served as their clinic, but neither Fergus nor Aileen showed any sign of moving. 'He's a financier, isn't he?'

Davina was taken aback. 'Yes,' she said, alarmed. 'But he's just as much committed to a life of service as you and Aileen are. It's a different kind of service, of course. Yours is to people and my father's is to his country. He isn't an advisor to King Fuad because he wants to be. He serves the British government in Egypt – often under very difficult circumstances – because he believes that his doing so is in the best interests of Britain.'

Fergus nodded – though he didn't look very convinced.

'And is your mother the Lady Conisborough who is the famous American high-society hostess?' he asked, finally picking up his doctor's bag and leading the way to the door.

'Well, she is American,' Davina said as they stepped out into a narrow cobbled street, 'and she does have a lot of friends. But I hadn't realized she was famous.'

With the air of a man trying to get to the bottom of things Fergus said patiently, 'Davina, is your mother the Lady Conisborough who is friends with Sir John Simon, the Foreign Secretary? And with Winston Churchill, who used to be Chancellor of the Exchequer and is the only person in the government who realizes what a risk to our peace Hitler is? The Lady Conisborough who is known to be a long-time friend of the Prince of Wales?'

'Yes,' Davina said, doubtful of the reaction this was going to meet with. 'How do you know so much about my mother's friendships?'

'The whole of the country knows about your mother's friends. Hannen Swaffer, at the *Daily Sketch*, writes about her every chance he gets. Nothing on earth would induce me to read *Tatler*, but you can bet your life her photograph is in it nearly every month. She's acknowledged as being one of the country's greatest beauties. Didn't you know?'

'No,' she said, feeling a little foolish. 'I didn't. And if my mother does, she wouldn't take it seriously. She's too busy being interested in other things to care whether she's a beauty or not.'

One of the things her mother was very interested in was Aileen Sinclair's plans to open a free clinic for women in Whitechapel.

'Tell me more about it, Davina,' she said, sitting in bed with a breakfast tray across her lap. 'Is it to be a general health clinic?'

'No.' Davina seated herself on the edge of the bed. 'It's to be a clinic to help stop the women who have nine or ten children and can't afford to feed them from having any more.'

Her mother, who had been in the process of

pouring herself a cup of coffee, spilled it over the embroidered tray cloth.

'Land sakes, Davina! You're a single young woman of eighteen! You can't be fitting women with diaphragms! Your father would have ten fits!'

Davina giggled. 'I wouldn't be doing anything like that. I'm not qualified to. And besides, by the time the clinic is up and running the season will be over and I will be back in Cairo.'

Her mother looked relieved, and then she said, 'What is the clinic going to be called, honey? Because if it's called a contraceptive clinic, or a family planning clinic, a lot of men won't let their wives be seen entering it.'

Glad that her mother was basically so un-shockable and sensible, Davina mopped up the spilled coffee with a napkin and said, 'Aileen intends calling it simply the Free Clinic because apparently men do kick up a fuss when their wives are given the power to have only the children they want. It's a fuss I don't understand because, since they are living in such dreadful poverty, half the time the babies they have die within a few weeks. Parts of Whitechapel are just as bad as parts of Cairo.'

Her mother said nothing, but looked grim, and Davina didn't know if it was because her mother disapproved intensely of the fact that she was familiar with such parts of Cairo, or because she was thinking of the women who, living in tenements full of damp and mould, with no running water and no sanitation apart from a lavatory that had to be shared with thirty or so other families, gave birth in unutterably squalid conditions.

'I'd like to meet the Sinclairs,' Delia said thoughtfully. 'They sound as if they could do with financial help to get their Free Clinic off the ground. Why don't you bring them to Cadogan Square this evening? Do it early, though. I'm dining with Margot at eight.'

Davina had great reservations about asking Fergus and Aileen to Cadogan Square, for she couldn't imagine either of them feeling comfortable being greeted by a butler and waited on by maids and footmen. But if her mother was going to sink some money into Aileen's Free Clinic, it was something that was going to have to be done.

'My mother would like to meet you both,' she said when she met up with them in the hideous little room that was to serve as their clinic for the day.

Fergus quirked an eyebrow and for a dreadful moment Davina thought he was going to decline the invitation. Then Aileen said, 'Well, that's only natural when you're spending every day with us. If I was your mother, I would want to meet us as well!'

The three of them travelled by tube from Whitechapel to Kensington and then walked from Sloane Square tube station to Cadogan Square.

As they approached the splendid porticoed entrance to her home, Fergus made the kind of sound in his throat that, for a Scot, could mean anything and which Davina suspected was disapproval at the private wealth it signified.

Bellingham opened the door and Davina was acutely aware that though she'd always taken a butler for granted, Fergus and Aileen most certainly did not.

'Fergus and Aileen, let me introduce you to Bellingham,' she said, trying to put things on as casual a footing as possible. 'Bellingham has been the butler here since before I was born. Bellingham, Dr Fergus Sinclair and Mrs Sinclair.'

'How do you do, sir, madam.' Bellingham inclined his head and at that moment the bell rang again and this time a footman opened the door.

To Davina's delight he opened it to Jerome.

'Davina, my dear,' he said as he stepped into the marble-floored hall and immediately gave her a hug and a kiss on the cheek. 'What a pleasure to find you here – and what a rarity. I understand you've more or less exchanged Kensington for Whitechapel?'

Smiling sunnily, happy for the opportunity to introduce Fergus and Aileen to the person she loved more than anyone else in the world, apart from her parents and Petra, she proceeded to make introductions. 'Sir Jerome is an MP, an old family friend and my honorary uncle,' she said to the Sinclairs and then, to Jerome, 'Fergus and Aileen are resident volunteers at Toynbee Hall. It's an–'

'I know exactly what Toynbee Hall is, thank you, Davina. I'm speaking there on the Liberal Party's stance on trade unionism in a week's time.'

Jerome, resplendent in a beautifully tailored dinner jacket, a red silk handkerchief in his breast pocket, shook hands with Aileen and Fergus. 'You get to the debates, do you? It would be nice to see you there next Wednesday.' And with easy familiarity he steered them towards the drawing room's double doors.

Davina could hear the sound of laughter and the clink of glasses. As the realization dawned that her mother was throwing one of her early evening cocktail parties, Davina's horror knew no bounds. All she could think of was that the three of them needed to leave the house immediately.

'Uncle Jerome!' she called after him urgently. 'Please stop!'

It was too late. The footman threw open the double doors and Jerome squired Fergus and Aileen into the drawing room as easily as if he'd known them for years.

Eyes swivelled in their direction. Several eyebrows rose, not so much at the leather elbow-patches on Fergus's jacket as at her and Aileen's cotton day dresses. Where Fergus was concerned, nearly every one of her mother's male friends dressed similarly when at their country estates, shabby, good-quality tweeds being *de rigueur*, and it was easy for everyone to make the assumption that Fergus had driven straight up from the country and had eccentrically not taken the trouble to change into clothes appropriate for the occasion.

The way she and Aileen were dressed was, however, a different matter as both her pink and white candy-striped dress and Aileen's Sunday-best floral cotton dress were grossly inappropriate wear for a high-society cocktail party.

Her mother, wearing a midnight-blue, seductively cut, lamé cocktail dress, her hair tamed into fashionable upswept sleekness, gave a cry of delight and headed straight towards them.

Any discomfort the Sinclairs might have felt at

303

being plunged into such an unexpected scenario vanished within seconds beneath Delia's American informality and her lavishly warm welcome.

'I've so much I would like to talk to you both about,' she said almost immediately. 'I've been wondering if Toynbee Hall organizes holidays for disadvantaged children. My husband's family home, Shibden Hall, is in Norfolk, within sight of the sea. We've had tenants in it for most of the years we have been in Egypt, but their tenancy came to an end some months ago. That being the case, it occurred to me it would make a cracking good holiday home for deprived children. What d'you think, Dr Sinclair? D'you think it's a feasible idea?'

Fergus, looking as bowled over as most men did on first meeting her mother, said, 'A feasible idea, Lady Conisborough? I think it's an absolutely grand idea!'

'Then let's talk more over a drink.' And tucking her hands through both Fergus's arm and Aileen's, Delia led them away from Davina and across the room, introducing them to various people as she did so.

Davina said apprehensively to Jerome, 'There's no chance of Sir Oswald Mosley dropping by, is there, Uncle Jerome? Because if there is, I'm going to have to get Aileen and Fergus out of here PDQ.'

'Not a hope. Delia went to one of his public meetings with Baba and said it was like a Nuremberg Rally. All banners, spotlights, martial music and black-shirted thugs giving violent short shrift to any hecklers. Mosley started raving about the Jews Hitler-style, and when Delia next saw him she told him that as a large number of her friends were Jewish he might find it more comfortable not to visit Cadogan Square again. And he hasn't.'

He shrugged his shoulders unhappily. 'I wish everyone had the same reaction, but they don't. Sylvia and her husband have become hard-line converts to fascism. At the meeting Delia attended, Girlington was on the platform with Mosley, dressed to the teeth in black pseudo-military garb. It makes it hard on Jack. The last thing his Foreign Office career needs is for him to be linked politically with the British Union of Fascists – even if the link is only via his mother.'

Vastly relieved that Sir Oswald Mosley wouldn't be making a demon-king appearance, and not knowing how best to carry on the conversation Jerome had started about Sylvia and her new husband, Davina looked around the room.

Petra's friend, the former Annabel Mowbray, was standing near one of the windows with her husband and a couple of people Davina did not recognize. Nor did she recognize the vast majority of the other people in the room. 'Who is the plain, neat-looking woman sitting on the sofa and chatting with Lady Portarlington?' she asked.

The corners of Jerome's eyes crinkled. 'That's your mother's bosom chum, Wallis Simpson. Have we to go over and have a word? I like her. She's full of wisecracking vitality.'

As they crossed the room towards Wallis, Winnie Portarlington, seeing their intention, rose to her feet, blew a kiss in Jerome's direction, then walked languidly over to join Annabel and her husband and friends.

'There's no need for introductions, Jerome,' Wallis said in an attractively rasping voice when they reached her. She turned to Davina, 'I've guessed who you are.' She flashed a lightning-quick smile. 'And I can tell from the way you are dressed that you didn't expect to walk into a cocktail party, but your dress is exactly the kind I like: unfussy, yet pretty.'

Davina was certain Wallis was being sincere, for of all the women in the room, she was the only one wearing a dress unadorned by sequins or bugles or beads. It was of black crêpe de Chine and instead of being slinkily clinging or sensu-ously floating, it was tailored to within an inch of its life, its only adornment a square-cut emerald pin. Her hands were large and, perhaps in order not to bring attention to them, her nails were unpolished. Her dark hair, parted in the centre and taken back in crimped waves over her ears, was so sleek she might have been Chinese. She looked very prim and proper and not at all as Davina had imagined she would look.

Wallis patted the space on the sofa vacated by Winnie Portarlington. 'Sit down and tell me all about yourself,' she said in the tone of a headmistress speaking to a prefect, and then, to Jerome: 'Delia may be a divine hostess, but not, apparently, where her daughter is concerned. Davina is still without a drink. Would you get her a cocktail, Jerome, please?'

Jerome looked startled and Davina didn't blame him. Her mother could be breathtakingly

306

direct, but for sheer bossiness Wallis beat her hands down.

'I'm afraid I don't drink cocktails, Mrs Simpson,' she said affably.

'Of course you do. Everybody does – and your mother makes swell cocktails. She should. I taught her.' Again there came the lightning-quick grin that took the sting out of her words. She looked across to Fergus and Aileen who were talking to a beautiful woman Davina didn't at first recognize. Then she realized it was the film actress, Merle Oberon.

Wallis took a sip of her highball and said musingly, 'Your friend's husband reminds me of the Prince of Wales, Davina. He has the same quiet manner and charm.'

It was said with an air of such proprietorial knowledge of the Prince that Davina, remembering all the gossip her mother had passed on to her with regard to Wallis's relationship with Prince Edward, could think of absolutely nothing to say in response. She was saved from having to reply by Wallis saying, 'Even in a cotton dress your friend looks spectacularly lovely. Tell me all about her and her husband. Who are they? Where are they from?'

And as Jerome handed her a very welcome glass of champagne, Davina proceeded to tell Wallis all about the pioneering work Fergus and Aileen were doing in London's East End.

SIXTEEN

The next day, before the three of them left Toynbee Hall for the school where they were to carry out inoculations, Fergus said to Davina, 'Your mother is an exceptional person.' He shifted his heavy doctor's bag from one hand to the other as they walked across the cobbled quadrangle. 'Offering Shibden Hall as a holiday home for East End children is such a generous gesture, I don't know how Toynbee will ever be able to thank her.'

'She doesn't need thanks,' Davina said, happy that the Sinclairs' introduction to her mother had turned out so well. 'She just doesn't like the thought of Shibden standing empty.'

Aileen linked arms with her. 'And she was *riveted* by the idea of a clinic giving free advice to women on contraception. She said she'd never seen a diaphragm and would I show her one.'

Fergus blanched and Davina's eyes nearly popped out of her head.

'Great God, Aileen!' Fergus said, when he'd recovered the power of speech. 'You didn't get one out at her cocktail party, did you?'

'No, silly.' She giggled. 'They aren't something I carry around in my handbag, Fergus.'

As they crossed a busy road to enter a narrow street of dingy and dilapidated tenement buildings, Aileen gave Davina's arm a squeeze. 'The financial help your mother has promised for the clinic is going to make all the difference to how soon it can be opened. I never imagined a viscountess being an instinctive socialist, Davina, but your mother is one. Through and through.'

It was, Davina knew, the highest accolade Aileen Sinclair could give.

A day or two later, for the first time, she spoke to Aileen about Darius, prompted into doing so by Aileen saying to her, 'I expect your mother is hoping that by being a debutante and going to lots of parties and balls you'll meet a nice young man and fall in love.'

They were seated at opposite sides of a table, writing up – in legible handwriting – Fergus's scrawled and barely decipherable medical notes.

Davina put her pen down. 'That's always the general idea, but I think by now my mother knows it isn't how it's going to be for me.'

Aileen finished the sentence she was writing and then looked up at her. 'Why not?' she asked, curious.

'My mother doesn't know why not – apart from the fact that I never want to live anywhere but Cairo, which is certainly not where any of the young men I meet at debutante balls and parties will want to live – but the real reason is that the only person I can ever imagine falling in love with is the son of one of my father's friends.'

She had never before put any of her feelings for Darius into words and she flushed a bright pink.

It was Aileen's turn now to put down her pen. 'But surely that's perfect? What could be better? I can understand your father may well view having spent money on a London season for you as having been a waste of time, but think how pleased he and his friend will be.'

Davina shook her head. 'It isn't like that. Darius is Egyptian and he hates the fact that Britain controls so much of what goes on in Egypt. For example, nearly all the wealth from the country's cotton crop goes into British pockets, and what doesn't, goes into the pockets of a handful of Egyptian landowners. None of it filters down to the peasants who work the land. My father doesn't realize yet just how fiercely anti-British Darius is, but it won't be long before he does. And then Darius is the last person in the world he would want me to fall in love with.'

'And how does Darius feel? Is he prepared to take on the world – and your father – in order to be able to marry you?'

Davina's pink flush turned a fiery red. 'We're just friends at the moment, Aileen. We've been friends ever since I was a little girl. And that's how Darius still thinks of me,' she added miserably, 'as if I'm still a little girl.'

'Then when you return to Cairo, you'll just have to convince him that you're not. And it may be that he's been holding off changing the nature of the relationship between the two of you because he knows that your father would disapprove.'

It was a point of view Davina hadn't thought of before and it cheered her. Well aware of how much she was going to miss Aileen when she returned to Cairo, she gave her friend a grateful smile and picked up her pen again.

An hour later she was watching Fergus stitch

the scalp of a young boy who had been hit over the head with a glass bottle by a British Union of Fascists' thug.

It was the kind of incident that was happening daily. As Fergus sent the boy on his way, suitably stitched and bandaged, he said heavily, 'This is the result of Mosley emulating Hitler and Mussolini. Fascist creeds always need a scapegoat and, like Hitler, Mosley's scapegoat is the Jews. The anti-Semitism he's stirring up is a political strategy and if we don't want to go down the ugly road Germany is going down, we are going to have to fight it tooth and nail.'

He took off his horn-rimmed glasses. 'The irony is,' he said, polishing them with a handkerchief, 'that if Mosley had stayed in the Labour Party he could have been a force for good, for when he was a Labour MP some of his economic ideas with regard to the ending of unemployment were brilliant.'

He put his glasses back on and she didn't tell him that she had met Sir Oswald Mosley in her own home. She was just deeply grateful that the occasion wouldn't arise again.

The next morning it was Fergus who was being treated for injuries received in a street disturbance. 'But what *happened?*' Aileen asked him, white-faced, as she dealt with the cuts and welts he had received.

'Mosley's thugs had set on a couple of Jewish youths. I couldn't stand by and do nothing, Aileen.'

'But did you have to get involved in the fighting?' Her hands trembled as she squeezed out a

311

bloodied sponge.

'Yes,' he said levelly. 'I did. And I'm going to become even more physically involved in fighting Mosley's vile politics. There's a British Union of Fascists' rally to be held at Olympia tomorrow evening and there will be a large number of protestors there. I shall be with them and I shall have hundreds of pamphlets with me. I'm not going to remain passive in the face of this kind of racial intimidation, Aileen.'

Later, when Davina and Aileen were alone together, Aileen said, still pale-faced, 'I shall go with Fergus tomorrow evening, Davina. If we want to show Sir Oswald Mosley that we don't want Britain to be a totalitarian state with him as its leader, then we have to oppose him at every opportunity there is. Fergus says that if there are enough protestors there, Mosley could well begin to lose his credibility.'

Not, for even one minute, did Davina consider not going with her.

What she hadn't realized was just how hard it would be to get into the exhibition hall. Traffic on the main road was at a standstill as a crowd of several thousand pushed and jostled, struggling to get near one of several entrance doors. Mounted police were out in force as were massed groups of Blackshirts. Though she and the Sinclairs weren't carrying a placard, scores of other demonstrators were and the Blackshirts descended on them, knocking them to the ground and kicking and punching as they wrested the placards from them.

To Davina's disbelief there was no protection

from the police. Bloodied demonstrator after bloodied demonstrator, still yelling protests, was dragged off by them.

'At this rate no hecklers are going to get into the meeting!' Fergus shouted, trying to shield Davina and Aileen from the worst excess of the crush as they pushed and shoved a way forward.

By some miracle they reached an entrance door.

By an even greater miracle they jostled their way through it.

'How many people d'you think are in here?' Aileen shouted to Fergus over the din as, five minutes later, she looked around the packed-to-capacity auditorium.

'Thirteen or fourteen thousand,' he shouted back to her. 'Possibly more.'

Everywhere Davina looked there was a sea of flags. The familiar red, white and blue of Union flags, black and yellow fascist flags, and swaying banners carrying the names of all the various London districts of BUF party membership.

Seating at the rear, sides and immediate front of the platform had obviously been reserved for family and distinguished friends, many of whom, to her horror, she recognized. In sharp contrast to the vast majority of those present – who were clearly working class and in working clothes – those in privileged seats were in evening dress. Baba Metcalfe was clearly visible, as was her sister, Irene. There was no sign of Fruity, but someone else who was clearly visible was the person she still, out of long force of habit, thought of as 'Aunt' Sylvia.

313

'There's Neil Francis Hawkins,' Fergus said suddenly, also looking down at the platform. 'He's Mosley's second-in-command. And there's John Beckett, a former Labour MP.'

A band, made up entirely of Blackshirts, began to play a rousingly patriotic march and she dragged her eyes away from Baba and Sylvia, scanning the main body of the hall.

'There's a shocking number of women present,' Fergus said. 'It isn't something I would have expected.'

Aileen agreed with him and Davina could hardly say Mosley's sexual magnetism was such that she wasn't at all surprised at the number of women tensely waiting for him to make his appearance.

The time when he was scheduled to speak came and went. Blackshirts lined the central aisle running from the main entrance to the large platform and as they waited for him to stride down towards it and as tension mounted to breaking point, Mosley's followers launched into a deafening rendering of the BUF anthem. Though Davina couldn't catch all the words she didn't need to, for it was set to the same emotively rousing tune as the Nazi *Horst-Wessel-Leid*. Hearing in England something that accompanied every rabble-rousing rally addressed by Hitler made the hair at the back of her neck stand on end.

Then great arc lamps were switched on, trumpets blasted a fanfare and, enveloped in a sinister greyish-blue tinge, Sir Oswald Mosley entered the hall.

Seeing the man she had met in the drawing

room of her home swaggering with shoulders back and chin and chest out down the central aisle of the huge auditorium to deafening roars of 'Hail Moslcy!', as if he were a latter-day Messiah, was a surreal experience. His arm was held high in the fascist salute. A squad of black-uniformed, flag-carrying paramilitary stewards preceded him, and behind him came four of his personal bodyguards.

The scene was pure Grand Guignol. In black boots, breeches and shirt, under the glare of giant spotlights and still with his bodyguard of muscular young men, he strode onto the platform to a storm of frenzied cheering.

When at last the noise dropped to a level over which he could be heard, he thumped the lectern with his fist. 'Thousands of our fellow country-men and women,' he thundered, 'have come tonight to hear our case and thousands more have rallied and joined the fascist ranks!'

A storm of rapturous foot-stamping broke out.

'This movement, which is represented here tonight, is something new in the political life of this country.'

Fergus leaped to his feet. *'And we don't need it!'* he shouted at the top of his lungs.

If Mosley heard, he showed no sign. 'It is our intention to challenge and break for ever the power of the Jews in Britain!'

Other protestors were on their feet now.

Blackshirts began running down the aisle in their general direction. As they did, Mosley finally acknowledged that hecklers had got inside the building.

'Ignore the interruptions!' he roared to his followers. 'They don't worry me and they needn't worry you!'

The cheers, underscored by valiant booing, were deafening.

As the rampaging Blackshirts reached the protestors nearest to them, there was no orderly escorting of them outside the building. The Blackshirts pitched into them with raised arms and fists. Men fell. Blood flew. Women screamed. Chairs were overturned.

Mosley stabbed the air with his fist. 'These protests are futile, for what is being represented here goes further, and deeper, than any other movement this land has ever known! This meeting is symbolic of the advance of the Blackshirt cause in the first twenty months of its existence. In that time fascism in Great Britain has advanced more rapidly than in any other country in the world.'

In other parts of the hall other fist fights between protestors and stewards were taking place – and not only fist fights. Davina saw a chair leg being wielded. A boot flew through the air and then a shoe.

Mosley was now prowling the platform as he spoke, his dark eyes flashing, his aura of sexual power palpable. 'And it is not because our people had to adopt it under the lash of economic necessity, as in other lands,' he continued with a sweeping gesture, 'but because they desired a new creed and a new order in our land. A creed which elevates the nation above the individual and faction.'

Davina could bear no more. 'Fascism equals Hitler, equals Mussolini!' she shouted as a fellow woman protestor, only yards away from her and

Aileen, was grabbed by two Blackshirts and bustled up the nearest aisle towards an exit, her arms twisted behind her.

It took minutes for the chaos around them to settle and when it did Aileen shouted urgently, 'Where is Fergus, Davina? Where has he gone?'

Davina looked around her, searching the various melees for sight of him. There wasn't any.

'I don't know. But we can't leave our seats to look for him, Aileen. We might never make contact with each other again if we do.'

With her stomach muscles taut with anxiety she heard Mosley thunder, 'Masses of our people have shown in no uncertain way that they are weary of the present order; weary of political parties and of the present parliamentary government...'

Suddenly, from the roof space a hundred feet and more above him a voice with an unmistakable Scottish inflection shouted: *'Down with fascism!'*

Davina's gaze flew upwards.

Beside her, Aileen screamed.

Fergus was balanced precariously on an iron girder, and as thousands of people drew in a concerted breath he began raining pamphlets down.

Mosley didn't even pause in his tirade but he had lost everyone's attention.

Arc lamps swung away from the platform and illuminated Fergus. Within minutes half a dozen Blackshirts had reached the girder and had begun approaching him from either side.

People directly beneath the girder scrambled out of their seats in case the men should fall on them.

Aileen, her eyes wide with horror, had both hands pressed to her mouth. Davina was praying harder than she had ever prayed in her life.

'The ex-servicemen who fought in the Great War are weary of the privilege of Conservatism,' Mosley continued as if nothing untoward was taking place. 'Our people are weary of the mass inertia of Socialism. The Labour Party is nothing but a Salvation Army taking to its heels on the Day of Judgement.'

As the Blackshirts on the girder came almost within reach of Fergus, he swung himself up onto an even higher girder and from there onto a platform that disappeared into the shadows of the roof. Within seconds he, too, was out of sight, his pursuers hard on his heels.

'What is wanted is a new creed,' Mosley declared with passion as the arc lamps swung back towards him 'What we are fighting for is nothing less than a revolution!'

From somewhere unseen came the sound of shattering glass.

That someone had fallen – and from a great height – was obvious to every single person in the auditorium.

Aileen and Davina didn't hesitate. In sheer terror they began pushing and stumbling past everyone seated between them and the nearest aisle, intent only on reaching Fergus; intent on finding out if it was Fergus who had fallen and, if he had, whether he was alive or dead.

Once in the aisle Aileen, with Davina hard behind her, broke into a sprint. A fight had broken out ahead of them. A missile intended for one of the Blackshirts hit Davina at the side of her head. She felt blood pour down her face and though she tried to stay on her feet, she couldn't. The world spiralled into darkness and, with Aileen's screams ringing in her ears, she buckled at the knees, falling senseless amid a forest of booted feet.

SEVENTEEN

When she regained consciousness Davina knew she was in a hospital bed and that it was the middle of the night, for the ward was dark.

'Fergus Sinclair?' she said weakly to the nurse who came to check on her. 'Did he fall? Is he hurt?'

'Quite a lot of people were hurt last night,' the nurse said briskly. 'And I don't know anything about the men who were brought in. You've had a very nasty knock to the head and you need to rest and not worry. We'll make enquiries about your friend in the morning.'

Though she tried to stay awake in order to ask any other members of the night staff if they knew whether Fergus was in the hospital, she fell almost immediately into a deep, exhausted sleep.

In the morning she opened her eyes to find her mother sitting next to her bed. 'Fergus?' she said again, before even wondering how Delia knew what had happened to her and where to find her. 'He was a hundred feet above the auditorium on a girder and then Aileen and I couldn't see him.

319

We only heard the sound of shattering glass. Is he all right?' Her grey eyes were dark with worry. 'Is he here in the hospital? Is Aileen with him?'

'He's in Men's Surgical and yes, Aileen is with him.' Her mother's lovely face was tense and drawn. 'He wasn't over the main drop of the hall when he fell. He's hurt badly, though, and at the moment Aileen is the only visitor allowed.'

'Was Aileen hurt as well?' she asked, feeling as if her heart was being squeezed within her chest. If Fergus was badly hurt, how long would it be before he was able to begin working again? And what of Aileen? What would happen to Aileen's plans for a clinic if Fergus was so badly injured that Aileen was going to have to look after him and not be able to work either?

'Aileen received some cuts and bruises in the melee, but otherwise she's all right. It was stupidly reckless of you to have gone to Olympia, Davina. You, of all people, should have known the kind of violence that was likely to take place.'

Davina had never known her mother be seriously angry with her before, but knew she was now.

'You've witnessed the street violence that takes place when Tom's thugs are let loose.' Her hands were clenched so tightly in her lap that the knuckles shone white. 'Fergus was grossly irresponsible in taking you and Aileen with him – and you were equally irresponsible in going.'

'I'm sorry, Mummy.' Then, well aware that even if she had known the outcome in advance, she would still have gone, she changed the subject. 'Are you going to take me home now?'

'Home?' Delia put a line beneath the crossness she felt. 'They may have said you had a sore head, honey, but it's a *very* sore head. Can't you feel how tightly it's bandaged? There's no way you're goin' to be comin' home for another two or three days.'

Davina didn't protest. Men's Surgical was probably only a short walk down a hospital corridor, and as soon as she was able to do it, it was a walk she was going to take.

It was the next day before she was able to walk without feeling sickeningly dizzy. On the pretext of leaving her bed in order to have a bath, she left the ward and, in her nightdress and dressing gown, made her way to the Men's Surgical ward.

Before she reached the ward itself a nurse hurried up to her.

'I'm afraid this is a men's ward, miss. You've got terribly lost. Would you like me to get someone to escort you back to your own ward?'

Davina was about to shake her head but then, remembering her still massive headache, said, 'No. And I'm not lost. A friend of mine, Dr Fergus Sinclair, is a patient on this ward. I know he isn't allowed any visitors other than his wife, but I'd like to know how he is doing and I was hoping to have a word or two with Mrs Sinclair.'

The nurse eyed her doubtfully. 'Dr Sinclair is still very poorly, but if you'd like to take a seat in the waiting room, I'll tell Mrs Sinclair where you are.'

'Thank you.' There was nothing Davina wanted more than to be able to sit down. The effort it had taken to walk the short distance from her own bed had left her feeling not only dizzy, but profoundly sick.

The waiting room was blessedly empty and she sat down gingerly on a slippery-looking leather chair and took deep breaths to fight off her nausea.

As it began to recede, Aileen opened the waiting-room door. Her square-jawed face was ashen with anxiety and there were blue circles beneath her eyes. She looked like a woman who had forgotten what sleep was.

Davina started to rise to her feet, but Aileen forestalled her.

'Don't get up, Davina,' she said, her voice breaking. Then, as if her legs would hold her upright no longer, she collapsed on the chair next to Davina's and took tight hold of her hand. 'Fergus has broken his back,' she said starkly. 'It's going to be months and months – perhaps a year – before he'll be able to walk again. They are going to do the bone grafts here and then, as soon as he can be moved by ambulance, they are going to transfer him to a hospital near our home in Caithness. He'll be in traction then to allow the bones to align properly as they heal.'

Davina closed her eyes for a moment, trying to take it all in. Fergus wasn't going to be paralysed. That was the main thing. It was the end, though, of his work in Whitechapel. And it would mean the shelving of all Aileen's plans for a clinic giving women free contraceptive advice.

As if reading her thoughts, Aileen said, 'When Fergus is recovered – and no matter how long that takes – we'll come back to Toynbee Hall, Davina. And there will be a free clinic for the women of

Whitechapel. It is just not going to be this year, that is all.'

Davina squeezed her hand, knowing that no matter when it was, her mother would still be a staunch financial supporter of it.

Aileen said quietly, 'I have some other news, Davina, and this time it's good.' Despite her exhaustion and her anxiety for Fergus, she smiled. 'I'm pregnant. I've known for two weeks. Fergus doesn't know yet. I was going to tell him on our wedding anniversary at the end of the month, but now I'm going to tell him just as soon as he's well enough to appreciate the news.'

'Aileen is having a baby? But that's wonderful, honey.' Delia's face lit up. 'It will give both of them something to look forward to during the long months of Fergus's recovery.'

Davina had broken the news when her mother was in Cadogan Square's high-walled rear garden, having afternoon tea *al fresco* with Wallis Simpson.

'Is Aileen the friend you introduced me to at the cocktail party?' Wallis asked. 'The young woman married to the doctor?'

Davina nodded.

Her mother waved a hand in the direction of a cane chair, indicating that she should join them, saying to Wallis, 'Dr Sinclair had a ghastly accident and broke his back. He's going to be able to walk again, but it will be a long time before he does. Now do tell me how your refurbishing of Fort Belvedere is going on. Are you meeting with lots of objections?'

'Not from David. He's given me a free hand.'

Wallis, bandbox-smart in a navy dress edged in white, flashed Delia a broad smile. 'And I just love re-fixing furniture, and decor. Lady Mendl is giving me a hand. We spent the whole of last week pulling up carpets, taking down curtains and sending the furniture that no longer goes with the Fort's new look into storage. There isn't one room that looks as it did in Freda Dudley Ward's time.'

'Or Thelma Furness's?' Delia asked naughtily.

Wallis's smile broadened. 'Or Thelma's. That gal really did have appalling taste, Delia. Her bedroom at the Fort was done in the most frightful shade of pink and the bedposts were decorated with Prince of Wales feathers!'

As her mother and Wallis shook with laughter, Davina, who wasn't remotely interested in how the Prince of Wales's favourite home was decorated, ignored the vacant chair.

'I won't join you, if you don't mind,' she said to her mother. 'I haven't seen Fawzia for ages and it's about time I did.'

'Then you'd better do it fast, Davina. She's going on a river cruise with Jack this afternoon. He'll be here at any moment.'

'Is Aunt Gwen going with them?'

'I don't think so.' Her mother avoided looking her in the eye. 'I don't think Gwen likes water.'

Davina pursed her lips disapprovingly, well aware of what Zubair Pasha's thoughts would be about such an arrangement, knowing he had been right in thinking that, where chaperoning skills were concerned, Delia's left much to be desired.

For the next few weeks Davina visited the hospital daily. Whenever she could, she persuaded Aileen to leave the hospital for a little while for a short walk to a café for elevenses or lunch.

'Fergus is going to be transferred to Inverness soon,' Aileen said as they sat having tea and sticky buns in the café around the corner from the hospital. 'I can't wait for him to be somewhere his parents can visit him, but I shall miss you, Davina.'

'I shall miss you, too,' Davina said sincerely. 'It will mean I'll see more of Fawzia – I have a guilty conscience where she is concerned – but Fawzia and I don't have much in common any more. All she can think about is attending high-society events and being the exotic centre of attention at parties and balls. When you and Fergus go to Scotland, I'm not going to stay in London. Even though the season isn't quite at an end, I'm going to return to Cairo. My mother will be disappointed but I don't think she'll raise any objections. She knows by now that the battle to turn me into a debutante has been lost.'

It turned out her mother was more than disappointed; she was seriously cross.

'It just isn't fair to Fawzia,' Delia said 'She is having a whale of a time and yanking her back to Cairo before the season is finished is nothing short of cruelty.'

'She doesn't have to come with me. She can stay in London, with you, and the two of you can travel out to Cairo together in a few weeks. I can go to Cairo alone.'

Her mother was about to leave the house to have dinner at Quaglino's with friends and, taking a leaf out of Wallis's book, was dressed with stunning severity in a narrow, backless sheath of black crêpe, with long sleeves and a high neck. The arrow-straight skirt skimmed high-heeled black suede shoes and her fiery red hair blazed like a candle flame.

She picked up her slim evening bag and said, 'No, Davina. You can't. You're only eighteen.'

Davina shook her head in disbelief. 'Of course I can. You were married when you were my age. And even before then you used to ride for miles and miles in the Blue Mountains, unaccompanied. All I shall be doing is catching a couple of trains and a boat. I have Chandler blood, remember? I'm quite capable of doing things without having to have someone watching over me.'

'Sweetheart, I've been all afternoon at Fort Belvedere watching the Prince of Wales – who will one day be King of Great Britain, Ireland, all British dominions overseas and Emperor of India – fetching and carrying for Wallis as if he were a slave and she were the Queen of Sheba. Where that relationship is going, heaven only knows and I'm beginning to have great concerns about it. What I don't need is to be concerned about you as well.'

She turned to pick up her chinchilla stole, revealing a supple, flawlessly creamy back.

'You don't need to be concerned about me.' Davina's voice was one of sweet reason. 'All you have to do is give me a kiss, send me on my way and tell me that you'll see me in Cairo in a month's time.'

'Land sakes, you really are the most exasperating child! All right, go back to Cairo by yourself – and don't blame me if you fall into the hands of white slavers!'

'I won't,' Davina said, loving her mother so much that it hurt, 'but white slavers aren't very likely. Daddy has already agreed to my plans and has bought me the tickets and I don't think white slavers travel first class.'

Four days later, when her train from Alexandria steamed into Cairo's chaotic main railway station, Darius was at the barrier waiting to greet her.

'How did you know I was coming back and what train I would be on?' she asked, tingling with pleasure as he took her small suitcase, from her hand.

'Petra told me. We don't usually converse or socialize, but she kindly made an exception in order that I would be here for you. She can't be. She's at Abdin Palace with Sir Miles. He's having a meeting with King Fuad. I don't think your sister is Lampson's official secretary yet, but she might as well be. Is that a bruise on your head? Have you had a bad fall?'

'Yes, but only after I was hit with a flying object.'

He quirked an eyebrow, but said nothing. She didn't mind. She wasn't ready yet to launch into explanations of what had happened at Olympia.

As she so obviously didn't want to talk about her head injury he said non-controversially, 'What are you going to do now you're home?'

'I'm going to spend as much time as possible in Bayram el Tonsi Street,' she said, checking that the horse pulling the gharry they had chosen showed no sign of ill-treatment.

'That's where the Old War Horse Memorial Hospital is, right?'

She nodded. 'And I'm going to approach the Anglo-American Hospital and see if they'll take me as a student nurse.'

He helped her into the gharry, saying to the driver. 'Garden City, *minfadlak*.'

He was wearing dark glasses and a white linen suit that looked as if it had been tailored in London. A group of heavily veiled young women stopped and stared at them.

Davina didn't blame them. Where looks were concerned, Darius was film-star class.

As they moved out into a tumultuous stream of cars, buses, bicycles and donkey carts, she leaned back against the cracked leather seat. In a little while she would tell Darius all about Toynbee Hall and the Sinclairs and Sir Oswald Mosley. For now, though, she just wanted to relish her happiness. The heat was overpowering, but she didn't care. Heat meant that she was in Cairo again, and being in Cairo meant that she was home.

EIGHTEEN

'And so it was hideous, Petra. The most hideous thing you can possibly imagine.' The two of them were seated in cane chairs on the lushly watered lawn of Nile House. Near by, the donkey Davina

328

had rescued munched happily on alfalfa grass. Thirty yards or so away, beyond a shelving stone embankment, the Nile flowed glitteringly past the foot of the garden, thick with white-sailed feluccas. Davina gazed unseeingly at them. 'All Aileen and I heard was glass shattering, and then as we struggled to get to Fergus I was hit on the head and went down like a ton of bricks.'

Petra adjusted her large, wavy-brimmed sun hat so that her face was in a little more shade. 'From the sound of it you were lucky not to have had your skull fractured.'

'And Fergus was lucky he wasn't killed.'

Their drinks were on a small table positioned between them and Petra reached for her glass of Tom Collins. 'How were things in London when you left?' she asked, stirring the ice cubes around with a straw. 'Did you see much of Jack while you were there?'

Her voice, as always when she spoke of Jack, was queerly abrupt and, again as always when speaking of him, her eyes didn't meet Davina's. Instead she looked with studied intensity across the Nile towards the hazy outline of the pyramids ten miles away.

'I didn't, though I would have liked to. All my time was spent in Whitechapel. I did see Uncle Jerome a few times. Since meeting Fergus he's become even more involved with Toynbee Hall than he already was. He's helping to set up a council of East End citizens, the aim being that they will take whatever action is necessary to try to put an end to the present street violence. The Archbishop of Canterbury is to be the council's President.'

A shutter came down over Petra's face at the mention of Jerome's name and thinking that it was because Petra was tired of hearing about London's East End, Davina said, 'What is the situation here, at the Palace? Why was Sir Miles Lampson meeting with the King?'

'Oh, the usual.' Petra stopped stirring the ice cubes. She popped a maraschino cherry into her mouth and Davina couldn't help noticing that it was the exact same colour as her vibrant-red lipstick and nail varnish. 'Street violence here never completely comes to an end, Davvy. The King took away Parliament's full constitutional rights ages ago – it now operates only in an advisory capacity – and the WAFD party is agitating for Parliament to have full constitutional power again.'

'And Farouk? Is he as exasperating as ever?'

Petra pulled white-framed sunglasses down her nose and looked at Davina over the top of them. 'Farouk,' she said, 'has the attention span of a gnat.'

Davina giggled.

Looking towards the donkey as it began a gentle ramble across the lawn, Petra took a sip of her drink and then said, 'What about Fawzia? We haven't talked about *her*. Is she enjoying playing the part of a debutante? According to Delia's letters she's received lots of proposals.'

'She's received shoals of them. Not, though, from the person she might well have accepted.'

'And who was that?' There was amusement in Petra's voice. 'The heir to a dukedom?'

'No.' Davina hesitated and then, aware that Petra had shown ages ago that she no longer had

330

the slightest romantic interest in Jack, said, 'The person she spent most time with was Jack.'

To her horror, Petra sucked in her breath and then let it out very slowly.

Terrified she had made a severe miscalculation, Davina said anxiously, 'It doesn't matter to you, does it, Petra? I mean, it was you who did the chucking, wasn't it?'

'Oh, yes. Most definitely. And of course it doesn't matter to me.' Petra shot her a bright, brittle smile, but there was no longer any amusement in her voice. 'If you don't mind I'm going to find some shade. The sun is giving me a headache. It's good to have you back, Davvy. I did tell you that, didn't I?'

As she watched Petra walk back to the house Davina was both surprised and touched at how much Petra had obviously missed her. And though Darius hadn't said so when he met her at the station, she was hoping he, also, had missed her very much.

'D'you fancy a ride out beyond the pyramids?' Darius said, standing with one foot on the first of the wide shallow steps fronting Nile House.

He was dressed in jodhpurs and boots, his white shirt open at the throat. Behind him, parked in the gravelled driveway, was a low-slung cream sports car. Wryly Davina noted that it wasn't a British car, but a German Mercedes-Benz.

'I thought it would give us a chance to catch up on things,' he added, making no attempt to mount the steps.

'Give me five minutes,' she said, her smile

331

radiant, 'and I'll be right with you.'

She didn't suggest that while she changed into riding clothes he should come inside to wait for her. The House had been a second home to Fawzia and Darius for over ten years, just as their mansion had been a second home to her and Petra. That for the last couple of years Darius had chosen never to enter it, regarding it as though it were part of an enemy camp, was something she had long learned to accept.

Ten minutes later, in a caramel-coloured silk shirt, jodhpurs and riding boots, her shoulder-length hair braided into a fat pigtail, she ran down the steps and across to the car.

'Why a German car?' she asked as she slid onto the cream leather seat beside him. 'Is it another one of your too-subtle-for-most-people-to-understand anti-British statements?'

'Yes, it's an anti-British statement.' He put the car into gear. 'But what do you mean about people not understanding them?'

His face was unsmiling, but then it nearly always was.

She knew him too well to mind.

'Well, it's like your never coming into the house,' she said as he drove towards the Kasr el Nil Bridge. 'I know why you don't any more, but I doubt if anyone else has even noticed. And you can't expect them to, not when you still go to the Sporting Club and other British hang-outs, such as the Turf Club and Shepheard's.'

'I go to those places because I am Egyptian and the vast bulk of Egyptians cannot.'

'But who knows that is why you do it? No one

knows apart from yourself – and me,' she added, aware that she as the only person he ever revealed his inner thoughts and feelings to.

He swerved to avoid a group of black-garbed women carrying large baskets on their heads.

'People are going to know soon enough.' His voice was harsh. 'I've had enough of WAFD's hope for change through political negotiation. The only way Egypt is going to free itself of the British is by taking far more extreme measures. And, together with people who feel like me, I'll soon be doing so.'

The car swooped up onto the bridge and a breeze from the river fanned her face.

She looked across at him. His jaw was clenched so tightly a nerve had begun to pulse at the corner of it.

Stifling her growing anxiety she said in a voice of sweet reason, 'Your father is one of King Fuad's key ministers. If you came out into the open as a revolutionary he would disown you. He'd have no choice.'

'And d'you think I'd care?' A lock of night-black hair fell over his forehead as he swung his head towards her. 'D'you know how long it is since Britain first promised to get out of Egypt? They promised to get out in 1883 – *1883!* And you're still here!'

'I won't be for much longer if you don't keep your eyes on the road. Mind the bullock cart, Darius. You're going to clip its load.'

Driving with only one hand on the wheel, he swerved past it.

'And it isn't only you British who have to go,'

he said, speeding off the bridge and onto the straight dusty road leading to Giza. 'Fuad and Abed al-Fattah Yahya Pasha have to go too.'

Abed al-Fattah Yahya Pasha was the Prime Minister and, having been appointed to office only recently, was not a man Davina knew much about.

As if she had asked about him Darius said, almost spitting the words, 'He's a Whitehall puppet. He and the King both dance to the British government's tune. And your High Commissioner, who reminds me very strongly of your father, does exactly the same.'

Davina remained silent. She'd briefly met Sir Miles Lampson, the High Commissioner, when he had visited Nile House, and she thought Darius rather astute in thinking him similar to her father in looks and personality. 'Lampson's going to be far more heavy-handed than his predecessor on anti-British student demonstrators,' her father had said after the limousine, bearing a fluttering Union Jack on its bonnet, had borne Sir Miles back to the Residency.

It wasn't a snippet of gossip she felt inclined to share with Darius when he was in such a fiercely anti-British mood. Neither did she think it wise to ask him what he intended doing for polo ponies and sports cars if his father were to disown him.

The road was now flanked on either side by fields of alfalfa and maize. They made a brilliant chequerboard of green and gold, interspersed occasionally by narrow irrigation channels and date palms. As she looked out at them, her arm resting on the top of the car's low-slung door,

Davina was both deeply sympathetic with his anger and impatience over Britain's refusal to give Egypt unconditional independence, and profoundly worried as to where his anger and frustration might lead him.

If he became involved in acts of terrorism his father would disown him. Her own father – if he were to know of it – would personally ensure that Darius was arrested and served a cripplingly long jail sentence. His career as an up-and-coming lawyer in one of the city's most prestigious law firms, would be at an end. Yet he was right in thinking that Britain had no intention of granting the country unconditional independence.

'The Foreign Office doesn't think the time is right for Egyptian independence,' her father had said when she had questioned him about it. 'Which isn't surprising, as Egypt is incapable of governing itself without British help.'

If that was what her very fair and just father thought, she knew there was no chance at all of anyone else in the British government hierarchy thinking any differently.

'Not one British minister would take the slightest interest in Egypt if it weren't for the Suez Canal,' Darius said, breaking in on her thoughts. 'Sometimes I wish the bloody thing had never been built!'

He swerved through the gates of the Mena House Hotel from where the stables were within easy walking distance. Once he was out of the car, his mood changed.

'D'you fancy riding to the Step Pyramid?' he asked. 'On the off-chance of you saying yes I've brought fruit and water with me.'

The Step Pyramid of Zoser, at Saqqarah, was ten miles south of the Giza pyramids and was where he had taken her on their very first ride together.

'As long as there's no chance of a dust storm,' she said equably.

'No chance at all. It's the wrong time of year.'

As they walked into the stables, he said, 'You haven't talked about London. What did you do there?'

'I met two of the nicest people in the world. People I will be friends with for the rest of my life.'

And when they rode into the vast expanse of the shimmering desert she told him all about Toynbee Hall, Sir Oswald Mosley's nightmare rally at Olympia, and the Sinclairs.

For the next year Davina spent most of her time at the newly opened Old War Horse Memorial Hospital in Bayram el Tonsi Street, and when she wasn't at the hospital she was out in the streets with another voluntary worker, buying broken-down horses so that they would spend their last days being lovingly cared for.

'The cruelty isn't always maliciously intended,' one of the senior volunteers said to her. 'You have to remember that an ex-cavalry horse needs far more food than a donkey or a mule and that their owners are so poor they aren't even able to adequately feed their children. Another thing to take into account is that the owners often don't realize that animals feel pain. Education is as important a part of our programme as veterinary care.'

She did her best to educate her friends.

'Never use a gharry when the horse looks half dead,' she said fiercely to all of them. 'Never ask a gharry-driver to hurry, no matter how late you may be. The horse will only get whipped. Never ever tip anyone who constantly whips or wears out his horse and never, *never*, travel more than four to a cab. The weight is just too much for the horse.'

Before long even her mother's acquaintances were paying attention to the condition of the gharry horses and Davina remembered Fergus telling her that to effect social change, education was essential.

Just before Christmas she was accepted as a trainee nurse at the city's Anglo-American Hospital. 'Though I don't start until the new year,' she said to her mother. 'And do please try to look a little happier about it.'

Her irritation more pretend than real, Delia said, 'I'd be even more pleased if you were engaged to marry one of your father's friends' sons – or any of the highly eligible young men you met when in London. Twice your father has gone to the extravagance of putting his daughters through a London season, the only result being that one of them is a glorified secretary and the other is about to spend her time emptying bedpans all day.'

'All that matters is that we're happy. Or at least *I'm* happy,' she said, not at all sure that Petra was.

Her mother made a sound that could have meant anything and continued with the letter she was writing to Wallis Simpson.

NINETEEN

At the end of January 1936, just after her mother had returned to London for three months, King George died peacefully at Sandringham, and a spate of anti-British demonstrations rocked Cairo.

'There was a running battle between students and police in Ezbekiya Gardens,' her father said when he came home on the evening of the largest demonstration. 'Twenty youths have been arrested. All university students. All young hotheads.'

An hour or so later, a deeply anxious Adjo asked Davina if he could have a word with her.

'I was there when the trouble started, Missy Davina,' he said, keeping his voice so low it was almost a whisper. 'There were young men all around the edge of the Gardens orchestrating what was happening. And one of the leaders of the demonstration was Zubair Pasha's son.'

'Darius?'

He nodded, and something small and tight turned over in the pit of her stomach.

'You could have made a mistake, Adjo,' she said. 'There were a lot of people and it must have been chaotic...'

Adjo shook his shiny bald head firmly. 'It was Darius, Missy Davina. I have known him since he was a small child. I could not possibly make a mistake about such a thing.'

'Then I think it best that no one else is told, Adjo. It would cause great trouble and great distress to Zubair Pasha. Darius could be arrested. He might even go to jail. And the students were just expressing what many Egyptians feel.'

'It is not a good way to express what we feel, Missy Davina.' Adjo's ebony face was grave. 'People could have been hurt. The police could have started shooting.'

'But they didn't.' Her mouth was dry, her heart hammering. 'I'll speak to Darius. I'm sure it won't happen again, Adjo.'

Three days later she did speak to Darius, and he told her that it would most certainly happen again; that demonstrating in such a way was his democratic right.

Davina wrote to Aileen:

If Darius was in love with me there's a chance he would listen when I tell him that being a member of WAFD is one thing and involving himself in acts of violence is quite another. Not being his girlfriend, I simply don't have that kind of influence.

In her reply Aileen asked:

Who is his girlfriend? From everything you've told me about him, there must be one. He doesn't sound the sort of man to live like a monk.

Davina wrote back, hardly able to believe the pain it cost her to face up to such a reality:

You are right to think Darius does not live like a

monk. He dates lots of girls and they are nearly always members of what is referred to in Cairo as the 'fishing fleet'. Debs who come out from England in the hope of snaring a wealthy suitor. They are always glamorous and sophisticated, and I'm not. Much as I'd like things to change I don't think they are going to. And as I've no desire to date anyone else, it looks as if I'm on the road to becoming an old maid.

Davina was also in constant touch with her mother and, now that David was King, the main topic of her letters was his love affair with Wallis.

At the end of February her mother wrote:

Things are moving ahead fast. Gossip is rife within the Palace circle. The King now never holds a party without Wallis acting as his hostess. She's such a straightforward kind of gal she doesn't realize the animosity this kind of preferential treatment arouses. And if the King realizes, he obviously thinks it's of no importance. As far as he is concerned, Wallis is his sun, moon and stars.

'I really cannot understand your mother sharing such salacious tittle-tattle with you,' her father said when he'd asked Davina what her mother's news was and she told him. 'She seems to forget you're still only twenty.'

'Lots of girls are married at twenty.'

He was seated in a leather wing-back chair in his study and she was perched companionably on one of its arms. It was late evening and she had come into his study to say goodnight to him.

'Well, I'm glad you're not. I don't want to lose

340

either you or Petra for a year or so yet.'

'That's not the impression Mummy gives. She seems to think that not ending our season with a wonderfully suitable engagement was a crushing disappointment to you.'

He chuckled. 'No, she doesn't. Not really. She just wants to keep abreast with her London friends and, as their daughters are all snapping up husbands, she wants you two to do so as well. And of course, as she's now spending so much more time in London, she'd like it if you and Petra were living in London – or in reach of London – as well.'

'It's you she wants living back in London, Papa. She told Petra she thought that might be happening last year and yet here you are, still in Cairo.'

'Yes ... and the odd thing is, after years of simply enduring being here and looking forward to being recalled to London, I now no longer want to leave Egypt. So many of my best friends in London are now dead – George Curzon, Herbert Asquith, Cuthbert Digby. And your mother has a whole new circle of friends all her own age. I can't quite see me fitting into King Edward's playboy set, can you?'

She slid her arm around his shoulders and dropped a kiss on the top of his head. His hair had receded at the temples and was rapidly thinning, but it was still the same pale gold colour as her own.

'No,' she said with a giggle, 'but not all your closest friends are dead. Uncle Jerome certainly isn't. He's very much alive and kicking.'

341

'Jerome?' He looked startled, as if the thought of Jerome being in London hadn't even occurred to him. After a moment's pause, he said, 'Jerome is actually far more your mother's friend than mine, Davina. He's a good bit younger than me, you know.' He frowned, deep in thought, and then he said: 'I feel sorry for him. If it hadn't been for his acting gallantly over his divorce, taking all the blame for it and so on, he would be in the Cabinet. Instead, he's languishing on the back benches, and lucky to be even there.'

Since marrying Theo and becoming a duchess, Sylvia's name had never been mentioned at Nile House. Remembering the sight of Sylvia at Olympia, it was something Davina was grateful for.

The doorbell rang and moments later Adjo entered the study to say that the visitor was Kate Gunn.

'Ah, yes.' Ivor rose to his feet. 'I was expecting her. Please send her in, Adjo.'

To Davina, he said, 'I have a report that needs typing up pretty urgently and Kate will make short work of it.'

She nodded, well aware of how reliant on Kate he had become. Sometimes she wondered if he hadn't become a little too reliant on her. Nearly everywhere he went, Kate went with him.

'If Delia doesn't mind, I don't see why you should,' Petra said dismissively when she had voiced her concern. 'And our mother is very, very fond of Kate. She's become family.'

It was true, especially as she had been part of their lives since they were small children.

All the same, as Davina left the study to go to her

342

own room, she couldn't help but wonder if Kate was also one of the reasons why her father no longer had any desire to leave Cairo for London.

A week later Davina received another letter from Aileen. She had got into the habit of always reading Aileen's letters in her favourite spot in all of Cairo, the belvedere in the Citadel, near to the Mohammed Ali Mosque.

Up there, at the highest point overlooking the city, there was nearly always a light breeze and it was possible to sit on the edge of the terrace and see right across Cairo to the pyramids at Giza and the seemingly endless desert beyond.

Saving up the pleasure she knew the letter would give her, she entered the Citadel through the Bab al-Gabal gateway and walked past the Mosque's arcaded courtyard to the low wall edging the terrace.

Though this was the heart of Islamic Cairo, there was always a sprinkling of Europeans eager to have their photograph taken against the backdrop of the magnificent view and today was no exception. Giving them a wide berth she walked to a quiet part of the terrace and sat down on the wall.

To the left of her was the Mosque, its huge dome covered in shimmering silver-coloured lead; its walls glittering with alabaster; its slender minarets piercing the brassy blue bowl of the sky. To the right of her the Citadel's ramparts fell away with dizzying steepness, affording a view she loved more than any other.

Cairo in all its turbulent, noisy density lay

spread out before her. Amid the jumble of narrow streets and bazaars she could see the roof of the orphanage where she had done so much voluntary work and, further away, the roofs of the Coptic churches of Babylon. Everywhere else there was a sea of domes and minarets spreading down to the broad glitter of the Nile. Though the heat haze was heavy she could see Garden City, the Kasr el Nil Bridge and Gezira Island. Most wonderful of all was the sight of Giza's three pyramids in the far distance. The most substantial, enduring monuments of all time, they looked ethereally insubstantial in the heat haze, almost as if they were floating in the air.

She rested her eyes on them for a few moments and then withdrew the envelope from her pocket.

Dearest Davina,

Prepare yourself for a big surprise! The Free Clinic is finally up and running in Whitechapel! It's been a long haul and we wouldn't have achieved it without the financial support of your mother and her friends.

Having it as a goal has helped Fergus's recovery enormously. He still limps, but that he is walking at all is a miracle we are deeply grateful for.

My sad news is that my mother passed away a month ago. I'm so glad that before she died she was able to spend time with her only grandchild.

I've enclosed a photograph of Andrew – he's a toddler now and running about all over the place. He's an absolute delight – the light of my life.

Deeply happy for her friend Davina rested the letter on her knee, wishing that Cairo was closer

344

to Britain and that she could give Andrew a hug and a kiss; wondering if the day would ever come when she, too, would have a son.

Once Davina began nursing training, she continued to help out at Dorothy Brooke's Old War Horse Memorial Hospital in any spare time she had.

Her way of life and Petra's way of life were now so different that the two of them could have been living in different cities. When her day's work at the Residency was over, Petra's social life was a frenzied round of parties. Swimming parties at the Mena House Hotel followed by horse riding across the desert to the Saqqarah pyramid, dances at Shepheard's – tea dances as well as evening dances. She never missed a polo match at the Gezira Club and played tennis there several times week. When not at Mena House or Shepheard's or the Gezira Club she would be at a dinner party with her friends from the Residency and the up-and-coming young diplomats stationed in Cairo.

The titbits of gossip she brought back from such dinners were always political. In early summer she said with unusual seriousness, 'You really must end your friendship with Darius, Davvy. He no longer has any truck with WAFD. Not now it's semi respectable. Instead, he's become associated with an anti-British group that are little more than terrorists. Even Fawzia has given up on him.'

'I know.'

'How?' They were sharing a quick breakfast together and Petra stared at her, a slice of toast held high. 'You hardly ever see Fawzia these days.

345

You're always either at the hospital or at Bayram el Tonsi Street.'

'Jack mentioned it in his last letter to me.' She poured herself a glass of mango juice. 'And I know from Darius that he's no longer on speaking terms with his father.'

Petra put the slice of toast back down on her plate. 'How,' she asked again, but this time with a different expression in her voice, 'does Jack know that Fawzia now has next to nothing to do with Darius?'

'Because Fawzia writes to him. Not just occasionally, but all the time.'

The skin tightened over Petra's cheekbones. 'Oh!' she said, and then, ignoring her toast and not looking Davina in the eyes, she hastily pushed her chair away from the table. 'I must get off. I'm going to be late. Bye, Davvy.'

In February Petra began regularly mentioning the name of Sholto Monck, a diplomat only recently stationed in Cairo.

'He's Anglo-Irish. Very dishy. Very sophisticated. I rather like him, Davvy,' she said, looking happier and far less brittle than Davina had seen her for a long, long time.

In June, they were married.

The wedding took place in London, at St Margaret's.

Davina was a bridesmaid, as were Fawzia and Sholto's younger sister.

Though the Conisboroughs were short on close relatives, her father had done his best to see that their side of the church was impressively represented with distant family she and Petra had only ever heard about and never seen, and with an army of distinguished friends.

Walking down the aisle behind Petra, Davina recognized the short, aged figure of Lady Asquith, swathed in her perpetual black as if at a funeral, Winston Churchill and his wife, Clementine, Sir John Simon and – to her surprise – Wallis Simpson.

With difficulty she tore her eyes away from Wallis's beautifully dressed, almost boyish figure. From being a woman whom only a few royal insiders had heard of, Wallis had become a woman the whole of high society was now gossiping about.

'Which wouldn't be the case if King George hadn't died,' her mother had said. 'As it is, now that David is King, his affair with Wallis simply can't be hidden from public notice any longer. Or it could,' she had corrected herself, 'if it wasn't for David bringing it to public notice every chance he gets. Insisting she act as hostess at a dinner party at which the Prime Minister was a guest and which, having been an official function, was duly noted in the court circular, was sheer stupidity. Poor Wallis's nerves are in shreds. She doesn't particularly want to divorce Ernest – they've always been quietly if not passionately compatible and Wallis has the deepest affection and respect for him – but that is what the King is pushing her to do. And when *that* becomes public knowledge the gig really will be up!'

Aware that nearly as many pairs of eyes were on Wallis as were on the bride, Davina continued walking down the aisle behind Petra to the strains of Mendelssohn's Wedding March. In a pew second from the front on the left-hand side, was Jerome. In the front pew were her Aunt Gwen, Pugh, and her mother.

Whether her mother was already crying she couldn't tell, but she knew that before the service was over her mother would cry. She was far too emotional not to.

Her father and Petra were now at the foot of the altar. With Sholto on her right-hand side, his best man next to him, Petra took her hand from Ivor's arm and handed Davina her bouquet.

And then Sholto and Petra stepped up to the altar.

Remaining in the nave with Fawzia at her side and Sholto's sister a step or two behind her, Davina focused her thoughts on the man who, in another few minutes, would be her brother-in-law.

He wasn't the brother-in-law she had wanted to have. Seeing Jerome in a pew set aside for family and close family friends had only made Jack's absence more cruelly obvious.

'Of course I've invited him,' Petra had said tartly when Davina had enquired whether Jack would be at the wedding. 'But he can't come. He has another commitment.'

Davina hadn't pushed it, but she'd been quite sure that if Jack *had* been invited, it had only been with the knowledge that whatever the date of the wedding, Jack would have found himself with another commitment that he couldn't break.

'Dearly beloved,' the bishop intoned. 'We are

gathered together here in the sight of God, and in the face of this company, to join together this man and this woman in holy matrimony...'

From the back, Sholto looked unnervingly like her father, being tall – at least six foot three inches – and slenderly built. Their colouring, too, was similar. Like her father, he had fair hair, though not fair enough to be truly blond – and like her father's hair, Sholto's was glassily sleek and smooth. His eyes, though, were not grey. They were a quite startling blue. He had a wide, mobile mouth and the kind of charm that so often goes with being Irish.

It was a charm that had won her parents over instantly, but for some reason it hadn't won her over. There was something about him she couldn't put her finger on – something just a little too glib and a little too smooth. Petra, though, was obviously certain she had at last found the man she wanted to spend the rest of her life with, and so, for her sister's sake, she was determined to get along with him.

'...which is an honourable estate, instituted of God, signifying unto us the mystical union that is betwixt Christ and his Church...'

She looked across at Fawzia. Over the last few months Fawzia had shown a side to her character that had previously been well hidden. Always a docile daughter – any other kind would have been inconceivable to Zubair Pasha – she had recently begun to show that beneath her dazzlingly delicate beauty there was a streak of steel.

'I shan't be returning to Cairo after Petra's wedding,' she had said to Davina when they had gone together for the last fitting of their brides-maid's dresses. 'Your mother has said I can stay on as a guest at Cadogan Square for as long as I want. My father is livid, but I'm twenty-two. I've pleased him for long enough and now I'm going to please myself.'

'...which holy estate Christ adorned and beautified with his presence and first miracle that he wrought in Cana of Galilee, and is commended of St Paul to be honourable among all men and therefore is not by any to be entered into unadvisedly or lightly, but reverently, discreetly, advisedly, soberly, and in the fear of God...'

Though Fawzia hadn't mentioned Jack's name, Davina was certain that Fawzia's motive in remaining in London was so that she would be able to spend time with Jack. Davina wondered what would happen if Jack were to propose to Fawzia. As an Egyptian Copt, Zubair Pasha would want only an Egyptian Copt as a son-in-law. She suspected Fawzia would be quite uncaring of his wishes. Like Darius, she would do in life what she wanted to do, irrespective of the consequences.

'...Into this holy estate,' continued the bishop, breaking in on her thoughts, 'these two persons here present come now to be joined. If any man can show just cause why they may not lawfully be joined together, let him now speak, or else hereafter for ever hold his peace.'

In the silence that followed Davina half expected to hear Jack's voice speaking out from the rear of the nave. She noticed that Petra's shoulders, too, had tensed, as if she was half expecting the same thing.

Nothing happened.

Wherever Jack was, he wasn't in St Margaret's, Westminster.

A few feet in front of her the bishop joined Petra's and Sholto's right hands together, saying, 'Those whom God hath joined together let no man put asunder.'

It was over and Petra was Mrs Sholto Monck.

A month later another romance began causing a furore that would soon rock not only family and friends, but also the nation. Delia wrote to Davina to say that the King's affair was becoming public knowledge.

Wallis has begun divorce proceedings against Ernest, and David – though I must stop referring to him as David now that he is King Edward – has chartered Lady Yule's yacht, the Nahlin, *and is taking her (Wallis, not Lady Yule!) on a Mediterranean cruise. They won't be on their own, of course, a whole coterie of friends is going with them – but I don't see how such a jaunt can be kept out of the newspapers.*

Thanks to self-imposed censorship by news-paper magnates loyal to the King it *was* kept out of the newspapers – but only out of British news-papers. American newspapers had a field day.

The passion of her mother's feelings showed in the flamboyance of her handwriting.

The American press are being absolute skunks. Instead of playing down the situation, they are play-ing it up with headlines such as WILL WALLIS BE

QUEEN?'Wallis is terrified that her relationship with the King is now endangering his position. Until now she's never really grasped just how taboo divorce is in royal circles and how utterly impossible it would be for the King to marry a woman who, in order to be able to marry him, will have been divorced not once, but twice.

She's written two letters trying to break things off with him – both of which he has ignored. What more the poor gal can do I really don't know. He's become totally dependent on her and is insistent that he is going to marry her no matter what the cost.

In October Davina learned that Wallis had been granted a divorce. Delia was distraught.

Which means that when it is made absolute in six months' time she will be free to marry and what will happen then is anyone's guess. Most of the people who professed to be Wallis's friends in the early days of her relationship with David, have distanced themselves from her – no doubt thinking it best to be critical in case he loses his throne over her and they have to be on the right side of Bertie. Though how brother Bertie will step into David's shoes I can't imagine. He doesn't have an ounce of David's charisma and the poor lamb can't utter two words without stuttering.

When, in December, the King abdicated and Bertie became king, announcing he would be known as King George VI, the family least surprised were the Conisboroughs.

In Cairo, too, a king was the talk of the day. King

352

Fuad had died in April 1936 and sixteen-year-old Farouk was the youngest king Egypt had known since the days of Ancient Egypt, when Tutankhamun had briefly reigned.

'Not that I think things will change much,' Darius said to Davina darkly and in a low voice when, fifteen months later, they attended Farouk's investiture. 'Even with the new treaty that's been signed granting Egypt independence – and it would never have been drawn up if it hadn't been for increased anti-British terrorist activity – the British still have control of the canal and British troops are still on Egyptian soil.'

The ceremony took place at Parliament, in the Hall of Deputies. In a green-velvet-draped box facing the Prime Minister's seat were the Queen Mother and other members of the royal family. Behind them were members of the court circle. Davina could see Zubair Pasha's distinctively stout figure quite clearly. Other rows were filled with members of both houses of Parliament and then came row after row of senior officials, Arab sheikhs and European dignitaries – including her parents and Sir Miles and Lady Lampson.

Those seated further back, as she and Darius were, were nearly all in blocks of seating given over either to Europeans, or to Egyptians and fellow Arabs.

By rights Darius and Davina shouldn't have been in close proximity to each other at all, but Darius had taken not the slightest notice of this segregation policy. The minute he had seen Davina he had made his way across to her, and the people seated next to her had simply had to squeeze up uncomfortably in order to give him room.

'He's young,' Davina whispered back as the gold crown that 3,300 years earlier had crowned Tutankhamun, was placed on Farouk's head. 'He's going to think and feel as you do, Darius. You'll get the kind of Egypt you want before very long.'

'Good,' he said, bending his head so close to hers that his lips brushed her ear. 'It's time Egypt changed, Davina. And it's time our relationship did as well.'

She gasped as the Iman placed the crown on Farouk's head, proclaiming, 'In Allah's name! Farouk, King of Egypt!'

'When we get out of here,' Darius said, his eyes holding hers, 'let's drive to Giza and ride into the desert.'

Even though there was a celebratory ball that night at the Palace, she didn't hesitate for a second.

'Yes,' she said, her heart hammering.

They left Garden City with champagne and a picnic of pitta, hummus and figs.

Getting out of Cairo wasn't easy. Thousands of people had flooded in from all over the country in order to be part of the general excitement and the streets and squares were jam-packed with flag-waving fellahin. Farouk's picture was in every window and fronted every balcony. Every so often the cry 'Long live the King!' would be taken up like a football chant by the surging crowds. The Kasr el Nil Bridge, usually choked with donkey carts and gharries, was filled with limousines and Cadillacs as guests invited to the ball began inching their way towards the Abdin Palace from palatial residences on Gezira Island.

By the time Darius's Mercedes-Benz swooped into Giza it was dusk and the pyramids were silhouetted against an orange-streaked lilac sky.

They parked at the Mena House Hotel, its gardens and balconies thronged with partygoers celebrating the new reign, and made straight for the stables.

Saqqarah and the Step Pyramid – and Davina knew they would be riding to nowhere else – was an hour's ride south and all the way, on their left-hand side, the Nile, engorged by the tropical rains of distant Ethiopia, was in full flood. As the spangling lilac dusk deepened rapidly to purple twilight and then to night, huge pools of water could be seen gleaming slickly black in the moonlight.

By the time the distinctive shape of the Step Pyramid loomed ahead of them in the star-studded darkness both they, and their Arabian horses, were wet with sweat. The complex around the pyramid, scattered with the ruins of tombs and shrines and courtyards, was blessedly empty and as Darius reined in and speedily dis-mounted, she reined in only feet behind him.

In seconds he was by her horse's side, his hands hot on her waist. Her hands went to his shoulders, and as she slid to the ground and he pulled her hard against him they went higher, up and around his neck.

'Why now?' she asked, her mouth a millimetre from his, a pulse beating wildly in her throat.

'Because it's time,' he said, and still holding her fast against him with one hand, he moved his other to the ribbon that held her hair from her face when she rode and pulled it free, sending her ivory-pale hair tumbling to her shoulders.

The blood surged through her body in a hot tide and then, as her horse moved restlessly behind her, his mouth came down on hers in swift, unfumbled contact.

It was a long, deep, sweet kiss, and when he finally raised his head from hers he said, still holding her close, 'Until now, you've been too young for what this kind of relationship between us is going to mean, Davina.'

'How can I have been too young?' she said unsteadily, so confounded with desire she could barely stand. 'I'm twenty-one. You could have kissed me years and years ago. You could have kissed me when I was seventeen.'

'No, I couldn't,' he said with a rare smile. 'When you were seventeen you were still wearing hairslides and short socks. Compared to other girls you've always been young for your age, Davina.'

'I haven't!' Davina felt a surge of indignation. Though it was hard to believe at such a magical moment she was, she knew, on the point of having an argument with him.

Realizing it, he said gently, 'Let's put a blanket on the sand and unpack the food and the champagne. And I'll explain just why our being in love would have been so difficult for you to handle a year or so ago – and will still be difficult for both of us to handle now.'

He took the blanket-roll off his horse and laid it beneath the black silhouette of a date palm. Then he set out the pitta and bowls of hummus and figs.

As he began pouring Heidsieck into the champagne flutes he had brought with him she sat on the blanket, a warm jacket around her shoulders, her legs curled beneath her.

'I chose my political course a long time ago, Davina,' he said, champagne fizzing over the top of the glass as he handed it to her. 'Because I'm so anti-British our friendship has always been disapproved of, but it's been tolerated by your family and the rest of the British community because of the respect your father, and my father, are held in. A full-blown love affair will be viewed very differently.'

'A full-blown love affair,' she said, her voice even more unsteady, 'is what I want.'

'It's what I want too.' At the blaze of passion in his eyes a tremor ran through her. 'Apart from your father's opposition – and make no mistake, Davina, his opposition is going to be fierce – there is also the opposition I shall meet with among my nationalist friends. And because I want to do something for my country, because I want to free it of British control and help make it a country that is strong and respected, my nationalist friends are important to me.'

'And with a British girlfriend you would lose all credibility with them?'

He shook his head. 'Not necessarily. Dating members of the "fishing fleet" is thought of as something of a joke – or at least it is among those

357

who are Coptic. But a British wife wouldn't be thought of as a joke.'

His eyes held hers intently.

She knew what he was waiting for. A sign that she was now mature enough to understand that nothing was going to be straightforward for them; that there would be no early engagement followed by a wedding acceptable to both their families and to both the Egyptian and British communities.

The moonlight fell across his handsome face, highlighting its harsh planes. She was aware, as never before, of the passionate intensity that was so much a part of his personality. Of his fierce intelligence. Of his utter commitment to the ideals he believed in. Of the sense of danger he carried with him.

She put her champagne glass down. 'I love you,' she said. 'I don't care what problems we face, Darius, just as long as we face them together.'

She saw the overwhelming relief in his eyes and realized with amazement that he hadn't been certain of what her response was going to be. Then as he also put his champagne glass down, the world tilted on its axis, and as he reached out for her with powerful, yet careful hands, she went down to him like wax, uncaring of everything but the knowledge that she was as central to his life as he was to hers – and that she had never been so happy in her life.

Shortly after Delia had left Cairo for London, Davina plucked up courage to tell her father about her new relationship with Darius.

'And so we're a couple now, not just best friends,' she told Ivor.

It was early evening and the two of them were in his study at Nile House. He had just come back from a meeting with Nahas Pasha, the new Prime Minister, and looked preoccupied, which was a pity, but couldn't be helped.

'Excuse me? *Excuse me?*' Ivor slapped a document he had brought home with him onto the corner of his desk and wheeled round to face her. 'Are you trying to tell me that you and one of the biggest political troublemakers Cairo has, are unofficially engaged?'

She had never seen him look quite so angry or so forbidding. Other people, often quite distinguished people, were, she knew, often intimidated by him, but neither she nor Petra had ever had any reason to be. As a father, he had never been overly affectionate, but he had always been approachable.

'Not exactly,' she said, wishing her mother was there to help her. 'I don't know when we can marry, but we are romantically involved. I thought it best for me to tell you so, before anyone else did.'

She had never seen her ice-cool, patrician-like father splutter, but he spluttered now. 'Romantically involved? *Romantically involved?* What, in the name of all that is holy, is that supposed to mean? Is his family aware of this "romantic involvement"? Can I expect Zubair Pasha to mention it to me when next we meet? It has to end, Davina. It has to end *now*. D'you understand? Darius is a dangerous young man. His politics

359

are dangerous and the ways he pursues them are dangerous.'

'You don't know that for certain,' she said, trying to sound reasonable and not provocative. 'Nearly everything that is said about Darius is rumour. There aren't any hard facts. If there were, he'd be in a British prison.'

'The only reason he's not in a British prison is because his father is so strongly pro-British! And as Britain needs every friend she can get in Farouk's court, Zubair Pasha isn't a man we would wish to offend by imprisoning his son – no matter how worthy of imprisonment he may be!'

He paced to the window.

'No more of this nonsense, Davina,' he said, struggling for control. 'I always felt it was a bad move allowing you to continue your friendship with Darius once it was obvious he was no friend to Britain. His politics have already caused his father great distress. Even Fawzia, I believe, has very little to do with him, and your continuing friendship with him is quite inappropriate.'

'Maybe so,' she said quietly, 'but it will continue, Daddy. And it will continue as a friendship that is also a romance. We are a couple and we intend to remain a couple.'

He paled. 'Then you had better make arrangements to live elsewhere, Davina. And that is my final word on the subject.'

It was her turn to look ashen. 'You're asking me to leave Nile House?'

'Only in order to bring you to your senses.'

'Under the circumstances I think you could be more understanding.'

'Circumstances? What circumstances?' He breathed in hard, his nostrils white.

'Kate Gunn,' she said.

And left the room.

'And I left the house as well,' she said the next day to Petra after she had rung her at work at the Residency and said she needed to have lunch with her. 'I've moved into the Nurses' Home. It will probably be quite jolly. The half-dozen girls I'm doing my training with all live in.'

Petra stared at her gentle-voiced, gentle-natured young sister. 'Are you telling me,' she said disbelievingly, 'that you and Darius are now red-hot lovers and that you had the nerve to tell Ivor so?'

'I didn't tell him that we were red-hot lovers,' Davina conceded. 'The expression I used was "romantically involved".'

'And Kate?' Petra asked, quirking a finely pencilled eyebrow. 'How long have you known about that little secret?'

They were on the terrace at Shepheard's, the position of their table giving a view of both the chaotically busy street below them and, at the side, the entrance to the hotel's Moorish Hall. The Hall, dimly lit by coloured glass, was a favourite masculine meeting place.

'I don't know,' Davina said slowly, looking towards the Hall and seeing several of their father's friends sitting around little octagonal tables, deep in conversation, drinks to hand. 'It didn't come as a sudden revelation. I just gradually realized the part she played in Daddy's life

361

and came to accept it.' She took a sip of her lime juice, and then said, 'Do you think Mummy knows it's an affair?'

'Oh, most definitely,' Petra said with the hardness that was so often in her voice when she spoke of their mother. She leaned back in her chair, her torrent of mahogany-red hair glinting and gleaming in the strong sunlight. 'Where Ivor and Kate are concerned there will never be a whisper of gossip – they are both too careful. You, however, are in a different position, Davvy. When news of you and Darius breaks, Cairo's crème de la crème will regard you as little more than an addition to the "fishing fleet".'

'They can regard me however they like,' Davina said with her usual quiet composure. 'I really don't care. All that matters to me is what my friends at the Anglo-American Hospital and the Old War Horse Memorial Hospital think of me. And as they are not interested in my personal life, their opinion of me won't change.'

Gossip among the British community about Davina's private life soon gave way to much more serious gossip as the war clouds that had been gathering in Europe for so long finally began impinging on Cairo. Everyone became aware that there suddenly seemed to be a far greater number of Germans in the city than there had been only months earlier. Farouk, it was claimed, rather liked them.

'Which could be a bit tricky if and when war is declared between Britain and Germany,' Sholto said languidly in Davina's hearing. 'The Anglo-

Egyptian Treaty of a year ago is pretty specific that if Britain declares war on a hostile nation, that declaration goes for Egypt as well – but if Farouk doesn't want to keep to that, it will be pretty hard to make him.'

As Christmas approached and Delia came out for her usual long stay over the holiday period, she brought news which she seemed to be both pleased about and yet very reluctant to break to Petra.

'But why?' Davina asked her, perplexed. 'It's four years since Petra ended her love affair with Jack and she's married to Sholto now. Why on earth do you think she will be distressed to learn Jack is to marry Fawzia? And why are they going to get married in London and not in Cairo? And why a Registry Office wedding?'

'I don't know why a Registry Office, darling, except that Fawzia is a Copt and Jack isn't, and that may have something to do with it. And I don't know why London, either, except that while Zubair Pasha likes Jack – and has enormous respect for Jerome – it probably isn't *quite* the marriage he would have wanted for his daughter. To be quite honest, like every other high-ranking Egyptian, he probably had hopes that she would catch Farouk's eye and become Queen of Egypt. Instead of which, Farouk is marrying Safinez Zulfiquar in January – though according to your father she won't be known as Queen Safinez, but as Queen Farida. Farouk has the same quirk about names beginning with "F" as his father. He believes it's lucky. Which means that if Fawzia had

363

remained in Cairo instead of making London her home, she might have had a chance.'

'She's too old. She's twenty-three. Farouk is still a month short of his eighteenth birthday and Safinez is just fifteen.'

'Sixteen,' her mother corrected.

'Fifteen,' Davina repeated. 'The official announcement that she is sixteen is only a sop to those who think fifteen a little too young.'

Her mother's presence in Cairo ensured that her father stiffly requested that Davina be at Nile House for the Christmas festivities. Knowing that he hated their estrangement just as much as she did, Davina did as he asked. He didn't invite Darius, but that hadn't mattered because if an invitation had been proffered, Darius wouldn't have accepted it.

At a Christmas Eve party at the American Legation, Davina saw the moment when her mother broke the news of Jack's impending wedding to Petra.

The great formal reception room was crowded and, perhaps out of deference to the Christmas spirit, Hitler's latest appalling antic – German parents having their children taken away if they didn't teach them Nazi ideology – wasn't dominating the conversation.

Petra was wearing a halter-necked backless gown of emerald-green lamé. Her thick mane of hair was coralled into a sleek chignon in the nape of her neck and her mouth was painted a vibrant, glossy scarlet. She had a glass of champagne in one hand and a jade cigarette-holder in the other. She was laughing at something someone had said to her and she looked sophisticated and *soignée* – and as if she was trying far too hard to enjoy herself.

It was an impression she had constantly given for years now – ever since she had returned to Cairo after her debutante season. It was as if she daren't stop partying and dashing from one social event to another; as if she would fall apart if she did.

Now, as their mother approached her, radiant in a mauve evening gown shimmering with crystal beads, Davina had a sense of deep foreboding. Perhaps her mother was right to be apprehensive about how Petra would take the news. Perhaps there was far more to Petra's break-up with Jack than she had realized.

She saw her mother touch Petra lightly beneath her elbow in order to gain her undivided attention. She saw Petra turn away from the people she had been talking to and flash their mother a wide smile. And she saw her mother begin to speak.

Petra's smile vanished.

The blood drained from her face.

The glass of champagne in her hand fell, spraying her gown and splintering into shards on the floor.

Neither of them took the slightest notice of the damage done to their gowns, or of the broken glass at their feet.

Other people did, though. Sholto, who had been at the far side of the room chatting with a young diplomat from the Argentine Legation, excused himself and began making his way towards her.

The American Minister hastened to her side.

And then, as Davina began crossing the room towards her, Petra turned on her heels and, ignoring everyone, ran from it.

It was an exit that Davina knew would be the talk of Cairo high society for weeks to come.

It was quite obvious that her mother was also well aware of this for she was saying loudly to those nearest to her, 'Poor gal. News of the death of a dear friend in London, I'm afraid. I chose a bad moment to break the news.'

Sholto, completely deceived, said merely, 'Then she probably wants to be alone for a while,' and made his way unhurriedly back to the Argentinian diplomat he had been in conversation with.

Her mother said in a low undertone, 'Please don't go after Petra, Davina. This is something she won't be able to talk about. Sholto is right. She'll want to be by herself for a while.'

Because Davina always trusted her mother's judgement she did as Delia asked, but it was hard – and it was even harder realizing that her mother knew something about Jack and Petra's break-up that she didn't.

Next morning, straight after breakfast, she left Nile House for the villa on Gezira Island that Petra and Sholto had lived in ever since their marriage.

Petra was sitting on the villa's terrace, an untouched breakfast on a cane table before her. She was still in her dressing gown and her hair was in unbrushed, careless disarray.

'Don't ask, Davvy,' she said wearily, raising a hand in a dismissive gesture before Davina even spoke to her. 'It was a bad time of the month. The news was unexpected and I reacted to it badly. The coffee is still hot. Why don't you have a cup and tell me what you are wearing to Farouk's wedding?'

As Petra so obviously didn't want to confide in her, Davina reluctantly went along with the abrupt change of subject; but she hated knowing there were secrets between them and desperately hoped that Petra would eventually open her heart to her.

She didn't do so.

Her extreme reaction to the news of Jack and Fawzia's wedding was something Petra never spoke about, but when Jack and Fawzia paid their summer visits to Cairo, she always behaved as though she was ecstatically happy for the two of them. Jack, too, seemed completely at ease. The only person who behaved with slight reservation was Sholto.

'And that's probably because he's jealous,' her father said when Davina mentioned it to him. 'Jack's been moved sideways into MI6. With war bound to break out at any moment, I rather think Sholto fancies himself as an Intelligence officer and doesn't like the fact that Jack has pipped him to it.'

Her father's prediction that war was not only in the offing, but imminent, proved to be only too correct. On 3 September Prime Minister Chamberlain announced in the House of Commons that, as from noon that day, Britain was at war with Germany.

'And Egypt?' Ivor said grimly. 'What about Egypt? Who is Egypt going to be at war with? Germany? Or us?'

PART FOUR

Darius

1940

TWENTY

Darius sat in the garden of Groppi's tea rooms. There were two Groppi's. The more famous one was on a corner of Soliman Pasha Square, but the Groppi's he preferred was in Sharia Adley Pasha, a little nearer to the Opera House. He liked its garden. It was small and intimate and never became as crowded as the Corner House Groppi's. White jasmine and purple bougainvillea climbed the trellised walls and for those sitting at the little tables there was always a feeling of secluded intimacy. He was early for his meeting, but he didn't mind. He had a lot to ponder and couldn't think of a better way of doing it than over thick Turkish coffee and pastries drizzled with rosewater and honey.

That Britain and Germany were now at war was a surprise to no one – nor was it too much of a surprise that the Egyptian government was, outwardly at least, complying with the terms of the Anglo-Egyptian 'Friendship and Alliance' Treaty. Martial law had been established. Known Nazis in the city – and there were a lot – had been interned in the Italian School in Alexandria. Other Germans had been interned in Cairo, rather appropriately in what had been the German school in the Bulaq district. Railways and aerodromes had been put at Britain's disposal. To all intents and purposes Egypt was keeping to the letter of the

Treaty. It was supporting Britain in the war it had declared on Germany and was cooperating fully. But Egypt had not declared war. And neither, Darius thought to himself grimly as he took a sip of the mint liqueur that had accompanied his coffee, would it.

He wondered if Sir Miles Lampson, no longer a High Commissioner but, since the signing of the Anglo-Egyptian Treaty, an Ambassador, was taken in by the dutiful actions taken by Ali Maher, the Prime Minister, and doubted it. Lampson was too smart not to realize Ali Maher would take for granted that his actions would, in Germany, be looked on as actions taken under British duress. Germany would be quite aware that Egypt would give no real help to a country it wished so heartily to be rid of.

He tasted coffee grounds in his mouth, pushed his cup away and ordered a refill from the waiter hovering near him. If Britain lost the war it had declared on Germany, then it would also lose its overseas imperial power – and that would mean the end of the British presence in Egypt. It was reason enough for not wanting to see Britain emerge victorious. Someone else who didn't want to see Britain emerge victorious was a Romanian he had become friendly with. Constantin Anton-escu was a diplomat at the Romanian Legation and it was Constantin who had arranged to meet him at Groppi's.

At a nearby table an elderly businessman in a tarboosh and Savile Row suit was sharing what Darius judged to be a few stolen moments with a beautiful Greek-looking girl young enough to be his granddaughter. At a table a little further away two Egyptian matriarchs were making great inroads into cream-filled cakes piled high on a glass cake stand. None of the four were paying him any attention – though he was sure the Greek-looking girl would have, under other circumstances – and he was certain that when Constantin arrived their conversation would be of no interest to anyone but themselves.

He looked at his watch, not because Constantin was late – he wasn't – but because he often looked at his watch in order to picture where Davina would be and what she would be doing. As it was now late afternoon and it was a Wednesday, he knew that she would be at the Old War Horse Memorial Hospital, putting skills she had learned as a nurse to veterinary use.

A shadow fell across the table. 'I see we have the garden more or less to ourselves,' Constantin said as the two matriarchs heaved themselves to their feet and, leaving an empty cake stand behind them, left the garden. He glanced over towards the besotted businessman and his companion, adding, 'I think we should have it completely to ourselves, though, before I begin telling you how I intend to help Germany win the war.'

That evening he and Davina went to the Continental Hotel for dinner. Opposite Ezbekiya Gardens, the Continental practically rubbed shoulders with Shepheard's. The Continental, however, boasted a rooftop restaurant with a small dance floor that they were particularly fond of.

As they walked through the crowded public

rooms they passed the entrance to the bar and there, in the centre of a noisy group of people and conspicuous by his height, Darius saw Sholto Monck.

He shot Davina a quick glance to see if she, too, had seen her brother-in-law. By the way she had stiffened and was very deliberately avoiding eye contact with Sholto, he guessed that she had.

'You don't like him, do you?' Darius said matter-of-factly as they took the caged lift to the restaurant.

'No. Not much.' As they stepped out of the lift, she added in explanation, 'He's not making Petra very happy.'

He left the subject alone until they were seated at a table near the dance floor and a bottle of Premier Krug was in an ice bucket beside them.

'Because of his drinking?' he then asked. 'Or because of his gambling?'

'I don't think she *likes* the fact that he spends more time propping up the bar in Shepheard's, or the bar downstairs, than he does with her, but his drinking is something Petra would take in her stride if everything else was all right between them.'

She didn't say anything about the gambling, but there was an unhappy frown on her face and he knew she was deciding whether to divulge something Petra would very probably rather he didn't know.

At last, toying with her champagne glass, she said, 'Sholto's background isn't all he's said it is and though Petra doesn't mind what background he comes from, she does mind his having lied about it. It's shaken her trust in him.'

'And in this background she didn't know about, was there another woman?'

'No. Sex doesn't come into it at all.'

She looked across to the small band. They were playing Cole Porter's 'Night and Day' but no one was dancing. It was too early.

Darius didn't say anything, just looked across at her.

Her fair hair was held away from her face with ivory combs, and fell in satin-smooth waves to her shoulders. Her evening dress was halter-necked, the shimmering material the same soft grey as her eyes. Her fingernails were painted silver and instead of her mouth being a fashionable crimson red, her lipstick was a pale rosy-pink. He thought she looked like an Ancient Egyptian moon goddess and it was a look that aroused him far more than Petra's more obvious glamour, or the hard sophistication of so many of the 'fishing fleet' girls.

Still looking towards the band, she said, 'Sholto lied to Petra – and to everyone else – about being Anglo-Irish. He isn't Anglo-Irish. He's simply Irish.'

'And there's a difference?'

'There is where class is concerned. The Anglo-Irish are the landed elite.'

'And so an Anglo-Irish son-in-law would have been acceptable to your father while a merely Irish one wouldn't have been?'

She nodded.

He gave a slight shrug of a white dinner-jacketed shoulder. 'Then it's quite obvious why

375

he practised a little deceit.'

'But not why he lied about it to Petra.' Davina took a sip of champagne and finally looked away from the band and towards him. 'It's also a question of money. Sholto always gave the impression that he had family money and that he would inherit considerably more, but in reality...' It was her turn to shrug a shoulder, but she didn't do it carelessly, as Darius had. She did it with deep unease. 'In reality there isn't any family to speak of and there isn't any money, though he behaves as if there were. Petra's terrified of what will happen when his bluff is called.'

'Your father will shore him up,' Darius said, rising to his feet and taking hold of her hand to lead her out onto the still empty dance floor. 'And I'm not surprised Petra is terrified. At the thought of breaking such news to your father, I would be too.'

After that evening's conversation Darius found himself watching Sholto Monck more closely, and on Constantin's advice he began to play down his fierce anti-Britishness.

'You have social access that very few Egyptians have,' said Constantin. 'It is something that could be very useful to your fellow nationalists. Think of it, Darius. In the home of a man such as Lord Conisborough you will be virtually at the heart of the British government in Cairo!'

Darius had seen the sense of the advice. Within a few months he managed to be on stiff social terms once again with Davina's father. Constantin's belief that Nile House was virtually the centre of British government in Cairo had, though, proved optimistic.

Although for many years Lord Conisborough had enjoyed the confidence of King Fuad, primarily as his advisor, his position had become defunct when Farouk became King. The sheer length of time that he had known Farouk – which was for most of Farouk's boyhood – ensured that for a while he continued to have a part to play at Abdin Palace, even though it amounted only to being a positive influence on Farouk where British interests were concerned. But the days when Farouk could be influenced by a man who had been his father's friend were long gone. Darius knew this from his own father, whose role at the Palace was now almost as defunct as Ivor Conisborough's.

'The problem is, he's too young for his position,' his father had said exasperatedly on one of the rare occasions when they had spoken together on almost friendly terms. 'He thinks more about his cars than he does about politics. Getting him to take the present situation seriously is almost impossible.'

Now in his late sixties, Ivor Conisborough had not been recalled to London and no longer held any high official position. He had not, though, done as everyone had expected him to do, and chosen to return to England.

'He's been in Cairo for so long that he can't bear the thought of re-acclimatizing himself to London,' Davina had explained. 'Most of his London friends are dead and when the Prime Minister let him know that there would be no wartime post for him he decided against returning. At least here, in Cairo, his long experience in Egyptian affairs makes him very useful to Sir Miles Lampson – so useful that he's been made an Honorary Attaché.'

He knew that she could also have added that her father would not have found it as easy to continue his relationship with Kate Gunn in London as in Cairo, but she hadn't mentioned Kate and he had resisted the temptation to do so.

Darius's visits to Nile House usually took place when he knew Lord Conisborough was elsewhere, and even then he always parked his distinctive Mercedes discreetly, a little way from the house. It was on one such visit, knowing that Ivor was to be at an official function, and he had arrived at the house in order to take Davina to the evening races at the Sporting Club, that he overheard her father in very intimate conversation...

Davina was still upstairs getting ready and he was enjoying a large gin and tonic in the drawing room. The spacious room faced the lawns and though its several pairs of French windows were open to the long wide terrace, he didn't hear Ivor's Rolls sweep up the front drive. What he did hear was Ivor's unmistakable cut-glass voice as, with a companion, and via the garden, he strolled around to the rear of the house and the terrace.

Darius drew in a deep breath of irritation, knowing exactly how unwelcome his presence was going to be. Determined not to be found looking awkward or embarrassed he sat down on a sofa and, one knee carelessly over the other, pretended to enjoy his drink.

Instead of entering the drawing room through the French windows, Ivor and his companion sat down in fantail chairs on the terrace.

'It's a shame your visit here is being kept to such a tight schedule,' he heard Ivor say. 'Petra and Davina would have loved to spend a little time with you.'

'I'll do my best to lunch with them at least once,' replied his companion, and Darius tensed in shock.

The voice was Jerome Bazeljette's.

'And so your brief from the Prime Minister is to assess Cairo's civilian wartime readiness, is it?' Ivor continued. 'Trust Chamberlain to be fussing about something so non-urgent.'

Jerome laughed in agreement and then said, 'Non-urgent or not, I was glad of the opportunity it's given me to speak to you face to face, Ivor. We have a problem, you and I, and it needs to be dealt with.'

He heard Ivor give a long, heavy sigh, as if well aware of what the problem was.

'You cannot allow Delia to remain on her own in London. The city is certain to be bombed,' Jerome said bluntly. 'Either you must return to London or, while there is still the means of doing so, Delia must join you here.'

'And is the problem that she doesn't want to come?'

Though he was yards away from them, Darius could sense Jerome Bazeljette's intense annoyance at Ivor not even discussing the possibility of his returning to London.

'Of course she doesn't want to come! Good

379

God, Ivor! If she comes we'll be separated for as long as this show lasts – and unlike the optimists in the Cabinet, I think it's going to go on a devil of a long time. And though I want to be separated from Delia as little as she wants to be separated from me, I want her to be safe – and she'll be far safer in Cairo than in London. Cairo isn't likely to be bombed.'

'It could fall into enemy hands. To the south of us is Ethiopia – part of the Italian empire. And the Italians are also to the west of us, in Libya. With Hitler and Mussolini hand in glove there's bound to be a build-up of German troops in both countries already.'

'Italy isn't as yet at war with us – and even if it were, any fighting would be hundreds of miles away, in the desert. Any real danger to Cairo and there would be a mass evacuation of British women and children to Palestine.'

Darius's head reeled: not at the speculation as to Cairo's safety as opposed to London's, but at the way the two men were talking about Delia Conisborough.

Ever since their trip together to Old Cairo he had maintained a distant, but quite definite, friendship with Delia. It wasn't a friendship he had ever discussed with Davina though she was aware that he liked her mother, and she was also aware that Delia was more than a little *simpatico* where his Egyptian nationalism was concerned.

Now he wondered how long she had been Sir Jerome Bazeljette's lover? And how long had Ivor Conisborough known that she was his friend's mistress? Did Petra and Davina know? Did Jack?

He hadn't seen much of Jack for years, but they had once been very good friends, albeit friends who had always tried to score points off each other. Did Jack know about his father's love affair with Delia?

'I need your help in persuading her to leave London,' Jerome was now saying. 'The two of you still have the kind of relationship where she takes great notice of your opinion and if you emphasized that she was *needed* here, it would probably do the trick. Winston is First Lord of the Admiralty again. There'd be no problem about her leaving England to join you.'

There was a short silence and then Ivor said gravely, 'Yes. You're right, Jerome. London is no place for Delia when any bombing raids that take place are bound to take place at night and she'd be on her own, apart from the staff. She must come here. Leave it with me. I'll make sure she does.'

Darius heard Jerome give a heartfelt sigh of relief and knew it was time to make an exit.

As quietly as possible he eased himself off the sofa and then, as he heard Ivor say, 'I think you'd better have a snifter before you hare off to the Embassy, Jerome. What is it to be? A brandy?' he walked soundlessly from the room.

Just as he reached the foot of the stairs Davina began coming down them. He instantly put his finger to his lips.

'Your father is home and on the terrace with a guest,' he mouthed to her, purposely not telling her who the guest was. 'Let's leave quietly and PDQ.'

She nodded and, slipping her hand into his,

allowed him to hurry her towards the front of the house and its main door.

A month later, two weeks after Jerome had returned to London, Delia arrived in Cairo – and she did not arrive alone.

'Good gracious! Fawzia is with her!' Davina exclaimed to Darius as the train from Alexandria steamed into Cairo's Central Station and she was the first to see the two figures leaning from an open window, both of them waving furiously with one hand as they held onto their wide-brimmed picture hats with the other.

She and Darius were not alone as a welcome committee. Lord Conisborough, Petra and Sholto were also with them, and Darius so wanted to see the way Ivor Conisborough greeted his wife that he barely reacted to the unexpected sight of his sister.

'Sorry you had to slum it on a troop train, sweetheart,' he heard Ivor say as Delia kissed him on the cheek while scores of soldiers streamed past them. 'Under the circumstances I expect your entire journey was ghastly.'

What Delia's response to this was he didn't hear as Fawzia had flung herself into his arms with a rare display of sisterly affection. He responded in kind, wondering if marriage had made Fawzia forget that they rarely had time for each other.

As he released his hold of her he saw the expression on Petra's face. It was an expression that when Fawzia turned towards her changed swiftly to one of delighted welcome, but he knew from that moment on that Petra was more appalled than pleased by his sister's return as Mrs Jack Bazeljette.

'Isn't this grand?' Delia said as, hemmed in by kitbag-carrying Tommies, they made their way down the platform. 'So nice to know you are doing well in your new law practice, Darius,' she said, referring to the fact of his growing professional reputation and flashing him her wide, beguiling smile.

'And what news of friends in London?' Ivor asked, returning her attention to himself. 'How is Margot Asquith? When Jerome was here he said she now went out very rarely.'

'She doesn't go out much, but I don't think she minds. Marie Belloc Lowndes keeps her company. They are both of an age – somewhere in their late seventies – and have been friends forever. They both have similar family concerns.'

'Which are?' Ivor asked as his chauffeured Rolls finally came into view.

'Anxiety about family abroad. Margot's daughter is in Romania. Her husband was the Romanian Ambassador in Paris until war broke out, and when he was recalled she went with him. Margot is terrified that she won't live long enough to ever see her again. As for Marie – all her family are in France and so she too worries constantly.'

As the chauffeur opened the rear door for them Ivor said smoothly, 'Fawzia is coming with us, and Petra and Sholto are following on. Davina and Darius have, I believe, an engagement they have to hurry off to.'

It wasn't true, but when Davina opened her mouth to protest, Darius squeezed her arm. That he had been tolerated in the family party to greet her mother – and, as it turned out, his sister – was a step forward enough. If Lord Conisborough didn't want him intruding any further on the family reunion that was quite okay with him. There would be other occasions when he would be at Nile House, and other occasions when nuggets of information, such as British pessimism with regard to France, would come his way.

His assumption was verified a few days later when he and Davina had tea with Petra at the Sporting Club. Over cucumber sandwiches and hummus Petra brought Davina up to date with more of her mother's London gossip. 'Delia seems to think Winston Churchill will soon be stepping into Chamberlain's shoes,' she said, adding with a wry laugh, 'Hitler will have to look to his laurels if he does. And she says someone else who will have to look to his laurels is Ivor's old friend, Sir John Simon. As Chancellor of the Exchequer he's apparently got himself a reputation for indecisiveness – and Winston won't want anyone indecisive around him.'

'And what about Uncle Jerome?' Davina asked as Darius continued to affect disinterest in the conversation by watching the cricket match taking place near by.

'Jerome?' A studiedly careless note entered Petra's voice. 'Jerome still doesn't have a ministry of his own, but Chamberlain has kept him very busy ever since war was declared. And as his relations with Winston have always been good, if Winston becomes PM, no doubt he will keep him equally busy.'

Later Darius shared the news about Churchill with Constantin, who said enviously, 'You probably know more about what goes on behind the scenes in the British government than anyone else in Cairo, Darius, apart from Lampson.'

Having Fawzia back in Cairo – and a Fawzia who was a married woman – was something of a mixed blessing.

'I don't trust this apparent abandonment of fierce anti-British feeling,' she said when he visited the family home – a home he hadn't lived in for years – to see her.

'I haven't abandoned it. I've just stopped giving noisy – and futile – expression to it.'

She was lying in a hammock slung from the lowest branch of the cedar tree that was the focal point of the lawn. The orange sundress she was wearing revealed a great deal of flawless olive skin and her fingernails and toenails were painted a searing scarlet.

'Father doesn't approve either,' she said, sensing his disapproval, 'but I'm a married woman now and I'm no longer answerable to him. I'm answerable only to Jack.'

'And where is Jack?' Darius asked. 'Still in London?'

He was lying sprawled on the grass, a drink close to hand.

She laughed. 'Would you believe me if I told you I don't know? London isn't Cairo. No one talks about where people are posted – that is, if they know. Most of the time they don't. It's the kind of security-consciousness Cairo could do with. I've heard rumours that the city is awash with spies and there's certainly enough loose talk for them to listen to. You wouldn't be a spy, Darius, would you?'

The look he gave her was withering. 'Hardly. What do I know of troop movements and troop numbers? What I am curious about is you. Why did you opt to come back to Cairo with Delia? I thought you were enjoying yourself in London.'

'I was when I first went there. But that was when I was single. Once I was married the fun faded a bit because going to parties without Jack was thought not the done thing – and though Jack's posting was London, he was always being sent to Paris or Madrid or Rome or somewhere for days on end, and sometimes for weeks on end.'

She sat up, swinging her long legs over the side of the hammock, her scarlet-painted toes touching the grass.

'And something else that took away from the fun,' she said with blunt frankness, 'was discovering that Jack doesn't have the kind of wealth I'd imagined he had, and so being on my own was boring. I couldn't shop the way I'd always shopped in Cairo...'

'When Father paid.'

'...and we didn't live in a grand house as I had imagined we would,' she said, ignoring his interruption. 'We lived in a small flat in Knightsbridge that would fit a dozen times over into this villa, or Petra and Sholto's villa, or Nile House.'

'And court social life?' he prompted.

She pulled a face. 'Court social life doesn't exist in England. King George and Queen Elizabeth are

386

the most boring married couple you could ever hope to meet and, even if they weren't, Jack scarcely knows them. It will be different here. With a King as young as Farouk, the Palace circle is bound to be one of great glamour.'

'It may be,' he said drily. 'I wouldn't know. I haven't been inside Abdin Palace since I was in my teens. As far as I'm concerned, Farouk is as useless and corrupt as his father and his grandfather, but as he's only three generations out of Albania, what can you expect?'

Fawzia wasn't interested in King Farouk's non-Egyptian ' heredity and didn't answer him. Instead, she said, 'I've heard rumours that he's already begun being unfaithful to Queen Farida. I wonder how generous he would be to a mistress? Do you think he would shower her with jewels?'

It was said carelessly, but Darius's eyes narrowed.

He knew discontent when he saw it. And he knew his sister.

'Stay away from Farouk,' he said bluntly. 'He would be far more trouble than you could ever handle.'

TWENTY ONE

Throughout February and March Allied troops continued to pour into the city. Everywhere one looked there were men in uniform: Englishmen, Scotsmen, Welshmen, Irishmen. Then the Commonwealth troops, the New Zealanders, South Africans and Indians, began to arrive. Khaki was everywhere. Cairo seemed to be drowning in it and Darius, like so many of his fellow country-men, gritted his teeth, appeared indifferent – and hated it.

'There are so many suede boots, fly whisks and swagger sticks in the Continental and Shep-heard's that it's nearly impossible to get a drink these days,' he said exasperatedly to Davina.

They were on his houseboat, the *Egyptian Queen*. Moored at Zamalek on the north end of Gezira Island it had been his home ever since he and his father had first had their differences with regard to British Occupation.

Davina was lying in the crook of his arm, naked apart from an ivory-coloured lace-trimmed silk slip. He was wearing a galabiya made of expensive black cloth lavishly edged with gold braid. When on the houseboat, he always wore a galabiya. West-ern clothes were for when he was making a public statement to the British and other Europeans.

As Davina slid her arm across his chest and he hugged her even closer, he thought about the British.

If they had been a thorn in the flesh before they had declared war on Germany, they were even more so now. Though Egypt itself was not at war, the city had become a wartime city. The Semi-ramis Hotel on the banks of the Nile had been turned into the military headquarters for British troops in Egypt and was known simply as BTE. A large block of luxury flats in Garden City had been commandeered as the General Headquarters

388

Middle East and, cordoned off with great rolls of ugly barbed wire, was known merely as GHQ. Open-air cinemas had sprung up everywhere in order to entertain the troops, the brothels in the squalid El Birkeh district were busy day and night, and everywhere the British Tommy was noisily – and often drunkenly – making his presence felt.

Hating that presence with every fibre of his being he sighed heavily. Constantin, he knew, avidly gleaned every little bit of gossip he could to relay it back to his superiors at the Romanian Legation. Where that gossip then went Darius didn't know, but he was fairly sure it was used in a way that would help the German war effort.

'And if Germany wins the war it will be the best possible result for Egypt,' he had said unthinkingly, a few days previously, to Davina.

She had been so horrified that it had nearly been the end of their relationship.

'I want an independent Egypt as much as you do,' she had said vehemently, 'but helping Germany isn't the way to achieve it. Have you any *idea* of what the world would be like if Hitler won the war? What do you think would happen to Egypt if Hitler was the victor? True, it would be the end of a British presence in Egypt, but the British would just be replaced by Germans. Instead of British soldiers at Suez, there would be German soldiers. German propaganda telling Egyptians any different – telling you that if they win the war they'll give Egypt independence – is just blatantly untrue. It isn't in Nazi Germany's nature to give any country its freedom. It's just the opposite.'

It was a valid point, and Darius knew it.

Constantin's way of helping the Germans to win the war was to run a network of informers – barmen, waiters, shoe-shine boys and prostitutes – to collect any information, however trivial, which might be useful to Berlin. He'd once thought that Constantin's way of doing things was in Egypt's best interests. Now he wasn't so sure. What if the only result of a German victory was for Egypt to find itself flying out of the frying pan and into the fire?

Yet if helping Germany win the war wasn't the route to total independence, what was? The anti-British demonstrations he'd taken part in and helped to organize since his student days were no longer feasible in a city where British soldiers were crammed cheek by jowl, and, even if they were, taking part in something so openly confrontational when Britain had its back to the wall would strain his relationship with Davina to breaking point. Yet there had to be something he could do; there had to be something he could involve himself in.

Davina stirred beside him, breaking in on his thoughts. 'Is it five o'clock yet, darling?' she murmured, her eyes still closed. 'I should go.'

She was temporarily assigned to a clinic in the north of the city and at that time of the evening the roads – and especially the Bulaq Bridge which served the northern end of Gezira Island – were choked with traffic.

'No,' he said gently. 'We have another hour.'

He lowered his head and kissed her. Her lips were like the petals of a flower and he felt himself tremble. That he cared for her so deeply always amazed him. He didn't care for anyone else

390

deeply, not even Fawzia. As for his parents – he'd been fond of his mother and intensely sorry when she had died. For his pro-British father he had only contempt.

At the touch of his mouth Davina's eyes opened. They were an unusual colour: grey, but grey holding the merest hint of blue. Many years ago, when Davina had still been a child, he'd heard her father liken the colour to English bluebells just before they opened. Whether the judgement was true or not he couldn't tell, never having seen English bluebells, but he'd always remembered the description.

Everything about her entranced him. Unlike Fawzia, and her Egyptian girlfriends, Davina's beauty wasn't voluptuous and obvious and was never used as a bargaining counter to get her what she wanted. Scheming – something that was meat and drink to Fawzia though she took good care that no one should suspect her of it – was alien to her.

And not only was she different from the Egyptian girls he knew, she was also different from the other English girls he knew. She never strove to look glamorous. Petra always looked glamorous. He couldn't even begin to imagine Petra without Hollywood-style glossy red lips and long lacquered nails.

Davina seldom wore make-up and when she did it was little more than a touch of powder on her flawless skin and a muted pink lipstick. She never dressed provocatively either. The girls of the 'fishing fleet' all dressed to attract attention. Though he was not Muslim, it was something he disliked. Davina's dress was always understated. Today when she had arrived at the houseboat she had been wearing her nurse's uniform, but if it hadn't been a working day he knew she would have just worn a simple cotton dress, her only jewellery her wristwatch.

As time ran out on them he watched her dress, his hands behind his head.

'I can get a taxi back to the clinic if you don't want to face the chaos of the early evening traffic,' she said as he made no effort to reach for his shirt or trousers.

'Then how would I know you'd got back safely?' he said, swinging his legs from the bed, amused at the mere thought of not wanting to be bothered to drive her back over the congested Bulaq Bridge into central Cairo.

She laughed, bending down to ease her feet into wedge-heeled sandals, her pale blonde hair falling forward at either side of her face like skeins of silk. 'I walk Cairo from end to end unescorted and well you know it.'

He did know it and he didn't like it, not when the city was choked with British Tommies. He didn't say anything, though. Davina had made Cairo her own over the years. Her work at the Old War Horse Memorial Hospital, which she still continued with despite her full-time nursing work, often took her into parts of the city even he would be loath to enter.

He tucked his white silk shirt into lizardskin-belted trousers, picked up his jacket and, with his arm around her shoulder, walked her across the houseboat's gangplank to where his car was parked, pondering yet again how he could work constructively towards the day when Egypt would be rid of the British for ever.

In April, as the Germans occupied Denmark and Norway, it began to be obvious that Germany was winning the war. A month later the Germans invaded France, Belgium, Luxembourg and the Netherlands. In June Italy declared itself to be at war with the Allies.

A few days later Constantin said, 'The head of the Italian Legation has been asked to leave. Though whether King Farouk's Italian friends within the Palace will go into internment with the rest of the city's Italians remains to be seen. Personally, I doubt that the King will be parted from them.'

Darius doubted it as well. Ever since King Fuad's day, a large number of the Palace servants had been Italian and Farouk had grown up with them and trusted them. If he refused to allow them to be interned it would be a source of great irritation to the British.

To his great delight, Farouk did refuse and, to his even greater delight, did so by taking advantage of the British Ambassador's Achilles heel. Sir Miles Lampson's wife was Italian, and the whole of Cairo was soon cackling at the King's riposte to the Embassy's demand that the Palace Italians be interned: 'When Lampson gets rid of his Italian,' Farouk was reported as saying, 'then I'll get rid of mine.'

Two weeks after Italy's declaration of war, France fell.

'It's unbelievable,' Petra said, looking pale with

393

shock when she joined Darius and Davina for pre-dinner drinks at Shepheard's. 'Nazi flags flying the full length of the Champs Élysées! German troops marching down it shoulder to shoulder! Swastikas on the Eiffel Tower and the Arc de Triomphe!'

They were sitting around one of the small octagonal tables in the Moorish Hall. Petra was wearing a gold lamé cocktail dress with a slashed neckline that left one golden-skinned shoulder completely exposed and Darius was aware that their table was the focus of much male attention. Sholto was supposed to join them briefly before he and Petra continued on to a party at the Spanish Legation, but there was no sign of him and Darius noticed that when her hand wasn't holding her champagne glass, it was constantly fiddling with her wedding ring.

'Mummy's hardly spoken to anyone ever since she heard.' Davina's voice was bleak. 'She'll rally, and become optimistic again, but at the moment she's in the depths of gloom. The only ray of light she can see is that Winston is now Prime Minister. It's something she says should have happened months ago; but now it has, she's certain the tide will turn.'

It was the kind of gossip that Petra and Davina thought of as family gossip and the insights it gave into British government and military morale always intrigued Darius.

'Poor Delia,' Petra said without, he thought, too much real sympathy. 'One minute she was over the moon at Winston becoming PM, the next she was devastated by one of his first actions –

394

interning that creep Sir Oswald Mosley.'

Darius's interest was caught. 'Why was she devastated? Mosley is a fascist, isn't he?'

'He is now, but he used to be a quite respectable MP, and when he was, he was on very friendly terms with Delia. His wife, who died a few years ago, was the daughter of Lord Curzon, an old family friend. Having known him for so long, my mother doesn't believe he would ever be disloyal to Britain – he was decorated for bravery in the Great War – and so she thinks his internment is quite unnecessary.' Her eyes flicked to Davina. 'What do you think, Davvy? You've met him. I haven't.'

Davina thought of the effect the demon king had had on her when she met him in the drawing room at Cadogan Square, and of the effect he had had on the thousands of people at the mass rally at Olympia. 'I think he might do anything,' she said quietly, not wanting to think too long about that evening at Olympia. 'I think Winston was probably very right to put him out of harm's way.'

Every table around them was crowded and people were constantly traversing the Moorish Hall on their way to the Long Bar.

A member of the diplomatic corps who had been standing at the foot of the great staircase, leaning against one of the two bare-breasted ebony caryatids that flanked it, spotted them and strolled across.

'If you are waiting for your husband, Mrs Monck,' he said genially, 'you may be waiting for some time. I've just left him at the Mohammed Ali Club and he's deep in a hand of chemin de fer. The King is gambling at an adjoining table and it's doubtful which of them is playing for the higher stakes. I'll say this for your old man – when it comes to cards he has nerves of steel!'

With good-natured laughter he left them, heading a little drunkenly in the direction of the terrace.

No one spoke and then, with an artificial smile towards the two of them, Petra rose to her feet. 'No use my hanging around here if Sholto isn't going to show,' she said, her voice studiedly casual. 'I think I'll give Kate a ring and see if she'd like to party with the Spaniards this evening.'

Darius smiled back at her in a way that indicated he thought there was nothing odd about her husband not meeting her as arranged, and wondered how she could continue such a carefree friendship with Kate Gunn when, as he knew via Davina, she was well aware of Kate's relationship with their father.

Whether either Davina or Petra was aware of their mother's relationship with Jerome Bazeljette was something he'd never attempted to discover. Certainly he didn't think Davina was aware of it. Petra, though, was far more worldly than Davina and it was just possible that she knew and was being protective of Davina by not telling her.

In August the Italians attacked British Somaliland from Ethiopia. With the war now very firmly taking place much nearer to them, tensions in Cairo increased. They increased even further when Italian troops crossed the border from Libya and established a base in the Egyptian desert.

Loose talk as to the number of German troops with the Italians was rife, but military gossip and rumour wasn't hardcore information about British tank numbers and battle plans, and it was these that Darius knew Constantin was hungry to get his hands on.

'And I will,' Constantin said to him as they sat at a small table at the rear of one of the city's most popular nightclubs. 'I'm in contact with a big fish now, Darius. A truly big fish.'

'Someone in the British military?'

'No, the British diplomatic corps.'

For once Darius was staggered – as Constantin had known he would be. When he'd got his breath back, he said, keeping his voice as low as Constantin had kept his, 'And how much German gold did that take?'

'I don't know. I didn't do the bribing. He's someone who has been on the Nazi payroll for years and he contacted me – in order to make use of me. Whatever his pay-off, I assume it's on par with our Prime Minister's pay-off.'

The rumour that the Prime Minister was being bribed with German gold was rampant throughout Cairo. The only thing that surprised Darius about it, if it was true, was that the Germans thought a bribe necessary, for though the King and the government abided by the Anglo-Egyptian Treaty and went through the motions of being pro-British, the widespread belief that Berlin would support Egyptian independence after a German victory ensured that the reality was very different.

Every Egyptian he knew was certain that Egypt would be better off if the Axis forces in the desert chased the British army into the sea.

The difficulty, of course, was in knowing just how many Axis forces there were in the desert, compared to British forces. The general consensus was that the British were heavily outnumbered. And what was known for a fact was that fighting was heavy.

Unable to see Davina, who was working a night shift, Darius left Constantin ogling his belly dancer and strolled down Soliman Pasha Street to a far more upmarket nightclub.

Within minutes of his arrival, the King made an entrance. Slickly suited and wearing dark glasses and a tarboosh, he was accompanied by a couple of people Darius didn't recognize, two aides-de-camp and half a dozen muscular bodyguards.

As a boy Darius had often accompanied his father to Abdin Palace, and despite Farouk being much younger he had spent time kicking a football with him in the Palace gardens, or, more accurately, kicking a football to him, for Farouk had never deigned to run after the ball. It had been attention Farouk, totally isolated from boys his own age and with only four sisters for company, had been pathetically grateful for.

Now, to his surprise, Farouk recognized him and threw his entourage into a flurry by not seating himself at the table permanently reserved for him, but by walking across to him.

'Good evening,' he said affably as Darius rose to his feet and reluctantly inclined his head. 'It is a long time since we have had the pleasure of

398

seeing you.'

'Yes, sir. Several years, sir.'

Farouk had been a handsome little boy and his good looks were still in evidence, though there was a chubbiness about his face that was beginning to blur it.

'Then let us make up for it,' he said, seating himself at Darius's table and leaving his companions, aides-de-camp and bodyguards standing a few feet away in awkward confusion.

Having no other option, Darius sat down again. Champagne speedily arrived. 'You are a great friend of Lord Conisborough, I believe,' the King said as it was poured.

Well aware that this wasn't how Ivor Conisborough would describe their relationship, he said evasively, 'I've known Lord Conisborough's family for nearly twenty years, sir.'

'Yes. Quite so. And his daughters? We see Mrs Monck at many events in Cairo. Like her American mother, she is a great beauty, is she not?'

'Yes, sir.' Darius wondered where this extraordinary conversation was leading. 'Mrs Monck is indeed very beautiful.'

He took a drink of his champagne. Farouk – a Muslim – ignored his.

'We think Mrs Monck looks very like Rita Hayworth and that it would be nice to see more of her,' Farouk said blandly, using the royal 'We'. 'Perhaps she would like to admire the art treasures of the Palace? Maybe you would like to invite her to do so?'

Darius nearly choked on his champagne, but recovered speedily and said with equal blandness, 'I'm sure Mrs Monck and her husband would be delighted by such an invitation.'

Farouk smiled and waved a finger in lazy admonishment. 'We find that English gentlemen are not as interested in art as English ladies. It has been nice renewing our childish acquaintance. But no games the next time we meet at Abdin. Only art and Mrs Monck.' He rose to his feet and the singer on the stage came to a deferential halt in mid-song as, surrounded by his entourage, the King crossed the nightclub to the table at which no one else was ever allowed to sit.

A few minutes later Darius exited the club, a pulse pounding furiously at the corner of his jaw. Behind him, the club's entertainer resumed singing. Out on the pavement Darius sucked in a great breath of air as he came to terms with the fact that his twenty-year-old king had asked him to pimp for him.

Farouk's unfaithfulness to his young wife was legendary and there was a widespread rumour that many court officials were now reluctant to attend court functions with their wife in case their wife attracted Farouk's attention. If she did, there was little the man in question – or his wife – could do about it. If they didn't comply with the King's Royal Command, the husband's career would be at an end. It was an unsavoury rumour and one that Darius, though he had little time for Farouk, had hoped was untrue.

Now he knew that it wasn't.

He lit a cigarette and began walking in the direction of the river. That Farouk would have the gall to attempt to add one of Lord Conisborough's daughters to his list of mistresses was so outrageous that Darius was still dazed by it. There were European women in the city who would be flattered at the thought of intimacy with a king, but Petra certainly wasn't one of them.

Despite his fury at the way Farouk was trying to use him, when he thought of Petra's reaction – if she were to know of it – the corners of his mouth twitched, and then, as he strolled past a couple of red-capped military policemen, he burst out laughing. The idea of Petra frolicking naked with Farouk among Abdin Palace's artworks was so surreal he almost wished he could share it with someone.

That he couldn't went without saying.

And what also went without saying was that when he failed to escort Petra to Abdin on the pretext of privately viewing its artworks, Farouk would take great umbrage. And when a king took umbrage, anything could happen.

TWENTY TWO

A few days later, at the office at which he carried out his advocacy work, Darius had an un-expected visitor.

'Lady Conisborough would like five minutes of your time,' his Egyptian secretary said, her eye-brows raised high. 'Shall I tell her you'll see her?'

'Of course I'll see her,' he said crisply, hiding his astonishment. 'Have tea sent in. Earl Grey.'

401

With one swift movement he swept the papers he had been working on into the top drawer of his desk and rose to his feet, wondering why on earth Delia was going out of her way to see him in such an unusual and private manner. Even Davina had never troubled to visit him at his chambers – mainly because it was a side of his life he always heavily downplayed.

'So you really *are* a lawyer, and you really *do* practise as one,' Delia said teasingly as she strode into the room, trimly dressed in St John's Ambulance Brigade uniform.

Though Davina had told him that at the outbreak of war her mother had joined St John's Ambulance Brigade he had never seen her in uniform before. He liked what he saw. The tailored black jacket and pencil-straight skirt emphasized how slim she still was and her black peaked hat made the blaze of her Titian-red hair seem more fiery than ever. The hat sported a jaunty striped cockade that he suspected was an honorary symbol of rank. It suited her outgoing personality, and not for the first time he found it remarkable that a woman in her mid to late forties could still be so breathtakingly dazzling.

'I always thought your legal practice was a scam,' she continued as she sat down, 'and that you simply claimed to be an advocate in order not to have people accusing you of being a playboy.'

He laughed and seated himself behind his desk and she said, 'I've come to see if you can supply me with names of potential punters for the Red Cross and Red Crescent Ball I'm helping to organize in order to raise money for the war effort. Lady Lampson and I have contacted everyone we know in the British community – which is everyone – and your father has kindly shared with us the entire contents of his address book. As your social circle is a much younger one and different yet again, I wondered if I could ask the same favour of you? I have four hundred tickets to sell and so I need all the help I can get.'

He thought of Constantin's reaction if she was to try to sell him a ticket to a charity ball in aid of the British war effort and said, keeping amusement out of his voice only with great difficulty, 'I can give you the names of some of my polo-playing friends, Delia, but the tally won't come anything close to four hundred.'

'Never mind.' She took off the gloves she was wearing. 'Every little helps.'

His secretary brought in the tea tray.

Delia checked the contents of the china teapot and then poured.

Watching her, he puzzled over what had been missing in the Conisboroughs' marriage that had resulted in her embarking on what appeared, from the conversation he had overheard between Conisborough and Sir Jerome Bazeljette, to be a long-standing affair with Sir Jerome.

The likeliest thing he could think of was that Ivor Conisborough had first been unfaithful and she had become unfaithful in retaliation. The odd thing was that their relationship seemed perfectly compatible, both knowing about and accepting the other's lover. He knew from the conversation he had overheard that Ivor Conisborough had remained friends with Delia's lover,

Jerome Bazeljette, and certainly Delia – who he was sure must be aware of her husband's affair with Kate Gunn – was accepting of her. Kate was often seen in her company at polo matches and race meetings at the Gezira Club.

If Delia and Sir Jerome's affair was so long-standing, Kate was too young to have been the first of Ivor Conisborough's mistresses. Conisborough had to have had a mistress way before coming out to Egypt – which meant the Conisborough marriage had been in disarray ever since Petra and Davina had been children.

He wondered again if Jack were aware of the nature of his father's relationship with Delia. Although Jack had married Fawzia, Darius found it difficult to come to terms with the fact that they were now brothers-in-law. When they had been boys and when Jack had frequently spent long periods of time as a guest at Nile House, the two of them had been friends, though it had always been a fiercely competitive friendship – as when they had both damned-near killed themselves when riding in opposing teams in the Gezira Club polo match.

It had been a while since the two of them had met. And now, putting even more strain on their relationship, Jack had moved sideways from the Foreign Office into Military Intelligence.

Before he could start pondering on the problems he could well face if Jack were to be posted to Cairo, Delia said with a complete change of subject, 'Something else I'm tryin' to do, Darius, is to think of ways of entertain' the troops when they are on leave. They need something to take their minds off the hideousness of the fighting in the desert. At the moment most of them simply flock to the El Birkeh district and then end up in the VD clinics. Alternatives are needed. D'you have any ideas?'

He couldn't think of another woman of her age and class who would so unselfconsciously bring the problem of prostitution and venereal disease into a conversation.

Aware of just how much he liked her, he said, 'You could try tea parties and concert parties or historical trips to the city's mosques and to the pyramids, but I doubt such activities will tempt soldiers away from the brothels – especially when women are in such short supply in the city.'

'But what about proper clubs for them? Somewhere they could get something resemblin' British food – tea and toast, eggs and chips, and home-made cake, for instance?'

'If the club in question also had hot showers, baths and a barber, then you just might be successful. And if the British weren't so class-conscious, there wouldn't be a need for such clubs. If privates and NCOs could go to Shepheard's, the Continental, the Gezira Club, the Turf Club, or any of the other decent places in Cairo that are out of bounds to anyone other than officers, the problem wouldn't exist.'

It was a provocative thing to say, but he was gambling on her being in agreement with him for she was, after all, an American. And he was damn sure American soldiers wouldn't put up with such fierce segregation when off duty.

His hunch proved correct.

She made a despairing gesture. 'I quite agree with you, Darius. But strict segregation between officers and other ranks has always been the way in the British army which is why, as so many places are out of bounds to him, it's so important that there are other places the British Tommy can go.'

Darius pushed his half-drunk cup of tea to one side. 'I'm not going to be able to come up with any alternative entertainment ideas unless I do so over coffee and some decent pastries. How about we go to Groppi's?'

'That's a grand suggestion,' she said with alacrity. 'I like Groppi's. They make the best sugared almonds in Cairo.'

And with the suppleness of a woman twenty years her junior, she rose to her feet and slipped her hand companionably in the crook of his arm.

'I understand you've been squiring my mother to Groppi's,' Davina said teasingly as they met up at the Gezira Club in order to watch an under-25's polo match.

'I'm not quite sure who was squiring whom.' Darius was wearing dark glasses but he still shielded his eyes from the sun as the ponies trotted onto the field. 'It was my idea that we go there, but only after she'd taken me by surprise at my chambers. She wanted a list of names of potential punters for a Red Cross and Red Crescent charity ball – and she also wanted ideas about how to keep the troops out of the El Birkeh district and the VD clinics.'

'Dear Lord! What did the two of you come up

with? Or would it be better for me not to know?'

'We came up with lots of things. Not least a well-run club providing everything the Hilmiya camp doesn't.'

The Hilmiya camp for British troops was a tram-ride out of the city at Heliopolis and it was common knowledge that apart from its sea of tents it boasted no facilities at all other than a bar and a not very adequate football pitch.

Ponies and players were now lined up in two opposing teams and as the umpire tossed the ball between them action exploded in a great clacking of mallets and urgently shouted orders. From then on, as they were caught up in the furious excitement of the match, all conversation between them ceased.

During the intermission they walked onto the field with other spectators and began the ritual of stamping the divots back in.

'Petra is a very happy bunny at the moment,' Davina said, searching out another clump of grass that had been unearthed by the quick stops and starts of the ponies, and toeing it back into the ground. 'She's just heard that one of her closest friends, Boudicca Pytchley, is coming to Cairo as an ambulance driver. Another of her old friends, Archie Somerset, is already in Cairo. She ran into him, completely by accident, at a party at the Scarabée Club.'

'Is he a regular soldier?'

'No. Special Ops.'

There were a whole clutch of outfits operating under the banner of Special Operations. All of them operated deep in the desert, reconnoitring and raiding behind German and Italian lines.

He was still thinking about the Special Operations units when the intermission came to an end and Davina broke into his thoughts by saying, 'Mother's had an awful dust-up with Sir Miles. She thinks he should be taking a stronger position about the army directive that wives and children of military personnel are to be evacuated and that only wives with official war work are to be allowed to stay on.'

They were nearing the stands and a welcome breeze sent the skirt of her ice-blue silk dress fluttering against her legs.

'And what was Sir Miles's response?' Darius asked, wishing he could have seen such a head-on confrontation.

'Oh, he agreed with her that the action was unnecessarily alarmist, but said it was something he could do nothing about. Not being a military family it doesn't affect us, and as Petra is a secretary at the Embassy and I'm a nurse, it wouldn't affect us even if we were. It's causing a lot of distress, though, and shoals of wives are now applying for military clerical jobs in order to stay.'

Not feeling the remotest sympathy for the shoals of English women desperate to stay on in a country that wasn't theirs, he slipped his arm around Davina's waist. It was a very tiny waist, its tininess emphasized by a crisp white belt.

'Let's miss the second half of the match. We can go to the houseboat.'

As they continued walking she leaned against him, loving the feel of his body close to hers, the faint smell of the lemon cologne he used and the fact that he wanted to make love to her so urgently.

They walked past the stands and, avoiding the Lido terrace that fronted the swimming pool and was always full of people they knew, who would no doubt delay them by talking to them, they left the club grounds by the Shari el Gezira exit.

Zamalek, and the houseboats moored there, was only a short riverside walk away and as they strolled along the river bank, her arm now as comfortably around his waist as his arm was around hers, she said, 'I think Fawzia must be becoming very friendly with Queen Farida. We went to Cicurel's department store yesterday to look at the new picture hats they have in and while we were there a police flunky came up to us and said Fawzia's presence was wanted at the Palace. He simply whisked her out of the store and into a limousine then and there. It was pretty rude of him, considering that she was with me.'

Darius stopped short. High above his head a kite circled slowly in a warm draught of air. 'Did the flunky say specifically that it was the Queen who wanted her company?' he asked, a nerve beginning to throb at the corner of his jaw.

'No, but who else could have wanted her presence at the Palace? If it had been the King she simply wouldn't have gone. Not unaccompanied. And I've heard your father say that Farida gets terribly lonely. It was probably at his suggestion that the invitation came.'

'Yes,' he said, his face and voice carefully devoid of expression. 'I expect you're right.'

The kite, spying prey, dived.

Davina, always on the side of the victim, winced.

As they started walking again, she said, 'I imagine your father would like it if Fawzia and Queen Farida became friends, because I think Fawzia is also lonely. My long working hours – combined with the time I spend with you – mean I see little of her, and she and Petra are always prickly with each other these days. The best solution would be if Jack were to be posted to Cairo. It can't be easy being a new bride and then being separated so abruptly from your husband. She must miss him very much.'

He didn't say anything. He was thinking of how discontented Fawzia already was in her marriage to Jack – and of how shocked Davina would be to know of that discontent and the mercenary reasons for it.

He was remembering Fawzia wondering aloud about how generous to a mistress Farouk might be. And he was pondering the oddity of there being no comeback from the Palace over his failure to deliver Petra there in order that she could, in Farouk's words, 'admire the art treasures of the Palace' with him. Was the lack of any such comeback because Farouk's interest had shifted elsewhere? And to a person even closer to him?

The next day he drove at high speed – or as high speed as was possible through streets choked with gharries, heavily-laden donkeys and military vehicles – to his family home in Garden City.

A long wall of the house faced a tree-lined boulevard and he swerved to a halt outside a wide, high gateway that was its only opening. It was too early for Fawzia to be at her dressmaker's or hairdresser's or to be enjoying mid-morning coffee and pastries with anyone, but not, he hoped, so early that his father would still be at home. He wasn't in the mood for filial courtesies.

As he slammed the low-slung door of the Mercedes behind him, a black Nubian, who had been sitting cross-legged in front of the heavy cedar-wood door of the gateway, leaped to his feet. It was his sole task to open and close the door to visitors and though he had been there ever since Darius was a child, Darius had no idea of his name.

Striding past him into the huge, rose-filled courtyard beyond, Darius's only thoughts were on whether or not his sister was behaving like a whore – and the line of action he would take if she was.

His father's major-domo hurried to greet him, his galabiya spotlessly white and edged with royal-blue braid.

On being told that Fawzia was having breakfast on the garden terrace – a terrace that looked out towards the Nile – he strode through the high-ceilinged, lavishly furnished rooms towards it.

When she saw him, her astonishment was so great she almost dropped the coffee cup she was holding.

'Darius! What on earth...? Nothing is the matter, is it?' She put the coffee cup down unsteadily onto the beautifully laid breakfast table. 'There hasn't been an accident? An incident?'

'There hasn't been an accident, but there has

certainly been an incident – though not a military or a political one.'

She went rigid and he knew instantly that she knew what he was referring to.

He said without preamble, 'Davina told me about your visit to the Palace the other day. She assumed it was a summons from Queen Farida, but I don't think it was. And I don't think it was the first such visit.'

Abruptly she pushed her chair away from the table and sprang to her feet, her rose-pink nightdress and negligee swirling around her ankles. 'What I do and who I see is my own business!' she said explosively.

'Not if it means you've become one of Farouk's whores!'

'I'm not a whore! I'm the mistress of my King!'

He'd never hit her, not even when they were children, but he slapped her face so hard her head almost left her shoulders. She staggered, let out a cry of rage and pain, and slapped him back with all the strength she had.

The urge to seize hold of her and give her the kind of beating she would never forget was almost too much for him.

Well aware of the danger she stood in, and heedless of it, she didn't back away from him. Instead, she moved so close that if they had been the same height they would have been eyeball to eyeball.

'You keep out of my affairs,' she spat, fire in her eyes, 'and I'll keep out of yours.'

'And just what the hell do you mean by that?'

'I mean that I know all about your friendship

with Constantin Antonescu – the Head of the Romanian Legation is a frequent visitor to the Palace – and if you come on heavy-handed about my having become Farouk's mistress, I'll tell Davina just how close your links are to Britain's enemies.'

'At least my loyalties are to my country!' Rage was streaming through him in a dark, dizzying tide. 'Where are your loyalties? What do you think Jack's reaction would be if he knew that in order to keep me quiet about your adultery, you were condoning my connection with the Romanians?'

'His reaction would be about as disastrous as Davina's would be if I were to tell her what you are up to.'

'And you think you know what that is, do you?'

'Oh, yes,' she shot back at him. 'I know.'

At the certainly in her voice, he said raspingly, 'Then you won't be surprised if I ask you to keep me informed of any interesting conversations you overhear at Abdin. If you have to whore, it may as well be for something more valuable than the jewels you're no doubt now being showered with.'

'That's quite a lot to ask, considering my husband is a British intelligence officer.'

Sometimes her effrontery was so shameless he almost admired it.

'You should have thought of your husband and his loyalties before you got into bed with Farouk,' he snapped as she seated herself once again at the breakfast table.

She crossed her legs. 'King Farouk,' she corrected with insolent composure. 'His Majesty, King Farouk, by the grace of God, King of Egypt and of Sudan, Sovereign of Nubia, of Kordofan and of Darfur. One of the richest men in the world and a man who is going to divorce Farida and make me his queen.'

'Sweet heaven,' he said devoutly. 'I do believe you think it's possible.'

'It's more than possible. It's already on the cards.' Her voice was full of amusement. 'Like you, I play for very high stakes – and I can't wait for the day when you have to comply with royal etiquette and walk away from me backwards.'

'That day, Fawzia,' he said through clenched teeth, 'will never come!' And he strode away from her, slamming the French windows so hard behind him as he re-entered the house that the glass in the frames splintered and shattered, falling at his heels in great ugly shards.

TWENTY THREE

'I don't care how many other parties are being given this Christmas, the party at Nile House is going to be the biggest and the best,' Delia said as she sipped a gin-sling on Shepheard's terrace. 'We have so much to celebrate. Dear General Wavell has chased the Italians all the way back across the Western Desert and there are now no enemy troops at all on Egyptian soil. It's a cause for great celebration, don't y'think?'

Her vivacity was always contagious and, keeping his true thoughts to himself, Darius said

414

mildly, 'What isn't quite such a cause for celebration is that it's rumoured Hitler is sending General Rommel to Libya.'

It was early evening and the terrace that looked out over Ibrahim Pasha Street was crowded with military personnel. When he had seen her there, quite by accident, she had been sitting with a woman friend, waiting for Ivor's arrival. When Ivor had failed to appear on time, the friend, having an engagement of her own to hurry off to and happy to leave Delia in Darius's company, had excused herself and left the two of them alone. Now Delia looked around at the sea of khaki at the other tables and said chidingly, 'It's a rumour I've heard as well, but not one we should be chattering about here.'

'Why not? I'm pretty sure every soldier in the city is aware of it.'

'Maybe so,' she said equably, 'but it doesn't do to take risks. According to General Wavell, the city is chock-full of German informers.'

Below the terrace, in the crowded street, a black chauffeured Rolls-Royce came to a halt. Recognizing it, Delia reached for her white muslin gloves and began pulling them on. She was wearing a dress and a broad-brimmed picture hat in pewter-blue, a colour he had never seen her wear before. It suited her, but then he had never seen her in anything that didn't. The brim of the hat, decorated by a single white rose, dipped low over her eyes, shading them from the sun.

Half a dozen tarboosh-wearing commissionaires hurried down the hotel steps to escort her husband up them. Tall and imposing, dressed

415

impeccably in a dark-grey suit and wearing a silver, grey-spotted bow tie, he cut through them like a knife through butter.

'I'm sorry I'm late, Delia,' he said as he strode up to their table. 'There are great shenanigans over Lampson's attempts to get the ministers and diplomats at the Hungarian and Romanian Legations expelled. Ah! Darius. How unexpected. Still, I'm glad that you've been able to keep my wife company while she waited for me.'

Darius, who fiercely wanted more information on whatever plans were afoot for the members of the Hungarian and Romanian Legations, knew it would be fatal to make a direct enquiry. Ivor Conisborough was far too shrewd not to find such interest suspicious. It was equally obvious that as far as Ivor was concerned he was now *de trop* and that it was time for him to take his leave.

A week later, when he was making Turkish coffee for Constantin aboard the *Egyptian Queen*, Constantin said, 'There's someone I want you to meet. Have you heard of a group of Egyptian army officers who go by the name of the Free Officers' Movement?'

Darius added sugar to coffee grounds and water in a small copper pot with a wooden handle. 'No,' he said, stirring the coffee grounds until they sank to the bottom of the pot and the sugar dissolved. 'Who are they?'

As he put the pot on the stove to boil Constantin came and stood at the galley's doorway. 'It's good you haven't heard of them. It means their security is watertight. The Free Officers'

Movement is a subversive organization within the army that is simply waiting for the right moment to rise up and trigger a revolution. I've arranged for you to meet with one of the officers in question. His name is Anwar Sadat.'

The day of his first meeting with Sadat was the day of the Christmas party at Nile House. By the time he arrived the long curving drive was thick with parked cars, as was the street outside. Adjo opened the door to him, resplendent in a royal-blue galabiya lavishly embroidered in gold. One glance over Adjo's shoulder was enough to tell him that everyone who was anyone in Cairo high society had arrived before him.

Sir Miles and Lady Lampson were clearly in evidence, as were the heads of all the foreign legations and their wives – the only exceptions being the heads of the Romanian and Hungarian Legations. The room was awash with be-medalled high-ranking military men and their bejewelled wives – there were two generals and three brigadiers in his direct line of sight alone.

Prince Mohammed Ali, Farouk's extremely pro-British uncle, was there, dapper in pinstriped trousers, a velvet dinner jacket and a jaunty bow tie. Only his tarboosh and the ostentatious cabochon ruby ring he was wearing singled him out as being non-European.

Princess Shevekiar was holding court in a far corner of the room. Avoiding her – and avoiding his father, who was deep in conversation with a broad-shouldered, tough-looking American of about his own age whom he had never seen before – he sought out Davina.

Her face lit up at the sight of him and he felt, as he always did when she looked at him in such a way, as if he had been punched in the chest and all the breath had been knocked out of him.

'Darling, isn't this wonderful?' she said, sliding her hand into his. 'Have you seen the Christmas tree? It's fake, of course, but it's even bigger than the fake tree at the Embassy. We only finished decorating it seconds before the first guests arrived.'

Her ivory-pale hair waved softly to shoulders that were naked. It wasn't often she wore a strapless evening gown – strapless evening gowns were far more Petra's style than hers – but the rose-pink, shot-taffeta gown looked magical on her.

'I want us to introduce ourselves to Petra's friend, Boudicca Pytchley,' she said, beginning to lead the way to where a tall, fair, plump young woman with beautiful hands was talking with Kate Gunn. 'She's with the Motorized Transport Corps and has only just arrived. All the newly arrived ambulance drivers in her medical unit are women, which has caused quite a flap at Hilmiya camp.'

'...thirty thousand Eyeties taken prisoner is rather a good Christmas present, what?' Darius heard a staff officer saying to Sholto Monck as, in making their way across the crowded room, they squeezed past him. 'And with Sidi Barrani now back in our hands it looks as if it's going to be victory all the way.'

Sidi Barrani was one of the villages on the Egyptian side of the border with Libya and, having occupied it in September, the Italians had been hopeful of making it a base for further operations. Even though the fact that it had been retaken was public knowledge, it was still a conversation Darius would have liked to have listened in on for longer.

He wasn't able to.

'And this is Boo and she's been Petra's friend for years and years and years,' Davina was saying and he had no option but to abandon his eavesdropping and allow himself to be introduced.

The first thing Boo Pytchley said, when the introductions were over, was: 'If Kate and Darius don't mind, I need to have a quiet word with you, Davina. Jack's father asked me to pass on some Toynbee Hall news.'

Her eyes had become suddenly very troubled, her voice grave. Though he was aware of her change of mood, it was obvious that Davina and Kate weren't.

'Oh, good.' Davina put her hand in his again. 'News from Uncle Jerome is always welcome. Though I must stop referring to him as "uncle". Petra says it's pathetically childish – she stopped calling him "uncle" when she was about thirteen.'

From the room beyond the one they were in came the sound of a jazz band launching into 'Jingle Bells' and Kate Gunn clapped her hands in delight. 'Jazzed-up Christmas songs! How utterly typical of Delia.'

All around them chatter and laughter competed with the efforts of a brilliant saxophonist.

'Boo has been telling us how absolutely ghastly life now is in London,' Kate said, raising her voice in order to be heard and surprising him by being the one to take the lead in the conversation. In all the long years he had known her she had never spoken to him before he had spoken to her. 'The Christmas food rations are measly. Sugar has been increased to only four ounces and tea to two ounces. I can't imagine how people are managing. It makes me feel very guilty when food is so plentiful here. I bought a whole armful of oranges this morning. Boo says Londoners have forgotten what an orange looks like.'

Not wanting to continue with the conversation, he made a sound she could take to mean anything. Though he was well aware that Kate was pleasant and personable and, according to Davina, had a deeply kind and loving nature, she had always bored him and was certainly boring him now.

He looked across the room to where Ivor Conisborough was chuckling at something Lady Wavell was saying to him, and he wondered how Ivor could possibly prefer Kate's company to his wife's.

Exactly on cue Delia descended on them, arms outstretched, a radiant beam of welcome on her face. 'Where have you been, Darius? I thought you were never goin' to arrive. Isn't the band grand? They've begun to play every Thursday night at the Continental and the minute I heard them I just knew I had to have them.'

She was wearing an evening gown of turquoise chiffon that floated around her in perpetual movement and there were diamonds at her neck and her wrists and threaded in her upswept fox-red hair.

He tried to remember that she was in her late forties, and failed.

Kate, at least a decade younger, looked colourless in comparison. Her mauve silk evening gown was halter-necked, the narrow fluted skirt embroidered with tiny purple flowers. It was a pretty dress and should have flattered her light brown hair and cream-and-roses complexion, but it merely looked a little faded and insignificant.

Delia slipped a hand affectionately through her arm and said, 'It's been so good, Kate, getting really up-to-the-minute gossip from London. Jerome took Boudicca out to lunch only days before she and all the other girls in the new medical unit set sail and he told her to pass on the information that Shibden Hall is packed to the rafters. Toynbee Hall have rehomed an entire East End orphanage there. And now,' she added, looking around at them, fizzing with vitality, 'y'all understand if I shanghai my daughter for a few minutes. Bruno was an early supporter of the Old War Horse Memorial Hospital and as he's so rarely in Cairo, he's eager for an update on what is happening there.'

Davina gave his hand a hard squeeze and allowed herself to be whirled off in her mother's wake.

'Bruno?' he asked, raising an eyebrow questioningly.

'Bruno Lautens,' Kate said as he watched Delia making a beeline for the man with the build of a middleweight boxer to whom his father had been talking a little earlier. 'He's an American archaeologist based in the far south, near the Sudanese border. Before the war he was an experienced desert traveller.'

'Golly.' Boo Pytchley was impressed. 'Where did that little nugget of information come from?'

'Lord Conisborough.' As she said his name a faint flush of colour touched Kate Gunn's cheeks. She took another sip of her champagne. 'He thinks Mr Lautens will be very useful to some of the people in Special Ops.'

That social talk was often so careless never ceased to amaze Darius. Any hope of further indiscretions on Kate's part was, however, dashed as Petra approached and kissed Kate, and then Boo, on the cheek.

'So glad you two have made friends,' she said, paying him not the slightest attention. 'And Archie has just arrived,' she said to Boo. 'If only Rupert was here as well it would be just like old times.'

'Rupert's my brother,' Boo explained to Darius. 'He's in the RAF.'

'Darius wouldn't know about being in the RAF – or being in anything else.' Petra's voice was blatantly caustic. 'He's not even in the Egyptian army. But then Egypt isn't officially at war with Germany – something it's always best to bear in mind, Boo.'

The inference was so obvious that it was then he knew she'd had far too much to drink.

'Oh golly! Really?' Startled and bewildered Boo looked around for a way out of the suddenly sticky situation and, seeing Archie, she said with deep relief, 'Excuse me for a moment, Petra. I'm just going to have a word with Archie.'

The minute she'd left them Darius said in a low

voice, 'Let's talk in the garden. Delia wouldn't thank either of us if we had a shouting match in here.'

For a second he thought she was going to refuse to leave the room with him, but then she gave a careless shrug. Her nearly backless gown was of silver lamé and clung sensuously to every voluptuous curve.

If Sholto Monck saw her leave the room with him, he gave no sign of it. It was an indifference he couldn't imagine an Egyptian husband displaying.

The garden was lit with fairy lights and there were almost as many couples outside as there were in. He strode onto the darkened lawn and then across it, heading towards the Nile. Somewhere on his right-hand side he could hear the jangle of Davina's donkey's bridle. Only when they had reached the foot of the garden did he turn round to face her.

'Just what the *hell*,' he said through gritted teeth, 'was that little scene about in front of your friend? You might just as well have said quite baldly that I'm not to be trusted!'

'Are you? I don't know. I'm not even sure if you know.'

The silver of her dress shimmered in the moonlight as she folded her arms tightly across her chest.

'I've never much liked you, Darius. You come with too many complications. And I don't like your affair with Davvy.'

'My affair with Davina hasn't anything to do with you.'

'She's my sister. It has everything to do with me.' For the first time he noticed that she had walked down the garden barefoot. 'What is going to come of it? Are you going to marry her?'

It was a question he asked himself almost every single day and when he didn't answer it – because he couldn't answer it – Petra pushed her glorious mane of hair away from her face and said explosively, 'Yet you won't give her up so that she can find someone who not only loves her, but will also marry her!' Her voice shook with passion. 'The last thing Davvy has ever needed in her life is you, Darius. You're trouble. You've always been trouble. And you're trouble now on a monumental scale – I can feel it in my blood and in my bones!'

And yanking her tight fishtail skirt up to her knees she whirled away from him and stormed in high temper back to the lights and the music.

He stared out grimly over the black-silk surface of the river and didn't begin walking back to the house until he'd finished smoking his cigarette down to a stub.

Back at the house one of the 'fishing fleet' girls was singing 'A Nightingale Sang in Berkeley Square' and nearly everyone was dancing. There was no sign of Davina, and taking a glass of champagne from a passing tray he went in search of her.

He found her in the small room the Conisboroughs referred to as 'the den'. She was laughing at something Bruno Lautens was saying. Archie Somerset was running a finger along the titles of the many books on the bookshelves, a paper party-hat on his head, a glass of whisky in the other hand. A girl who had arrived at the party with one of Archie's friends had her arm hooked proprietorially over Lautens's shoulder.

At his entrance Davina looked towards him, her eyes lighting up at the sight of him. 'We're taking a breather. Bruno's got some very funny stories. The fellahin south of Aswan believe Hitler is a Muslim!'

He gave a polite smile, not at all liking the admiring expression in Lautens's eyes when he looked at Davina.

He was just about to suggest to her that they return to the crush when Boudicca Pytchley pushed past him into the room.

'Oh goodness, what a party! Your mother has just promised she'll sing "Dixie". Look, I must have a few words with you, Davina, and it's as quiet here as anywhere.' She drew in a deep, steadying breath. 'Jack's father asked me to tell you that a doctor and his wife you used to know at Toynbee – Dr and Mrs Sinclair – were killed in a car accident at the end of November. It was dreadful. They were both killed outright and there's a child ... a boy...'

That Boo so obviously didn't realize just how close Davina and the Sinclairs had been, only added to the hideousness of the moment.

Davina gave a low, terrible cry, and as her legs gave way it was Bruno who was closest to her and it was Bruno who caught hold of her and lowered her into the nearest chair.

'Where...?' she croaked thickly, her face chalk white. 'How...?'

'It was at a place called Dunbeath, in Sutherland. I hadn't realized the Sinclairs were such close friends, Davina.' Boo's voice was full of remorse. 'If I'd known ... if I'd realized ... I would have taken more care in breaking the news to you.'

'I think Davina needs to be on her own to get over the shock,' Darius said brusquely, wanting them all out of the room.

Davina said again, as if he hadn't spoken, 'How, Boo?'

'It happened on a coast road, and from what Sir Jerome said it was at night. The road was steep and there was a sharp bend. The driver of the other car was drunk. The crash was head-on.'

Davina shuddered so violently, Darius thought she was going to collapse completely.

'Fetch her a brandy,' he said abruptly to Bruno Lautens. 'And a shawl, or a blanket of some kind.'

That no one had ever had the nerve – or been foolish enough – to speak to Bruno in such a way before was quite obvious to everyone in the room, but at the sight of Davina's ashen face Bruno merely said, 'Sure. Will do.'

'Their little boy...' Davina's teeth were chattering so hard she had difficulty getting the words out. 'Andrew. Was Andrew hurt?'

'He wasn't with them. I don't know why. Sir Jerome didn't say. He did say, though, that Dr Sinclair's parents died last year and there are now no relatives on either side of the family to take care of him. Muriel Scolby went to the double funeral and when she realized the situation she brought Andrew back down to London with her. With the family solicitor's permission, he's now living at Shibden Hall.'

'And can he be adopted?'

The question was so unexpected that Boo blinked.

'Well, yes,' she said, 'I suppose so. Though he may be a little old now to be easily adopted: he's five. Sir Jerome mentioned that adoptive parents prefer babies or toddlers. Older ones don't seem to have much of a chance.'

'This one will.' Davina's teeth had stopped chattering and the light in her eyes was almost as fierce as the tone of her voice.

Bruno strode back into the room and Darius took the glass of brandy and a tartan car rug from him. He pressed the glass of brandy into Davina's hand and then laid the blanket around her shoulders.

Her eyes locked with his. 'When this bloody war is over,' she said unsteadily, her face like parchment, 'I shall adopt him, Darius. It's the least I can do for Aileen and Fergus.'

He felt beads of sweat break out on his forehead. The difficulties they faced in marrying had always been colossal, but even if was possible for him to survive the difficulty of having an English wife – and if he wanted the future Sadat had mapped out for him that difficulty was virtually insurmountable – he could never, in a million years, overcome the difficulty of having a British stepson.

He couldn't, though, tell her so when the Pytchley girl, Bruno Lautens and Archie Somerset were clustered so anxiously around her. Instead he said heavily, 'I think we should leave Davina alone for a little while.'

'Yes, of course, old chap.' The speaker was

Archie and as Archie duly opened the door, the incongruous sound of Delia singing 'Dixie' filled the room.

TWENTY FOUR

Later that night, back on the *Egyptian Queen*, he sat in darkness on the deck, a cigarette in one hand, a glass of arak in the other. Talking Davina out of adopting the Sinclair child wasn't an option: for one thing, he knew he wouldn't be able to; for another, he fully sympathized with what she intended doing. The Sinclairs had been her close friends. If their child was now left with no family and no one to turn to, Davina wouldn't be the person he loved if she hadn't responded as she had.

Over the river the sun was beginning to rise. From somewhere on the bank he could hear a pelican moving. He tossed the glowing butt of his cigarette overboard and thought of Sadat and of his meeting with him.

'You're a lawyer,' Sadat had said. 'And a skilled lawyer will have a vital part to play when the war is over and we, the Free Officers, take control of Egypt. And we won't want newcomers in positions of power. We'll want men whose loyalty and commitment have been forged now. A Minister of Justice who has been with us from the beginning.'

From anyone else he would have taken such a remark as empty daydreaming, but Constantin had told him enough about Sadat for him to know that Sadat was a hard-nosed realist, not a dreamer.

'There's a whole new breed of officers in the army now,' Constantin had said. 'And they are ready to stage an uprising as soon as the moment is right. Their real leader is an officer by the name of Gamel Nasser. Anwar is his deputy.'

What Constantin hadn't told him was that Anwar was in his early twenties. He had been expecting someone far older and, for a moment, he had been severely disconcerted. The shock hadn't lasted.

'It isn't only the British we need to be rid of,' Anwar had said bluntly. 'It's the monarchy. As long as there is a monarchy Egypt will remain poor and backward. All our country's wealth – the wealth from our cotton, from our canal – goes into the pockets of a handful of self-indulgent and corrupt men. There has to be change. The King is a parasite and has to go. The great landowners have to go. Parliament, as it exists, has to go. Everything must be ripped up by the roots and a new start made.'

A future such as the one Anwar painted – where the old feudal estates were broken up and given to the peasants, where the wealth from cotton was reinvested by a responsible government and put into the building of a modern state – was so far beyond anything he had ever dared to hope for once the initial goal of ridding Egypt of the British was attained, that he had been mesmerized by it.

By the time Anwar had left the houseboat,

Darius had known where his future lay. Together with Anwar and Nasser and the idealistic young officers they had gathered around them, he was going to be instrumental in the rebirth of Egypt. Above all, he was going to ensure that it was never again subordinated to another nation.

'And that includes Germany,' Anwar had said, stuffing tobacco into a pipe. 'We can't run the risk of putting misplaced trust in Germany. I know that at the moment, with the British having chased the Italian troops back into Libya, it looks as if the tide of the war is turning against Germany, but it won't be so for long. Hitler will send German troops to put spine into the Italians – and he'll do so under a first-class German general. When that general arrives, it is imperative we have direct contact with him. We can't stage an uprising that will help him take Cairo unless we have a guarantee that when the war is over, Egypt will be independent.'

It was so much what his own concerns were that he hadn't had a second's hesitation about it. 'What kind of contact?' he had asked. 'Wireless contact?'

'Only to arrange the meeting,' Anwar had said, lighting his pipe. 'Our intention is to fly one of our officers across the desert in a military aircraft for a personal meeting. It's risky, of course. When the British realize he's heading for enemy lines they'll try to shoot him down, and unless the Germans are expecting him, they'll blast him from the sky before he can land. They have to know when and where to expect him. As Constantin is already in touch with Berlin by wireless transmitter, Berlin will tell him the wavelength needed for their headquarters in Libya and, when the time is right, we'll be able to make contact with it.'

Darius lit another cigarette and poured himself some more arak. Golden light was now streaking the sky and gilding the surface of the Nile. In a few more hours Davina would, he knew, be with him.

He wondered how much he could safely tell her.

And he wondered if it was fair to tell her anything at all.

'I didn't break the news to my mother of Aileen and Fergus's deaths until breakfast time,' she said as she sat down wearily on one of the sun deck's sunloungers. 'I just couldn't bring myself to do it last night when she was having such a wonderful time.'

'And this morning?'

She winced. 'It was terrible. She admired both of them so much and had grown very fond of them, particularly Aileen.'

Her eyes were red-rimmed, her face etched with grief.

Seeing her pain was like feeling a knife twist in his heart.

'Would you like a coffee?' he asked, wishing there was some way he could comfort her.

She nodded. 'Yes, please. But not Turkish.'

Leaving her on the sunlounger he went down the companionway to the galley. Though he hadn't been to bed he had long since changed out of the Western clothes he had worn to Delia's

431

party, and into a galabiya. It was black, trimmed with narrow silver braid and as he caught sight of his reflection in the glass of the saloon door he was quite sure that he had never looked – or felt – more Egyptian than he did at that moment.

When he returned to the sun deck, he said, 'I've been introduced to a most remarkable young man, Davina. His name is Anwar Sadat and he's an army officer.'

And he told her all about Sadat's vision of an Egypt without foreign interference and without a corrupt monarchy or a corrupt Egyptian elite. And he told her how Sadat envisioned a place for him in the new republican scheme of things. He knew he should also be making clear to her just how difficult such a future would be for him if he were not only married to an English girl, but had a British stepson as well.

Because of her still raw distress over her friends' deaths, there was no way he could bring himself to do so.

Always able to read each other's minds, she did it for him.

'I doubt if the Free Officers envision a future Minister of Justice who is married to an English-woman,' she said, her voice filled with despair. 'And my adopting Andrew only complicates matters further, doesn't it?'

He wanted to say that no, it didn't. And because they had always been truthful with each other, he couldn't.

She put the tips of her fingers to her forehead as if trying to ease a pain that was too much to bear. 'Perhaps we should end things now, Darius.

Perhaps it would be easiest...'

He seized hold of her by her arms and pulled her roughly to her feet. 'No,' he said fiercely, knowing it was something he wouldn't, yet, be able to survive. 'Whatever will have to be done eventually doesn't have to be done now. It will be years before the Free Officers' dream comes to fruition. And it could well be years before you are able to adopt Andrew. Who knows how long this bally war is going to go on for? Who knows who is going to win it and what the circumstances will then be? For now, we go on as we've always been. Together. Anything else is simply not an option.'

She sagged against him, weak with relief.

His arms closed around her and as he hugged her to him he knew he was only forestalling a day that would have to come sometime, and when it did come, joy would go out of his life forever.

A month later a Romanian diplomat friend of Constantin's was expelled from the Romanian Legation on suspicion of spying. The Legation, however, was not closed down.

'Can't be, old boy,' Archie Somerset said in his infuriating English public-school accent to Bruno Lautens, in Darius's hearing. 'You have to remember that Egypt's not at war with Romania – or anyone else for that matter. Much as Ambassador Lampson would like to close the Hungarian and Romanian Legations, he can't. Getting rid of a diplomat so clearly a spy he may as well have had a label proclaiming it plastered across his forehead, was the most Lampson could do. It must make him crazy with rage. I know it

433

does me.'

Archie was the kind of hail-fellow-well-met type of Englishman that most annoyed Darius. Always jolly, always joking, he would disappear from Cairo for weeks on end and then turn up again with pale marks around his eyes left by sand goggles, and with no explanation other than that he had been 'in the blue' – British slang for the Western Desert.

When he was in Cairo, Archie was everywhere. No matter what the party, Archie was a guest. And Darius regularly ran across him in places British soldiers normally never surfaced. One day Archie said to him, 'How about a party on your houseboat, Darius? That's what houseboats are for, aren't they? A bit of music, a lot of dancing. Have you got a radiogram? I've got plenty of records you can borrow if you have.'

He had replied, stony-faced, that he never held parties.

Darius had even begun to wonder if Archie was the British contact giving so much information to Constantin.

The British euphoria over the collapse of the Italian advance changed to an atmosphere of tension in February when General Erwin Rommel landed in Libya at the head of two crack Panzer divisions.

Even before the month was out the Afrika Korps made their arrival felt by launching into an engagement with British troops at El Aghelia, the point in Libya where, a couple of months earlier, the British had run the Italians to a standstill. There was no running German troops to a standstill, and the prospect of Rommel striding into Shepheard's and commandeering the best suite suddenly seemed a very real possibility.

Sadat, using Constantin's wireless transmitter, contacted Rommel's headquarters in Libya from the *Egyptian Queen*. As a trained army wireless operator and using a code Constantin gave him, he made short work of the complicated procedure. To Sadat's great consternation, no reply came back.

In March, as more successful attacks were launched by the Germans, Britain's Foreign Secretary, Anthony Eden, flew into Cairo in order to take an on-the-spot report of the situation back to Churchill. He was accompanied by the Chief of the Imperial General Staff, Sir John Greer Dill, and by Sir Jerome Bazeljette.

Though nearly every moment of the three men's time was spent in discussions with the military hierarchy – and with Farouk and Prime Minister Ali Maher – Jerome did manage to squeeze in an appearance at a party thrown for him by Delia.

Darius – along with his father – received an invite.

Their hostess was radiant. Wryly Darius wondered if he was the only person – apart from her husband and Jerome – who was aware of the reason for Delia's glowing happiness as, with her arm tucked through Jerome's, she stayed close by his side while he renewed his acquaintance with people he knew from his pre-war visits to Nile House.

'Sylvia and Girlington are at Skooby for the duration,' he overheard Jerome say to Lady Tucker, the wife of an army general.

He hadn't a clue who was being talked about.

Aware he was eavesdropping, and of his puzzlement, Davina glided past him and whispered helpfully, 'Sylvia is the former Lady Bazeljette. The Duke of Girlington is Theo, her present husband. Skooby is one of their many homes and is a castle in the north of England.'

His lips twitched in amusement, but it was an amusement that vanished when Fawzia entered the room on their father's arm.

She looked ravishing, as always. Her blue-black, satin-shiny hair was coiled in an elaborate chignon. Her cocktail dress was ruby-red brocade, and magnificent diamonds he had never seen before were at her ears and at her throat. He regarded them cobra-eyed, certain that whatever she may have said to their father, they had not been given to her by her husband.

He remembered Anwar Sadat's passionate promise that when the Free Officers' Movement liberated Egypt from the feudal chains of its past, Farouk and all he stood for would be the first to go. For Darius, as he looked at the waterfall of diamonds hanging from his sister's ears, that day couldn't come soon enough.

'You'd forgotten that Sir Jerome is my father-in-law and that I was bound to be here, hadn't you?' she said when their father had moved off to speak to Ivor. 'Unfortunately he has no more news of Jack than I have. The last we heard he was in Palestine.'

436

Darius said nothing. Palestine was, though, too close to Egypt for comfort. Now that Sadat was attempting to contact Rommel from a wireless transmitter onboard the *Egyptian Queen*, the last thing he needed was a British intelligence officer turning up in Cairo – especially when that intelligence officer was both a brother-in-law and a friend.

From close behind them they both heard Delia, who had become temporarily detached from Jerome's arm, saying cheerily to Lady Tucker, 'It's so dandy getting reliable news of the Duke and Duchess. When I heard the Duke had been given the governorship of the Bahamas my heart sank. It's so far from Europe I couldn't imagine either of them feelin' it was anything but a form of exile, but apparently the Duke is doing a cracking job and Wallis, who is just as sweet as she can be, has thrown herself heart and soul into Red Cross work.'

Darius could see Lady Tucker's face, and it was a picture. He had long ago realized that no one in the British community had a good word to say about the woman for whom King Edward VIII had renounced his throne, but Delia always left no one in any doubt as to where she stood on the issue of Wallis Simpson. Wallis was her friend and, as she said often, 'a grand gal'.

While the conversation continued to take place behind him, with Lady Tucker stiffly changing the subject to Delia's highly successful club for all soldiers in the ranks, he watched Davina as she threaded her way through the guests in order to reach Jerome's side. Her cocktail dress was pale blue and simply cut, her shoulder-length fair hair held away from her face by a mother-of-pearl comb. Though she was twenty-five, she looked barely twenty and he was strongly reminded of an illustration he had once seen of Alice in the children's storybook, *Alice in Wonderland*.

Jerome's reaction to her approach was to give her an enormous, avuncular bear hug. Petra, he noted, was keeping her distance from Jerome, though he also noted that her eyes followed him wherever he went. Hard as he tried to read the expression in them, he couldn't. The expression was too guarded. All he could assume was that she was well aware of the nature of Jerome's relationship with her mother and that she wanted as little to do with him as possible.

The conversation between Jerome and Davina had become earnest and as he lip-read the words 'Shibden Hall' and 'Andrew', tension churned in his guts. He turned away, not wanting to lip-read any more; not wanting to be reminded of the devastation that would take place in his life on the day Davina adopted Andrew.

Leaving the party early, he arrived back at the *Egyptian Queen* not long after midnight to find Constantin seated on one of the deck's sun-loungers.

'What's the matter?' he asked abruptly, not in the mood for a late-night chat. 'I thought I'd told you I'd be at the Conisborough party for Sir Jerome Bazeljette this evening?'

'Did you? I'd forgotten. Still, if you're not in the mood for a drinking session I'll wander off.' He waited for Darius to dissuade him then, as

Darius didn't, he heaved himself to his feet. *'Noaptre buna,'* he said, wishing him goodnight in Romanian.

"Night,' Darius said, knowing he'd been inhospitably churlish and, with thoughts of Davina's intended adoption of Andrew Sinclair still on his mind, not caring.

By April Rommel was advancing on Egypt at such a pace that the British, fearful that the Egyptian army units stationed on and near the frontier would throw in their lot with Rommel, ordered that they be replaced with Allied troops.

'And our generals acquiesced!' Anwar exploded. 'If only Rommel had come back to us, agreeing to meet with one of our officers and agreeing to sign the treaty I've drafted, it would have been the perfect time to have staged an uprising. As it is, there is still no word from him. Why, Darius? Why?'

By May the war in the desert had grown tenser and was being conducted on such a vast scale that the streets of Cairo were clogged with dispatch riders, trucks packed with equipment and men, and ambulances bringing in the wounded from the front. The number of tanks engaged in the battles being conducted was astronomical and the talk in the Long Bar at Shepheard's was that the Germans could be expected to arrive at the pyramids at any moment.

Tobruk, a coastal town of great strategic value because of its deep harbour, had been encircled by Rommel and Darius didn't expect anything else to be the talk of the day. He was wrong. The news Davina took the trouble to break to him herself was news that, where the British community was concerned, superseded even that of what was happening at Tobruk.

'My parents are divorcing,' she said to him, white-faced, as she stepped aboard the houseboat.

'Sit down,' he said. 'I'll make coffee.'

Only when the coffee had been made did he allow her to begin talking again.

'My father is going to marry Kate,' she said dazedly. 'And the incredible thing is, my mother doesn't mind. She says that as Kate is thirty-nine and is desperate to have a baby, it's best they marry now before it's too late for her to have one.'

Davina passed a hand across her eyes. 'I feel so odd about it, Darius. Knowing Kate was having an affair with my father was one thing. I came to terms with that knowledge ages ago. But I never dreamed my father would divorce my mother so that he and Kate could marry. He and my mother have always been so close. He's always talked with her about absolutely everything. And that is how my mother says it will stay. She says that they will always be each other's best friend.'

She took a sip of her coffee and then said, utter bafflement in her voice, 'My mother almost seems *relieved* by my father asking for a divorce. She says it is something that couldn't have happened when my father was an official government advisor to King Fuad and when he acted in the same capacity to King Farouk. A divorce then would

440

have meant his immediate recall to London and the end of his career. In England, divorcees aren't even allowed to attend court. Their social life would have taken an enormous battering. Now, even if that happens, I don't think either of them cares. And it probably *won't* happen because the war has changed everything. People think differently now, and behave differently.'

'Where will Kate and your father marry?' he asked, bemused.

'I don't know. In the Church of England, people who have been divorced can't have a church wedding. My mother is hoping – as it matters to Kate so much – that after a civil marriage ceremony they might be able to have a blessing in the English cathedral.'

'If that's what your mother is hoping for, then I dare say it will be what your mother gets,' he said, wondering whether, before very long, Davina was going to have to face the even more profound shock of realizing that her mother had taken news of being divorced with such equanimity because of her long-lasting and obviously deep love for Sir Jerome Bazeljette.

'Who is going to be the one to move out of Nile House?' he asked, intrigued as to how the three protagonists were going to survive the deluge of gossip about them.

'My father. He's already moved into a house here, on Gezira Island, close to the Sporting Club.'

She looked exhausted and he said abruptly, 'Let's go to Fleurent's for lunch. You can tell me about Petra's reaction to the news over a glass of wine.'

According to Davina, Petra hadn't allowed her even a glimpse of what she was really feeling. What she had done, instead, was to affect great indifference. It wasn't a reaction shared by anyone else in the British community. Wherever he went, Darius heard the Conisborough divorce and Lord Conisborough's intended remarriage being discussed. For any another couple of their social standing it would have been social death. The Conisboroughs, however, rode out the storm with admirable élan, thanks mainly to Delia, who behaved as if nothing very extraordinary had happened and who continued to give the best parties in Cairo at Nile House.

In order not to prejudice the divorce proceedings, neither Ivor nor Kate was present at any of them, but even the most blinkered of Cairenes realized that if Delia could have had them there, she would have had them there.

'Of course, she's *American*,' Darius often overheard in Shepheard's or Groppi's, but it was always said with admiration, not condemnation.

'She's sassy,' he once heard Lady Lampson say, using an American-expression often used by Delia.

It had amused him. He'd wondered if Lady Lampson also regularly told her husband that the gig was up.

As the first shockwaves of the Conisborough divorce began to die, conversation everywhere reverted to the continuing siege of Tobruk. The garrison there consisted of the Australian 9th

Division, under General Morshead, and British troops who had withdrawn there before the start of the siege.

'They make a total of twenty-five thousand men,' a brigadier bragged in Shepheard's Long Bar.

It was the kind of careless talk to make Constantin euphoric.

Two days later a coded message was received from Rommel. He was agreeable to a meeting with a member of the Free Officers' Movement and would give consideration to the treaty the officer would be bringing with him. To guarantee the safety of the plane flying the officer over German lines, the date and time of his flight needed transmitting back as a matter of urgency.

Sadat's voice, as he said over the telephone, 'I'll be at the houseboat tonight at midnight, to transmit,' was taut with tension.

Darius and Davina had a party to go to that evening – in Cairo there were always parties to go to – and this one was being given by Momo Marriott, wife of Brigadier Sir John Marriott. Momo, who was nearly as popular a hostess as Delia, had transformed the basement of her house into a lavish private nightclub.

Even though it would mean him leaving the party early he didn't for a second consider not going. All the usual crowd would be there, which meant that Bruno Lautens would be there. And he knew that Bruno was deeply smitten with Davina and that there was nothing more Bruno would like than to be able to spend time with her when he, Darius, wasn't around.

The moment he and Davina stepped into Chez Marie, which was the name Momo had given her nightclub, they were swallowed up in a glittering throng of Cairo's elitest socialites, for Momo went out of her way to play hostess to many European royals who had sought sanctuary in Egypt when their countries had been overrun by the Germans.

King Zog of Albania was dancing with his wife, Geraldine. King Victor-Emmanuel of Italy was also dancing, though not with his wife. Prince Wahid al-Din, Princess Shevekiar's son, was standing by the bar talking with Petra. Jacquetta, Lady Lampson, was laughing at something Sholto Monck was saying to her. Winston Churchill's son, Randolph, who was in Cairo as a press officer, was there, flirting with Momo.

There were a score of glamorous 'fishing fleet' girls; an entire contingent of British officers on leave from the front; a rowdy bunch of New Zealanders, also on leave from the front, and an even rowdier bunch of Australians; a whole clutch of Embassy personnel; many members of upper-crust Egyptian families, both Syro-Lebanese and Coptic. The singer Momo had purloined from the Scarabée Club was singing Johnny Mercer's 'Jeepers Creepers' and Archie Somerset was doing an energetic quickstep to it with Boo Pytchley.

'Squeeze through the crush and get a couple of glasses of champagne!' Davina shouted to him over the noise of the music and the laughter. 'I'll wait for you here!'

He launched himself into the fray and as he did Princess Shevekiar accidentally bumped into him.

She was elderly and he immediately steadied her.

'Thank you so much,' she said regally, not seeming to recognize him, and then, looking in the direction in which he had left Davina, she said, 'Lady Russell Pasha has just pointed out to me what a wonderful match Bruno Lautens would be for Davina Conisborough. He's a widower with a young son, did you know that? His little boy would make a perfect stepbrother for the child Davina is going to adopt.'

Darius swung round. Several quickstepping couples now separated him from Davina, but she was no longer standing alone. Lautens was with her. Seeing them together like that, from a distance, rooted him to the spot. It was as if he had suddenly been transported in time to the future: a future where the war was over and he was part of the government of an independent Egypt. A future where Andrew Sinclair was Davina's adopted son. A future where, because he had ended his relationship with her, she and Bruno had married and he, Egypt's Minister of Justice, was doomed to seeing them together, as they were now together, at every social occasion he attended.

He tried to think how he would survive such a hell, and knew he wouldn't be able to. Passionately as he loved his country and wanted to hold the highest office in it that he could, he knew in a moment of blinding revelation that high office would never be able to compensate him for losing Davina. She was as essential to him as breathing was. So what if her father was English? And so what if the child she was to adopt was Scottish? It was something the Free Officers'

Movement would simply have to accept.

And if they didn't?

If they didn't, he would still have Davina, and as long as he still had Davina then his life would be worth living.

As the singer on the tiny rostrum started to sing 'All the Things You Are,' he began, for the first time, to understand just why King Edward VIII had renounced his throne rather than give up Mrs Simpson.

He began weaving a way through the dancers towards Davina. He felt as if he were doing so in slow motion. He felt as if he might never reach her. He was aware of Bruno Lautens turning round towards him at his approach, but he wasn't interested in Bruno Lautens.

She smiled at him. It was the smile that had entranced him when she had been little more than a child, and that entranced him still. It was the smile that would entrance him as long as he lived.

He took her hands and held them tightly in his – and he knew that if Petra was to ask him now if he was intending to marry Davina, the answer would be that of course he was; that any alternative to the two of them being together for the rest of their lives was utterly and totally unthinkable.

PART FIVE

Jack

1941

TWENTY FIVE

Jack's satisfaction when his commanding officer told him he was to be transferred to British Intelligence in Cairo was so deep it was all he could to prevent himself from punching the air.

'You'll still be under the umbrella of Security Intelligence Middle East, but you'll liaise with SIB, Cairo's Special Investigation Branch.'

His commanding officer shuffled paperwork into a file.

'All the usual rules apply. You can wear civvies or the uniform of any other rank below your own as the situation necessitates. And the situation, I may tell you, is grim. Someone in Cairo is passing on classified information to the enemy. Your task is to hunt out whoever it is, before Rommel is on the terrace at Shepheard's ordering himself a beer.'

He leaned forward, resting his elbows on his desk and steepling his fingers.

'I see from your file that your wife is Egyptian and is living in Cairo,' he said, frowning slightly. 'It's a situation that could prove good cover for intelligence work, but generally speaking I think I'd keep it under my hat. And there'll be no married quarters. Army wives, apart from those of brigadiers and generals, were evacuated a year ago whether they wanted to be or not. Not many went willingly and so you can see the bad feeling

449

that would arise if you were seen enjoying connubial bliss.'

Jack nodded. The minute he'd heard of his transfer his thoughts had flown to Fawzia and the difficulties the nature of his work would cause to their reunion. Their not being able to live together would ease those difficulties immeasurably.

He flew from Jerusalem to Cairo crammed uncomfortably in a Wellington bomber, and as the Wellington's engines thundered in his ears he was aware, to his shame, that his thoughts weren't centred so much on Fawzia as on Petra.

The last time he had seen her was when he and Fawzia visited Cairo during the summer before war was declared. She'd spent as little time as possible in his company, and on the occasions she couldn't avoid him she hadn't wanted to talk to him. She hadn't even seemed to be the same woman. She had been so taut, so tense, so buttoned-up that it was as if she were going to explode at any moment. He understood only one thing: if she had ever been in love with him, she was so no longer. Their affair was over. Finished. Kaput. And just to make sure he had got the message she had married that long thin streak of shallow facile charm, Sholto Monck.

Monck, he knew, was still in Cairo and because of his position at the Embassy, he was someone Jack was going to have to rub along with. It wasn't something he was looking forward to.

As the Wellington's wheels put down at an airstrip near to Hilmiya camp he exerted considerable self-control and put all thoughts of Petra on

450

hold, allowing the anticipation he always felt when returning to Cairo to flood through him, for Cairo was, without, doubt, his most favourite city in all the world.

Stepping out onto the tarmac and breathing in the familiar hot, spicy air, he determinedly thought only of the upside of everything. After eighteen long months he was about to be reunited with his wife, and though his marriage had always been far shakier than he had ever openly admitted, it was a marriage he was determined to make work.

He was also about to be reunited with people who, apart from his father, were closer to him than members of his family. Delia was certainly closer to him than his mother had ever been. When he thought of his childhood and of being loved and cherished and mothered, it was Delia he thought of. Delia, not his mother, had been the one who had spent time with him, who had turned up at school sports days with his father in order to cheer him on in rugger matches and cricket matches, and who, with Petra and Davina also in tow, had taken him to the zoo and the circus and the cinema. As for Davina: she was the baby sister he had never had. Being reunited with Davina was going to be pure pleasure. A reunion with his brother-in-law was something he was looking forward to, too.

He knew from several sources – Davina's letters, Delia's letters, his father's trips to Cairo – that Darius had put his anti-British activity on hold not long after war had been declared. That he had was certainly going to make things easier where their family relationship and their friendship were concerned. He wondered whether they would be able to manage a game of polo together; this time with both of them playing for the same team.

A young lieutenant saluted then courteously took his briefcase from him and led him across to a waiting staff car.

'It's a filthy city, Major Bazeljette,' the lieutenant said, assuming it was his first time there. He slid behind the wheel, put the jeep into gear and said even more helpfully, 'And the bloody wogs are a nightmare. You can't trust them as far as you can throw them – not that you'd want to throw them anywhere because that would mean having to touch them,' he added, chuckling at what he thought was his very funny remark.

Jack rested a foot against the jeep's dashboard, and with his knee comfortably bent almost against his chest, he took a packet of Camels out of his Jacket pocket. 'My wife is an Egyptian,' he said, lighting up.

The jeep slewed almost off the road. 'I'm sorry, Major!' The lieutenant's spluttered apologies were abject. 'I didn't know... Didn't think... Oh, Christ!'

Jack didn't tell him it was all right and not to worry. He let him suffer. The news that his wife was Egyptian would, he knew, now spread like wildfire. That this was directly opposite to the advice he had been given before leaving Jerusalem didn't bother him. It would save him from hearing the word 'wog' being bandied about every few minutes and that, for his temper's sake, was of prime importance.

Hilmiya camp was six miles from the centre of Cairo and, as it was an approach to the city he had never made before, he settled back to enjoy the ride. The narrow road was so congested with army traffic that there were times when he thought it would have been quicker to walk.

Quicker, but far more exhausting. It was July and the heat was so intense that beneath his khaki shirt he could feel sweat trickling down between his shoulder blades. By the time the Citadel and the gleaming white alabaster walls of the Mohammed Ali Mosque came into view, he was gasping for an ice-cold beer.

As they entered the city the bars and pavement cafés were thronged with troops who had all had the same idea as himself. There were British uniforms, Australian and New Zealand uniforms, Free French, South African and Indian uniforms. Always a crowded, noisy, dusty and hectic city, Cairo was now a noisy, dusty and hectic city explosively bursting at the seams.

Almost submerged under the endless sea of khaki there were, though, plenty of old familiar sights. Sherbet-sellers still weaved their way through the crowds. Beggars still crowded every corner. Old men in dirty galabiyas pushed hand barrows piled high with fruit and vegetables through the traffic, dusty leather slippers slapping against their bare heels. Overloaded, scrawny donkeys fought with buses and cars for road space and survival. Trains crawled down the centre of the roads, some passengers squatting cross-legged on their roofs, others balancing with death-defying fervour on their running boards.

At Ezbekiya Gardens the ancient bandstand was still standing. At the corner of Opera Square Cicurel's department store still boasted a window display of hats so fashionable they would have done a shop in the Champs-Élysées proud.

The long wailing notes of the muezzins calling the faithful to prayer sounded as they motored down Kasr el Nil Street and then, minutes later, he caught his first glimpse of the Nile.

It was a sight that had always made his heart slam against his chest, and the sight of its olive-green water dotted with white-sailed feluccas made it slam now.

His driver swerved left into a road that flanked the river bank, heading straight for GHQ, the British Army Headquarters in Garden City.

GHQ was situated in a modern block of flats called Grey Pillars at the southern end of Garden City, not far from his father-in-law's palatial family home and close to Nile House. Knowing that a reunion with Fawzia and a visit to Nile House were going to have to wait until he had hit base with his new commanding officer he fought down his impatience and wondered if his CO in Jerusalem had got it right when he had said that his prime task was going to be the hunting down of one specific spy.

Brigadier Haigh, the Director of Military Intelligence, left him in no doubt that it was.

'The bugger's got to be caught, Major, and so far we've no lead on him at all. All we know is that the German military know what we're going to do before we do it. The information getting to them could be coming from anywhere. The former

Prime Minister, Sirri Pasha, is still a force politically and is so pro-German he'd inform the Germans of our plans at the drop of a hat – given the chance. The King is no different. Ambassador Lampson has a terrible time getting him to toe the line.'

That the brigadier regarded Lampson's relationship to the King as that of a schoolmaster to a fractious pupil would have been comic if it hadn't also been the kind of attitude that made good relations with the Palace well-nigh impossible.

Hoping to aid his superior officer's understanding without finding himself on the first plane back to Palestine, Jack said mildly, 'With Egypt not being at war with Germany itself, sir, but unwillingly caught up in our war, Farouk is always going to be fractious. It can't be much fun for him having his cities full of foreign troops and his desert crawling with tanks.'

'The bugger's lucky to have us here!' the brigadier snapped. 'If it wasn't for us, the Italians would have swarmed into Cairo a year ago and sent him packing. You're here, Major Bazeljette, because you have pre-war knowledge of the city and because you studied Arabic at Oxford. Being a Gyppo-lover isn't part of requirements – and it won't make you many friends.'

Wisely keeping any further thoughts to himself Jack saluted and made a judicious exit.

The next two hours were spent in familiarizing himself with his office and his staff. Grey Pillars was a rabbit warren on a massive scale. Scores of what had once been separate flats had had their walls ripped out and partitioning put up to make

455

offices and cubicles out of every available inch of space. Narrow corridors linking what had been one flat with another were thronged with harassed-looking army personnel hurrying along with huge files in their arms.

His own corner of the rabbit warren came furnished with a desk, a chair, a filing cabinet, a wastepaper basket, a telephone and, much to his great relief, a window.

'And I'm Doris, your typist, sir,' a pleasant-faced young woman in army uniform said, walking into the room and putting a huge sheaf of files on the desk. 'I'm also the typist for six other intelligence officers, so sometimes if you want me you have to shout quite loud. Would you like a cup of tea? Some of these files haven't been dusted off for months. You'll probably find them thirsty work.'

It wasn't the way he'd been addressed by WACs when he'd been in Jerusalem, but he far preferred a free and easy working atmosphere to a stiff and formal one and, as she was wearing a wedding ring and as her friendliness wasn't in the least flirtatious, he said with equal ease, 'A cup of tea would be just the job, Doris. I was told my staff included a Captain Reynolds and a Corporal Slade. Is either of them about?'

'Captain Reynolds has been transferred to another unit, sir. We're expecting a replacement, but he hasn't shown up as yet. Corporal Slade is hunting down a staff car for you. Nothing in Cairo is quite as organized as you might be used to. I believe Corporal Slade is also checking out your quarters. Or rather, finding you some quarters.

Sleeping space is like gold. As you are Intelligence you'll probably find yourself sharing a flat with a couple of other intelligence officers. The barracks are packed to overflowing.'

An hour later, after meeting with his radio-room staff and the corporal in charge of them, but with Corporal Slade still nowhere in evidence, he left Grey Pillars to make the short walk to Fawzia's family home.

It had been eighteen months since he had last seen her, and when they had parted it had been in steaming anger after a furious, blistering row.

The row had been about money. Fawzia simply could not understand why they didn't live the same type of lifestyle in London that Delia lived when there, or that his mother and Theo Girlington lived.

'But your father is a baronet and your mother is a duchess!' she would say time and time again, 'so why are we living in a flat that would fit into my family home a dozen times over?'

That the flat was palatial by London standards made no difference to her. It wasn't a mansion in Cadogan Square – and the equivalent of a mansion in Cadogan Square had been, he had found out far too late, what she had expected.

Jewellery had been an issue too. His wedding present to her had been a diamond and emerald brooch that had been his paternal grandmother's. The family tiara that in normal circumstances would have been given to her was in the posses-sion of his mother, and she, despite the fabulous jewellery collection that had come her way when she married Theo, had shown not the slightest desire to relinquish either it, or any other items of Bazeljette family jewels. To compensate for the lack of them, his father's wedding present to Fawzia had been a splendid tiara from Aspreys.

Fawzia's false expectations when they had married were not expectations that could be made good. His Foreign Office salary and the private income that had been left to him by his Bazeljette grandmother ensured he was relatively well off, but he wasn't rich. Even looking to the future he had no expectations of being rich on the scale Fawzia thought of as being rich, which meant being rich on the scale that her father was rich.

That she'd had so little idea about what the realities of being Mrs Jack Bazeljette would be, he blamed on himself. In Cairo she had been brought up in a luxuriously cocooned world. Though she had been friends with Petra and Davina she had never, apart from the lessons they had shared as school girls, lived as they lived. By the time she was fifteen, Davina was doing voluntary work at the orphanage and travelling unaccompanied on public transport. Fawzia, he knew for a certainty, had never been on a Cairo tram in her life.

When she had stayed in Cadogan Square with Davina in order to share Davina's London season with her, and had later shocked her father to the core by announcing she wasn't going to return to Cairo after Petra's wedding but was going to stay on in London as Delia's guest, she had been almost as equally cocooned. Delia had been far stricter about where Fawzia could and couldn't go, and who she could, or couldn't go with, than she had ever been with her own daughters.

At London balls and parties everyone Delia allowed Fawzia to meet was either cash rich, or land rich, or both. That Fawzia had assumed he too was heir to half of an English county had never occurred to him. And he doubted whether it had ever occurred to Delia either.

When he reached the heavy cedar-wood door set in the high blank wall he spoke in Arabic to the Nubian guarding it. Seconds later, as the door creaked open, he stepped into the familiar shade of the colonnaded courtyard, fraught with tension at the thought of the reunion about to take place.

The fountain in the centre of the courtyard trickled water. Lizards clung to its bronze, verdi-gris-coated base. A large Ispahan rose dropped pale pink petals onto the mosaic tiles it overhung.

Two sufragis ran to meet him dressed in blind-ingly white galabiyas sashed in crimson. Hard on their heels was Zubair Pasha, a welcoming smile on his walnut-dark, heavily lined face.

'So you are finally back in Cairo, Jack!' he said exuberantly, steaming up to him and clapping both hands on his shoulders in a gesture of affec-tion. 'Fawzia said you would move heaven and earth in order to be posted here. She will have to be moved out of her present bedroom – it isn't large enough for the two of you. I will have the double guest bedroom made ready immediately. And where is your kit? Have you left it at the gate-way?'

'No kit, I am afraid.' Jack's answering smile was rueful. 'Orders are that I don't draw attention to the fact that I have a wife in the city. The whole-sale evacuation of army wives has made doing so insensitive, apparently.'

Zubair raised his eyebrows slightly, but it was in understanding, not bewilderment. After a life-time at Abdin with first King Fuad and then Farouk, if anyone knew the nuances of pussy-footing around sensitive or potentially sensitive situations, he did.

'You must have a welcome drink,' he said as a sufragi appeared at their side with two rosewater-scented drinks on a silver tray. 'And while you are drinking I will explain to you that Fawzia is not at home, but is at Nile House. She spends a lot of time at Nile House, with Davina.'

Grateful that Zubair Pasha showed no inten-tion of delaying him with a traditionally long Egyptian welcome, Jack drank the sickly sweet drink and minutes later was making his way down the elegant winding roads of Garden City to Nile House.

Adjo greeted him with restrained but deep affection.

There was nothing unrestrained about Delia's greeting.

She was in the drawing room arranging yellow lilies in a crystal vase and when, at his request, he walked in on her unannounced, she dropped the lily she was holding and with a cry of delight ran towards him, a smile of blazing pleasure on her face.

'Jack! How grand!' she gasped as he hugged her tightly. 'We'd no idea you were going to be posted here! Did Fawzia know? And if she did, how could the little minx have kept it to herself?'

'No one knew,' he said, filled with the huge sense of well-being Delia always imparted to those she loved. 'I didn't know till two days ago. Is she here?'

'Here?' Delia stepped away from him. She was now in her late forties and her beauty was more full-blown than it had once been, but it was also bone-deep and he knew that she would never lose it. She was wearing a straight-skirted cornflower-blue linen dress, the waist cinched by a broad, white leather belt. 'No, she isn't here,' she said, looking a little startled. 'Apart from running into her at parties I haven't seen Fawzia for weeks and weeks. If she isn't at the Palace, she'll be at home.'

'She isn't at home,' he said easily, not letting the faint sense of disquiet he was beginning to feel, show. 'And why should she be at the Palace?'

Delia tucked her hand comfortably into the crook of his arm. 'She's always at the Palace,' she said as she began to walk him towards the French windows and the terrace beyond them. 'Farouk neglects his little queen quite disgracefully and Farida relies on friends such as Fawzia for company – sometimes too much so. Davina says that more than once when she and Fawzia have been out together a royal car has drawn up, a court flunky has announced that Fawzia's presence is required at the Palace and Fawzia's been borne off whether she's really wanted to go or not.'

A pergola had been built over the terrace since he had last been at Nile House and as they stood beneath the shade of the vine growing over it and

461

looked down towards the river, he said, 'Zubair Pasha didn't mention Fawzia's Palace visits. He said she spent most of her time with Davina.'

'Well, she probably would if she could,' Delia responded drily, 'but spending time with Davina is difficult for anyone. Every nurse in Cairo is working eighteen hours out of every twenty-four – and then some. And Zubair Pasha isn't well-versed any more in what's going on at Abdin. Pride will prevent him from saying so to you, but he's been out of favour with the King for some time now – probably because he's far too openly pro-British for the King's comfort.'

As they began walking again, this time down the terrace steps and onto the lawn, she said, 'Now what other news d'you need bringing up to date on? There's the divorce, of course. Ivor is at last going to make an honest woman out of Kate, and he will, hopefully, finally father a son and heir. Needless to say, everything is extremely amicable – though I think Cairo society rather wishes it wasn't, as it would make things so much more interesting for them. Back in England, Shibden Hall is full to capacity with evacuees and orphans – including an orphan I think will soon be a member of the family.'

If the news that she and Ivor were divorcing was a thundering surprise, it wasn't a totally unexpected one. The news about an orphan who was about to become a member of the Conisborough family was, however, a complete mystery.

'The orphan,' he prompted, seeing with amusement that the lawn no longer rolled in immaculate splendour down to the banks of the

Nile, but that the bottom two-thirds of it had been turned into a field in which several aged donkeys were contentedly grazing.

'Davina's friends, Aileen and Fergus Sinclair, were killed in a road accident in Scotland. Toynbee Hall was notified and Muriel Scolby, the receptionist and office manager at Toynbee, notified your father. She also went to the funeral. When she realized there were no grandparents or aunts and uncles to take care of the Sinclairs' little boy, she took it upon herself to do so. Being wartime, officialdom was only too happy to let her. For the moment Andrew is at Shibden, where your father visits him as regularly as he is able. The long-term plan is for him to come to Cairo. Davina is going to adopt him.'

They reached the stone wall that was the Nile's embankment and she said, 'As for Shibden, when the war is over, it will remain a children's home. Ivor has no use for it – he and Kate intend remaining in Cairo – and though I shall return to London when the Allies have put paid to Hitler, I won't have much use for it either – and the days of keeping a house Shibden's size in order to use it only on high days and holidays are long gone.'

She turned to face him, the light breeze from the river tugging at hair that was still a defiant Titian-red. 'The same goes for Sans Souci, of course,' she said meditatively, 'but Sans Souci is different and I have every intention of spending long periods of time there when the world has regained its sanity.' The smile that could light up a whole room split her face, the laughter lines around her mouth and her eyes deepening. 'And when I do go back to Sans Souci,' she said in a sudden burst of confidence, her husky voice fizzing with happiness, 'I shall do somethin' I've wanted to do for twenty-eight years, Jack. I shall take your father with me.'

It was, he knew, the broadest hint possible that when her divorce was finalized, she and his father were going to spend the rest of their lives together.

Knowing that one of the questions he'd longed to ask was no longer necessary, he finally asked the most necessary question of all.

As the roaring of the lions in the Gezira zoo echoed faintly across the water, he said, keeping his voice casual with superhuman effort, 'How is Petra, Delia?'

TWENTY SIX

'Petra,' Delia said, turning her back to the river and looking towards the house, 'is fine. You will stay for a late lunch, won't you? Then we can catch up on all sorts of other gossip. Boo Pytchley is in Cairo, and so is Archie Somerset. I don't think Petra has had news of Rupert and all we know of Annabel and Fedya is that Fedya is in the RAF. Suzi, of course, it's impossible to get news of. What life is like in German occupied Paris is hard to imagine, but at least Suzi isn't Jewish. I say my prayers every night for the French who are. As for Magda...'

464

She tucked her hand once more in the crook of his arm and they began walking back to the house. 'As for Magda, I sincerely pray she no longer thinks Hitler is the Saviour of Germany. In the days when she so admired him he hadn't yet shown his true colours and it has to be remembered that there was a time when much of English high society shared her admiration. In 1936, when Ribbentrop was the German Ambassador to London, he was accepted socially nearly everywhere. I met him twice when we were both guests at the same dinner party. Sholto, I believe, met him even more often in similar circumstances. As for poor Wallis...'

She lifted her shoulders in a gesture of despair.

'According to your father there's a rumour going round that she and Ribbentrop were lovers. It's the usual bunk. Wallis would never have put her relationship with David at risk in such a way. Why people are such skunks about her is beyond me.'

It was a familiar refrain of Delia's, and as they walked up the wide shallow steps leading to the terrace he was thinking about Petra again and of how infuriatingly unsatisfactory Delia's brief comment about her had been. He was fairly sure he knew why she'd been so vaguely offhand and why she had so immediately changed the subject. It was because she didn't want him causing waves in Petra's marriage to Sholto. It was because she didn't want to see his marriage to Fawzia come to grief. She was sending the message loud and clear that it was out of order for him to show any undue interest in Petra; that his doing so could only lead to heartbreak, and the heartbreak would be his.

And she was quite right about the dangers. British social life in Cairo had always revolved around only a handful of venues: the Gezira Club, the Turf Club, Shepheard's, the Continental, both Groppi's, the Mena House Hotel, the Scarabée, Fleurent's, the Mohammed Ali Club. That they would meet continually went without saying. For Petra, happily married to Monck, such meetings would be of no great consequence. For him, they would be of such consequence that the already shaky foundations of his marriage could very well totter.

And he owed it to Fawzia not to let them.

Filled with the steely resolve to make his marriage work, he stepped into the shady coolness of the dining room and began paying attention to Delia's conversation once again.

'Your father doesn't get to ride half as much as he would like these days,' she said as they took their places at a beautifully laid table. 'In Virginia he'll be able to ride to his heart's content.'

With amusement he saw that the table was laid for two: Adjo had taken it for granted that he would be staying for lunch. He also noticed how Delia's face glowed as she mentioned his father.

'When I was a girl,' she said, her green eyes growing dreamy with memory, 'I had the most wonderful horse, his name was Sultan. I miss him still. Saying goodbye to him was one of the hardest things I've ever had to do.'

A young sufragi, who had a look of Adjo about him and was, Jack suspected, probably one of

Adjo's great-nephews, poured the wine and then left them in privacy to enjoy their meal.

'Was that when you left Virginia after marrying Ivor?' he asked, breaking off a piece of warm pitta bread and dipping it into a dish of hummus.

'Yes.' She sounded unusually thoughtful and instinct told him to remain silent.

She took a black olive from a blue and white glazed bowl, bit into it and then said; 'He wasn't in love with me when we married, although he was deeply attracted to me and had a genuine affection for me – an affection that has lasted, I'm glad to say.'

It was something he had long suspected, but hearing her suddenly speaking of it so frankly was a shock. He said carefully, knowing he was on dangerous ground, 'But if he didn't love you, why did he marry you?'

She put a tongful of fava bean salad onto her plate and added a stuffed sweet pepper. 'He was a widower who had no heir. I was young and he thought I would be able to provide him with a son – probably with several sons. As it was, after Petra and Davina there were no more children. Considering how great his disappointment was, he took it mighty well.'

Things that had never previously been spoken of between them were now being said and it was such an opportunity to ask the kind of question he'd been burning to ask for years that he forgot all about eating.

'If Ivor didn't love you,' he said, 'who did he love?'

Her eyebrows rose slightly, as if it was a

467

question she was surprised he'd had to ask. 'Why, your mother, of course,' she said.

Her eyes held his with perfect candour.

'Your mother was the love of Ivor's life from when he was a young man. He was in love with her when he married Olivia, and he was in love with her when he married me – and she remained the love of his life long after she ended their affair and married Theo Girlington.'

There was no bitterness or resentment in her voice and he realized that all bitterness and resentment and deep, deep hurt were long over with.

'Kate, who is so utterly different in every way from your mother, brought personal happiness back into his life.' Her affection for Kate was clear in her voice. 'I've always been grateful to her for that. With luck she'll be able to give him the son he has waited for, for so long.'

Asking her about her own personal happiness was unnecessary. He knew with whom her own happiness lay. There was, though, one question he absolutely had to ask while she was in such a starkly honest mood.

'Why,' he said, as she took a sip of her wine, 'did you object so strongly to the thought of my marrying Petra?'

The instant the words left his mouth it was as if the air in the room had been violently sucked out of it. The tension was so thick, it was palpable.

She stared down into her wine for a long, long moment and then, as she took a deep steadying breath, the door of the dining room opened and Fawzia walked in. Her blue-black hair was looped into a knot on the top of her head. Her skin gleamed pale gold. In her flawless face her kohl-rimmed eyes were as dark as sloes. She was wearing a vivid emerald brocade dress more suitable for a cocktail party than the early afternoon and she looked like a princess straight out of the Arabian Nights.

'Daddy told me you were here!' she said a trifle breathlessly. 'Isn't this wonderful? To be together again like this?'

He rose from the table and closed the space between them in quick strides, agonizingly aware that the moment between Delia and himself had been lost and that it would not come again.

As he held her close, kissing her with as much passion as Delia's presence allowed, he was aware that her perfume was as unsuitable for an afternoon as her dress. It was heavy and exotic and very, very sexy.

'How long are you here for?' she asked, her arms still around his neck as he finally lifted his head from hers. 'Your father was in Cairo with Mr Eden a few months ago, but only for three days. Then they flew off to have important talks somewhere else. Ankara, I think. Is that what you will be doing, Jack?'

'No,' he chuckled, amused at her naivety. 'I've been posted here and will most likely be here for the duration of the war. We can't live together, though. Did your father tell you? We're going to have to behave like illicit lovers.'

She gurgled with laughter. 'But that will be fun! Will you be in an apartment, or in barracks?'

'An apartment, but it won't be mine alone. I'll

be sharing it with a couple of other officers.'

She gave a small pout, but it was one that signalled she was going to accept the difficulties they would be living under. He was deeply grateful. Not many wives would have been so understanding, and it indicated that Fawzia had done a lot of growing up during their eighteen-month long separation.

'Adjo is bringing some champagne,' Delia said, as they came to join her at the table, their arms around each other's waist. 'So if you two happy people can bear to delaying haring off together for just another few minutes, we'll drink it in cele-bration. D'you have a staff car yet, Jack? If you haven't, you can borrow my car, because the best place for a little privacy is still the Mena House Hotel.'

Thirty minutes later, in Delia's racy, open, drophead coupé they were on the road leading to Giza, the pyramids – and Mena House.

The straight road he had been used to skim-ming along in pre-war days with only goats, sheep and heavily laden donkeys and camels to slow him down, was now chock-a-block with army traffic heading out to the Western Desert.

A mile out of Cairo Fawzia's hair suddenly tumbled free of its pins and cascaded past her shoulders, long and heavy.

He took his eyes from the road to shoot her a swift, amused glance. 'You must have put your hair up in an awful hurry.'

'Pins can never be trusted,' she said lightly, a flush to her cheeks that he couldn't for the life of him see the reason for.

When they finally reached Mena House the rooms there were as chock-a-block as the road from Cairo had been. However, Fawzia was the married daughter of Zubair Pasha and her father's name carried a lot of weight.

A room was found for them – and not just any room. It looked south, giving a glorious view of the pyramids.

'It's a good job we can't see the Sphinx from this angle,' she said as he tipped the bellboy and closed the door. 'It's covered in sandbags – presumably in case the Germans attempt to bomb it.'

He wasn't interested in the Sphinx.

He was only interested in taking her to bed.

Considering the protected way Fawzia had been reared and her years of strict schooling at the Mère de Dieu, her abandonment in bed had always both surprised Jack and given him great pleasure. Now, within seconds of beginning to make love to her, he knew that during the long months of their separation she had changed.

She was no longer delightfully abandoned in bed.

She was lasciviously wanton – and skilfully so.

Certain of what her new expertise signified, his brain screamed at him to halt what he had now started, but his body wouldn't allow him to stop. It would have been as physically impossible as flying. It was like being on a roller coaster with no way of abandoning the ride until it came to a cataclysmic, earth-shattering, explosive end.

As he finally collapsed with a drumming heart amid the tangled sheets, exhausted and sheened with sweat, he knew that she hadn't been faithful to him. That she'd had – and possibly still had – a lover. A lover who, if the sexual tricks she had revealed such a knowledge of were anything to go by, was Egyptian, not English.

He slid from the bed, picked up his khaki shorts from the floor and put them on. Then he scooped up his shirt and took a packet of Camels and a lighter from one of its pockets.

Fawzia didn't move. She was lying on her back making small purring sounds, her arms stretched out flat above her head, her eyes closed.

He remembered almost the first words she had said to him: 'How long are you here for?' He had thought she was desperately anxious to be reassured that he wasn't in Cairo on a visit as fleeting as his father's visit had been. Instead, her anxiety had been just the reverse. She had been hoping to hear that in forty-eight hours or so he would be on his way back to Palestine or to somewhere else. Anywhere else. And her easy acceptance of the fact that they were not to be allowed to live together hadn't been a sign of mature understanding on her part. It had been relief. Her dress, the exotic scent she was wearing, the way her hair had been so precariously pinned, this all made sense now. When she'd heard the news of his arrival she had been with her lover – and she had come to him straight from her lover's bed.

He walked to the window and stood looking out towards the pyramids, his guts twisting deep in his belly.

He'd known, when he'd been transferred from Jerusalem to Cairo, that he was going to have emotional difficulties to face when he arrived. This difficulty, though, was one he hadn't seen coming. It had come straight from left field.

He inhaled deeply, knowing that he had to come to a decision about how to handle the situation before he left the room. One thing was obvious: he had to be fair.

They had been apart for eighteen months – and it was wartime. Old values, old standards, all previously accepted ways of behaviour were tossed out of the window in wartime. She hadn't known they were about to be reunited. If she had known she would, no doubt, have ended the relationship with her lover immediately.

He wondered how many people knew about it. Someone, for instance, had told her of his arrival and somehow he didn't think the someone had been her father. Though he knew that Zubair Pasha would have much preferred an Egyptian son-in-law, he couldn't imagine him condoning Fawzia's adultery. The person who had known where to find Fawzia and who had told her of his arrival was more likely to have been a house sufragi in Fawzia's confidence, or, even more likely, her personal maid.

Delia, too, quite obviously did not know that Fawzia was being unfaithful to him. It was one secret that Delia would never, in a million years, have been a silent party to.

It didn't mean, though, that other people weren't aware of the other man in Fawzia's life, or that, even if they weren't, they wouldn't become aware of him in the future if the affair continued.

Behind him he heard Fawzia stir.

He turned around. As she pushed herself up against the pillows, her silk-black hair grazing her breasts, he said tersely, 'Your lover, Fawzia. Who is he? I need to know.'

Her face took on a blank, impassive, shuttered expression. It was an expression he was familiar with. When it was necessary, Egyptians were more skilled at hiding their thoughts than any other race of people he had ever met.

'I don't know what you mean,' she said pettishly. 'I don't have a lover.'

There was a large brass ashtray on a nearby table and he ground out his cigarette in it. 'Don't make this any harder than it needs to be, Fawzia. I'm not a fool. I know you have a lover and I know that you were with him only a couple of hours ago. What I need to know is his name.'

He saw something flicker in her eyes and read what it was immediately. She thought he knew of her affair via his intelligence work. That he had been told of it even before he left Jerusalem.

Angrily she swung her legs from the bed and stood up. 'If you know that I am having an affair, then you also know who I am having it with.' She snatched a black lace-trimmed bra from a chair.

'I don't, as it happens.' He watched her as she put on the bra and reached for a pair of silk cami-knickers. Though she wasn't tall, her body was magnificently proportioned: her breasts full and deep, her waist so narrow it was literally a hand-span, her legs slim and exquisite.

Knowing Fawzia's body would never again have the power to move him, he said, 'What I do know is that your father believes you've been spending time with Davina when, according to Delia, Davina has no spare time to spend with anyone. Delia believes you've been spending time at Abdin with Queen Farida, but I very much doubt that you've been anywhere near the Palace. So where have you been? And who have you been with?'

From the far side of the rumpled bed she glared at him with the venom of someone who has been tricked and who, if she'd realized how little he knew, would have kept her mouth very firmly shut.

'You're the intelligence officer!' she hurled at him. 'You find out! I'm not going to tell you!'

The desire to seize hold of her and to shake her till her teeth rattled was almost more than he could control. Bunching his fists so hard the knuckles gleamed white, he said through clenched teeth, 'I'll find out all right. And when I do I'll make sure he never attempts to make contact with you again!'

'And how are you going to do that?' she spat, stepping into her brocade dress.

'I'll let him know that if he does, it will be the very last thing he does.'

It wasn't an idle threat. He was as toughly built as a Commando and just as useful with his fists. Bare-knuckled bouts at his public school had been deemed character-building. He'd never been in a fight yet when he hadn't truly thrashed his opponent.

As she slipped her feet into her high-heeled sandals, her whole mood changed. Pushing her heavy fall of hair away from her face she said in amusement, 'You'll deck my lover? A lover I have no intention of giving up? And in public?'

His eyes, as they held hers, were like pieces of splintered slate. 'Yes,' he said, white-lipped. 'That's a pretty accurate description of what I'll do Fawzia.'

As if it was the funniest thing she'd ever heard, she began laughing.

He reached for his shirt and pulled it on over his head. 'I'm going back to GHQ,' he said. 'And I'm going alone. You'll have to get yourself a taxi. As you've no intention of breaking off with whoever it is you're sharing a bed with, we won't be having another reunion. It's over, Fawzia. Lover-boy is welcome to you.'

Controlling her laughter with difficulty she said, 'And will you still punch him on the jaw when you find out his identity?'

'Oh yes,' he said grimly, yanking the door open. 'That's a pleasure I've no intention of forgoing.'

She began laughing again and he slammed the door on her, knowing, as he strode away, that his unwise marriage was irrevocably over.

As Delia's bright yellow sports car was brought from the car park for him, he resolved to tell Zubair Pasha at the first opportunity that the marriage was over. He wouldn't tell him why. He would simply say that he and Fawzia had always been incompatible and that it was a mutual decision. What Fawzia chose to say in explanation would be up to her.

He punched the starter motor into life, deciding to tell Delia as well. He knew she would believe that his ongoing feelings for Petra had played a major part in the break-up of his mar-

476

riage and that she would be deeply perturbed, but it couldn't be helped. She'd had enough secrets kept from her in the past, without there being another.

It was five o'clock by the time Jack got back to Grey Pillars, and with the heat of the afternoon over the place was a hive of activity again.

'I've left another sheaf of files on your desk,' Doris said efficiently as he strode into his cupboard-sized office. 'Captain Reynolds's replacement hasn't arrived yet. Corporal Slade has found you a comfy billet with two other officers in a flat on Sharia el Walda. He says it's pretty shabby, but the location would be hard to beat. It's so near to the Embassy, you can see into the Embassy garden.'

'Thank you, Doris – and now a mug of tea if you can rustle one up,' he said, flopping into a battered swivel chair, putting his feet up on the desk and reaching for the fat pile of files. 'Two sugars, please.'

And then, with the paddles of a ceiling fan rotating creakily above his head, he settled down to do his reading. Two hours later he knew the names of all the pro-British informers on the British payroll – and the names of many anti-British informers.

'Though who the anti-British informers pass their information on to, we're not sure,' said Slade, a young cockney, when he handed a key to the Sharia el Walda flat to him. 'The Romanians are always suspect. One of their number has already been expelled. Peter, the barman in the Long Bar at Shepheard's, is also a favourite bet but, to be honest, sir, there's not much to back up the suspicion. The only thing anyone's sure of is that the enemy is getting military information and that it's coming from an A1 source. Which has to mean from someone within GHQ or the Embassy.'

Having come to that conclusion long ago, Jack merely nodded, tucked the key into his pocket and went on with his reading. Rommel had apparently earned himself the nickname of 'the Desert Fox' and Jack wryly noted that the nickname was often used even in official communiqués.

On the military front, though the Australians, with some British help, were still holding out at Tobruk, Rommel had the port city encircled and all the major British offensives now taking place were being undertaken in order to relieve it.

None, so far, had been successful. Despite the huge number of tanks and troops engaged in the offensives, Rommel's fiendish use of 88mm anti-aircraft guns as anti-tank guns ensured that every British offensive ended in a murderous defeat. The enormous guns were dug deep into the sand in a U-shaped formation with their snouts disguised by sand-coloured tents. Even with field glasses it was impossible to distinguish them from sand dunes.

Rommel's trick was to send light tanks on a fake attack on British positions. When British tanks engaged in battle with them, the Panzers would withdraw into the U-shape, and at nearly point-blank range the enormous Flak guns would then open fire. The result was carnage of epic proportions with the British tanks erupting into blazing infernos.

It made for grim reading and Jack's mood lightened only when Doris waltzed in on him again. 'Captain Reynolds's replacement has arrived, sir. Shall I send him in?'

'Pronto, Doris, please.'

He swung his legs off the desk and, as he did, Archie walked into the room.

Jack's eyes widened, and as the realization dawned that it was Archie who would be his second-in-command, all the misery, anger and tension of the afternoon vanished.

He rounded the desk in a flash. 'Archie, you old sonofagun!' he said, giving him a great bear hug. 'I thought you were with Special Ops?'

'Ah, well. You know what thought did, old mate,' Archie said comfortably, a wide grin splitting his homely face. 'It thought wrong.'

'Let's go for a beer.' Jack snatched his peaked cap off the corner of his desk. 'We've a lot of catching up to do – and when we've done that, you and I have a spy to catch.'

Three days later Jack was in the Khan el Khalili bazaar in order to pay a visit to a seller of fruit and vegetables. A reliable informer, a barber, had told him of a conversation he had overheard between a father and a son. 'The father is a greengrocer and the son is in the Egyptian army,' he had said. 'The son wants money to pay his mess bills and his father won't give him any unless he lands him a British army contract for vegetables. His exact words were, "You'd do better to get that contract instead of involving yourself with crazy army plots

479

that are bound to fail.'"

The term 'crazy army plots' was one that couldn't possibly be ignored and Jack thought he could see a way of getting hard inside information about them.

The Khan el Khalili was a mammoth maze of twisting alleys so crowded with jutting rows of narrow stalls that it was only possible for two people to pass each other by coming into jostling, physical contact. The bazaar sold far more than just fruit and vegetables. It sold perfumes, rugs, spices, silver, alabaster and jewellery so fine that it was the one place in Old Cairo Europeans could always be found.

As he pushed a way through the noisy crowds, Petra suddenly stepped out of a dark shop doorway a few yards in front of him, her arms full of silks.

He came to such a sharp, abrupt halt that the Arab walking immediately behind him – who was hauling a goat along at his side – tripped hard over his heels.

'*Maaleesh,*' he said. as the Arab struggled to regain his balance and the goat bleated. 'Sorry.'

Petra, too, had come to a halt. With the shopkeeper standing beside her she was examining the silks in sunlight coming from a gap in the long tin roof above their heads.

It was the first time he had seen her since his arrival in the city. Her glorious mass of mahogany-red hair fell in a turbulent riot of deep waves to her shoulders, pushed away from her face on one side with a tortoiseshell comb. Tall and slender and graceful she was wearing a white linen suit, its skirt arrow-straight. Her scarlet sandals were wedge-heeled and sling-backed, her legs suntanned and bare of stockings.

He felt as if his heart had ceased to beat.

She was completely preoccupied with what she was doing, frowning in concentration as she fingered first one roll of silk and then another.

He saw, as if he had never seen them before, the long thick sweep of her eyelashes, the faint hollows under her beautifully sculpted cheek-bones, the rich, generous curve of her mouth.

In that moment he knew that his love for her, and his need of her, were so deep and absolute they would never end.

And she no longer loved him. For years he'd been trying to hammer that information into his head and still there was a part of him that couldn't accept it, that refused to believe it. He'd tried to move on; he'd tried to find happiness with somebody else. And the culmination of that had been the hideous scene between himself and Fawzia at Mena House.

In bitter despair he stood and drank in the sight of the woman he'd loved for as long as he could remember, and as he did so she raised her head from the rolls of silk and their eyes met.

He saw shock jar through her. One of the rolls of silk slipped from her hands and the shop-keeper darted forward to catch it. He forced himself into movement. Striving to look relaxed and at ease he strolled up to her.

'Hello,' he said as she clutched a roll of crimson cloth to her chest. 'I wondered when we'd run into each other. Did your mother tell you I was

481

back in the city?'

'Yes.' The word came out clipped and short as if someone had just punched her, hard. 'Your being posted here was bound to happen, though, wasn't it?' she said, her voice now as falsely bright as if she was talking to a casual acquaintance. 'You know Cairo so well and you speak Arabic. Not many intelligence officers in Cairo do. Ivor says it's a wonder you weren't sent here a year ago.'

'I wish I had been. Can I take that roll of silk from you before it follows the other one?'

Without waiting for her response he lifted the silk from her arms. As his hands touched hers, she trembled.

'Could we go for a drink together, Petra?' A pulse was throbbing at the corner of his jaw in exactly the same way a pulse always throbbed at the corner of his father's jaw when he was under intense emotion. 'The Terrace at Shepheard's, or perhaps coffee at Groppi's?'

'I ... no.' She looked around wildly as if for a way of escape. 'It isn't possible, Jack. I have an appointment...'

'Sholto,' he said, determined to keep her talking for at least a few moments longer. 'How is he? He's someone else I haven't run into yet.'

'Sholto?' Her face took on a shuttered expression that wasn't a world away from the expression that had come down on Fawzia's face when he had asked her who her lover was. 'Sholto's fine, thank you. And now, I'm sorry, Jack, but I really do have to go.'

Shattering all the stallholder's hopes of a hefty

sale, she turned swiftly away from him and plunged into the sea of humanity streaming down the narrow alleyway.

Jack didn't follow her because he knew she didn't want him to.

Within seconds, as the crowds pressed around her, all he could see between a bobbing mass of white turbans, red fezzes and black veils, was her Rita Hayworth mane of hair and her shoulders. He wasn't sure, but as she disappeared from view he thought that her shoulders were shaking – almost as if she were crying.

TWENTY SEVEN

'I wasn't sure the powers-that-be were going to agree to the grocery contract,' Archie said a few days later as they reviewed the successful outcome of what they referred to as their 'greengrocer and son' operation.

'They had to.' There was wry amusement in Jack's voice. 'It was the only way of getting the son to give any information. Once the British army contract for vegetables was in place I had him exactly where I wanted him. It was a case of talk or lose the contract – and by bluffing that I knew far more than I did about his "crazy army plots", as his father referred to them, I scared the living daylights out of him. The poor devil thought he was going to be charged with conspiring against the security of the state if he didn't cooperate.'

Archie lit a cigarette. 'And so we now know there's a group of Egyptian army officers itching to rise in revolt and we have the name of one of the ringleaders. Captain Anwar Sadat,' he said with great satisfaction. 'I'm not surprised the brigadier is pleased.'

It was late evening and they were in Jack's cubbyhole of an office. Doris had long gone, as had the great majority of people who worked at GHQ. Jack was in his favourite position – slouched comfortably in his swivel chair with his feet on the table, his ankles crossed.

'It doesn't bring us any nearer to finding our spy, though,' he said, a deep frown pulling his eyebrows together. 'The kind of information the German military is getting isn't the kind of information a captain in the Egyptian army would be privy to. For a lead to the spy we're after, we need to be looking much closer to home. From now on I'm interested in every high-ranking officer at GHQ who has an Egyptian girlfriend. That's the way I see the information being obtained, Archie. Via pillow talk, or via a girlfriend having access to a briefcase and private papers.'

'And Sadat?' Archie, asked. He was perched on a corner of the desk, one leg swinging. 'What is our next move to be where he's concerned?'

'Our informant will continue to give us information – he's too deeply compromised now not to – and wherever possible, Sadat will be followed. I've given that task to Slade. If Sadat is in contact, in any way, with the chap we're after, we'll soon know and then we'll have the satisfaction of seeing Sadat's friend put against a wall and shot.'

484

He glanced down at his watch. 'It's past mid-night, Archie. What say we mix work with plea-sure and begin a trawl of the nightclubs and take note of every likely officer we see with an Egyptian girlfriend? Where shall we start? The Kit-Kat or the Sphinx?'

'There's a small club off Kasr el Nil Street, near to the Turf Club, that would be a good starting-off point. The belly dancer there is the best I've ever seen.'

'Let's give it a try, then.' Jack lifted his feet from the desk and reached for his belt and holster. He was quite sure that his theory about a British officer with an Egyptian girlfriend was the right one. He couldn't imagine a British officer know-ingly passing secrets to a German spy, but Cairo was a city where, given the number of troops that were in it, women were in chronically short supply. If a man could get himself an Egyptian girlfriend then he would, even though the chances of the girlfriend caring for anything other than his money were somewhere around the nil mark.

A German spy in Cairo would also have an Egyptian girlfriend, the difference being that she would be in love with him and willing to do anything that would help Germany win the war. That being the case she would be the perfect bait for any gullible, sex-starved British officer with access to military top secrets.

And that was how he saw the information being obtained. When her boyfriend was asleep the girl would copy the papers in his briefcase and then pass the copies to her German lover. The German, a full-fledged spy with transmitter and codebook, would then transmit the information to the German military.

Before he'd left Jerusalem he'd assumed that tracking down such an officer would be relatively straightforward. There couldn't, he had thought, be that many officers at GHQ with access not only to top-secret documents, but to top-secret documents they had the clearance to take out of the building in a briefcase. Such an officer had to be extremely high-ranking, which would automatically cut down the list of suspects.

And then he had seen the number of high-ranking officers crammed into Grey Pillars and had known that even if his theory about how a German spy was getting hold of British military secrets was correct, tracking down the officer responsible was not going to be easy.

The club off Kasr el Nil Street was exceedingly small and the minute he stepped through its beaded curtains he doubted any officers of the type they were after would be found in it.

'Welcome to club King Cheops, Major,' a waiter said, swiftly taking in the crowns on Jack's shoulder straps. 'Would you like champagne? Company? We have very nice girls at King Cheops. Very good dancers.'

'We'd like a table and two Stellas,' Jack said pleasantly. 'And no company. Not tonight.'

As they were led across to a table directly in front of the stage Archie raised his eyebrows.

'You said that "not tonight" as if you'd welcome female company another time. I thought you were a happily married man?'

Jack sat down. 'My marriage is over. And I

don't want any commiserations, because I don't need them. Now, how long d'you think we're going to have to wait until your belly dancer comes on stage?'

They sat through a dreadful acrobatic act and an even more dreadful snake-charming act and then, as there came a roll of drums, the tension in the little club mounted and the noisy clientele at the other tables became even noisier.

'Zahra's good. Really good,' Archie said in happy anticipation, raising his voice so as to be heard. 'I reckon her father must own the club, because I can't see any other reason for her not being in demand at the Sphinx or the Kit-Kat.'

When Zahra glided barefoot onto the tiny podium dressed in gold sequins and a chiffon hip skirt, bracelets on her arms and ankles, and tiny cymbals on her fingers, Jack could see that she was exceptionally beautiful in exactly the same way as Fawzia was beautiful. Her kohl-rimmed eyes were doe-shaped and slanted, her eyebrows perfectly symmetrical arches, her waist-length hair a gleaming blue-black curtain.

Over the years he had seen many belly dancers during his trips to Cairo, and as the familiar sinuous music began and Zahra's hips swivelled slowly and sensuously he thought that perhaps Archie was right and that she was far too good a dancer for the club that they were in. Strings of beads hung down from her bra to just above her belly button and as the music became faster and she began shimmying, the beads swayed and swung erotically against the sheen of her olive-toned flesh.

Beside him, Archie had hunched forward, mesmerized. Under other circumstances Jack was pretty sure he would have been similarly mesmerized, but tonight he had too much on his mind. Earlier that afternoon, when Brigadier Haigh had congratulated him on having infiltrated the subversive group of officers within the Egyptian army, he had also given him a grim warning: 'Now that Claude Auchinleck has replaced General Wavell as C-in-C, it's going to be all systems go to relieve Tobruk. With a big push like this in the offing it's vital no information is passed on to the Germans. Whoever their spy in Cairo is, he's got to be found, Jack.'

It was, Jack reflected as he took a deep drink of his Stella, a task easier said than done.

The music had now become frenetic. With her spine arched and her head thrown back, her gleaming curtain of hair swinging down to her buttocks, Zahra's hips were gyrating faster and faster.

It was then, as her dance and the music climaxed, that he saw Darius.

He was seated with another man at a corner table just out of range of the stage lights, and as their eyes met Jack knew Darius had been observing him for some time. Later he was to wonder whether, left to his own devices, Darius would have made his presence known.

For now he merely said to Archie, 'I've just seen an old friend. It might be a good idea if you wandered down to the Kit-Kat. This place is far too seedy for the officer we are looking for.'

'Will do,' Archie said as Zahra exited the stage

488

to a storm of applause.

Jack didn't hear him. He was already halfway to Darius's table. Seeing his approach, the thin-faced man who had been sitting with Darius rose to his feet and walked off speedily in the direction of the bar.

Darius also rose to his feet. 'I'd heard you were in town,' he said as they slapped each other on the back in an old friends' gesture. 'Are you just passing through or here for the duration?'

It was reminiscent of the way Fawzia had greeted him and he said wryly, 'As far as I know, I'm here for the duration. How are things? The only person I've caught up with so far is Delia.'

He purposely didn't mention having spoken to Petra. His feeling about her were so painfully intense he knew he couldn't carry off speaking about her without revealing them.

'What about Fawzia? Surely you've seen her?'

'I have – and we aren't a couple any longer. Our marriage is over. She's been seeing someone else and has no intention of giving him up. I'll be filing for a divorce just as soon as I get a minute's time.'

There was no surprise or commiseration from Darius. With an expression in his voice Jack couldn't quite place, he merely said, 'And do you intend naming the boyfriend as co-respondent?'

'Of course I'll be bloody naming him! And if you know his identity I'd appreciate you telling me who he is. I have more to do at the moment than chase around Cairo hunting down my wife's lover.'

A crooner had come on stage and the tiny dance

floor was crowded with smooching couples.

As the small red-shaded lamp on their table flickered, as if it had a loose connection, Darius remained infuriatingly silent.

'Come on, Darius,' he said impatiently. 'This is no time to restart the tradition of scoring points off each other. I haven't the time for it. I may not look as if I'm working, but I am. I've another half-dozen clubs to visit before I hit the sack.'

Darius poured champagne, saying with a crooked smile, 'So you've come to the King Cheops hunting down a German spy?' Ignoring the ice bucket, he stood the bottle on the table. 'Rumour has it the city is crawling with them. You'll probably have a cell full before morning.'

'I doubt it, but what I do want before morning is the name of the man I'm going to thrash,' he said bluntly, refusing to be baited. 'I'm assuming he's an Egyptian.'

'You assume right, but I'm not sure you're going to get your own way about thrashing him – or citing him as a co-respondent.'

Suddenly there were no longer two of them at the table, but three. Zahra, dressed in a scarlet cocktail dress that looked as if it had been bought in Paris, approached the table and sat down, saying, 'Where has Constantin gone, Darius? Do you know?'

'The bar, I think. Let me introduce my brother-in-law to you – though he doesn't intend remaining my brother-in-law. Zahra, Jack Bazeljette. Jack, Zahra. Her boyfriend is a friend of mine.'

Jack registered Zahra's shock at discovering that Darius was on such close family terms with

490

a British major. Her shock didn't surprise him. He doubted that Darius had previously mentioned he had a British brother-in-law.

'The name, Darius,' he said, barely able to keep his patience in check, 'and then I'll be on my way.'

'Farouk.' There was naked disgust in Darius's voice. 'And in case there's any mistake about which Farouk, the Farouk in question is His Majesty, King Farouk, King of Egypt and of Sudan, Sovereign of Nubia, of Kordofan and of Darfur – and if you attempt to lay a finger on him his aides will have your head off your shoulders, and if you attempt to cite him as co-respondent in your divorce action your government will have you cashiered.'

Jack knew instantly that Darius wasn't teasing him, for everything now made sense. Fawzia's amusement when he had said he intended seeking out her lover and giving him the hiding of his life; the cavalier way royal aides had whisked her off to the Palace no matter where she had been or whom she had been with. The Queen had never been the object of her visits there. It had always been the King. And because it was the King there wasn't a damn thing he could do about it.

One word of accusation from him and he would be stripped of his rank and booted out of Egypt before he could bat an eyelid. Not only that, any word of accusation would be utterly pointless, for Farouk would merely deny everything.

In furious frustration he slammed his fist down on the table.

The table tottered.

The bottle fell.

Champagne soaked the lamp and its wiring, and as the snake charmer reached the high spot of his act, bending forward to kiss the head of the hooded cobra swaying before him, the lights fizzed and fused, the club was plunged into chaotic blackness and pandemonium broke out as everyone thought a raid was in progress.

It was, Jack often reflected later, a fitting end to his and Darius's reunion.

A week later Jack had the kind of lead he'd been praying for. The monitoring section of his unit picked up an unidentified transmitter in the Gezira/Zamalek area. 'We've picked it up a few times now,' his signals officer said, 'and it's broadcasting in code. Must be our guy, don't you think?'

'It's some bastard up to no good. How long is he on air for?'

'Not long, sir. Too short a time for us to be able to pinpoint his exact position. We'll just have to hope he soon gets a bit chattier.'

That afternoon Jack drove out to Gezira Island deep in thought. Until now he had been working on the assumption that though top-secret information wasn't being obtained by a German, it was being transmitted by a German. It had been the only scenario that had made sense to him. Now it did so no longer, because not only was Gezira Island one of the least crowded areas of Cairo, it was also one of the most elegant and expensive. Which made it the very last place a man needing to meld unobtrusively into the background was likely to hide.

Dominating the southern end of the island was the Sporting Club and it was inconceivable that anyone could be transmitting from there. Also on the southern end of the island were a hospital and a delightful area of tree-lined avenues boasting palatial houses, their residents mainly British officials connected with the Embassy. It was where Petra and Sholto lived. It was where, if they didn't live in Garden City, every British diplomat lived.

He took the road that rounded the island's southern tip. On his left-hand side the Nile began to flow once again undivided, its waters glittering a myriad different shades of green under the hot rays of the afternoon sun. On his right-hand side were the little visited Khedeiwi Ismail gardens, where meandering gravel pathways were flanked by acacias and shaded by purple-flowering jacaranda trees.

As he began motoring up the west side of the island he came almost immediately to a bridge leading to Giza and the pyramids. Known as the English Bridge, it marked the beginning of a whole line of houseboats. He slowed the jeep to a standstill and lit a cigarette, regarding them thoughtfully. A houseboat would make quite a good hideaway – but not for a German. In a community such as Gezira's houseboat community, everyone would know each other. A stranger would be instantly obvious, and a stranger with an accent even more so.

Determining that at first light he would have every houseboat searched and every houseboat owner questioned, he stubbed out his cigarette and put the jeep again into gear.

Within minutes he was driving along the western boundary of the Sporting Club. Beyond the Sporting Club were botanical gardens, and with these behind him he was in the residential district of Zamalek. Several palatial houses faced the Nile, though this time, from the names on their high, carved gateways, it was clear that the owners were rich Egyptians and not British.

He drew to a halt yet again and smoked another cigarette. Had he been barking up the wrong tree? Was it a royal aide he should really be hunting down? But would a royal aide have access to British military plans?

The Zamalek end of Gezira didn't end in a rounded curve, but in a sharp angle. He drove each and every quiet street that lay within the angle and then began driving in the direction of the Bulaq Bridge. Here, before he reached the bridge, there were more houseboats, but only a few, and the area they were in was far more deserted than the area of houseboat moorings adjacent to the English Bridge. Resolving that in the morning he would also have those searched and their owners questioned, he continued down the east side of the island until, once, again, he was at the Kasr el Nil Bridge.

Driving past the two bronze lions that guarded the entrance to the bridge he reflected that if his signals officer was correct, somewhere within the circle he had just circumnavigated a transmitter was being used to relay military secrets to the Germans. Though the homes of rich and influential Egyptians couldn't be searched without far more evidence than he currently had, the houseboats could be searched and his gut feeling was that such a search would be satisfyingly successful.

That evening he met with Brigadier Haigh, liaised with the Commander of the Egyptian Police Force – and had dinner with Davina.

It always amused him that though she was a part of Cairo on a level he knew no other English girl to be, she still looked as English as if she had arrived in the city from the Home Counties only days ago. Her pale blonde hair was held away from her face by a dark-blue Alice band and she was wearing a grey pleated skirt and pastel blue twinset, her jewellery a single string of pearls.

'It's so absolutely wonderful to have you in Cairo, Jack,' she said when they had ordered from the kind of menu people in heavily rationed Britain could only fantasize about. 'We've hoped and hoped you would be posted here. I haven't seen Fawzia since you arrived – I see very little of her these days as Queen Farida monopolizes all her time – but she must be over the moon at being reunited with you.'

He'd ordered a bottle of Chablis Premier Cru and as the waiter filled their wine glasses he said, 'I thought your mother might have brought you up to date where Fawzia and I are concerned.'

She shook her head. 'Things are so manic at the hospital that I now live in the Nurses' Home and, apart from phone calls, I haven't spoken to my mother for an age. When we do speak the lines are so bad we never touch on anything really personal.'

Jack waited till the waiter had left them and

then said; 'Fawzia and I will be getting divorced, Davina. Our marriage was never one with very deep roots. We each had expectations of the other that neither of us could fulfil and she's now heavily into a love affair that's far too important to her for her to consider ending it.'

'But she can't be!' Davina looked both shocked and totally bewildered. 'Fawzia loves parties of course – and there are lots of parties in Cairo. But if she had met someone at a party, word would have spread. Cairo thrives on gossip. It just isn't the kind of thing that could have been kept secret. And besides, I don't know when she would have found time for an affair. She's nearly always at the Palace, keeping Queen Farida company.'

He shot her a wry smile. 'You're right about her being always at the Palace, but it's not the Queen she's with when she's there. It's the King.'

Davina gasped, her eyes as wide as saucers. 'You can't mean it! King Farouk's got an awful reputation as a lecher – but King Farouk and *Fawzia?*'

'Why not?' he said reasonably. 'She's exceptionally beautiful. She's Egyptian and from a good family. Zubair Pasha is a member of the Senate and he's served as a minister in one Cabinet or another for over thirty years. Farouk will have seen Fawzia at the Palace several times when she visited it with her father. When she returned to Cairo from London she must have come to his attention almost immediately. And from Fawzia's point of view there's a lot to play for. Farouk is one of the richest men in the world, and, knowing Fawzia, I'm pretty sure she already has a fabulous collection of jewels safely squirrelled away. And he's probably led her to believe he may divorce Farida and marry her. Can you imagine how Fawzia feels at the possibility of becoming Queen of Egypt?'

'But she'll be a divorced woman! And a divorced woman who is a Copt! The King will never marry her. Even if he wanted to, he *couldn't* marry her!'

'He isn't a British king, Davina. He can't be forced into abdication by his Prime Minister in the way King Edward was. I must admit that his marrying her isn't very likely, but Farouk's never given a damn about tradition and convention.'

'And what if he doesn't marry her? What will happen to her then?'

'Then he'll provide for her – even if he doesn't want to.'

Despite the hard certainty in his voice she said, not understanding, 'But how can you be so sure? He's an autocrat. No one can make Farouk do what he doesn't want to do. Not his Prime Minister. Not Sir Miles Lampson. No one.'

Suddenly his face was no longer the face that had been so dearly familiar to her ever since she was a child. It was no longer full of easy affability and good humour. It was the face of a man who could be very tough. And who intended to be very tough indeed.

'Farouk will provide for her – and provide for her lavishly, because I'm going to make him,' he said grimly. 'Fawzia and I have too much shared history for me to stand by and see her being treated shabbily. I may not be able to cite the

King in my divorce action, but I can still put the fear of God into him. And I'm going to, Davina. Trust me.'

She looked so unhappy at the thought that he abruptly changed the subject.

'Tell me about the little boy you are going to adopt. What is his name? Angus? Alfred?'

'Andrew,' she said, the sparkle back in her eyes. 'At the moment he's at Shibden Hall and your father is maintaining contact with him. I think he's going to love it out here in Cairo. I know when I was a child I would have simply loved spending time onboard the *Egyptian Queen*.'

'The *Egyptian Queen*?'

'Darius's houseboat at Zamalek.'

The trio had been playing slow waltzes in order that as many couples as possible could squeeze onto the dance floor. Now they began playing something more uptempo.

Jack couldn't have cared less what they were playing. In his mind's eye he was seeing again the handful of houseboats moored in the quiet area north of the Bulaq Bridge. In a matter of hours they, along with every other houseboat moored on Gezira, would be swooped on by his men and by members of the Egyptian Police Force. If there was anything remotely suspicious on the *Egyptian Queen* it would be found.

And what he was passionately hoping now was that the *Egyptian Queen* would be as clean as a whistle.

TWENTY EIGHT

Jack's tension the next morning, as he oversaw the large search operation he had put in place, was enormous. When, many hours later, it was concluded, crushing disappointment and over-whelming relief swamped him in equal waves.

His disappointment was because, despite every houseboat having been rigorously searched, no radio transmitter was found. His relief was that Darius was as in the clear as every other house-boat owner.

'How many bearings indicated that the trans-mission you picked up was sourced on Gezira?' he demanded of his signals officer. 'Could your triangulation have been wrong?'

'No, sir. I've got three different bearings on it. It's so accurate that next time sonny boy starts transmitting our monitoring unit stands a chance of being able to jam his messages.'

Jack drummed his knuckles on his desk. Jam-ming the messages was all very well, but the Ger-man listening station would tell the transmitting radio operator that he was being jammed and then there would be no more transmissions – and no hope of catching the radio operator in the act. Even more importantly, there would be no hope of catching the spy supplying the information being transmitted. All that would happen was that when transmissions began again, they would be from a different locale. Alexandria, possibly. Or even the desert. Rommel would continue to get vital British military information and any chance of the tables being turned on him would be lost.

And it was that chance of turning the tables that was so vitally important. If they could capture the radio operator in the act of transmitting – if they could get hold of his codebook – then they could broadcast false information to Rommel that Rommel would take as being gospel. And that could mean the difference between winning the war in the Western Desert, or losing it.

'And with stakes like those to play for, we've got to allow the transmissions to continue,' Brigadier Haigh said, grim-faced, when he told Jack what Downing Street's take on the problem was. 'Once we jam them, he'll know we're on to him and go to ground. But we can't allow them to continue for long. And we've got to lay our hands on that codebook. With that in our possession we can scupper Rommel once and for all.'

Back in his own office Jack studied the file that was the only tangible result of the massive search operation. It listed the name of every houseboat, the name of every owner and, if the occupier was different from the owner, the name of every occupier and any relevant details.

Opposite the name *Egyptian Queen* the name of the owner was given as Darius Zubair and his occupation was listed as that of a lawyer. The officer in charge of searching the *Egyptian Queen* and questioning Darius had made a note to the effect that Darius had been extremely cooperative.

Deep in thought, Jack closed the file. He was

still deep in thought when Archie walked in on him.

'So what's our next step to be?' Archie asked glumly. 'Do we simply keep methodically checking up on the private life of every officer with clearance to take top-secret information out of the building?'

Keeping to himself for the time being the information that Darius was one of the houseboat owners, Jack said briskly, 'We'll keep as many people as we can spare doing that, but I think we should be looking at Embassy staff as well. Gezira is the place where most of them live. I know tradition has it that no British diplomat can ever even be suspected of treason, but there's a first time for everything. What's that you have in your hand? Another file resulting from the search operation?'

'No. Sadat has left Cairo for Manqabad in Upper Egypt. It's his official army posting, so no surprise there.'

'None at all. If he is on friendly terms with our spy and our spy's radio operator he won't be maintaining contact with them in Manqabad, so we can forget about Sadat for the moment – though make sure there's a paid informer at the train station. The minute he returns, I want to know.'

He ran a hand through his hair. 'I'm going to ask Haigh for clearance to speak with Sir Miles Lampson. Someone is going to have to tell our Ambassador that his diplomatic staff will be coming under SIB surveillance. Wish me luck, Archie. Lampson stands six foot six, weighs in at eighteen stone and is going to be one very angry man.'

Lampson was so angry Jack thought he was going to explode.

'A member of my diplomatic staff a spy?' he thundered when Jack had explained the reason for his visit.

'It's a possibility, sir. Transmissions are being made to Rommel from Gezira and–'

'*A member* of my *diplomatic staff a spy?*'

'–we need to know just what kind of military information Embassy staff are privy to–'

'*A MEMBER OF MY DIPLOMATIC STAFF A SPY?*'

'–and then sift through everyone with access to the sort of information that is being leaked,' Jack continued manfully as the Ambassador's face went from indignant red to choleric purple.

It took a full half-hour for Sir Miles to gain control of his temper. When he'd done so, Jack got the information he was after.

'Embassy staff at attaché level are allowed to see anything they feel it necessary to see, Major Bazeljette. Their authority comes from the highest possible source.'

'And that includes military information?'

'Of course. And if you think for one moment that a member of my staff is leaking such information to the enemy, then you are stark raving mad. You should be looking for a German, not an Englishman. And if not a German, you should be investigating officers in the Egyptian army. If a leak is coming from anywhere, that is the most likely source.'

Jack didn't trouble to point out that the British

military scrupulously kept the Egyptian army ignorant of the kind of information that was being leaked. He didn't need to get into an argument with Sir Miles. Embassy attachés had access to military information and that was all, for the moment, that he needed to know.

As he left the Embassy he reflected that as Farouk couldn't possibly be as intimidating as Sir Miles had been, it was high time he had his confrontation with him.

'Where to, Major?' Corporal Slade asked him as he slid into the passenger seat of his staff car. 'Back to GHQ?'

'No, Slade. The next stop is the Palace.'

'The Palace, sir?' Corporal Slade looked at him as if he'd said the moon.

'Yes, Slade. The Palace. Now get a move on, will you? I want to see the King before he starts on one of his gargantuan lunches.'

'The King, sir?'

Slade was looking at him as if he was suffering from heatstroke and a hospital would be a more appropriate next stop.

'Either you start driving this minute, Slade, or I turf you out and drive myself there. Please, for the love of God, get this damn jeep into gear!'

It wasn't far from the Embassy to Abdin but, as always in Cairo, a short distance could take a long time to cover. Today it was tanks that were causing a major traffic jam as they rolled in the direction of the Kasr el Nil Bridge and the road that led to the battlefields of the Western Desert and Libya.

As Slade drove past a small alleyway off Sultan

503

Hussein Street he saw Sholto Monck getting out of a Chrysler and stepping into a small café – and then he saw who Sholto was with.

It was the man who had been at Darius's table with him the night he and Darius had met up again. The man who was Zahra's boyfriend.

There was no reason at all, of course, why one of Darius's friends shouldn't also be friends with Sholto: Sholto was, after all, Davina's brother-in-law. All the same, it seemed both a strange and a surprising friendship, and as Slade battled on through the traffic towards the Palace, Jack wondered just how long it had been going on.

Once they reached Abdin they were forced to an ignominious halt.

Jack showed his SIB warrant card that gave him carte blanche to go anywhere he wanted, but it cut no ice with the guards at the Palace gates.

It was a reversal he had fully expected and he telephoned Haigh. 'I've spoken with Sir Miles and now I need to speak with the King,' he said tersely through the usual static. 'Get Sir Miles to sort it out for me, would you?'

Two hours passed. Jack spent the time sitting in his jeep at Abdin's gates with Corporal Slade.

'Do you mind me asking what we're doing here, sir?' the young Londoner ventured as the day's heat grew ever more intense and beads of sweat rolled down his face.

'I have an issue with King Farouk, Slade,' he said, thinking that that was, perhaps, the understatement of the year.

Just when he thought he wasn't going to be able to stand the heat for another minute, one of the guards walked towards him.

'His Majesty will not see you. The First Chamberlain will see you,' the guard said bluntly as other guards opened the giant gates. 'His Majesty does not give audiences to British army officers. His Majesty only speaks with generals and with the British Ambassador.'

Jack nodded, as if accepting the situation, but as Slade drove into the Palace grounds he was determined that Farouk *would* see him, no matter how many underlings he had to argue his way past.

Leaving an unhappy Corporal Slade sitting in the jeep, he entered the Palace and was shown into an ornate anteroom where he was offered tea.

Tea always prefaced any dealings with Egyptians – even the buying of a carpet demanded the ritual of tea-drinking before a purchase was concluded – and Jack knew better than to attempt the impossible by trying to hurry things along.

After an age of time had passed an aide appeared.

'The First Chamberlain will see you now, Major Bazeljette. If you will please follow me...'

Jack followed him. It was his first time in Abdin and he found the Oriental beauty of the rooms stunning. The main public chamber of the Palace, the Byzantine Hall, was as long as a rugger pitch with a high, gilded ceiling, exquisite mosaics and an awesome number of massive chandeliers. When they reached the end of it, there were still other rooms to walk through before they arrived at the room in which the First

Chamberlain was waiting. He was wearing a tarboosh, but his suit could have been tailored in Savile Row.

'I understand from your Ambassador that you have Special Investigation Branch business to conduct with me,' he said, making no attempt at polite small talk. 'Is it, perhaps, to do with the safety of His Majesty?'

'No. His Majesty's safety is very adequately taken care of, I believe. And my business, First Chamberlain, is not with yourself, but with His Majesty. I trust the Ambassador made that quite clear?'

The First Chamberlain breathed in so hard his nostrils turned white. 'His Majesty is not at the beck and call of British majors, Major Bazeljette! Nor is he at the beck and call of the British Ambassador! If you would please state your business and—'

At the far side of the room a door was ajar. Jack's sixth sense told him that the King was behind it – and listening.

Not allowing the First Chamberlain to finish his sentence, Jack said, speaking in a voice that would carry clearly, 'Perhaps His Majesty is unaware that Bazeljette is an uncommon name in England and that there is no other Major Bazeljette in Cairo. If he could be informed that I am the Major Bazeljette whose wife is the daughter of Zubair Pasha, and that my reason for seeing him is bound up with a delicate family matter, perhaps then he will see me. If not, of course, I am only too happy to lay the matter before you, or anyone else who—'

506

The half-open door slammed wide.

The First Chamberlain flinched.

The King glared at him.

'I'll speak with Major Bazeljette alone,' he said with an imperious gesture of dismissal, a huge cabochon emerald weighing down his little finger.

As the First Chamberlain fled, Jack regarded his wife's lover with interest. Though his huge appetite ensured he was already beginning to look a little portly, the King was a good-looking young man – the emphasis being very much on the adjective 'young'. Sovereign for five years, he was still only twenty-one. Jack had heard it rumoured that Sir Miles Lampson often referred to King Farouk as 'the boy' and could well understand why. The 'boy', however, had the kind of absolute power British kings had lost three hundred years ago.

'Many thanks for granting me this audience, Your Majesty,' he said, giving the bow protocol demanded, when what he yearned to do was land a very solid fist on the royal jaw.

The King, dressed very similarly to his First Chamberlain in an exquisitely tailored suit, and wearing a tarboosh, inclined his head.

And waited in stony silence for him to continue.

Jack had thought very carefully about how he was going to gain his objective with Farouk, without ruining Fawzia's life into the bargain. Any suggestion from him that he intended making Fawzia's affair with Farouk a public scandal would, he was fairly sure, simply result in Farouk instantly ending his affair with her. And as there was no question of his and Fawzia's marriage being patched together, such an outcome would, for Fawzia, be disastrous. What he wanted for her was some kind of protection for when the affair came to an end of its own accord.

He cleared his throat. 'It has come to my attention, Your Majesty, that a very eminent member of the court circle is having an affair with my wife, the only daughter of Zubair Pasha. Zubair Pasha has, I believe, held many Cabinet posts in Your Majesty's government.'

Farouk continued to regard him in silence, but his eyes had taken on a distinctly nervous look.

Jack said pleasantly, 'In order not to cause embarrassment to Your Majesty by citing a member of your court circle in a divorce action, I shall not be doing so. Nor will the divorce, when it is obtained, reflect in any way on my wife's reputation. Gallantry demands that she be seen as the innocent party.'

'Quite so,' Farouk said, now with relief in his eyes. 'English gallantry. A very commendable quality.'

Jack gave a nod of agreement. 'Indeed it is, Your Majesty. Which brings me to the crux of what I wish to speak with Your Majesty about.'

Farouk put a pudgy hand into his jacket pocket and began running worry beads through his fingers.

'I feel it would be gallant, on the part of my wife's lover, to make provision for her in the event of his not obtaining a divorce and marrying her. Such a provision would enable her to leave the relationship with the dignity that will come of knowing that she was, while the affair lasted, truly thought a great deal of. It is the kind of magnanimous gesture an English gentleman would make,' he said, knowing damn well that if it was, it was a pretty rare one, but seeing no reason why Farouk shouldn't be led up the garden path as far as he could take him. 'A chivalric, knightly gesture.'

'Ah, yes.' Farouk was beginning to look happier. 'Quite so. When Prince, I had an English tutor. I am familiar with historical instances of romantic English chivalry.'

'Then I think you will agree with me, Your Majesty, that the time to make the promise of such provision is not when an affair ends, for then it only brings complications when emotions are painfully raw, but that a written promise of such provision should be made by the gentleman in question now – and lodged with Zubair Pasha's lawyer who will, if the time comes when it is necessary, expedite everything without the gentleman in question having to be further involved in any way.'

The worry beads continued to rattle and click.

Jack waited.

'And what sort of … provision … in the event of the affair coming to an end, do you think this particular gentleman of my court should make, Major Bazeljette?'

'Not knowing the extent of the gentleman in question's wealth, I think perhaps Your Majesty, as his King, would be the best judge of that. Perhaps Your Majesty could indicate the kind of provision you deem it gallant for him to make?'

Farouk pursed his surprisingly small rosebud lips and then drew a gold-backed notebook and gold pen from one of his inner pockets. He scrawled down a figure, looked at it, and then wrote something else down.

Then he showed what he had written to Jack.

With great difficulty Jack remained nonchalant. 'That would be very satisfactory, Your Majesty,' he said, continuing the charade that they were talking about someone other than Farouk himself by adding, 'And now perhaps I could wait while you confer with the gentleman in question and a legally binding document is drawn up? I shall then deposit the document with Zubair Pasha's lawyer. Fawzia will know nothing whatsoever about her lover's chivalric action until the day comes when it is requisite for her to know. And perhaps,' he added in a moment of devilment he couldn't resist, 'perhaps that day will never come? Perhaps her lover will divorce his wife and marry her?'

Farouk's dark eyes gleamed. 'Perhaps he will, Major Bazeljette,' he said, holding out a hand for Jack to shake. 'And though I know that such an event would surprise you, it would not surprise me. And now, if you would like to return to the anteroom, an aide will bring the document to you very shortly.'

And with that Farouk exited the room fast, on feet that were very nimble for such a plump young man.

As he realized that he had achieved his objective, Jack let out a deep sigh of relief. Not only had the King made ample financial provision for

510

Fawzia, he had also stipulated that the title deeds of a palatial St Tropez villa be made over to her. It was, Jack thought, with sneaking admiration for Farouk's far-sightedness, a very good way of ensuring that if and when the affair came to an end, Fawzia would, very conveniently, be living several hundred miles away.

And if the affair didn't come to an end? As he left the Palace, the document guaranteeing Fawzia's future in his breast pocket, he couldn't help reflecting wryly that Fawzia would make a quite spectacular Queen of Egypt.

The next morning, as he set about prising from the Embassy a list of the names of Embassy staff, together with their biographical details, Brigadier Haigh put his head around the door. 'Just thought you'd like to know your father is about to land at Heliopolis airfield,' he said in a manner far more genial than usual. 'He's here to chinwag with Auchinleck and give Churchill a first-hand account of our situation. I keep forgetting what a bigwig your father is. If you want to join the reception committee, you may.'

Knowing that his father would probably have no time to spend with him, apart from a few minutes at the airstrip, Jack was out of Grey Pillars within minutes.

'Where are we going, sir?' Corporal Slade asked as he put the jeep into gear.

'Heliopolis airport, to meet a plane.'

'Anyone important, sir? It's not the Prime Minister, is it? Or the Foreign Secretary?'

'No, Slade,' he said as Slade slewed the jeep out

511

into Sharia Qasr el Aini, 'it's someone far more important than that.'

Completely mystified, Slade shot him a quick glance, narrowly missing a camel plodding down the centre of the road.

Jack, who had a growing affection for young Slade, grinned. 'I'm going to meet the Prime Minister's envoy, Sir Jerome Bazeljette, Slade.'

'Blimey.' Slade was impressed. 'Fancy you having the same name as a nob like that. I bet he won't half be surprised when he finds you have the same monniker. I don't think he's more important than the Prime Minister, though, Major. If you don't mind me saying so, that is.'

Jack chuckled, in high good spirits. 'I don't mind you saying so, Slade. But in my books he is. Now, how about we try to avoid this flock of sheep holding up traffic and take a short cut through El Ahmer?'

They reached the airstrip just as the plane landed. As Jack vaulted from the jeep, he saw that Ivor was there to welcome his father on behalf of the Ambassador and a brigadier was there to welcome him on behalf of Sir Claude Auchinleck. There were a couple of minor aides also standing on the runway and as Jack strode to join them, and Ivor gave him a nod of greeting, the door of the plane opened.

His father had never looked like a conventional Englishman of his class. Though his hair was now silvered at the temples, Sir Winston Churchill's envoy was still so dark-haired and swarthy that it seemed as though the blood of a country far hotter than England ran in his veins. And the scar through his left eyebrow made him appear not only raffish, but as if he would be an ugly customer in a fight – a fight that he wouldn't need much excuse to get involved in.

Instead of immediately descending the steps that had been run up to the door he paused, turning round to speak to someone behind him. A second later a sandy-haired little boy stepped uncertainly out of the plane's shadowed interior to stand beside him.

'Dear God,' he heard Ivor say disbelievingly from a few yards away, 'he's brought the Sinclair orphan with him. Now how the devil did he get permission to do that?'

As the brigadier's eyes nearly popped out of his head, Jerome walked down the steps, his hand reassuringly on Andrew's shoulder.

'On behalf of Sir Miles, welcome to Cairo, Sir Jerome,' Ivor said, mindful to observe the strict formalities, as the occasion demanded.

Jerome shook his old friend's hand hard. 'It's good to be here, Conisborough. As you see I have a young companion with me. I shall be dropping him off at Nile House before continuing with my schedule. Will Davina be there, do you know?'

'It's not likely, Jerome,' Ivor said, forgetting about the formalities and the presence of the brigadier and the aides. 'She works, breathes and sleeps at the hospital, but I'll have a message sent to her – and to her matron. I think I can guarantee she'll be at Nile House by the time you and Andrew arrive there.'

Jerome gave a nod of thanks and turned his attention to the brigadier. 'I believe I'm to meet with General Auchinleck at 1300 hours. Is that correct?'

'Yes, sir. At General Headquarters, sir.'

It was just after ten o'clock and Jack noted that his father looked deeply pleased at the pocket of time he had been given.

'As for you, Major Bazeljette,' his father said, his mouth tugging into a smile as he greeted him last of all. 'Who dropped word to you of my arrival?'

'Brigadier Haigh, sir,' he said with a grin, as mindful as Ivor had been that this was a formal occasion, not a family one.

'Then I'm sure Brigadier Haigh will be happy for you to accompany Andrew and me to Nile House,' Jerome said, adding in a low voice as he turned away from the small reception committee, 'The ride into Cairo might be the only time we get to talk to each other, Jack.'

Hoping passionately that the male secretary who had accompanied his father would be travelling in a separate car, thereby allowing him to talk freely not only about family affairs, but also about his mammoth difficulty in running Rommel's spy to earth, he strode across to where Slade was waiting for him.

'You're to return to GHQ on your own, Slade.'

'Yes, Major.' Slade was bewildered. 'And how will you be travelling back to Cairo, sir?'

'I'll be travelling with my father, Slade,' he said, and as Slade's jaw dropped, Jack walked back to where Jerome and Andrew were seated in the rear of a black limousine, waiting for him.

'Andrew, I'd like to introduce you to my son,

Jack,' Jerome said as the big car swung away from the airstrip. 'Jack wasn't much older than you now are when he first came out to Cairo and stayed at Nile House. You'll find living there very different to living at Shibden Hall, but you'll soon get used to it.'

Andrew gave both of them a shy smile. 'I already like the sun, sir. The sun doesn't shine much in Norfolk.'

With the knack he had of putting children at their ease, Jerome said, 'Jack and I have quite a lot of talking to do, Andrew, and only a little while in which to do it. It would be best if you tried not to listen to any of it and concentrated on looking out for camels and a glimpse of the pyramids. Anything you hear I'd like you to keep to yourself, okay?'

'Okay, sir,' Andrew said solemnly. 'I'm going to be a Cub Scout. I'm good at keeping secrets.' And he turned his back to the two of them and began looking very intently out of the window.

'I'm here for forty-eight hours, Jack.' Jerome gave Jack's hand a fatherly pat. 'It's the usual thing. Winston wants me to talk with Auchinleck and Sir Miles Lampson and get the feel of the mood out here. Needless to say, I'm going to squeeze in as much time with Delia as I can, though it won't be easy. Incidentally, my secretary is going straight on to General Headquarters and Ivor isn't following us to Nile House. He doesn't want his divorce from Delia to be scuppered by the accusation of collusion. Now, what is your situation with the brief you've been given?'

Jack's response was unhesitating. 'It's grim. My

515

monitoring group have targeted a transmission in code being sent from the Gezira Island area. So far they haven't pinpointed its exact location, and I doubt they'll be able to. The bugger transmitting doesn't stay on the air long enough – and nor does hc transmit that regularly, either. I reckon he's only a radio operator, not the spy himself, but if we could trace him we'd then be able to lay hands on the big fish. It has to be someone with access to military secrets, and we've scrupulously checked every bloody brigadier and colonel at GHQ with authority to take top-secret information out of the building. None of them has come up with the kind of dodgy Egyptian girlfriend who could be gaining access to the information and passing it on.'

As the limousine neared Cairo's poverty-stricken outskirts he paused for a second, and then said, 'I've now realized that Embassy staff at attaché level have authorization to see whatever military information they deem necessary, and so they are my next line of enquiry. Getting information on names and background isn't easy because the Embassy thinks I'm barking up the wrong tree. I don't think that, though. I've got a gut instinct about the leak coming from the Embassy and I want to follow it through. When you get back to London, I'd greatly appreciate it if you would send me the kind of information I'm after.'

'Will do. Your brief allows you to go anywhere and interrogate anyone, doesn't it?'

Jack nodded.

'Then don't be afraid of tackling Embassy staff head-on. If, because of information Rommel is receiving, Tobruk falls, then Cairo will be his next stop. And the domino effect won't stop there. If he takes Cairo, he'll have control of Suez and, once that happens, we'll lose our route to India, Singapore and Australia, and access to the Arabian oilfields.'

He didn't add that then the war would be over, with the Allies defeated and the Axis Powers victorious, because he didn't need to.

The prospect of the Allies losing the war was so horrendous that they were silent for a minute or two and then, as the limousine became clogged in the chaotic traffic of Kasr el Nil Street, Jerome said, turning the conversation to family matters, 'How is Fawzia, Jack? I should have asked you earlier. Was your posting to Cairo quite a surprise for her?'

'It was. And not a pleasant one. We've agreed to divorce.'

Jerome's eyebrows rose but to Jack's relief he made no comment and Jack realized that the news hadn't come as a complete surprise – though he was pretty sure that when he tossed Farouk's name into the ring his father was going to be poleaxed.

As the limousine began cruising through the wide leafy streets of Garden City Jerome said, 'I've asked whether the Royal Horse Artillery could organize an *ad hoc* polo match while I'm here – and if so, whether you and Darius could be guest players. It isn't a forgone conclusion that I'll have the free time to watch it, but if the arrangement is in place the faint chance is always there.'

'Brilliant. I've barely seen Darius since I've

been here and I've seen far too little of Davina.'

His father was, he knew, about to ask after Petra, but time had run out on them. They were cruising up to Nile House's porticoed entrance and Andrew was saying, round-eyed, 'Is this where I'm to live? Right next to the river?'

Jack could see Davina's little Morris parked on the far side of the drive and as Jerome said to Andrew, 'It is indeed, Andrew. And at the rear of the house there are donkeys in a lovely long garden,' Davina hurtled out of the house.

The chauffeur opened the nearside rear door for Jerome while Davina ran round to Andrew's side of the car. 'Welcome to Nile House, Andrew,' she said with a beaming smile, opening his door for him. 'I'm Davina, and please don't look so startled. Nile House isn't a hospital. I'm only in nurse's uniform because I've come straight from work in order to be here to welcome you.'

'That's all right,' Andrew said comfortably as he stepped out of the car. 'And I didn't think it was a hospital,' he added as she held out her hand and he slipped his into it, 'because hospitals don't have gardens and donkeys, do they?'

'Jerome! *Jerome!*' If Davina had run out of the house, Delia – wearing a dress in the brilliant turquoise colour she so loved and looking nearer to thirty-eight than forty-eight – came out of it as if her feet were winged, her arms wide, a blazing smile of joy on her face.

With a shout of exultation Jerome strode towards her, and as she threw herself into his arms he swung her off the ground and around and around, as if she were a young girl.

It was extraordinary behaviour for a statesman in late middle-age and a still married, though about-to-be-divorced, aristocratic leader of British Cairene high society, and Jack was grateful there was no one there to witness it but himself, Davina, Andrew – and a rather startled chauffeur.

'You must have a welcome drink,' Davina said to Andrew, and with Delia once more in touch with the ground they followed her and Jerome into Nile House. 'A welcome drink is traditional and Adjo, who will have arranged that the drinks are all ready and waiting for us, is impatient to meet you. When I arrived in Cairo, Adjo was my very first Egyptian friend and I'm sure he'll soon be your friend, too.'

In the relative coolness of the vast drawing room Jack took off his peaked cap, laid it on a low glass table and accepted from a sufragi one of the rose-water-flavoured drinks he found so sickly sweet. Jerome and Delia still had their arms around each other's waist and he looked across to Davina to see how she was taking this blatant statement of the open way the two of them now intended conducting their relationship.

She was showing not the slightest sign of being startled by it and he realized that, like him, she had probably known for a decade what the lie of the land was between his father and her mother.

'I'm just going to show Andrew his room,' she said as Andrew manfully downed his drink, 'and then, as Matron has given me the rest of the afternoon off, I'm going to spend it showing Andrew around Cairo.'

'I'm seeing General Auchinleck at one o'clock,'

Jack heard his father say to Delia. 'Then I'm having a meeting with Sir Miles Lampson. Tomorrow I shall be going into the desert to have a look at our forward positions. Winston wants a first-hand account. A polo match has been arranged, but whether I'll be able to get to watch it is doubtful. Other than that, this next hour is all the time we're going to have together.'

Aware that their conversation was becoming increasingly personal, Jack moved away, and until Davina and Andrew rejoined them he stood at the open French windows, looking down the long sweep of garden towards the river.

'I can see the pyramids from my bedroom window,' Andrew said with great satisfaction when he and Davina came back into the room. 'And Davina is going to take me on a sailboat on the river. Adjo says the sailboats are called feluccas.'

'I shall be staying here for a little longer,' Jerome said to Jack, putting his arm around Jack's shoulders. 'You can take the limousine if you need it – just as long as you send it back.'

'I don't need it, Dad. If I don't see you at the polo match, have a safe flight back to London.'

Aware that it was highly possible they wouldn't see each other for a long time they hugged and then, following in Davina and Andrew's wake, Jack walked out of the room and out of the house.

Davina and Andrew were already piling into her open-topped little Morris and she asked him if he wanted a lift.

He shook his head. 'I'm going back to Grey Pillars. Getting in and out of the car would be more trouble than it's worth.'

It was then he realized he'd left his cap behind.

With a sigh of irritation he turned back towards the house.

As he walked from the entrance hall into the drawing room there was no sign of Adjo or any of the sufragis – and no sign of his father and Delia, either.

He picked up his cap and then, as he walked from the room, he heard the sound of laughter from the floor above him, and footsteps running down the corridor leading from the head of the wide, curving staircase.

Seconds later there came the slam of a bedroom door.

He looked at his watch. It was eleven forty-five. As he walked out into the fierce sunlight he grinned to himself, knowing very well why his father had been so relieved at finding that he had at least an hour free before he had to leave Nile House for his meeting with General Auchinleck.

The polo match took place two days later, on the day his father was to leave. As it was such an impromptu match the only spectators were family and friends. Neither Jack nor Darius cared. For the first time ever, they found them- selves playing on the same team and as their ponies twisted and turned and galloped hard it was as if the years had rolled back to the days before the war, when they were just two young men who had a prickly, competitive friendship and no worries.

Jack was playing in Number Three position and

as he hit the ball, feeding it to Darius, in Number One position, he gave a whoop of triumph. Despite the Royal Horse Artillery riders playing like dervishes, Darius, he knew, was going to score.

Riding like a barbarian, Darius defeated all the opposing team's efforts to block him and thwacked the ball straight between the posts. Elatedly Jack stood up in his stirrups, his polo shirt soaking wet, unable to remember when he had last enjoyed himself so much.

Lunch was a family picnic in a quiet corner of the Sporting Club's flower-filled grounds. To Jack's disappointment, Darius had an urgent meeting with a client and so wasn't able to be with them. Sholto, who hadn't been at the polo match, wasn't with them either.

'So far, I've never seen Petra and Sholto together,' Jack said to Davina as they sat a little distance from where Petra was spreading a white tablecloth on the grass and Delia was unpacking from a giant hamper the picnic food prepared by the club's chef. 'When I asked Delia how Petra and Sholto were, she simply said "fine" and changed the subject. When I asked Petra how Sholto was, she simply said "fine" and changed the subject. From which I gather that things are far from fine.'

'You're probably right, but I truthfully don't know, Jack. Petra never speaks about her marriage. And so no one else ever speaks about it either.'

As Delia lifted silver cutlery from a hamper, Andrew said chattily, 'When we had picnics in

Caithness, my mother always used to sing the Happy Song.'

'The Happy Song?' Delia had begun cutting a large quiche into slices. 'Now what song would that be?'

'I think it can be any song, just as long as it's always the same one. It's the song you sing when you are really happy. Our Happy Song was "The Bonnie Banks of Loch Lomond". Don't you have a Happy Song?'

'I don't think we do, Andrew.' There was regret in Delia's voice as she slid a slice of quiche onto a plate.

'Oh yes, we do.' Davina's contradiction was immediate. 'It's "Dixie". You've been singing it at every happy family occasion ever since I can remember.'

'That's true, Delia.' Jerome, lying on the grass with his weight resting on one arm, looked at her with a gleam in his gold-flecked eyes. 'Though I remember an occasion, on the day we first met, when Ivor specifically forbade you from ever doing so.'

'Ah, well.' Delia's voice was full of naughty mischief. 'That was when dear Ivor thought he'd got himself a very different kind of wife from the one he actually had. How about I sing it now? Would you like that, Andrew?'

Andrew nodded and Delia handed the plate of quiche to Jerome and then launched into the song that reminded her of Sans Souci and Sultan and long exhilarating rides in the lush rolling countryside of her birth.

Jack looked across at Petra. All morning she

had done her best to put as much space between them as possible. She had hardly spoken to anyone else, either. More often than not, when he had looked across at her she had been looking towards his father, an expression in her eyes that he couldn't, for the life of him, fathom.

As Delia came to the last verse, they all joined in the chorus with enormous gusto. Afterwards Petra said, her voice strained, 'I'm going for a walk. I won't be long, Jerome. I'll be back to say goodbye before you leave.'

It was a reminder that the car that was to take Jerome to the airport was already standing by and in less than an hour he would be speeding to Heliopolis in it.

Jack watched her walk away. He knew she was bitterly unhappy. Everyone else knew she was bitterly unhappy. And she wouldn't talk to him about her unhappiness; she wouldn't let him close to her in any way at all.

He stood up, and arousing a great deal of interest he began running after her.

She was heading in the direction of the club-house and he caught up with her at the beginning of the lavender-lined pathway leading towards it.

Seizing hold of her arm, he swung her round to face him. 'Talk to me,' he said urgently, breathing hard. 'We may not be lovers any more, but we can at least be friends! Don't keep yourself so shut off, so isolated. I love you. I've always loved you. And because I love you I want to help you. Tell me what's wrong.'

'I can't!' In the strong sunlight he saw that there were deep circles carved under her eyes, and her skin was so pale it was almost translucent. 'There's so much wrong, Jack! It isn't just you and me – it's other things. Things I can't speak about; not until I'm sure.'

'What kind of things?' There was a different sort of urgency in his voice now, for her green-gilt eyes were frantic with an expression he'd seen all too often in interrogations. She was frightened – and he had to know why, and what of.

'Later, Jack. I just need a little more time.' Her face was bloodless. 'Please give my apologies to Jerome. I can't go back and say goodbye. Not now.'

She tried to turn away from him, but he held her fast, his heart pounding. 'You have to tell me what it is you're so scared of, Petra,' he said fiercely. 'I'll slay every damned dragon in the world for you, but I have to know what the dragon is. I love you with every fibre of my being. You can trust me with your life!'

'I know that, Jack! Please don't ever think I don't know that!'

A whole mob of people coming down the pathway swarmed around them and Petra twisted so suddenly and violently that this time she escaped his grasp. He tried to catch hold of her again, but a woman in the small group that was now between them stumbled and fell in front of him and by the time he had disentangled himself from her, Petra was yards away, running in the direction of the car park.

Sidestepping the woman, who was anxiously examining her grazed knees, he was about to sprint after Petra when a club official hurried up to

525

him. 'There's an urgent phone call for you from General Headquarters, Major Bazeljette, sir,' he said briskly.

Uttering a swear word he seldom used, Jack gave one last look after Petra and then headed for the clubhouse at a run.

The caller was Archie.

'Sorry to disturb your family thrash, Jack,' he said apologetically, 'but thought you should know that Sadat's in Cairo again. The minute our railway informer rang in with the gen, I set Slade on his tail and Slade has just contacted me to say that Sadat has boarded a houseboat on Gezira.'

Jack felt as if a ton weight had just slammed into his chest.

'On the south of the island?' he said, praying to God it was one the houseboats near to the English Bridge.

'No.' Archie was happily oblivious of Jack's concern. 'North. At the Zamalek end. The name of the houseboat is the *Egyptian Queen*.'

TWENTY NINE

Jack fought the temptation to head straight to Zamalek. No law was being broken and Sadat was being tailed only because he was known to be a member of a subversive group within the Egyptian army. His being so wasn't a crime for which he could be thrown into a British prison. Only if the Free Officers came out in open rebellion could action be taken against him. Keeping close tabs on him was, however, vital; yet if he became aware that wherever he went in Cairo he was being tailed – and he certainly would become aware of it if a British intelligence officer showed up on the houseboat – keeping close tabs on him would become impossible. So all Jack could do was step up the surveillance on him – and instigate surveillance on Darius.

It was the very last thing in the world that he wanted to do.

Once back at GHQ he hesitated, and hesitated some more over doing it. In the end, though, he knew he had no option. That Sadat had made contact with the owner of the *Egyptian Queen* was now a matter of record – as was the owner's name.

It went without saying that at the first opportunity he was going to confront Darius about his meeting with Sadat. Darius may have successfully fooled people into believing that his days as a fierce nationalist and an anti-British agitator were over, but Jack now knew differently. The war hadn't caused Darius to see things from a different perspective. All he had done was go undercover.

He wrote a terse report for Brigadier Haigh. Rang Petra's home number and received no reply. Rang Nile House only to be told that Lady Conisborough had not yet returned from accompanying Sir Jerome to the airfield in order to say goodbye to him. Then, just as he was about to send his report to the brigadier, the brigadier sent for him.

With Sadat's file tucked beneath his arm he

made his way along the warren-like corridors to Haigh's sanctum.

When he entered it, it was to find that the Director of Military Intelligence was not alone.

He had a friend of the Conisboroughs, Bruno Lautens, with him.

As an experienced intelligence officer Jack was well trained in remaining impassive in surprising situations, and although it took some doing, he remained impassive now.

'Sit down, Jack.' Since the reminder that Jack's father was a close intimate of the Prime Minister's, Brigadier Haigh's attitude towards him had become increasingly matey. 'Circumstances require that the three of us have a very private talk.'

'Circumstances?' Not looking towards Bruno, Jack put the file down on Haigh's desk.

The brigadier looked at the name on the file and tapped it with his forefinger. 'Yes, Jack,' he said meaningfully. '*These* circumstances.'

Bruno was seated in a club chair to one side of the desk. Jack took the club chair facing the brigadier.

'The latest update in this file,' Brigadier Haigh continued, 'will detail Captain Anwar Sadat's unexpectedly speedy return to Cairo and his having gone straight from the railway station to Gezira Island and to a houseboat owned by your Egyptian brother-in-law. Or at least, that is what I *hope* you've found fit to detail. I know all this, Jack, because we're not the only ones interested in Captain Anwar Sadat. The Americans, too, have a strong interest in him and are keeping him under surveillance. Mr Lautens is a high-ranking American intelligence officer.'

Jack quirked an eyebrow in Bruno's direction. 'I'd heard you were an archaeologist?' he asked. 'Was that just a front?'

Bruno's quick grin was affable. 'No. I'm a pukka archaeologist. It was when I was on a dig down near the Sudan border that I was recruited by Washington.' He looked towards Brigadier Haigh. 'Do you want me to put Major Bazeljette in the picture, or would you prefer to, Brigadier?'

Haigh pursed his lips and then said; 'I shall, if you don't mind. America's take on the Free Officers' Movement, Jack, is that when this war is won, America and Britain are going to need the men who are members of it in order to build the kind of modern Egyptian state that Britain and America can work with. That the monarchy's days are numbered is something we all know. Farouk is as corrupt as they come and is certainly not the man to hoist Egypt into the twentieth century. There's a feeling, however, that Gamel Nasser, who is the Free Officers' kingpin, probably is.'

'And does this ... scenario ... assume an Egypt that is completely free of a British presence?' Jack asked, looking from the brigadier to Bruno and back again.

'America doesn't like imperialism,' Bruno said pleasantly.

'And we have to be realistic,' Brigadier Haigh said heavily. 'I don't have a second's doubt that we're going to win this war but, when we do, the world is going to be a different place. It may very well be that the Americans are right and that in

529

the post-war world there will be no place for Britain in Egypt. On the outside chance that they are right – and on the even more slender chance that Nasser and Sadat will be the men we shall then find ourselves dealing with – my orders are to keep a tight watch on them and on their friends, but not so tight that we won't be able to come to an accommodation with them, should the occasion ever arise.'

'And is Darius Zubair counted as being one of those friends?'

Bruno leaned forward in his chair, his big hands clasped between his knees. 'Not only a friend but, according to our intelligence reports, a potentially leading member of whatever government Nasser may one day form. And that it *is* Nasser and his friends who one day form it is vital if the danger of the Muslim Brotherhood taking control of Egypt is to be avoided. That isn't a future any of us want to contemplate.'

'No, by God,' Haigh said with feeling. 'And so the long and the short of it, Jack, is that you keep your brother-in-law and Sadat under surveillance, but that you so do with an eye to the broader picture. Savvy?' And not troubling to open the file Jack had brought in for him to read, the brigadier handed it back to him.

'Yes, sir.' Jack rose to his feet, saluted and left the room.

When he got back to his own office he locked the file safely away and tried Petra's phone number again. Once again there was no reply.

Archie came in and thumped a pink-docketed report down on his desk. 'A British Gladiator

530

took off without authorized clearance from the Hilmiya airstrip two hours ago,' he said. 'Seems there was an Egyptian at the controls and radar tracking had him heading straight for the German lines. Our blokes tried to shoot him down before he crossed them. They failed, but a stray German gunner did the job for them. What the pilot was up to is anybody's guess.'

'Leave it with me. I'll send a report in to Haigh in the morning. I understand you've got a hot date with Boo tonight?'

Archie grinned. 'I have, but I've some paper-work to finish off first.'

Jack was in no mood for paperwork. When Archie began pounding away in a corner of the office on a battered typewriter he tried Petra's number again. This time the number didn't ring unanswered. This time it was unobtainable. A phone being out of order wasn't an unusual occurrence in Cairo and controlling his im-patience he said, 'I'm off home, Archie. I'm in need of a stiff drink and a reviving shower.'

Home, the flat he shared with two other intelligence officers he very rarely saw, was only a five-minute walk away, but between setting off from Grey Pillars and arriving at his door, dusk fell. It did so in spectacular fashion, as it always did in Cairo: pale yellow light turning fiery orange before plunging into deep purple twilight.

He knew the instant he stepped into the narrow hallway that no one else was at home. Relieved, he made straight for the bathroom and turned the creaky shower full on. The phone rang before he'd even had the chance to take off his shirt and, certain it would be a 'fishing fleet' girl for one or other of his flatmates, he walked back out of the bathroom and into the hall to answer it.

'Thank God you're there, Jack.' There was an edge to Archie's voice he'd never heard in it before. 'Petra showed up here minutes ago in a state of great agitation. She said she had to see you. When I said you'd just left for the flat she asked for the address. I offered to escort her over, but she refused point-blank. She was nearly hysterical and so I thought it best to let her have her way rather than risk making things worse.'

'And she left GHQ how long ago?'

'Two minutes. Maybe three.'

'Stay by the phone in case I need to contact you.' He slammed the receiver down. Whatever the cause of Petra's distress, he knew it was something extremely serious. She'd been scared when she had spoken to him earlier on – and Petra wasn't the kind of woman who scared easily. Nor was she the kind of woman to give way to hysteria.

As he strode into the bathroom and turned the shower off, the doorbell rang.

He was at the door in a flash, yanking it open so fast that she half fell across the threshold.

To his stupefaction he saw she was clutching a battered German prayer book to her chest.

He put an arm around her, taking her weight.

'I have to talk to you, Jack...' She was gasping for breath. 'I have to tell you...'

'Tell me when you're sitting down with a brandy inside you,' he said brusquely.

'No.' She shook her head violently, her torrent of hair tumbling over his arm. 'There isn't time...

I don't even know whether he's so injured he'll still be there, or whether he'll be gone.'

'He? Sholto?'

She nodded and, fighting to keep hysteria at bay, said, 'He's a spy. I've had suspicions for months, but when I found this–' her fingers tightened on the prayer book – 'when I found this, I was sure. So sure that I confronted him... He just laughed and then he lunged at me. We fought at the top of the stairs and I tripped him and he tumbled down them and banged his head on the newel post and that's where I left him, unconscious and bleeding. But when he comes round he won't stay there! Not now he knows I know.'

He didn't ask why she'd been suspicious of Sholto for months. He didn't ask what was in the prayer book.

He dialled his own number at GHQ.

Archie answered.

'Our man is Sholto Monck,' he said without preamble or explanation. 'He's at five Sharia Aziz, Gezira Island. Go there direct with a squad of armed men. I want him taken into custody no matter what diplomatic protection garbage he gives you. And I want him taken alive. Get a jeep and an armed officer to me and I'll meet you there. Got it?'

'Got it,' Archie said, stunned but unquestioning.

Jack took his Colt from its holster and strode into the bedroom. Tugging open a drawer he took a box of bullets from it. As he began fully loading the revolver, Petra said unsteadily from the doorway, 'Sholto isn't Anglo-Irish as he pretends.

533

He's Irish – but only half Irish. I was looking for something – anything – that would give me the certainty I needed and I found this in a box of books which he brought with him to Cairo and never unpacked.'

He put a handful of bullets into his top pocket, slammed his revolver back into the holster on his hip and took the dusty prayer book from her.

On the flyleaf, written in German spidery handwriting, was a list of family birth dates. The last name on the list was Sholto's. Against his name was his place of birth. It was Munich.

'What made you suspicious?' he demanded, taking fierce satisfaction from knowing that his suspicions where the Embassy was concerned had been right all along.

'Lots of things.'

Knowing the jeep would be with them within seconds she spoke first.

'He had so much money it was as if he were printing it himself – and I became sure the money was coming via a diplomat at the Romanian Legation. He only ever met with Constantin when he thought no one would see them together. And Constantin's colleague at the Romanian Legation was expelled for spying.'

She took a deep shuddering breath and pushed her hair away from her face. 'Then there's the contempt he has for Sir Miles and everyone else he works with at the Embassy – though it's a contempt he keeps well hidden from everyone but me. The realization that his motive in marrying me was so that he could gain contact with Ivor and those of Ivor's friends who move in the highest possible governmental circles. The fact that when he drinks heavily and talks in his sleep he does so in German. In the early days he laughed it off by saying he'd been dreaming he was twenty-three again and studying German for his Foreign Office exams. I used to laugh too. But that was before I began to know just how different the real Sholto Monck is from the Sholto Monck the world sees.'

The jeep screeched to a halt outside the flat.

He gripped her shoulders. 'You're to stay here. If he's already left Sharia Aziz he'll be on the hunt for you in the hope he can find you before you tell anyone what you know. Don't go to Nile House. It's one of the first places he'll make for. I doubt he knows this address, but there's going to be an armed man with you until I get back. Got it?'

She nodded. 'Be careful,' she said, her voice breaking, terror for his safety naked in her eyes. 'I couldn't bear it if anything happened to you. It would kill me, Jack. Truly.'

In the sudden, blinding knowledge that no matter what had gone wrong between them, she loved him still, he pulled her towards him, kissing her hard.

A minute later, leaving her leaning against the wall of the hall with tears streaming down her face, he was in the jeep's driving seat, saying savagely to the officer he had ejected from it, 'You're to let no one – *no one* – into this flat until I return. The woman in it is Lord Conisborough's daughter and you guard her with your life. Understand?'

'Yes, sir. Absolutely, sir.'

With a squeal of tyres Jack careered away from the kerb, heading for the Kasr el Nil Bridge, his foot hard to the floor, the palm of one hand almost perpetually slammed full on the jeep's horn.

It was dark now and though the streets were lit, they were dimly lit, for to comply with half-hearted blackout restrictions all street lamps – as well as car headlamps – were dimmed with blue paint. The bridge was as crowded with traffic as always and he fumed and swore as it took a seeming eternity to cross. He glanced at his watch. With luck, Archie and the squad of men he would have with him would already be in Sharia Aziz, and in another five minutes, six at the most, he would be with them.

As he swerved off the bridge onto the island he began heading immediately for the wealthy residential area favoured by the Embassy's diplomats. And then he saw the road leading off to the north. The road leading to Zamalek and the handful of houseboats moored there.

He remembered how expertly Darius had hidden the fact that he was still as anti-British at heart as ever. He remembered how the *Egyptian Queen* had been Sadat's first port of call when he returned to Cairo. He remembered how Constantin, who, according to Petra, was hand in glove with Sholto and probably the means by which he was receiving money from Germany, had been sitting with Darius the night he, Jack, had first made contact again with Darius – and how speedily Constantin had disappeared when he had seen the uniform he was wearing. He remembered seeing Constantin with Sholto as the two of them entered a café off Sultan Hussein Street.

If Darius was deeply involved with Anwar Sadat and the Free Officers' Movement, was he also, via Sholto and Constantin, involved in a quite different form of anti-British activity? Was Darius a German spy as Sholto Monck most definitely was, and as he was now sure Constantin was?

He brought the jeep to a screeching halt, perspiration beading his forehead. It was a possibility. And as he looked at the fork in the road and realized just how very near to each other Darius and Sholto lived, he acted on gut instinct and, slamming the jeep into life once more, slewed onto the road leading towards Zamalek, dread in his heart at the thought of what he might find.

The riverside road curved up the island past the Sporting Club and past the turn-off to the Bulaq Bridge. On the far side of the bridge the lights of restaurants and cafés glimmered and flickered. On the far north-east side of the island there were no such lights, only dense palm groves reaching down to the water's edge.

Twenty yards or so away from the moorings he cut the engine and rolled to a standstill, then, making as little noise as possible, he walked towards the *Egyptian Queen.* The lights in the state room were on, though the curtains were drawn. Darius's Mercedes was parked beneath nearby date palms. There was no sign of any other car, though even in the darkness it was easy to tell that another vehicle had recently churned up the ground.

As he stepped onto the gangplank he could

hear a woman crying, but no sound of voices.

With a hand resting on his revolver he crossed the deck and began to descend the ladder leading to the lit saloon. There was a sharp intake of breath and the crying stopped, but neither Darius, nor Sholto, challenged him.

They weren't there.

Only Zahra was there.

'What do you want?' she demanded, recognizing him at once. She knuckled her tears away; tears, he now realized, that had been tears of fury. 'If you've come to see your brother-in-law, he's gone. They've all gone.'

The anger and bitterness in her voice were scorching.

'They?' he asked, as if it wasn't of too much importance, knowing that if he began asking urgent questions she would remember that as well as being Darius's friend and brother-in-law he was also a British officer, and that the minute she did he'd get nothing further out of her. At the moment, by a blessed miracle, she was treating him as if he were a fellow conspirator.

'The Sholto man dragged me and Constantin here because he said his cover had been blown and that an emergency evacuation plan had to be put in place. He needed Constantin here in order that he could send a wireless message for him.'

Jack's heart felt as if it had ceased to beat. In one sentence, by confirming that though his men hadn't found it, somewhere aboard the *Egyptian Queen* had been a wireless transmitter, she had branded Darius a spy.

'What message did Constantin send?' he said

538

tersely. 'What is the plan?'

She shot him a withering look. 'How do I know what message he sent? He transmits in code. It was after he had that the row started.'

'The row?' Precious minutes were ticking away, yet he knew he couldn't lose his temper with her. To lose his temper with her would be fatal.

'The Sholto man said Darius and Constantin had to go with him and they didn't want to. Constantin said that even if the Sholto man's cover was blown, his wasn't, and that even if it was, as a diplomat, the worst that could happen to him was that he would be expelled and sent back to Bucharest. And that if he was sent back to Bucharest he would make sure I was able to join him there.' Her voice shook with explosive fury. 'I won't be able to join him now the Sholto pig has taken him with him to Germany!'

'*Germany?*'

None of his long training in keeping ice-cool in whatever situation he was plunged into, could keep him ice-cool now.

Zahra was too out of her mind with fury to even register his stupefaction.

'The Sholto pig said a plane would land at Malaqua and take them to Tripoli.'

Jack had never heard of Malaqua, but if a German plane was to land there it had to be deep in the desert and presumably close to German positions across the Libyan border. Which meant Sholto, Constantin and Darius were heading into an area that only a British Army Long Range Desert Patrol would be able to find and reach.

'Darius didn't want to go.' Zahra was so angry at

Constantin's betrayal in leaving her behind that she was happy to tell him everything. 'But the Sholto man said he had to drive him and Constantin at least as far as El Laban where he had a Bedouin contact who knew the desert route to Malaqua. And he said they had to take the transmitter with them so that they could keep in touch with the people who were sending the plane.'

Jack knew El Laban. It was a scattering of mudbrick houses set around an oasis thirty miles or so further south than Saqqarah. He'd been there years ago, with Darius, but whether he could find his way there alone, and at night, was another matter. He was, though, going to give it a hell of a try.

Knowing that he'd got all the information he would get from her and that what he was about to do could cost him his entire professional future – if not his life – he turned on his heel and scrambled back up the ladder and onto the deck.

Ten minutes later he was driving fast across the English Bridge, heading for Giza. Even though it was night the road was still busy with carts and camels and military trucks. He tried to work out how much of a start Darius, Constantin and Sholto had on him. Sholto must have recovered consciousness only minutes after Petra had fled from the house. While she had gone straight to Grey Pillars, he had gone to the houseboat, picking Constantin and Zahra up en route. How long would that have taken? How long would it have taken Petra to reach Grey Pillars and then to drive to his flat? Fifteen minutes? Twenty? And how long had they been in the flat before the jeep arrived and he had raced off to Zamalek? Four minutes? Five?

He swerved past an armoured car. At a rough estimate Darius, Sholto and Constantin were a good fifteen minutes ahead of him. And if he didn't catch up with them before El Laban, he wouldn't be able to catch up with them at all. A Bedouin who knew where he was going could travel the desert at night. Jack couldn't, not when, with blue-painted headlamps, he might not even be able to see the tracks of Sholto's car. And day or night, no one went into the Sahara unaccompanied. It was a death sentence. And he had no emergency supply of water with him. No clothes suitable for enduring the desert's crucifyingly cold night-time temperature.

Dark fields of sugar cane stretched out on either side of him and then, in the moonlight, the familiar triangular shape of the pyramids reared blackly against a star-pocked sky.

The road to the Western Desert veered off one way, towards the battle front. Another road, far narrower, led to Saqqarah.

Within yards of racing down it he was stopped by two military policemen. He flashed his SIB warrant card at them and they waved him on. Sholto's diplomatic identity card had, presumably, carried equal weight.

The road was one he knew well. Ever since he'd been a boy, whenever he'd visited Nile House he had hired a horse from the Mena House Hotel stables and ridden to the Step Pyramid, sometimes with Darius, sometimes with Petra or Davina.

541

Davina.

He couldn't even begin to imagine Davina's agony if Darius were to leave Egypt with Sholto and Constantin. And his leaving Egypt wasn't the worst scenario. The worst scenario was him remaining behind and there being evidence against him that he, Jack, knew nothing about; evidence so damning that not even his links to Sadat and Nasser would save him from a firing squad.

There were coils of barbed wire on both sides of the road and in the distance, to the left of him, something that looked suspiciously like a skull-and-crossbones minefield sign. He kept near to the middle of the road, mindful that the verges would be soft deep sand. A motorbike zoomed out of the darkness towards him, the rider wearing a blue and white Signals Corps armband.

He was shivering, freezing to death without the benefit of a heavy jacket. What the devil was he going to do if and when Sholto's distinctive Chrysler came into view? He was banking on the fact that he wouldn't have to draw his revolver on Darius.

But what if Darius was certain that with Sholto and Constantin captured he too would face a firing squad? What if Darius gave him no chance to explain the deal Jack knew could be struck because of Darius's links to Sadat and Nasser?

In the brilliant moonlight the Step Pyramid came into view. Jack's stomach muscles tightened. From here onwards his only chance of catching up with the Chrysler was by being able to pick up the Chrysler's wheel marks on whatever desert track Sholto had taken.

Cursing the dimness of his headlamps he circled round and round on the hard-packed sand and then he saw the tyre marks he was looking for. Praying that his petrol was going to last he swerved onto the track leading away into the depths of the Sahara and jammed the accelerator pedal flat to the jeep's floor.

As he covered mile after mile, with the Sahara stretching out on either side of him as vast as all eternity, his tension mounted. What if the tracks he was following weren't the Chrysler's? What if he was following tracks made by an army vehicle? What if he lost the tracks and couldn't find them again? If his petrol ran out it would be highly unlikely that anyone would ever find him and there was only enough water in the jeep for a day – two at the most.

After an hour or so he began seeing scrubby bushes in his headlamps and then he picked out the stark black silhouette of date palms. His relief was overpowering. Even if it wasn't El Laban, it was at least an oasis – and an oasis meant water.

Minutes later he saw mud walls that he recognized and he knew that unless Sholto was still in the village making preparations with his Bedouin friend for an arduous journey into the heart of the desert, his own particular journey had come to an abortive end.

There was no way at all that he could enter the oasis silently. In the desert the faintest sound carried for miles and El Laban's inhabitants would have been aware of his jeep's approach for the last ten minutes. None of them, however, appeared to be curious.

As he cut the engine and stepped out of the jeep, his hand on his revolver, there was no sign of any human movement. And no sign of a car.

In the starlight a skinny dog growled at him. From behind one of the mudbrick houses a donkey brayed. In the centre of the ramshackle collection of houses was the village well, and sitting on its waist-high, circular wall, one leg drawn up to his chest, the other swinging free, was the dark outline of a familiar figure.

'Who,' Darius asked conversationally, 'is going to shoot first, Jack? Am I to shoot you? Or are you going to shoot me?'

THIRTY

Jack stopped walking. 'Where's Monck?' he demanded, not deigning to answer the question.

'He's long gone. And there's no way you can catch him up, Jack. Not without a tame Bedouin as a guide.'

'I need a cigarette.' If Darius had a gun – and it was too dark for Jack to know for sure if he had, or if he was bluffing – he didn't want Darius thinking his hand was going to his Colt and not to a packet of Camels.

He took the cigarettes out of his shirt pocket. 'Want one?' he asked.

The moonlight was bright enough for him to see Darius nod.

He lit his own cigarette and, not yet prepared to close the distance between them, tossed a cigarette and his lighter to Darius.

'What is at Malaqua?'

Darius lit his cigarette. 'An abandoned Italian airfield. Nothing else. Another six hours and Monck and Constantin will be in Tripoli.'

'And how do you feel about that?'

'About Monck getting away?' Darius shrugged. 'I'm indifferent. About Constantin? Constantin would be better off not getting on the damn plane. It's an option I doubt Monck will give him.'

Jack inhaled deeply. 'Tell me about Monck. For how long has he been Rommel's spy in Egypt?'

'For as long as Rommel has been in North Africa. But he's not actually Rommel's spy, Jack. According to Constantin – who told me all this not long after Monck contacted him, without, though, disclosing Monck's name – he's Ribbentrop's spy and he's been spying for Ribbentrop since 1933. What the pay-off was in 1933, I don't know. The pay-off now is the promise that he'll be given a leading role in the future German government of Britain – assuming, of course, that Germany wins the war.'

Jack was so stunned it took him a moment or so to take onboard what Darius was telling him. He'd been a junior diplomat in the Foreign Office when Ribbentrop, as Hitler's Special Commissioner, had begun regularly visiting London and unofficially meeting with the Prime Minister at the time, Ramsay MacDonald, and with MacDonald's Foreign Secretary, Sir John Simon.

He'd met with a lot of other people too. In

those days, when war with Germany was still six years away, Joachim von Ribbentrop had been a popular guest at many society dinner tables. Jack remembered Delia telling him of a dinner party at which Ribbentrop and, among others, the Prince of Wales and Wallis Simpson were guests.

Had Ribbentrop's brief been to snare the Prince of Wales into ever closer friendship with Hitler so that when he became king, he would be king of a country Nazi Germany could count on as an ally? German blood in the royal family was strong and not only did Edward have a host of German relatives, he also spoke German flawlessly. To Hitler, it would have seemed a viable possibility.

Ribbentrop had obviously set out to target other British aristocrats as well. He remembered him being a guest of Lady Cunard's, and seeing him in the company of Lord Rothermere. When German Intelligence unearthed the fact that Sholto had a German father, Ribbentrop must have thought he had struck gold. As, in fact, he had.

'And Monck contacted Constantin, in order for Constantin to act as his radio operator?'

'That would seem to be about it.'

'And did so from aboard the *Egyptian Queen*?'

'That would seem to be about it as well.'

Jack sucked in air on a rasp and when he had himself under control again, said icily, 'The transmitter. Where the devil did you hide it?'

'Inside a radiogram. Below the turntable. All your men did, when they searched the houseboat, was lift the lid. And now you know all that,

546

Jack, what are you going to do about it? Because if you're thinking of taking me back to Cairo to face charges of spying I think it's only fair to tell you that I'm not going to let you.'

He moved his hand slightly and Jack heard the sound of metal grazing the top of the well wall. Whether it was a revolver, or merely the cigarette lighter he had thrown to him, he couldn't tell.

Determined to find out, he threw his half-smoked cigarette away. 'If that's what I wanted to do,' he said, steel in his voice, 'then I'd do it. And it may come to that if you don't see sense.'

Darius remained silent, the tip of his cigarette still gleaming red in the darkness.

'Why did you throw in your lot with the Germans, Darius? They're slaughtering Jews in their thousands and you're well educated enough to know that Arabs, too, are a Semitic people. You can't really believe that if Egypt supports Hitler, and Hitler wins the war, he will repay that support by allowing Egypt to govern itself, free of all German interference? It's as likely as pigs flying.'

'It's a possibility, and any possibility is better than none.'

'There's another possibility I like far better.'

'And what's that?'

'Throw me back the lighter so that I can light up another cigarette and I'll tell you.'

The lighter came winging through the darkness towards him.

He caught it, hoping that from now on there would be no further sound of metal scraping mud-brick.

'Until tonight I didn't know about your involvement with Sholto. And I didn't know Constantin was his radio operator. What I did know, though, was that you have close links with the Free Officers' Movement – and particularly close links with Anwar Sadat. The Americans know about it too. And are very interested in it.'

'The Americans? Of what interest is Egypt to the Americans?'

'America will end up coming into the war – and when it's won, Egypt will be of great importance to them. They are republicans and anti-imperialists, Darius. The Egypt they will want to have dealings with will be an Egypt without a monarchy, and without a British presence carrying with it, as it must, the baggage of an imperialist past. Which is exactly, I think, what the Free Officers' Movement wants as well.'

Darius was again silent, but Jack knew he had his full attention.

'In such an ideal situation the government of an independent Egypt would be up for grabs. The Muslim Brotherhood have huge popular support. A Koran-based, Mullah-led government would not, however, be the easiest kind for Western powers to work with. America prefers the idea of an Egypt governed by Nasser and his friends.'

'Are you sure? Aren't you forgetting that Nasser and Sadat are both Muslims?'

'No, I'm not forgetting. What matters to the Americans is that though they are Muslims, they've never gone along with the extremism of the Muslim Brotherhood. And you are a Copt. American Intelligence believes Nasser and Sadat have earmarked you for a role in any future

548

government they may one day form and the Americans – always looking to the future and always having plans in place for whatever the future might bring – want to nurse you along as their main contact in that government.'

'Which means they wouldn't want to see me shot me as a spy?'

'Which means they very definitely wouldn't want to see you shot as a spy.'

'Then that's just as well – for the British.' Dry, dark humour entered his voice. 'The British wouldn't, after all, want to shoot an innocent man, would they?'

The silence that followed was so profound that Jack could hear his heart beating.

'Run that past me again,' he said, terrified he might have heard wrongly.

'I said that the British wouldn't want to shoot an innocent man.'

'And are you innocent?' The hope that Darius was, was so overpowering that Jack felt giddy with it. 'Explain.'

Darius flicked the ash from the end of his cigarette. 'I always knew Constantin liked to gather whatever information he could that would be useful to the Germans. It was all petty stuff. Things barbers, waiters, prostitutes overheard. And as far as I knew, all he did with it was report it to his superiors at the Legation. And then he told me that a "big fish" at the British Embassy had contacted him. On the surface it was pretty startling information, but I didn't think the big fish was a serious spy. I reckoned Constantin was just doing a bit of bragging. And Constantin never told me his name.'

'So when did you know that it was Monck?'

'When he boarded the *Egyptian Queen* two hours or so ago with Constantin and Zahra in tow and a revolver in his hand.'

'It's a nice try, Darius, but it doesn't explain why the transmitter was aboard the *Egyptian Queen* – and why British Intelligence has been picking up regular signals from it.'

'That's easy.' Darius tossed his cigarette stub into the darkness. 'It was Constantin who introduced me to Sadat and, before you ask, I don't believe Sadat knew about Sholto, or that Sholto knew about Sadat. Constantin had many irons in the fire and he kept them all separate. Sadat was mulling over whether an uprising within the Egyptian army – an uprising timed to help Rommel take Cairo – would be beneficial or not to Egypt. He didn't have faith in the promises Germany had made about giving Egypt full independence and so he'd drawn up a treaty. That was why Constantin brought the transmitter to the houseboat. So that Sadat – who is a signals officer – could make direct arrangements with Rommel for member of the Free Officers' Movement to fly to Libya with the treaty in the hope that Rommel would sign it.'

The dog, which had been quiet for a while, began barking again.

Jack thought of the British Gladiator that had been shot down as the Egyptian pilot flew over the German lines. Whatever arrangements Sadat had made with Rommel for his officer's safe arrival, those arrangements hadn't filtered down

550

to the machine-gunners on the Libyan border – and the machine-gunners had inadvertently done Britain a big favour.

It wasn't something he was going to take up with Darius now, though. Pointing out that any signed treaty wouldn't have been worth the paper it was written on was something Bruno Lautens' superiors could point out to Darius later.

He said, 'Transmissions to Rommel with regard to an officer flying out to him wouldn't account for the number of transmissions we picked up from the *Egyptian Queen*.'

'No, probably not. Throw me another cigarette.'

Jack took another cigarette out of the packet of Camels, lit it from his own cigarette, and walked close enough to Darius to be able to hand it him.

There was no gun, he noticed, either in Darius's hand or on the top of the well wall.

'I think what happened,' Darius said, 'was that after Constantin's colleague was booted back to Bucharest on charges of spying, the Legation, or wherever else Constantin was transmitting from, became too hot for him. Once the transmitter was aboard the *Egyptian Queen* for Sadat's use, I think Constantin, when he could be sure I would be absent, was using it to transmit for Sholto. I once found him onboard, with no cause to be there, when I came home early from a party.'

Jack not only wanted to believe him. He did believe him.

Turning round so that his back was to the well, he prised himself up on it so that they were sitting companionably next to each other.

'Just out of curiosity,' Darius said, pushing a lock of straight black hair away from his brow, 'how did you reconcile the idea of me being a British spy with my being in love with Davina? And before you answer that, you'd better let American Intelligence know that I'm going to marry her, even if it queers the pitch for me with Nasser and Sadat.'

'It wasn't an idea I liked – but I know how deep your passion is for a British-free Egypt. I thought it was a length you might be prepared to go to. And I don't think marrying Davina will queer your pitch with Nasser and Sadat. She's half American, for one thing. For another, her long track record of voluntary work among the fellahin is testimony of her loyalty to Egypt. Did anyone else think you were a spy, by the way? Did Petra?'

Darius grinned and shook his head. 'No, though Petra's never liked me too much, mainly because she thought I was going to make Davina unhappy. When she knows differently, I'm hoping our relationship will change. Fawzia assumes I'm a spy, though. And Fawzia will always assume I'm a spy. It's the reason I never wasted time trying to convince her otherwise. Just to clinch the fact that I'm not, I've got something for you. I pocketed it when Constantin's attention was elsewhere.'

From his back trouser pocket he withdrew a slim, dog-eared, paperback book.

'It's Constantin's codebook,' he said as he handed it over. 'No transmitter, though. That's on its way to Tripoli.'

As Jack's fingers closed on the book, he knew that Darius had given all the commitment that

American Intelligence and British Intelligence would ever need from him. The transmitter on its way to Tripoli was of no importance whatsoever.

He thought of Sholto Monck, also on his way to Tripoli.

'I would have liked,' he said fiercely, 'to have seen Monck put before a firing squad and shot.'

Darius's mouth tugged into a wry smile. 'He didn't much like you, either. On our drive out here he had quite a few choice things to say about you. One of them I should pass on to you.' He took a long draw on his cigarette. 'He told me that Petra is your father's daughter.'

Jack chuckled. 'What? Of course she isn't. When I was six my father had mumps. It doesn't often render men infertile, but it did with my father. It's why I'm an only child. And there's a seven-year age difference between Petra and me. You can work out the maths for yourself.'

Darius quirked an eyebrow. 'Then perhaps you should have a word with Petra. According to Sholto, your mother's husband, Theo Girlington, told her donkey's years ago that your father was her father, and she's believed it ever since.'

Jack ceased to breathe. The world, as he knew it, stopped revolving.

In one flashing, cataclysmic moment, everything was clear to him.

He knew now why Petra had fled London, and him, in such distress.

He knew why she had been terrified of having the slightest intimate physical contact with him.

And he knew why Delia had so fiercely vetoed their love affair. She'd had suspicions; suspicions she had obviously never voiced to his father, suspicions she had kept a secret.

A secret that was now dust in the wind.

He sucked in air. The world began revolving again.

'Come on,' he said to Darius, joy roaring through his veins. 'It's time the two of us got back to Cairo.'

Together they walked across the beaten earth of the village square to his jeep.

He slid behind the wheel. In Cairo Petra was waiting for him, just as Davina was waiting for Darius, and he knew now – had known from the moment he had seen the terror in her eyes when he had left her to hunt Sholto down – that she still loved him. That she had always loved him, just as he had always loved her.

He put the jeep into gear, and as he headed out of El Laban he began whistling 'Dixie' as loudly and as jubilantly as his lungs would allow.

AUTHOR'S NOTE

In 1948 King Farouk divorced Queen Farida and married a commoner, Nariman Sadeq. On 23 July 1952, the Free Officers rose up in revolt and Farouk was forced into exile. He lived the rest of his life in Monaco and Italy. In 1954 Nasser became President of Egypt and remained President until his death in 1970. Anwar Sadat was selected to succeed him. President Sadat was assassinated by Muslim extremists in 1981.

ACKNOWLEDGEMENTS

My thanks to Carol Smith for sparking off the idea that Cairo was something I absolutely had to write about and for sustaining me with fun, friendship and good advice as I did so. Thanks also to Claire Bord, my editor; to Clare Parkinson, my copy-editor; and to the entire team at HarperCollins. Thanks also to my agent Sheila Crowley and to Linda Shaughnessy. Jim Walker OBE was invaluable in sharing his wartime memories of Cairo with me. Mrs Ragaa Gafaar was a wonderfully informative guide to the city. Several books were of great help: *Zamalek* by Chafika Soliman Hamamsy; *Operation Condor* by John Eppler; *I Spied Spies* by AW Sansom; *Cairo, Biography of a City* by James Aldridge; and particularly Artemis Cooper's wonderful *Cairo in the War*.

This Large Print Book for the partially sighted, who cannot read normal print, is published under the auspices of

THE ULVERSCROFT FOUNDATION